Praise for Emily Bain Murphy's *THE IVORY CITY*

"*The Ivory City* will have you mesmerized by the magnificent sights of the 1904 World's Fair—the perfect backdrop for danger, deceit—and one determined young woman's quest for justice."

—Michelle Collins Anderson, *USA Today* bestselling author of *The Flower Sisters*

"I'm a total fan girl over Emily Bain Murphy's writing! Like all her novels, *The Ivory City* is a story to savor—a mosaic of rich description, witty banter, and brilliant themes. I loved touring the opulent St. Louis Exposition with her and experiencing its fleeting grandeur from a multitude of perspectives and places, all while trying to figure out exactly what happened at the fair."

—Melanie Dobson, award-winning author of *The Wings of Poppy Pendleton* and *Catching the Wind*

"Grace Covington is the perfect amateur detective mixing charm and ingenuity in this richly detailed murder mystery set against the vibrant backdrop of the 1904 St. Louis World's Fair. A delightful read!"

—Julia Kelly, international bestselling author of *A Traitor in Whitehall*

"Vividly drawn with rich historical detail, *The Ivory City* is a sizzling mystery filled with intrigue, glamour and good old-fashioned romance that brilliantly ignites against the backdrop of the St. Louis World's Fair. Emily Bain Murphy's latest novel is a sheer delight!"

—Alyson Richman, international bestselling author of *The Time Keepers* and *The Missing Pages*

"A compelling mystery played out against the atmospheric backdrop of the 1904 St. Louis World's Fair, *The Ivory City* is a pleasure to read."

—Nilima Rao, award-winning author of *A Disappearance in Fiji*

THE IVORY CITY

THE IVORY CITY

EMILY BAIN MURPHY

NEW YORK

This is a work of fiction. Names, characters, business, events, and incidents are the products of the author's imagination. Any resemblance to actual persons, living or dead, or actual events is purely coincidental.

ISBN 978-1-4549-5782-9 (paperback)
ISBN 978-1-4549-5783-6 (e-book)

Union Square & Co. books may be purchased in bulk for business, educational, or promotional use. For more information, please contact your local bookseller or the Hachette Book Group's Special Markets department at special.markets@hbgusa.com.

Printed in Canada

2 4 6 8 10 9 7 5 3 1

unionsquareandco.com

Cover design by Patrick Sullivan
Cover art: Alamy: Neil Baylis (face), History & Art Collection (city), Bill Waterson (body); Shutterstock.com: bomg (borders), Graphic Effect (aura)
Interior design by Christine Heun

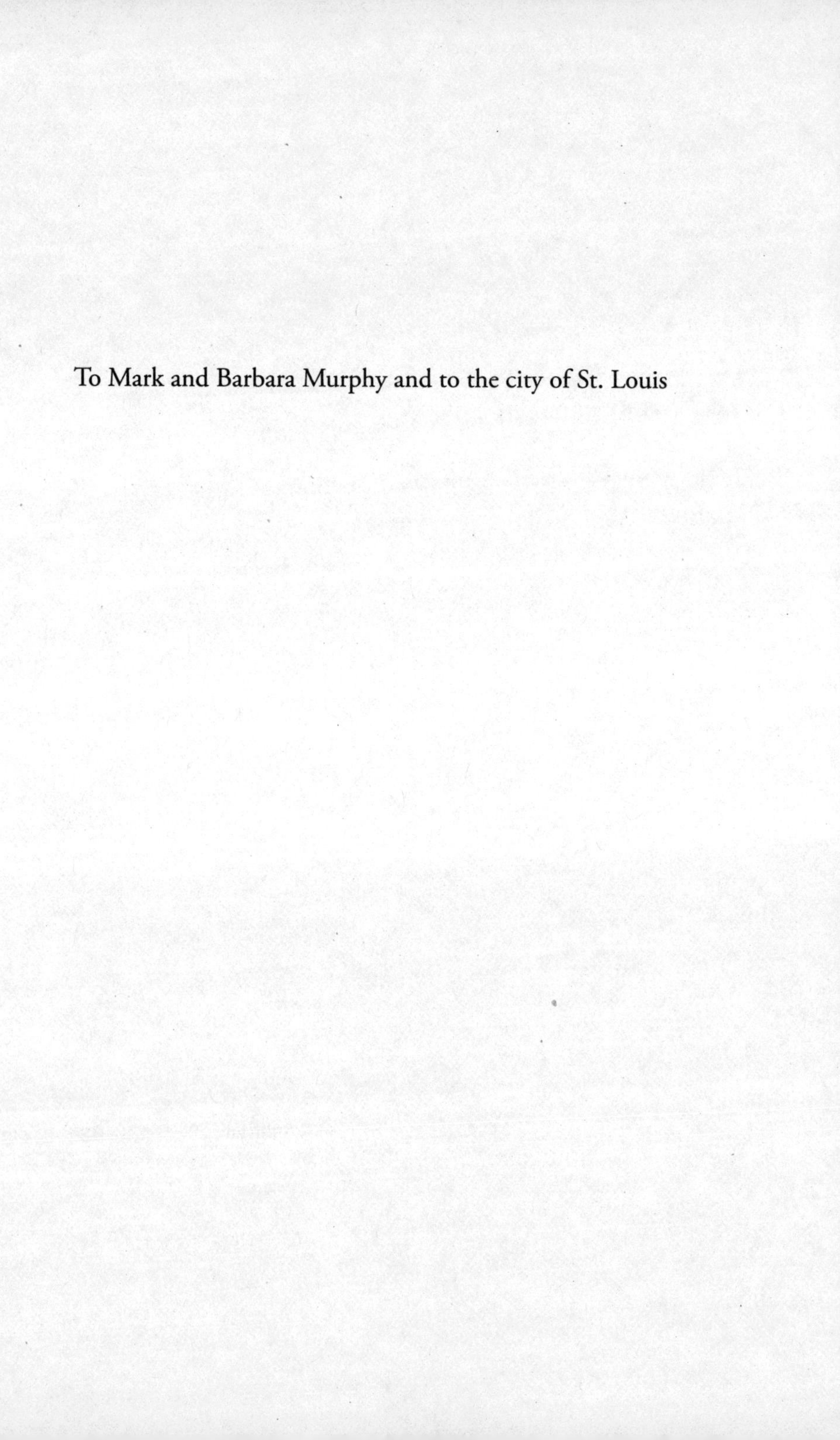

To Mark and Barbara Murphy and to the city of St. Louis

Open ye gates!

Swing wide, ye portals:

Enter herein, ye sons of men!

Learn the lesson here taught

and gather from it

inspiration for still greater accomplishments!

—David R. Francis, opening day
of the 1904 World's Fair

The past is . . . beauty. It is also burden.

It is where we go, many of us,

to remind ourselves who we are

and even sometimes to find out.

—Eddy L. Harris

Oakland
Engine House
Hotel Inside Inn
Concourse Drive
Arkansas
Pennsylvania
Maine
Kansas
Nebraska
West Virginia
Shaft House
New York
Colorado
Montana
Outside Mining and Metallurgy Exhibit
Wisconsin
U.S. Bird Exhibit
Park Commissary and Boarding Co.
Michigan
Cement Exhibit
South Dakota
Disciples of Christ
Oregon
Texas
INTRAMURAL RY
U.S. Government
Mines and Metallurgy
Kentucky
Germany
Hoo Hoo
Fine Arts
Tennessee
Restaurant
Cook & Sons
Liberal Arts
Sunken Garden
Festival
Hall
Grand Basin
Education
Social Economy
Jerusalem
Morocco
Electricity
Machinery
Machinery
Japan
Manufactures
INTRAMURAL RAILWAY
Town Hall
Library
Restaurant
City
Lindell Pavilion
Varied Industries
Transportation
Flower Beds
Closure
Engine Ho.
Station 2
Tyrolean Alps
Irish Village
Asia
The Paris
Cairo
Battle Abbey
Lindell Boul.
Plaza
THE
PIKE
Chinese Vill.
Hagenbecks
Japanese Village
Old St. Louis
Siberian R.R. & Divers
Naval Exhi
De Giverville Ave.

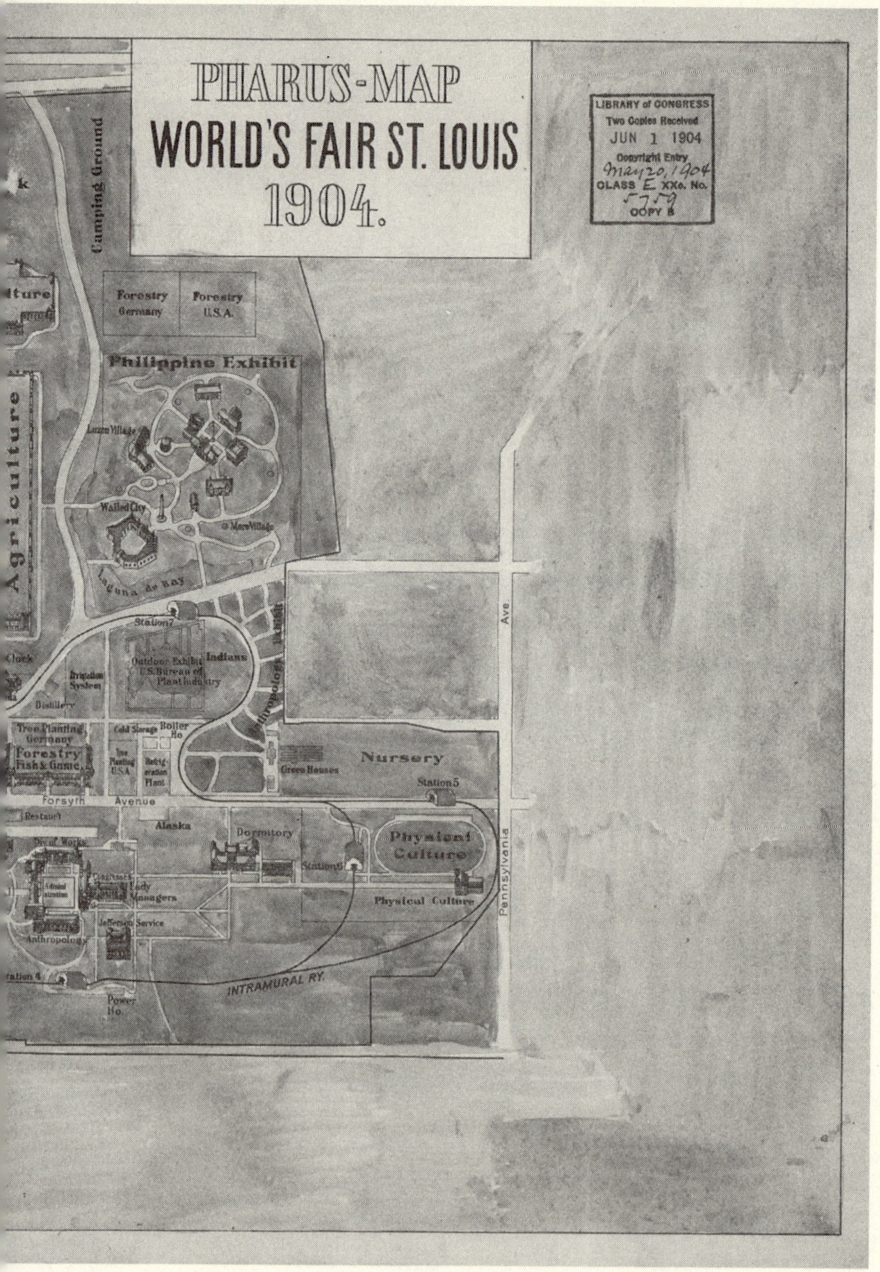

PHARUS-MAP
WORLD'S FAIR ST. LOUIS
1904.

Camping Ground
Forestry Germany
Forestry U.S.A.
Philippine Exhibit
Luzon Village
Walled City
Moro Village
Laguna de Bay
Agriculture
Station 7
Outdoor Exhibit U.S. Bureau of Plant Industry
Indians
Anthropology Exhibit
Irrigation System
Distillery
Tree Planting Germany
Forestry Fish & Game
Cold Storage
Boiler Ho
Tree Planting U.S.A.
Refrigeration Plant
Green Houses
Nursery
Station 5
Forsyth Avenue
Restaurant
Alaska
Dormitory
Div. of Works
Physical Culture
Station 6
Lady Managers
Physical Culture
Jefferson Service
Anthropology
Station 4
Power Ho.
INTRAMURAL RY.
Pennsylvania Ave.

PROLOGUE

CHICAGO

NOVEMBER 28, 1903

Approximately Five Months and Five Days Before the Murder

Grace Carter Covington was dressed in layers of clothing—a fur coat and muff surreptitiously stolen from her aunt, a satin gown spun from her dreams, and even silk undergarments that didn't belong to her—but she hadn't realized quite how naked she would feel without her cousin Lillie there.

The mansion in front of her was intimidating, its carved limestone ablaze with lights against the winter night sky. Lit paper lanterns and rose-filled votives floated in two pools that flanked the entry walk like outstretched wings. Beyond it, warm strains of ragtime music beckoned them forward. A light snow was beginning to fall.

Grace took a step out of the carriage with her cousin Oliver at her side. He was utterly at ease, but this was his world, not hers, and it made her feel even more out of place. He must have felt her suddenly stiffen because his hand found hers within the fur muff.

"You're understandably nervous," he said sympathetically, squeezing her hand. "Given how the rich in Chicago select a guest at every party to be pecked to death by their pet geese."

"Your attempts to relax me are alarming," she muttered. But he laughed and the sound did make her calmer. She felt the tension melt a little from her shoulders as she tugged at the slip beneath her dress, one that Lillie had lent her before collapsing back onto her bed that evening. Lillie, Oliver's sister and Grace's best friend in the world, was normally at her right hand, but she had suddenly come down with a fever and had insisted Oliver and Grace go without her.

"We didn't come all the way to Chicago for you to sit at home with me," Lillie cried. "Especially not in *that* dress." Lillie had ordered two gowns for herself but, unbeknownst to her mother, had one modified to meet Grace's measurements instead. It fit Grace like a glove: pale blue satin with panels of embroidered flowers and a curve of wisteria vines trailing down her arm.

It was without question the most beautiful thing she had ever put on her body.

"It's the party of the century," Lillie had said. She waggled her eyebrows, her face flushed with fever. "That is, of course, until the Ivory City next spring."

And so Grace had given her cousin's fevered cheek a kiss and arrived with Oliver on her arm.

"Mr. Oliver Carter and Miss Grace Covington," the butler announced.

The grand foyer was filled with Chicago's most elite society members, all of whom now turned to examine them.

Oliver whispered in her ear. "I suppose this is as good a time as any to share that I've never forgiven you for squashing that orange down my pants."

She snorted as he bowed to the crowd. "Nor I you," she whispered, "for the melted chocolate in my bed."

"You really were a formidable eleven-year-old," he said.

She curtsied to the crowd, and for a moment she thought of her older brother Walt, and what it might have been like to arrive on his arm. But that was a dream for another life. She no longer knew where

Walt was, a thought that pinched like too-tight shoes. She hoped he was somewhere warm tonight. Saying a small prayer under her breath for him, like she always did, she brushed the trailing wisteria along the skin of her arm and handed her borrowed fur coat to the butler.

"The Chicago rich pecking you to death was actually a bit of a metaphor," Oliver said as they moved to join the crowd. These were the people that Oliver and Lillie belonged to, as heirs of the Carter Merchant Company their shared great-grandfather had built. Once, in a different world, these would have been Grace's peers, too. But her mother Nell had chosen the shame of falling in love with a working-class man and the disinheritance that came along with it. As it turned out, all manner of heinous sins could be forgiven a person, except for the deliberate rejection of her own class.

"You don't say," Grace said, as Oliver took a flute of champagne from a passing tray. She followed his line of sight to a young stage actress she recognized from back home in St. Louis.

"Is that—?" she asked.

"Harriet Forbes," Oliver said. "Yes."

"Ah," Grace said with a wry smile. "And here I thought you'd brought me along for my scintillating company and sparkling conversation."

"Well that, of course, darling," he said, suavely turning away from Harriet, "but if people are talking about you they won't be talking about us."

"Thank you, cousin," she said. "I love being used as a decoy. Please remind me to decline your next hunting invitation."

He laughed. "Let me reward your invaluable service with a punch."

"And a petit fours, please, at the very least," she called after him. He raised his right hand in acknowledgment without looking back, shaking his head as though he were smiling. And she, without being asked, made her way through the crowd toward Harriet Forbes. Grace loved her cousins better than anyone and would do anything short of murder to help them.

"Hello," she said warmly to Harriet as she approached. Outside of situations like this one, Grace normally had no problem making friends—*she* wasn't the person concerned about her status, or lack thereof. And perhaps because she wasn't doing this for herself, but for her cousin, she found that her nerves were suddenly gone. "I'm Grace Covington," she said, curtsying.

"Harriet," the woman said. "Forbes." She wore her hair pulled up with ribbons, and earrings that were a cluster of dangling garnets. Her cream dress spilled over with dark roses.

"Yes, I saw you in Ibsen's *A Doll's House* last year," Grace said. Harriet had played the titular role and they had all been smitten with her—apparently none more so than Oliver—even though Grace knew that her aunt would rather burn off her own fingerprints than welcome an actress into the family. "You were luminous."

"You're too kind," Harriet said. She had a deep, sultry voice, and Grace's own heart lifted when Harriet took her by the arm and led her around the party. She stole glances at the walls gilded with patterns of gold, the intricately painted ceilings, and the vibrant Gobelin tapestries. Real, cascading flowers were strung in lines of blooming lace around the ceiling like crown molding.

"Are you from St. Louis, then?" Harriet asked. "I don't remember seeing you at the last Governor's Ball."

Grace's eye caught on a handsome man who was standing on the staircase landing, surveying the crowd as though he were observing a distant experiment. Chandeliers hung above his head like webs strung with heavy water droplets of crystal. When he turned his face to the side, she glimpsed a port-wine stain stretching along the length of his jaw, curling up toward his mouth like a shadow. She thought his dark eyes were striking, even though his mouth remained clenched, and he didn't smile. It was as if a cloud hung around him, a concentrated rainstorm in the middle of a spring garden. She stole another look at him as the guests took to the marble floor, dancing, and wondered what made him look so unhappy.

"No, I'm not from St. Louis," Grace said to Harriet. "But I have family there." She subtly guided Harriet toward Oliver. "Please allow me to introduce my cousin, Oliver Carter."

Grace had been to all manner of parties before—backyard jigs with whiskey, harmonicas, and fiddles, and late-night after-hours piano concerts at her father's restaurant ("shameful—it's little more than a speakeasy," her aunt had scoffed). She was surprised that the electric energy she felt here was almost the same, even though the black-and-white checkered floor of her father's restaurant had been traded for a marble ballroom overflowing with orchids and potted palms. It was a philanthropic event for a new botanical garden, and half of St. Louis's elite society had traveled to Chicago for the verdant party amid a deep winter.

And yet Grace's eyes kept sliding back to the sullen young man on the stairs.

His gaze met hers and she immediately looked away.

"Oliver," a young woman called, parting the crowd toward them. She wore a ball gown made of silk and golden metallic thread, with an intricately embroidered front panel and a fan to match. Her dark red hair glittered with pins as she eyed Harriet with unmasked disapproval.

Harriet was undeterred, instead staring boldly back.

"Where's Lillie tonight?" the red-haired woman asked, turning to Oliver.

"Under the weather, I'm afraid," Oliver said. "Lillie is my sister," he hurriedly clarified for Harriet. And then he offered her his hand. "Miss Forbes, would you care to dance?"

Harriet smiled.

"Grace," Oliver said, shooting his cousin a look of apology over his shoulder. "This is Miss Allred."

The woman snapped open her fan with a sharp twist. "Frannie," she said.

But Oliver was already gone.

Grace bit back a sigh. If only Lillie were there, they would be eating chocolates while pretending to use the lavatory and secretly evaluating all of the women's fashions and the eligible bachelors.

"Are you well-acquainted with Mr. Carter?" Frannie asked, delicately fluttering her fan. "I'm *quite* good friends with his sister, Miss Lillie Carter. Very close friends. Do you know her?"

"I do," Grace said. *We share blood,* she wanted to add. *In fact, at this exact moment, I'm wearing her undergarments.*

Her eye caught again on the man who was standing above the crowd as if he owned the house, observing them all.

"Excuse me, but who is that gentleman over there?" Grace asked.

"Well, that's Theodore Parker, of course," Frannie said, as if it were the most obvious thing in the world. "This is his family's manor." She seemed surprised that Grace didn't know. It was exactly the sort of detail Oliver wouldn't care enough to mention, which was why despite his spoiled nature, she liked him as much as she did.

Frannie's green eyes narrowed. "What did you say your surname was?" she asked.

"I didn't," Grace said. She hesitated. "It's Covington."

"Covington," Frannie repeated primly, thinking. She fanned herself as if the fan itself was frantically trying to escape her grasp.

"Where were you educated? Woodlawn? One of the Sisters?" she asked.

"No," Grace said. "My mother taught me herself."

A slight frown creased Frannie's face. "Were you living abroad, then?"

Grace shook her head. She smiled, determined to stay at ease despite the line of questioning.

"Oh." Frannie's own smile was falling. "Are you part of the New York Covingtons, then?"

"No. I live in Kansas City."

"And how have you come to be acquainted with Oliver Carter, then?" Frannie asked, tilting her head.

Grace's voice never wavered. "He's my cousin."

Understanding flitted across Frannie's face, and her pretense of politeness fell away. She recoiled.

"I've just seen someone calling to me," she said flatly.

She curtsied, and Grace dipped into a pointed curtsy of her own.

It seemed that her family's reputation had preceded her. Perhaps her mother's slight of choosing a common, working-class man over the future governor of Missouri could be forgiven. But Grace's older brother Walt was whispered about from Kansas City all the way to the grapevines of St. Louis society, solidifying opinions about how far Grace's family had fallen. It would be all but impossible for any of the Covingtons to be welcomed back into this kind of society again—regardless of how Grace's cousins felt about her.

Grace bit her lip. She knew she didn't fit here. She didn't know why she kept attempting to try. But—yes she did. Because she loved Lillie and Oliver and wanted to be in their lives, to be allowed in their world. And because she wanted to help assuage her mother's guilt.

Grace couldn't stand the thought that her mother might regret marrying her father. Not that she regretted having *them*, per se—but Grace had watched the way the guilt ate away at her mother over Walt. Nell blamed herself for her children's reduced position in life, for the unfortunate choices Walt had made, the way St. Louis society had shut them out and their social circles in Kansas City had recently shunned them. But if Grace could somehow find a way to be accepted—if she could make a good enough match despite their circumstances—her mother might stop blaming herself. And then Grace wouldn't have to see the hollow way her mother's skin was beginning to hang at her neck, the bruise-like circles beneath her eyes. Perhaps her parents would dance at night in the kitchen again when they thought no one was there. Maybe she would stop finding her mother in Walt's room, staring at the faded drawings he'd made when he was seven.

Grace sighed. Frannie had left her standing awkwardly and alone on the fringes of the party. She turned away, cursing Oliver less for his abandonment and more for forgetting the petit fours he'd promised her, when a man with an aggressively oiled mustache suddenly stepped into her path.

"Hello," he said. His eyes were slightly unfocused. "Would you care to dance?"

He looked at her neckline lasciviously and she tried not to shudder.

"I'm afraid I can't," she said. "But thank you."

"Can't," he said, subtly moving to block her way. His face hardened. "Or won't?"

He seemed alarmingly angry about the slighted invitation, and she tried to catch Oliver's eye, but he was completely enraptured with Harriet. Once again, she wished desperately for Lillie. The only two people she knew at this party were completely wrapped up in one another, oblivious to the outside world, and to her sudden predicament.

"I'm afraid I have to—" she began to say, stepping back, when someone came up beside her.

"Dance with me," the man beside her finished. "No need to take offense, Alexander. It's just that she already promised her hand to me."

She looked up to see Theodore Parker looking down at her. He still had a slight frown on his face, but even so, he was infinitely more agreeable than the man who seemed unable to take no for an answer.

"Yes," she said gratefully to Theodore. "I was just looking for you."

They pushed past the scowling Alexander and Theodore swept her out onto the dance floor, his hand on her waist.

"Thank you," she said as the music began, just as he brushed her foot with his own.

"I'm sorry," he said at the same time.

She smiled.

"You should know I don't usually dance," he said, looking pained. "Especially with women I don't know." His hand adjusted on her waist. "That is, if I can help it."

"Thank you for making an exception to assist a woman in distress. You should know I don't make it a habit of needing rescues by strange men," she said. "If I can help it."

The shadow of a smile crossed his face, and her heart strangely fluttered.

She was very aware of the weight of his hand on the curve of her waist, the grip of the other holding her gloved palm.

"The next time you're approached by an unwanted suitor, perhaps you could say you've drunk too much wine and are on the way to being sick," he offered dryly.

She laughed and secretly sent up thanks to Lillie for making her practice dancing with Oliver, so that at least this felt natural, and she didn't have to concentrate on counting steps. But she wasn't used to the shoes, and she wobbled a bit in them.

"That's not actually true, is it?" he asked, suddenly looking at her closer.

"No," she said, amused. "I don't really drink."

He nodded. "Nor do I. Though I find it helpful when I'm forced into parties I wouldn't otherwise choose to attend."

"Would this be one of those parties?" she asked.

He twisted his mouth wryly and cleared his throat instead of answering. She liked the smell of him, deep cedar and fall leaves and tobacco.

"Do you reside here in Chicago?" he asked. "Surely not. I've never seen you before."

"Just visiting," she said. "But I'd like to see more of the city someday. Which I will now always associate with this kindness." She curtsied to him as the song came to an end.

"I don't know your name," he said, bowing to her.

"Grace," she said.

"I'm Theodore," he said.

She loved that he wasn't conventionally handsome, the way the port-wine stain skimmed along his right jaw line and curled up toward his mouth.

He caught her staring at it just as Oliver approached.

"May I cut in?" Oliver asked.

"I'm sorry," she said, catching Theodore's eye. "But I've drunk too much wine and I was just on my way to being sick."

Theodore imperceptibly snorted and for a moment tightened his grip on her.

"I'm kidding," Grace said, laughing, and she felt his hand relax. "Mr. Parker, this is my cousin, Oliver Carter of St. Louis. Oliver, while you were otherwise engaged, this kind gentleman saved me from a ghastly fate, and I'm forever indebted to him."

"Then so am I," Oliver said, extending his hand. "Mr. Parker."

"Theodore," he corrected, taking Oliver's hand with a solemn expression. His dark eyes had a depth to them, his jaw like cut glass.

She felt a lightning bolt in her belly as he looked at her. There was a weightiness about him that suggested he didn't smile much, but that when he did, it was a prize worth the effort it took to win.

"Thank you for the dance," he said, bowing to her. "It was a lovely diversion, and now I'm afraid I've been promised elsewhere."

She felt the disappointment settle in her body as he left them and made his way over to a group of ladies, including Frannie Allred, who had been staring in their direction. She immediately glanced away.

"And are we making any inroads with the talented Miss Forbes?" Grace asked Oliver, falling into step with her cousin easily. They'd been dancing together for twelve years, since she was ten and he was nearing thirteen. Being with him was like coming home.

He groaned. "Somehow I turn from my handsome charming self into an uncontrollable blathering oaf whenever I'm near her."

"She must have a penchant for blathering oafs, then," Grace said, glancing over his shoulder, "as she's coming this way now."

He flushed a little and she found it endearing. With his name, wealth, and good looks, he'd always erred dangerously close to becoming a rake, and she'd never known him to be this nervous around a lady before.

"And what of you, cousin?" he asked. "No one has pecked you to death yet?"

"Miss Allred certainly tried."

Oliver rolled his eyes. "I've never understood why Lillie deigns to be friends with her."

"Lillie is an angel who is friends with everyone," Grace said.

"Even us," Oliver said, dipping her.

"Even us," Grace said, laughing. He twirled her, and her dress spun at her ankles, and she decided that she was glad that she had come. Perhaps someday she would meet a man who saw her for who she was, without the trappings of the family name her mother had thrown away, her father's honorable hard work that somehow made him pitiable, her cousins' elevated reputation, the tragic choices her brother had made. Perhaps someone would simply see her—passionate and loyal and sharp-tongued, with a strong nose she'd never particularly liked and aristocratic cheekbones she'd inherited from her late grandmother.

She was secretly glad to feel beautiful in her own skin tonight. For the dress Lillie had made for her, and the flowers she had pinned in her honey-plaited hair. Almost nothing she wore that evening belonged to her, but she felt a pleasant confidence finally returning that was all her own.

Which is why she was surprised by the way her stomach dipped just a little when she observed the intimate way in which Theodore was speaking to Frannie Allred. Glancing over at her, then sharply looking away.

Grace stiffened. So Frannie would tell him who she was. She suddenly felt nervous, her warm confidence draining away as if a door had swung open and let in a draft. She worried about the expression she would find on his face when she looked up again. But she needn't have. By the time she did, he was gone.

If only Lillie were there. Grace suddenly couldn't wait to return to her cousins' rented Chicago home, tuck herself into bed, and tell her beloved cousin everything over warm biscuits and morning coffee tomorrow.

"Don't mind her," Harriet said as she appeared beside them, her eyes cutting from Frannie to Grace. "Miss Allred's never spoken to me before tonight. My family name only goes back two generations, and her minimum requirement is three."

Grace laughed, and when Oliver began to stammer something almost incomprehensible again, Grace excused herself, taking a champagne flute merely to have something to hold. She climbed the stairs. Wound silently through the maze of hallways that coiled through the back half of the grand house, hearing the party fade. Through the magnificent arched windows, she could glimpse the balconies overlooking a lawn of green topiary mazes and lit lanterns floating in the pond. *What would it be like,* she wondered, *to have this sort of wealth at one's fingertips? To never be questioned as to whether you deserved to enter a room?* She thought of what awaited her back in Kansas City. Finding a nice working-class man, like her father. Perhaps even needing to work herself.

She tightened her grip on the champagne glass. She wasn't afraid of hard work. She didn't think herself above it. But she did fear losing Lillie and Oliver the way she had already lost Walt—a thought she almost couldn't bear. She stepped out onto the balcony to escape it. The frigid wind was a shock, and she hadn't considered how little protection the dress would offer from the cold, when she ran into something—someone—solid. She felt the moment of shock when she realized it was the body of a man.

"Excuse me," she said with a mixture of exhilaration and embarrassment. She barely missed splashing her glass down the front of Theodore Parker's high, white-starched collar. He caught her wrist and rescued the glass from her in one smooth motion.

She caught a whiff of his scent again, stormy smoke and leaves, and a wide smile leapt to her lips before she could help it. He was staring at her with an imperceptible look, and her smile faded.

He raised an eyebrow.

"Did you follow me out here just to ruin my suit?" he asked coldly, brushing away the drops of champagne that had apparently found their mark. He sniffed the glass she'd been holding and narrowed his eyes. "Not a drinker, you said?"

Her heart instantly sank as he continued to look at her cruelly, all his warmth from a few minutes ago gone. What a fool she had been. So this was who Theodore Parker truly was—a completely different man than when he had believed she was a woman of high society. Someone who pretended that snobbish airs bothered him, when he had been putting them on more than anyone. The wind stung her, but the way he was looking at her hurt more.

She braced herself in her ill-fitting shoes. Her ego was already smarting after the probing looks from the crowd, after her interactions with Frannie. She'd never had much patience for simpering to begin with, and whatever allotment she had was long gone at this point. These people were no better than she was, or her mother and father, or perhaps even her disgraced brother. Her eyes flashed.

"I was just in search of some pleasant company," she said, curtsying low. "I guess I'll have to keep looking."

To think she had found him devastatingly handsome a handful of moments ago. She almost relished the way his face darkened with surprise. She was about to turn away when he caught her arm.

"And what do you consider to be pleasant?" he asked. "A rich man in want of a wife?"

She almost laughed. She had never been good at hiding her emotions, something she heard far too often from her mother and Lillie, and she felt the amusement and pity for him plainly cross her face.

"I wish your future wife the best of luck, and most patience," she said. "For I find that many riches tend to dull the most promising men into petulant boys."

He dropped her arm, looking confused, and she continued. "However, *I*, as I'm sure you've heard, come from a line that marries for partnership rather than purse strings—a legacy I fully intend to continue. Good evening, sir," she said.

He didn't need to know how her heart had sped up at the sight of him, or that his criticism of her pierced straight to the bone. After all, was it wrong of her to want to make a desirable match, to marry above her station? To ease her mother's worry, to stay in her cousins' lives? She still wanted love above all else—but she was ashamed nonetheless. Face burning, she delicately took her champagne glass from his hand and went in search of Oliver.

"You look positively radiant tonight, cousin," Oliver said when she found him. "How did you find the fresh air?"

"Invigorating," she said curtly.

With a pricked heart, she drained the rest of her glass and promised herself she would never speak of Theodore Parker again.

CHAPTER ONE

ST. LOUIS

APRIL 30, 1904

Three Days Before the Murder

Grace had spent many of her summer days growing up within the elegant oak-paneled walls of the Carter mansion on Forest Park, despite the best intentions of her aunt. Grace resented the way her aunt Clove had cast out her mother, but her uncle Reginald had insisted that civilized people did not punish the innocent for the mistakes of their forbearers. So Grace and her brother Walt were to be given a fresh start and a chance to redeem their family line for the next generation.

Walt had squandered his chance in spectacular fashion and threatened to take Grace's out as well, yet somehow it still hung like a charm on a thin string, winking in the light. This was in large part because her cousin Lillie had adopted her from their first breaths and insisted upon bringing her along to high society functions. But what Grace had secretly loved more than any of Lillie's introductions to balls or dinner parties was the way the late-afternoon light splashed across the Carter mansion's parquet floors; how she and Lillie had grown up believing the cast-iron fountain in the back courtyard was a magical, wish-granting spring; the way Lillie's well-fed corgi Lulu padded around the house with a bell collar muffled by her fur.

It wasn't the riches of the Carter mansion that called her back again and again, but the sense of family. Though it would never be her home in name, Oliver and Lillie had planted seeds in her heart that were not easily uprooted.

"Turn around," Lillie ordered. She untied the sunhat from around Grace's throat. Lillie was a stunning beauty, with her mother's sculpted cheekbones and fair complexion, her father's bright eyes and his kindness. Grace was utterly in love with her.

Grace had arrived a week ago, taking the train from Kansas City, and they had spent every afternoon sitting beneath parasols in the backyard, eating sandwiches and drinking lemonades with frozen blueberries floating on top while the frantic sound of hammering thundered around them. It was impossible to go anywhere in the city without seeing the lavish art nouveau posters plastered on every pole and building for miles—an image by Mucha of an elegant woman in a tangerine dress, grasping the hand of a Native American chief in a ceremonial war bonnet behind her.

Grace and Lillie had written to each other of little else for months. The jewel of Forest Park stretched on in an endless green vista near the Carter house, its fountains and rolling hills visible from all of the south-facing front rooms. But over the last three years it had been steadily transformed into a different world. Ten thousand workers had poured in to create fifteen hundred new structures: palaces with domed cupolas, fountains and waterways and intricate canals for boats to float by grand halls and colonnades; a mile-long promenade of shops and restaurants; a Ferris wheel, an intramural railroad, and even a working roller coaster. It was an entire miniature city built to last seven months, a world's fair to be combined with the summer Olympic Games. It was also a testament to progress: what collective humanity could accomplish, as well as marking the hundred-year celebration of the Louisiana Purchase. "The Ivory City," the press had dubbed it.

The eyes of the entire world were turned toward St. Louis, waiting for the future to be made there. And Grace desperately wanted to be there, too, in its crucible, secretly hoping she'd be touched by something valuable in proximity.

"You're sure you don't mind if I go tonight?" Lillie asked, bringing an earring to her lobe. She studied Grace's face in the mirror's reflection.

"Of course not," Grace said. She tried not to feel the needle-prick of jealousy that Lillie and Oliver were invited to the fair's exclusive opening night's party. She was grateful that she got to go at all, tomorrow, and every day before she returned to Kansas City on the train next week. "I bet I can see the fireworks from the balcony," she said. "And in my nightdress, without the crowds."

"But you'll be here alone," Lillie said.

Grace scoffed. "I'll wait up for you to return and you'll tell me *everything*," she said. "And I won't be alone. Lulu and I will be here together indulging in a cup of tea and some dark chocolate, won't we, Lulu?" She scratched the dog's neck.

"I don't know," Lillie said. "Perhaps I'll just stay. We can make a girls' night of it."

"Don't you dare, Lillie Alice Carter, I would never forgive you," Grace said. "Oh! I almost forgot. I have something for you."

Partly to distract Lillie, she jumped up and fetched a box. She had spent three weeks fashioning what was inside—a necklace of round porcelain beads she had painted to look like an intricate bow pattern of floral lace. She'd used a horsehair paintbrush as thin as a whisper and sharp as a blade, and it had turned out beautifully. Lillie gasped, examining it closely. Then she insisted that Grace help her put it on.

As she fixed the clasp around the slender curve of Lillie's neck, Grace could hear the roar of a massive crowd cheering nearby.

Fifty thousand people—perhaps even one hundred thousand people. It sounded like the crash of an ocean wave in the middle of the country.

They both turned toward the window. Lillie's fingers flew to her mouth.

"Stop biting," Grace said automatically.

Lillie wrinkled her nose as she looked at her ragged nails. "Mother is going to have a conniption when she sees my hands."

"Nail-biting *is* the surest indication of a person's debauchery, more so even than gambling, wantonness, or prostitution."

Lillie threw a hat at her.

"Wear these," Grace said. She rummaged in Lillie's wardrobe and found a pair of satin gloves. Her eyes fell on a dress that shimmered pale blue, shot through with silver threads and exquisitely embroidered appliqués of beaded flowers. It was one of the many dresses Lillie would wear later in the week. Her eyes lingered on it.

There was a knock on the door.

"Everyone decent in there?" Oliver called.

"The jury is hung," Grace said. She went to open the door. "But fully dressed? Yes."

He waltzed in dressed in tails, a bow tie, and a top hat.

"You look lovely, as always, Sister," he said, giving Lillie a kiss on the cheek. Grace returned to pinning Lillie's hair.

"And I have a surprise for you." He dangled a box wrapped with a ribbon in front of them. "A riddle. One very decadent offering is hidden within this box. It is a single item that cannot be shared, and yet it's a gift to you both."

With a flourish, he set it in front of Lillie. "Can you guess what it is?"

She squealed. "You do the honors, Grace," she said, pushing it across the vanity, where Grace picked it up. It was as light as the discarded shell of a bird's egg. She resisted the urge to shake it.

"Don't keep us in suspense!" Lillie said. "Open it!"

Grace pulled at the ribbon, her face flushing. She opened the box and inside was a piece of paper.

Its gilded edge caught the light.

Invite One
Opening Night Fete of the World's Fair
Private Entrance
Under and Over the Sea

She turned toward Oliver, eyes shining.

A ticket.

Lillie shrieked, plucking it from her hands.

"A ticket? Another ticket for Grace?"

"Yes. A gift to you both."

"You are the most brilliant, delightful, delicious brother," Lillie said.

Grace could hardly catch her breath. "Thank you," she said, throwing her arms around Oliver. She kissed his neck. "Thank you."

"Oh, but quickly!" Lillie said, glancing at the clock on the fireplace mantel. "The carriage will be here soon! We have to find you a dress!" She threw open her wardrobe and began tossing gowns on the bed. "And now you'll get to meet my friend Frannie!"

Oliver buried a laugh in a cough and gave Grace an apologetic look.

Grace had never told Lillie how horrible Frannie Allred had been to her that night at last winter's Botanical Ball in Chicago. Her stomach turned a little at the thought of seeing Frannie again. It brought back the way Theodore Parker had looked at her like she was a piece of mess on the bottom of his shoe; the way the two of them had dissected and humiliated her together. She'd hidden it from Lillie, who would have been injured on Grace's behalf. And Grace couldn't bear to hurt her cousin, even if the wound had traveled through herself first.

But who cared about any of that now. The presence of Frannie Allred was a small price to pay for a ticket to the event of the century. Grace's gaze fell on the silver-blue dress she'd been eyeing earlier.

"Yes," Lillie said, immediately scooping it up. "It's so you."

"It won't fit me," Grace protested.

"So we'll pin it."

"Your mother will have a fit."

"Good. It will distract her from my nails." Lillie thrust the dress at Grace. "Now go put it on."

Grace held it to her chest and hurried to the guest room. Her heart was pounding. So the week at the Ivory City would start sooner than she had planned. She was thrilled—and yet the memory of Frannie Allred and Theodore Parker in Chicago was the least of the secrets she'd been keeping. The start of the fair meant she was one step closer to having to tell Lillie and Oliver the truth: she could no longer be part of their world. Her fingers shook a little as she pulled on Lillie's dress and pushed earrings into her ears. Lillie came in with pins to help the dress better fit Grace's shape. She fussed with the folds until it fell to her liking, then gasped with delight, steering Grace toward the bronze-framed mirror. "Can you believe it?" Lillie said, clasping Grace from behind. "This is about to be the best week of our lives."

Grace squeezed her back. She held the entry ticket carefully in her hand, as delicately as a living thing. Then she pinned back her hair and hurried to follow her cousins down the hand-carved staircase.

"What's this?" Aunt Clove asked coldly. She rose with barely disguised irritation when Grace appeared in the soaring foyer. Aunt Clove's satin train was wrapped around her feet, swirling behind her on the marble floor, as she tied on her formal feathered hat. "Lillie, I thought you were saving that dress for the president's dinner, not so that Grace could wear it for an evening in at home."

"Ollie found her a ticket for tonight," Lillie said. "Isn't it wonderful, Mother?" She swept around Aunt Clove, beaming. She looked even more beautiful when she beamed. "I of course lent her a dress and told her she could come with us in the carriage."

"Wonderful," Uncle Reginald said, and he winked at Grace behind Aunt Clove's glower. He was dressed in tails and drinking a martini.

Grace squeezed between Oliver and Lillie, poring over the opening day's program as the carriage wove through the crowded streets. She traced the labyrinth of canals that fed into the Grand Basin, the various palaces, the colonnade of states and nations, the train lines, the stretch of Pike that was dotted with restaurants and rides. The air was scented with fire, sugar, and smoke, and an evening parade appeared to be ending, with the First Missouri Infantry taking care to control the crowds.

Lillie squeezed Grace's hand. She wore a slate gray dress, the stormy color of the sea. It had cream tulle pulling it off her shoulders and pink roses sewn in bunches along the hem, all tied together with her satin cream gloves.

"I'm told that President Roosevelt is here for the Opening Ceremonies," Aunt Clove remarked. She craned her neck to look out the window, something that gave Grace great pleasure. She had never seen her aunt crane at anything before.

"And tonight's event is in a special area set apart from the riffraff," her aunt continued, watching a woman dressed in an enormous floral hat and carrying what appeared to be a peacock under one arm. "Thank God," she muttered.

Oliver poked Grace in the ribs, daring her to laugh.

She dug her nail into Oliver's hand, and he bit back a yelp.

"We'll enter tonight's dinner by gondola," Aunt Clove said. Her hat had feathers on it that threatened to tickle Uncle Reginald, who gently batted them away. "We're expected to meet the Haddings there."

"Oh, look!" Lillie said, examining the program. "A performance with Harriet Forbes! We loved her in *A Doll's House*!"

Oliver stilled beside her, and Grace was studiously careful to avoid his eyes.

"Oh, Lillie, of all the things to be excited about. An *actress*," Aunt Clove said, as though it were something contagious.

Grace was the only one in the family who knew Oliver had been secretly courting Harriet Forbes for the last four months.

She swallowed. The three of them—Oliver, Lillie, and Grace—each had secrets, she knew. Confidences that Lillie and Oliver had given to her but were keeping from each other, and she suddenly felt all of the secrets she was holding pressing against her ribs. She would never use the things she knew against her beloved cousins—no, they were closer than brother and sister to her, and sometimes she felt like the glue that held them together. She was never happier than when she was between them, Oliver handsome in his silk topper with his cut jaw and boyish smile, and Lillie stunning in her Doucet gown and lilac spray earrings.

They lived in a glittering world where they loved everyone and were beloved in return, and sometimes Grace felt like she actually belonged. They shared the same ancestors and lent her power where she had none.

Meanwhile, the darker part of her whispered that secrets were likely the only form of power she'd ever have.

The Missouri Infantry kept the streaming crowds at bay along the tree-lined cobblestone road long enough for them to disembark at the entry gate. Their tickets were examined, and just before they entered the fairgrounds for the first time, Grace's aunt pulled her aside.

"Grace," she said, with barely veiled fury. "You're far from a child anymore." She leaned forward, her words pressed to Grace's throat like a knife. "This is the last time your presence will be permitted to taint my children's company."

Grace turned to hide the slight from her cousins, as she always did.

"Thank you for your gracious welcome, as always, Aunt Clove," she said bitingly.

Her aunt blanched at the menacing undertone that for the first time ever, Grace had allowed into her voice. Usually, she held it behind the dams along with all of the other burning things she thought but could not say.

But this was her last week with her cousins. It had already been decided, even before her aunt said anything. She had returned from that party in Chicago knowing that she couldn't make herself fit. It was time to go back to Kansas City and make a life there. One that Lillie and Oliver couldn't fit into either. They had outgrown one another, and they couldn't pretend otherwise anymore. She would tell them at some point that this week was the end. And though the thought nearly broke her, she couldn't ask for a more memorable way to tell them goodbye.

The poster of the woman in the tangerine dress gestured them forward, into the Ivory City.

A spray of golden fireworks exploded above their heads, falling toward the cupola of the Palace of Electricity.

Lillie grabbed Grace's hand and squealed, pulling her inside.

The World's Fair was beginning.

❧

Grace had observed the Ivory City being built from afar, watching the construction from one of the ten bedrooms on the second floor of the Carter mansion. She'd seen the carved ivory columns, the soaring domes of the Palaces, the strips of manicured grass flanking the pavilions and stone bridges reminiscent of Venetian canals. She'd watched the rising silhouette of the enormous Ferris wheel that had claimed the lives of twelve men during its construction. But nothing had prepared her for being within the city herself.

Paved walkways bordered the lush emerald grass of the music pavilion, sculpted by viburnum bushes that burst with fragrant white blossoms as big as snowballs. Flags representing more than thirty countries unfurled to welcome them in a colorful promenade along the great entrance.

"I can't believe it," Lillie breathed. The breeze ruffled the curled ends of her hair.

A sparkling pond named the Grand Basin lay at the end of the pavilion, spattered with boats, gondolas, and arcing fountains. And beyond it rose Festival Hall, an immense, round dome that was set up on the hill like an elaborately decorated wedding cake. It was the most stunning building Grace had ever seen, intricately carved and lined with stately columns. Water poured out from a fountain set at its front like an open mouth, cascading into stacked levels of fourteen waterfalls. Grand sets of wide, magnificent steps rimmed either side of these flowing cascades like an embrace, and fountains gracefully arced into the Grand Basin while being lit from below.

Even Aunt Clove, for once, seemed unable to find fault.

Laughter and accented voices drenched the air as tens of thousands of people crowded by in their hats and finery. Concession tents sold puffed rice, crystal clear water, and scoops of vanilla ice cream in fluted glass dishes. As they passed the sunken gardens, electric lamps began switching on in their posts, and the night air became perfumed with sugar and roasted nuts, honeysuckle, and primrose blossoms. They strolled alongside bursts of pink and yellow spring tulips, smelling fragrant hyacinth, redbuds, and lilacs. Elation was something Grace could almost taste in the air. She couldn't believe she was there, alive in this moment, in a place so immersive and magnificent. She didn't know how she would ever return to real life.

"My darling, my dearest, my delight," Oliver said to Grace just before they passed a hundred-foot column honoring the Louisiana Purchase at the head of the Basin. He linked elbows with her, every bit the dapper gentleman, tipping his top hat at every acquaintance they passed.

"I know that tone," she said drolly. Over the years, they'd grown quite proficient at holding private conversations and sharing morsels of secrets while they casually walked just out of earshot of his parents. "What do you want?"

Oliver shot a nervous glance in Lillie's direction to make sure she wasn't listening. "Just a small favor," he said.

"And here I thought you'd brought me along, once again, for my scintillating company and sparkling conversation," she said.

"I always bring you along for that," he said. "And for your loyalty, benevolence, and discretion."

His eyes searched hers, pleading.

"Just tell me what it is," she said, cutting him a look. "You already know I'm going to say yes."

"In a few minutes we'll enter the Under and Over the Sea attraction," he said. "Gondolas will take us through a winding maze of canals before dropping us off at the private dinner. And I'm wondering if you'll share a boat with me."

"Of course," she said. "I thought you were going to ask me something *hard*."

"Well . . ." He gave her a slightly devious grin. "I'm hoping you'll be willing to swap boats with Harriet in the middle."

"Ah. I see," she said, cocking an eyebrow. "Then whom will *I* be sitting with? Will I be engaging in hand-to-hand combat with some notorious axe murderer on the way to dinner?"

"No, although if you were, I do hope you know my money would entirely be on you."

"No need for flattery, Oliver, I've already said yes."

"The only other person who knows about my feelings for Harriet is my closest friend, and he's already agreed to help. So no pressure," he said, batting his long eyelashes, "but ensuring my forever happiness is at this point all up to you."

She relaxed. She knew Oliver's best friend. A preppy, foppish young man named Evan Waxwell who rather inordinately loved croquet. Fine. It would be slightly painful, and perhaps scandalous if they were caught, but they could talk about mallets and wickets or whatever he wanted.

"Of course," she said. She wanted to say, *I would do anything for you.* Especially this week—the last time she could help him, even though he didn't know it yet. Instead she said, "If your mother finds out, she's going to throw me out of the boat and drown me in the lagoon."

"Don't be silly. She has standards," Oliver said. "That's a Paul Poiret she's wearing."

Grace snorted.

She followed Oliver into the immense opening of the Under and Over the Sea ride, where they were ushered in by guards who unlatched a red velvet rope for them. The building had intricately sculpted towers that rose almost two hundred feet above their heads. Inside was a soaring foyer, its heavenly ceiling scattered with delicately painted domes. It was quiet and cool after the vibrant crush of humanity in the fairgrounds. Inside, waiters offered them drinks that looked like small vases made of frosted glass and topped with violets. Grace drank hers from a striped straw. It tasted like nothing she'd ever had before, sparkling and floral.

"To us!" Lillie said, toasting Grace and Oliver. As soon as they'd raised their glasses, Lillie's eyes fell on someone in the crowd.

"Frannie!" she cried. She moved forward to give Frannie a kiss on the cheek and then pulled her back toward them. "You know Ollie, of course. And this is my beloved cousin, Grace," Lillie said. "Grace, this is Frannie Allred."

Frannie was dressed in a forest-green dress that set off her small waist and dark red hair. She gave Grace a smile that never reached her eyes.

"Oh yes, we've met," she said, as if they were old friends. "How do you do, Grace?"

Grace smiled wanly.

"We must ride together on the gondola," Frannie said, taking Lillie's arm and turning her away. "I have so much to tell you."

"I can't wait! And Grace must come, too."

"Oh, there's only room for two," Frannie said, her voice somehow both syrupy and sad.

Lillie frowned. "Well—"

"I'll ride with Grace," Oliver quickly volunteered.

"Yes. It's fine. I'll go with Oliver," Grace said. She gave Lillie an encouraging nod. Then she returned Frannie's disingenuous smile with a dazzling one of her own.

They were shown to a wide marble staircase leading down into a darkened pavilion, which was cavernous and lit inside to look like the night sky. Boats with gondoliers were lined up, lilting on the dark waves.

They waited with a handful of other guests in their finery while Aunt Clove and Uncle Reginald climbed into the first boat.

Then Lillie shot Grace an apologetic look and climbed into the second boat with Frannie.

"This is a clever little trick," Grace said to Oliver as he helped her into the third. They pushed off from the pavilion and began to glide across the inky waves. A lantern hung from the back of their boat. The starry lights reflected in the dark, swirling tidepools left by the stroke of the oar. From somewhere in the distance, she could hear the deep pounding of drums. They echoed her own heartbeat.

Oliver spoke quietly to the gondolier, who gently pulled over beneath the first bridge in the underground lagoon, where another boat was waiting in the shadows.

"Thanks, mate," Oliver said, handing him a hefty wad of bills.

"Hi, Harriet," Grace said, looking into the shadows beneath the bridge. She smiled with genuine delight as Harriet stepped into the boat.

"Thanks for this, Grace," Harriet said.

"My pleasure. I'm forever in service to clandestine young love," Grace said. Oliver helped her balance as she prepared to board the second boat.

She looked at the gondolier as she stepped across, beginning to greet her partner in crime, Evan. He reached up to steady her and keep her from falling.

But it wasn't Evan who was taking her by the hand.

No, Grace thought, freezing. *No, no, no.*

It was Theodore Parker.

CHAPTER TWO

GRACE FALTERED, losing her balance just enough to almost fall into the water.

"Careful," Theodore said roughly, catching her.

She regained her footing and shoved him away, sitting down roughly on the seat.

"I thought you were meant to be his best friend Evan," she said sharply.

He frowned, his eyes flashing. "And I thought *you* would be Lillie," he retorted.

The gondolier pushed off into the glittering lights of the lagoon, and Grace dug her fingernails into her crossed arms. She was going to *kill* Oliver.

"Why did he say you were his closest friend?" she stewed. "He didn't even know you six months ago."

Theodore snorted. "Things have a tendency to change, you know. I moved to St. Louis, and he's shown me about."

"Perhaps things have a tendency to change, but certain people don't," she said bitterly.

She narrowed her eyes, kicking herself. If only she had told Oliver what kind of a man Theodore really was last winter. Well, that was one more secret that would need to be revealed before the week was over. She relished the way Oliver would react and could practically see him stripping off his coat and flexing his fists, the way he had done many times before to come to her and Lillie's aid.

She sighed and slipped off her gloves—Lillie's gloves—which had been splattered by water.

"Still a Covington, then, I see?" Theodore asked cruelly, gesturing to her naked ring finger. He swallowed hard, the handsome mark on his jaw darkening.

She clasped her hands together and flushed. "You're still unattached as well? How shocking," she said, turning away.

She couldn't believe how even now she remembered the way his strong arms felt around her, dancing. How he had saved her from that wretched man at the party only to become an even worse fate. Their gondolier steered the boat and turned a curve into a new lagoon, this one lit like a southern bayou. It was filled with the echoing sounds of bullfrogs, floating paper boats, and glowing lanterns. Fireflies flickered in the darkness. Her eyes lit when she saw them and she bit back a sound of awe. If she was with anyone else in the world, it would have been terribly romantic. She turned away from Theodore, reaching down to touch one of the lanterns. It was made of delicate rice paper and the candle inside flickered. Between the boats and lanterns were lily pads.

If only Grace's mother could see this right now. But then, of course, she had grown up in this world, too—it was Grace who was the outsider. Last week, her mother had sat on the bed while Grace packed her trunk for St. Louis, listening to Grace explain why the time had come to embrace reality. Her childhood had been like playing dress-up in a life not meant for her. At one time, perhaps they had both hoped that she might overcome her family name, might make a match that would mend the rip her mother had left behind. But it was apparent that people didn't forget. Perhaps if her mother hadn't fallen so far. If she hadn't been engaged to the most eligible bachelor of their time, only to elope with Grace's father instead. It had been an enormous scandal. People whispered about shotgun weddings and decisions soaked in booze rather than reason. But her parents had married for love, and Grace had never admired anyone more. She wanted what her parents had, and perhaps she could find it, too. Just not in Lillie and Oliver's world.

Although admittedly, her own felt very, very far away right now.

"Wow," she heard Theodore say under his breath. The canal curved around a bend and the gondolier steered them toward a re-creation of Switzerland. There was a small, quaint Alpine town set in front of a backlit range of purple-hued mountains. The village roofs were entirely made of flowers, and there was even a working clock tower. The ever-present frown on Theodore's face slightly receded, and something close to wonder came into his eyes.

She caught a whiff of his scent, that smoke and forest, and that night at the ball half a year ago came hurtling back at her. How could a person she had known for less than an hour have had such an impact on her? It was infuriating.

"Maybe you can find someone who wants to marry you in Switzerland," she said sweetly. "It can only help your case if she doesn't understand a word of English."

It was as though he had forgotten she was there. His face instantly darkened and the wonder in it shuttered, and for a moment, she strangely felt as though it were she who had lost something.

"Are we almost there?" he asked the gondolier. He looked at Grace dead-eyed. "This has been the longest boat ride of my life."

Grace strained toward the sound of lively music approaching in the distance. She couldn't shake the fact that she still found him vaguely handsome, even with his atrocious personality. She was glad he would never know those secret thoughts, which would only further inflate his already overblown ego.

"You have traveled much, before, no?" the gondolier asked Grace. He flashed her a smile and his mouth was filled with gold teeth.

"Yes," Theodore said, at the exact moment that Grace said, "Not really, no."

Theodore colored, realizing he had spoken out of turn, and looked away.

"But I hope to," Grace said. "Someday." She dipped her fingers into the cold water of the lagoon. "Where should I go, if I had the choice?"

The gondolier smiled again. "Italy," he said. "Venezia."

"That would be lovely," she said, smiling back. "Though this is likely the closest I will ever get."

She said it without a hint of bitterness. Her future in Kansas City could still be a beautiful one. She would rather be there amid pleasant people who had big ideas and small pocketbooks than spend the rest of her life surrounded by people obsessed with nothing but class and money and the precise order of their forks.

"What is your name?" she asked the gondolier.

"Giorgio," he said.

She felt Theodore's eyes on her, watching her with curiosity, and perhaps a bit of surprise. Maybe he'd never seen people of lower classes interact with one another before.

"Tell me, Giorgio," she said. "Do rich people in Italy seem to care an inordinate amount about the proper order of their cutlery?"

"Er," he said, sweeping the oar with a quizzical look. "Cutlery?"

"Never mind," she said, and Theodore snorted.

At least she could escape him soon. Beyond the final bend of the canal was a replica of a Spanish courtyard. Warm lights spilled across its cobblestone square and a neoclassical cathedral rose up behind it. Tables were set around a central fountain, where musicians milled around playing a bandurria, castanets, an accordion, and a flamenco guitar.

Grace bent down to hide herself from her aunt and uncle's gaze as their gondola floated past the party, and Theodore shot her a look of annoyance when her leg grazed his own—as if she had planned it. As if she were trying to *seduce* him. She wanted to tell him not to flatter himself, but it hardly seemed worth the effort. Instead, she drank in the scene, pretending that she really was in Spain. If she would never actually go, there was no harm in imagining it, was there? Guests in their finery were nursing glasses of vermouth or creamy leche *merengada* topped with cinnamon sticks. Some were perched on the fountain made from a mosaic of painted tiles, and there were colors and music everywhere, and ceramic pots spilling over with crimson carnations and pink roses. Grace was itching to leave the boat and find her cousins. Her heart soared. This night was already beyond her imagination. Thankfully the boats unloaded at a pier in the shadows so that she and Theodore were able to disembark without being seen.

"Thank you, Giorgio," Grace said to the gondolier, and ignored Theodore's perfunctory hand to step out of the boat. She marched toward Oliver, seething, and let herself be only slightly distracted by the hundreds of candles that flickered in a cascade of votives from the cathedral.

"Is that real?" she asked Oliver breathlessly, reminding herself that without him, she wouldn't even be here.

"Drink?" he replied instead of answering, handing her a half-frozen leche *merengada*. "They're meant to be for dessert, but I couldn't help myself." He didn't seem remotely apologetic about what he'd just put her through on the boat ride over. After all, she supposed, why would he? She'd never mentioned Theodore to him, and Theodore must not have said anything about their encounter to him, either. Oliver looked radiantly happy as he clinked his glass with hers in celebration. "You look lovely," he said to her, but his eyes were still on Harriet, who was making her way around the party. Grace relaxed a little, feeling her annoyance melt away. She would tell him the whole story later, at a time that wouldn't ruin this night for either of them. For now, she'd just leave all thoughts of Theodore Parker behind and have as much fun as possible. She wanted to remember this week forever. She would drink deep of its intoxicating nectar, even if it hurt her all the more later.

"I absolutely insist you try this." Lillie placed a small plate of citrus-marinated olives and impossibly thin strips of *jamón* into Grace's hands.

"Just make sure to use the right fork," Theo said under his breath, so that only Grace could hear.

"Oh, I can think of many good uses for this fork right now," Grace retorted as they were ushered to a round table in the courtyard to sit down for dinner. There were large, vibrant clay plates set on a mosaic-patterned tablecloth. Oliver and Lillie were seated across the table. Grace's name was scrawled in elegant script on a place card between a man named Earnest Allred and . . . Theodore Parker.

She sighed and swept into her chair, dejectedly eating an olive.

"Well, I suppose that's two things I've never done before tonight," a man said, taking his seat next to her.

"Arrive at dinner by gondola?" she asked, turning toward him and pointedly away from Theodore's brooding presence.

"Visited fake Spain and had the pleasure of your acquaintance," the man said. "I'm Earnest." He extended a hand to her. "Allred."

"I'm Grace," she said, "Covington. I'm Oliver and Lillie Carter's cousin," she said clearly, so that Theodore could hear her—so that she could prove to him that she had nothing to hide.

Theodore cleared his throat into his water glass.

Grace examined Earnest as he said hello to Theodore and Harriet. He had strawberry blond hair, dimples like Oliver's, and a friendly face. He seemed quick to laugh and was everything that Theodore wasn't. As such, she took an instant liking to him.

The waiter lit the candles on the table and served them bowls of something he explained was called *salmorejo*.

"Your surname is Allred?" Grace asked Earnest, taking a bite of the soup. It was rich with cream and tomato, one of the most flavorful things she'd ever tasted. "You're related to Frannie, then?"

"Her brother," he clarified, stealing a look at where Frannie was engaged in conversation with Oliver. He made a knowing face at Grace. "I take it you've met?"

She smiled a little into her spoon as she took another bite of soup.

"Some of us have expensive taste in my family," Earnest said, taking out a copy of the fair's weekly program. He smoothed it out in front of him. "And some of us just like things that are beautiful."

He winked at her.

She flushed, enjoying his attention as Theodore sat beside her in stony silence.

"What are you most interested in viewing this week?" he asked, moving the program between them so she could see it. They bent together. She could smell his cologne, cinnamon and anise. She loved the warm light of the candles filling the cavern, flickering off the stone walls. She loved the intimacy of this private space, dinner with fifty people while tens of thousands of others walked in hidden crowds around them.

She traced the canals on the map that ran to the Palace of Electricity. "I want to see something historic and meaningful."

"And here I am just wanting to ride the observation wheel," he said, laughing. She smiled. Earnest had none of the airs of his sister. He was friendly and engaging, with an easy smile.

As a bonus, Frannie was glaring at them from across the table. And the chance to annoy Frannie and Theodore all in one go was almost too delightful to pass up.

Theodore turned and opened the question to the rest of the table for discussion. "What are you most looking forward to this week?"

"The Palace of Lights ball," Frannie said.

"The Pike," Harriet said immediately. "And I love to scream my lungs out on roller coasters. But—it's ridiculous—" She smiled a dazzling, self-deprecating smile. "These days I find I have to sing instead, so I don't injure my voice."

"Well, that's it. I want to hear Harriet scream-sing," Lillie declared. "And I want to eat fairy floss. And see acrobats. Theodore?"

Theodore swallowed. "I'd like to see the inventions," he said stiffly. "Thomas Edison himself is supposed to be at the Palace of Electricity overseeing some of them."

"Speaking of marvelous inventions," Oliver said. "I'm determined to try that waffle wrapped around ice cream. A cone, they call it."

"Hear! Hear!" Lillie said, raising her glass of Spanish cider. They cheered and as they ate paella and mussels, Earnest told Grace about his background growing up in St. Louis in the dynasty of the Allreds, who were known for their propensity to make money in lead, mercantile, and railroads. He'd wanted to go into aeronautics, but his parents had recently died, and he had inherited the family business instead.

"Oh. I'm sorry for your loss," she said. Her eyes flicked to Frannie with a newfound sympathy. Grace's parents were at home, patiently waiting for her to finish her St. Louis adventure and walk back through the door into their lives. Frannie would never have that experience again.

"Thank you," he said. "I can tell that you mean that." He gave her a small smile, then listened with interest as she told him about growing up in Kansas City and her father's restaurant.

"His vision is to be the next Delmonico's," she said. He had even taken her there once, on a trip to New York with her mother. Her father knew the chef and they'd been given a tour after hours. She remembered the cartoon drawings sketched across the menus, the rich sweetness of the ice cream and berries the chef had served them in the gleaming kitchen. Earnest's attention to her as she described it was flattering. She felt Theodore's eyes drift toward her.

When they stood, she was glad to realize that they had barely interacted.

"Are you always this sullen at parties?" she asked, gathering the train of her dress in her hand as she got up.

"You talked enough for the both of us. Half the table, really," he said.

She pulled on her gloves with a sharp, exaggerated precision. At least there had been no dancing tonight. Just intimate conversations over low-burning candles while flamenco guitars played in the background.

Perhaps too intimate. She noticed that Harriet and Oliver were bent toward each other, talking. Harriet was giggling at something he said and their faces drew nearer, sharing a confidence. Oliver was beaming, staring at Harriet with unmasked adoration.

Lillie was taking notice, too, glancing at them. Grace would have to tell Oliver to confess the truth soon or make a concerted effort to tone down his affections.

She didn't see Aunt Clove approaching until she was practically on top of them.

"Aunt Clove!" Grace exclaimed, attempting to block her. But the look of adoration on Oliver's face was unmistakable as he beamed at Harriet, and Clove's own face had settled into an alarming frown.

She stared at the space between them with something nearing a scowl. Oliver paled.

And Lillie stood beside them, looking confused.

Grace was just trying to decide what to do next when Theodore stepped forward.

"Mrs. Carter," he said, bowing formally to her. "It's a pleasure to see you again."

"And you, Theodore," she said, clearly still distracted. She began fanning herself in distress.

Theodore wove between Oliver and Harriet, then made a show of putting his hand at the small of Harriet's back.

"Mrs. Carter, have you met my . . ." He hesitated, his voice breaking a little, then cleared his throat. "My Harriet?" he asked.

Harriet smiled warmly and leaned in first toward Theodore, and then toward Aunt Clove. "How do you do?" she said, extending her hand. "I hope you don't mind that I've joined the party."

Aunt Clove visibly relaxed. "Of course not, dear," she said, her fan slowing. "I've always said that any friend of the Parkers . . ."

She stepped back, relieved.

"Hawthorne Shaw is here tonight," she said, turning to Lillie. "I'd love to introduce you." She threw one last glance over her shoulder at Theodore and Harriet and added in a low voice, "Theodore Parker is set to inherit eight million dollars. I would've hoped he'd set his eyes a *little* higher."

"Oh, Mother," Lillie said, rolling her eyes. "You know how this talk of money bores me."

Finally, Lillie broke free of her mother and came to take Grace's arm. She spun her around, then whispered in her ear, "Hurry, before my mother tries to marry me off to a man thrice my age." They giggled and darted together up the stairs to exit the Spanish plaza and into the humid St. Louis night perfumed with flowering azaleas and dogwood trees. Grace's head swam with joy.

"What you did back there with my mother was brilliant," she heard Oliver say in a low voice to Theodore. She turned to catch his look of pure gratitude.

Theodore didn't smile. "You know," he said dryly. "If you plan to make her the grandmother of Harriet's children, she's likely going to find out at some point."

"I know, I know," Oliver said. "I'll have to come clean soon. But if you could just play along a little longer . . . it will help my family warm to the idea of Harriet. Please."

Theodore worked his handsome jaw.

"I can get down on my knees and beg if debasing myself would help," Oliver offered.

"Fine," Theodore finally agreed. He grimaced. "Are we the only two who know?" he asked, tilting his head toward Grace.

Oliver nodded. "Yes. I'd trust my cousin with my life."

Theodore gave Grace a shrewd look that seemed to peer into the very depths of her. He frowned but surprised her when he bowed his head to her in a show of respect. "Well then. Bound together by the secret."

She narrowed her eyes and nodded, curtsying back.

Then she turned away. Oliver seemed so grateful to Theodore that she decided to hold her tongue. What a confusing man Theodore Parker was, a coin that kept flipping and showing different faces. But all the favors to her cousin in the world wouldn't make up for the dark side of him she had seen that night in Chicago. She wouldn't trust him as far as she could row a ship.

"Shall we meet back here tomorrow, then?" Lillie asked, pulling on her cloak. "We'll be sophisticated and cultured and tour the exhibits and the gardens. I want to eat an ice-cream cone and see the giant working clock fashioned entirely out of flowers."

"And then eat fairy floss and ride the carnival rides until we're sick," Harriet said.

"I love our little party," Earnest said, in a manner that seemed true to his name. And true to her own nature, Frannie hmphed.

Oliver's eyes were positively shining.

And Grace saw her dreams of her last, intimate week with her cousins fading away.

"Will I see you both tomorrow?" Earnest asked Grace and Lillie quietly. Grace nodded, and he bowed, a beautiful grin lighting his face. "Until then."

Theodore tipped his hat in a wordless goodbye at them all, his jaw tightening as Aunt Clove and Uncle Reginald approached.

"May I see you home?" Theodore asked, pivoting toward Harriet. "My driver and groom will accompany us." Harriet met his gaze and nodded.

Under the watchful eye of Grace's aunt, he escorted her into his waiting carriage.

"And then there were three," Oliver said, taking Lillie and Grace each by the arm.

Look at me, the jam in the sandwich, he used to say when they were children. *The sweet that holds it all together.*

The seedy part, I think you mean, Grace would reply.

The part that never fails to leave behind a sticky mess, Lillie would add.

Grace smiled at the memory.

"You seem to have enchanted Earnest Allred at dinner," Oliver said slyly to Grace as they strolled down the promenade. "Perhaps we'll make a permanent St. Louisan out of you yet."

"Oh! Don't tease me like that! Wouldn't that be everything, Grace?" Lillie squealed. "We could see each other every week instead of twice a year!"

Grace shook her head, laughing. "He was merely being a *gentleman*, Oliver, something understandably hard for you to recognize."

She should tell them now that this week would be the end, but she couldn't bring herself to. Instead, the image of Theodore's stormy face flashed across her mind.

Oliver watched the Parker carriage leave with Harriet inside, so trusting of his new friend Theodore. Grace hoped that her cousin's belief in him wasn't misplaced. She let Lillie take her by the arm, putting her head on her shoulder.

"Doesn't this feel like the kind of week that could change our lives forever?" Lillie said.

"Yes," Grace said quietly. She already knew that it would. Electricity crackled through the air like a coming storm.

New futures would be forged this week in the Ivory City, and beloved childhoods put to bed.

But for now, Grace thought, they were all together, and she knew no greater joy.

CHAPTER THREE

MAY 1, 1904

Two Days Before the Murder

The next morning, they ventured to the Pike. It was a one-mile stretch of amusements that ran from the Plaza of St. Louis to University Way, and by nine o'clock it was already teeming with people. Grace took Lillie's hand, and they walked beneath Lillie's parasol past the towering German Tyrolean Alps. The restaurant situated beneath its snow-covered peaks sat twenty-five hundred guests at a time and served over eighty kinds of wine. There were bazaars with merchants shouting, advertisements for gladiators battling in Ancient Rome, a mosque from Constantinople, an Irish village featuring a reconstruction of the Blarney Castle.

They followed a family chatting in Arabic and two men arguing in French and settled on breakfast in Cairo.

The café was set in the morning shadows beneath the balconies and striped awnings of a brick street teeming with fairgoers, camels, and monkeys. Oliver ordered them *ful medames* and flatbreads called *aish baladi*, and they drank black tea with fresh mint leaves, poured out of a teapot with a tall spout and served in clear glasses. Grace sipped her tea, taking note of the flavors so she could recount them to her father later. To her right, someone rode by on a caparisoned camel, holding an umbrella, and it was almost impossible to believe that she was in the heart of St. Louis.

"I had no idea Harriet and Theo were courting," Frannie said to Lillie, delicately selecting a date from the china. She wore kid gloves, and her hair was pulled up in a pompadour. The brooch at her neck was so overlarge it looked almost as if it were strangling her.

Grace snuck a subtle glance at Oliver. "I think it's brand-new," she said warily. "Probably nothing serious."

"Careful, you'll start to sound jealous," Frannie said, smiling with a little too much teeth.

Oliver squeezed Grace's knee under the table, and she bit back a snort.

Earnest's blond hair was curling in the morning humidity. His woolen suit probably cost more than a month of meals at her father's restaurant, Grace thought. He caught her eye and smiled, relaxing back in his chair. "This tea is good enough to make me wonder if something's in it. Does anyone else almost feel intoxicated?" he mused.

"Speaking of which, Grace, how *is* your brother?" Frannie asked under her breath. She dabbed her napkin on her mouth, eyelashes fluttering.

Grace's hand froze around her glass. Oliver stiffened next to her, but a brass band had begun to play on the street and no one else had heard the slight.

"Frannie, I was looking forward to seeing the lions and tigers later," Oliver said, throwing his napkin on the table in her direction, "but thanks to you, I've already had my fill of cattiness today."

Frannie made a sound, taken aback by Oliver's brazenness, and Grace would have laughed if an image of Walt hadn't flooded into her mind. He'd been gaunt the last time she'd seen him. She felt the way her chest had squeezed, as though she hadn't been able to catch her breath.

When she was a young girl, Walt had made elaborate slides for her doll Sanders from the baking pans in their father's kitchen. Once, he had constructed a luge that stretched all the way from the kitchen down to the entrance of the dining room. Sanders had shot across the floor so fast that it had nearly tripped Johnny, the dishwasher, and Walt had rushed to steady the tower of dishes just before they crashed to the floor. Grace and Walt had laughed until they were dizzy. "Walter, I think you're destined to be an engineer," their mother had quipped, and Grace remembered the way the sun had caught around her shining face like a halo. Now Grace's gaze slid to the Ferris wheel in the distance, and she felt a dull surge of anger. Her brother had been meant for so much more.

"How did they make these intricate buildings so quickly?" she asked to get the image out of her mind. She practically had to shout to be heard over the clanging commotion on the street.

"It's staff," Earnest said, reaching out to stroke the carved quoin beside his chair. "Plaster and fiber and paste. Like papier-mâché. It will come down as easily as it went up."

"All style," Theo said, stroking the tie at his throat. "No substance."

"I know some people like that, too," Grace said airily.

Theo was just about to say something back when Frannie let out a gasp.

"Earnest!" she said.

A gush of bright, red blood was running from Earnest's nose.

He reached up to touch it with his hand, as if surprised.

"You're bleeding!" Frannie cried.

"I recognize that, Frannie," he said calmly.

Drip. It fell from his nose to the tablecloth, where it bloomed like a grotesque flower. Or a bullet hole.

Hurriedly, Grace pulled a handkerchief from her pocketbook and handed it to him.

His fingers brushed hers as he took it.

"Blast," he said, holding the handkerchief to his nose. "This hasn't happened to me since I was a kid. I'm so sorry."

"Please, don't apologize," Grace said. "Just take care of yourself."

"Oh, no, I insist—doesn't every lady like a little blood with her breakfast?"

Grace laughed. "No. But I do love a man who can keep me guessing," she said.

"I'm mortified."

He was suddenly so shy and embarrassed, and she found it charming. She would take a man like this over a pompous ass like Theodore any day.

"Just keep holding pressure," Lillie said, moving to help him. "Yes, like that. There you go."

"Thank you," Earnest said, looking up at her. "This is very kind of you."

"Lillie, darling, I had no idea you were good with blood," Oliver said.

Lillie's eyebrow faintly twitched.

"One of us has to be good in an emergency," she said breezily. "And it certainly isn't going to be Mother. Or you."

"It's true, I faint dead away at the sight of blood," Oliver said. "And I inherited that trait straight from her. That and her adorable little nose."

"Earnest," Frannie hissed. "Are you quite under control now?"

Her face was flushed, and a dark part of Grace was pleased that the attention Frannie had tried to direct toward Grace's brother had suddenly shifted to her own.

"You might want to put your head between your legs, dearest brother," Lillie said to Oliver. "You're looking a little green."

"Nothing a little breakfast ice cream can't fix," Oliver said, tossing enough money on the table to cover the entire bill. "My treat, Earnest. Perhaps a cold ice-cream headache will fix that nosebleed right up. Onward!"

Earnest stood, the nosebleed abated. He clutched Grace's handkerchief at his side, still offering apologies.

She tried not to notice the way that crimson had darkened the delicate monogram her mother had stitched into the hem, creeping along the ivory lace like an ominous shadow.

❧

Under the striped awning of the cart, Grace insisted on paying for her own ice cream.

She felt Theodore Parker's imposing stare, with his perfectly tailored three-piece suit, gloves, and cane. Her cotton and lace dress might have belonged to Lillie, but her treat was rich with cream and a hint of peppermint, and it tasted even sweeter knowing that she had bought it herself.

"Miss Covington," he said flatly.

"Mr. Parker," she said, eyebrow arching.

The morning sun was growing hot, and Grace felt a trickle of sweat beneath the lace of her high collar as a magician passed by in a parade, handcuffed and trapped in a cage with a live tiger. The tiger hissed, saliva dripping from its mouth.

"Ah, look! A reenactment of the night we first met," Theodore said.

"It must have made quite an impression on you," Grace said. "I hardly remember it at all."

"Touché," he said with something almost bordering on amusement. "Just don't forget your *spoon*," he added under his breath, his eyes smoldering.

"It's the future, Mr. Parker, haven't you heard?" she said. "I won't even need one."

As the parade cleared, she saw a discarded newspaper on the ground and stooped to retrieve it. Her face burned a little upon the realization that no one else in their party, save maybe for Harriet, might even think of picking up a trashed newspaper from the street. They would simply buy a fresh one. She smoothed it out quickly, trying to cover her faux pas as she caught up with Lillie. It was a gossip rag called the *Fair's Fare* by Sam Whitcomb.

"Look!" she whispered to Lillie. They put their heads together to scour the salacious rag as they navigated between the throngs of the Pike, smelling saffron and sweat and perfume, weaving around vendors selling sweet milk, freshly brewed iced tea, and loaf cakes for 10 cents apiece. "Harriet's in it!" Lillie said.

"'GIRL ABOUT TOWN HARRIET FORBES SEEN WITH RECENT ST. LOUIS TRANSPLANT AND THE CITY'S MOST ELIGIBLE BACHELOR,'" she read. *"'Marked by birth in more ways than one, he's reportedly worth almost $70K a year.'"*

"St. Louis's *most* eligible bachelor? Hmph. I resent that," Oliver said.

"What utter trash," Theodore said with disdain, his port-wine stain deepening. His jaw was stark and handsome, his face somehow even more striking when his eyes were like fire.

"The news is out now," Lillie teased.

Theo shot Oliver a look of daggers, and Oliver responded with a subtle, sheepish shrug.

Surely this charade could come to an end now, Grace thought. Lillie's keen eyes glanced between Theodore and Oliver, always picking up on everything. She was sharp and she knew something was up.

"And look—he claims someone from the Cinch was spotted going into the Tunnels," Oliver said.

"The Cinch?"

"The business leaders of St. Louis," Earnest said. "The politicians don't run the town. They do."

"What are the Tunnels?" Lillie asked.

Oliver and Earnest exchanged an uneasy look. "Nothing the ladies need to know about."

Harriet waited until the men kept walking. "It's a seedy drug market," she whispered behind her gloved hand. "There are a few tunnels that run beneath the Pike from the Tyrolean Alps."

The thought made Grace feel suddenly ill.

"I guess I'm full from breakfast" was all she said, shoving the last of her cone into Oliver's hand.

"Since when have you ever not wanted ice cream, Grace Carter Covington?" he asked, but he devoured it without waiting for her answer.

"Come," Lillie said, noticing Grace's fallen temperament. "Let's go watch small children ride on that simply enormous tortoise."

Grace crumpled the gossip rag in her hand. The massive ivory palaces in the distance shone in the sunlight, shimmering like a dream. In Hagenbeck's Animal Show there was an elephant going down a slide, and a female photographer standing on stilts to capture a photograph. Small boys chased one another in sailor suits, and one girl was crying over a melted ice cream. Grace and Lillie stopped to admire the giant working floral clock, created with varying shades of centaurea, verbena, and twelve-foot-tall numbers made of red coleus. The marching bands were awash in bright brass sounds, and the scent of chocolate melded with the scarlet and pink begonias.

As they stepped inside the massive Palace of Agriculture, the floral scent dissipated into ripe fruit and rich, freshly-pressed olive oil. There was a huge roaring bear made of prunes and a wine temple draped with clusters of grapes in the California exhibit; a temple constructed entirely of multicolored corn cobs; and the Liquid Carbonic Company's soda fountain, which was flanked with potted palms and a wide bar staffed by waiters in crisp white uniforms. Grace ate and laughed until her stomach ached. She'd never seen so many people, so many inventions. It felt as though she'd opened an invitation from the world and glimpsed the swirling calligraphy of the card beneath. Doubt cut through the delight she felt, hollowing it like a knife. Could she really go back to Kansas City after this?

Why couldn't she just be happy with what she had?

She remembered being a young girl, hiding behind an urn during one of Aunt Clove's dinner parties. Lillie and Oliver had made a brief appearance to be shown off and petted, and Grace had snuck down the stairs herself, for just one glimpse.

She'd hid behind the chinoiserie and watched the champagne-infused laughter, the intricately set table of flowers and candlesticks, the guests in their shimmering gowns, and told herself she didn't care that they didn't want her. But she'd shrewdly observed their manners. She didn't want to be invited, she told herself, hugging her knees to her chest—she just wanted to be adequately prepared in case she ever was.

Now, beneath the columned, towering ceilings of the Palace of Transportation, she passed a revolving steam engine and shook hands with a man she'd never have dreamed she would meet—the inventor Thomas Edison—then followed Earnest through the rows of hundreds of gleaming new-fashioned American automobiles and motorcars while he considered buying one. His eyes shone as he examined the machines one after another, sitting in the plush red seats.

"But how will you finance one of my shows if you buy one of these, Mr. Allred?" Harriet said playfully, running her fingers along the hood of a jet-black American Mercedes. "Don't think I don't remember your promise."

His eyes crinkled as he winked. "I haven't forgotten."

Grace didn't even dare touch the automobile. How strange to be around people for whom money was no object. It felt like magic.

And she couldn't deny how flattered—and perhaps even a little frightened—she felt that Earnest had seemed to take an interest in her. Why would he want her when Lillie was right there?

He tilted his paper cone of puffed corn toward her so that she could try it.

"I have a little surprise for tonight," he said conspiratorially. "Do you like surprises, Miss Covington?"

"That all depends. When they involve death, dismemberment, or disaster? No. But if they involve dinner, dancing, or dessert . . . then . . . yes."

Earnest smiled and leaned closer to her ear. "How about defiance of gravity and displays of wonder?"

"Then do say more," she said breathlessly.

"I believe something will happen tonight that will make history and the future meet. It's in the very air itself. Can you feel it?"

The crackle in his voice gave her a sudden thrill.

"What do you think, Miss Covington? Would you like to see history made?"

His excitement was contagious. She felt the spark down her spine. To be where history happened. That's what she wanted from this week. To be near enough to touch it.

She nodded.

"Save a dance for me tonight, won't you, Miss Covington?" Earnest asked. He kissed her on the hand, then Lillie's, and helped them into their carriage.

"Could this day have been any more perfect?" Grace breathed, collapsing into the velvet seat as soon as the door was closed.

"He likes you," Lillie said, her smile stretching wide. "My darling, he must see what I see, which means he is going to fall effortlessly in love with you." She brought her forehead to touch Grace's, beaming, and they both squealed.

❧

Grace soaked her sore feet in gloriously hot water before lacing them into slippers and donning a gorgeous oyster silk dress covered in embroidered flowers for the Dragon Ball. The nephew of the emperor of China, Prince Pu Lun, had built a replica of his summer palace in the Chinese pavilion and was throwing an elegant party for those lucky enough to gain the invites: red and gold, and stamped with an official chop. The Cinch had determined which households were invited, and Grace's uncle had overruled Aunt Clove and said she was allowed to come.

Aunt Clove was in a huff about that, hovering and eavesdropping more than usual, wanting to know how the fair had gone.

"Did you see the statue of the president of the United States of America made out of *butter*?" Aunt Clove asked. "How crass."

"No. But we saw the X-ray machine and a horse that does math, which was decidedly more impressive," Lillie said.

"Was that actress there today?" Aunt Clove asked. "The one with Theodore Parker?"

Oliver smiled bitingly. "Her name is Harriet, Mother."

"It's an odd pairing, certainly. I'm sure Mrs. Parker would be rolling over in her grave," Aunt Clove said. "Will she be there tonight, then?"

"Mrs. Parker? No. Last time I checked, she was still dead."

"Oliver. Stop being cheeky. You know very well I meant that actress."

"*Harriet*," Oliver said.

Lillie was watching Oliver carefully.

His face remained smooth and with the perfect amount of nonchalance when he pulled on his gloves and said, "I have no idea. I guess we'll find out when we get there."

He was a chillingly good liar, Grace noted—and between him and Aunt Clove, she didn't get to speak to Lillie privately until they were entering the Chinese pavilion.

Lillie was dressed in a red silk dress with an exquisite, intricate pattern of lace over the bodice that was mirrored along the hem. The neck was high but draped with strands of lace that emulated delicate necklaces. Her hair was pulled up with pins in the shape of gold lotus blossoms that caught the light.

She was nothing short of stunning. Several heads turned wherever she moved.

Lillie didn't seem to notice.

The Imperial Chinese pavilion was set beside the Belgium exhibit and just in front of Cuba. The Ferris wheel was visible in the distance, peeking out from beyond the elegant, upwardly sloping eaves of the vibrant red entrance gate. They passed through it and stepped into the Chinese pavilion, which had a fragrant rose garden, a goldfish pond, and an intricate pagoda carved with six thousand pieces of wood, ivory, and ebony. Red Chinese lanterns hung from the timbers, delicately swaying with the evening breeze.

"I need your help tomorrow evening," Lillie whispered to Grace, taking her arm. "Can you distract Oliver for me so I can slip away?"

"What do you mean, distract him?" Grace asked. "We're in the middle of the fair. Shall I propose a game of croquet?"

"I'll pretend to go off with some friends tomorrow evening. I just need him and my mother to not be asking questions. It shouldn't be hard." Lillie's fingertips grazed her blood-red lips. Her hair smelled like it always did, clean and faintly of lavender. "Not as though he hasn't been distracted enough lately," she said under her breath.

Grace paused. "What do you mean?" she asked.

Lillie's eyes scanned the crowded palace, pausing for a moment on Harriet. She almost seemed to say something.

"Never mind," she said.

"Look," Grace said, eager to change the subject. "There's the prince."

Prince Pu Lun was speaking with the fair's president and organizer, David Francis. He was flanked by bodyguards and wore small circular spectacles. His ornate silk robes were intricately embroidered with gold-wrapped thread that shimmered in the light.

"Cheers." Lillie accepted a teacup, raising it to Grace just as Adolphus Busch, the St. Louis beer brewing magnate, presented the prince with the gift of a brand-new carriage.

The crowd exploded with applause.

Grace sipped her tea, which was strong with jasmine, and followed Lillie toward the open-air balconies, where the sunrise was beginning to streak across the sky in shades of soft pink and lilac. She knew, even without having to ask, where Lillie was going tomorrow: the Evening Dispensary. She was the only one who knew Lillie's secret and she held it close to her breast, as careful as an infant, knowing what it would cost Lillie if high society—or worse, her own mother—found out. Sneaking off to help female doctors at the underground women's clinic was dangerous, but it wasn't wrong. It was noble, actually, and that was why Grace was willing to help her. She loved her good, good cousin. Her smart and wickedly funny and kindhearted cousin. She gave Lillie an affectionate kiss on the cheek, just because she could. For one more week at least, she could do that whenever she pleased. And then she glanced over her shoulder, scanning the room for Earnest.

"Cousin," Oliver said, finishing his drink. "You look lovely tonight."

"Thank you," Grace said. She smoothed down her dress. "So does Harriet," she added, so that only Oliver could hear.

"She looks happy," Oliver said, as Harriet laughed throatily at something Theo said. And she did. She was beautiful, wearing a black dress patterned with iridescent shells that caught the dim light. Theodore was sharply handsome in a tailored black suit, his face all angles in the shadows.

"Indeed," said Grace lightly. "Mr. Parker is playing his role well."

Too well? she wondered. She wouldn't put it past Theodore Parker to be the sort of man to steal his friend's love. And, a darker part of her thought, if Harriet was merely out for money and status, then Theo had even more to offer her than Oliver.

She felt almost violently protective of her cousins. She wanted their every happiness. And yet she knew how money distorted things. How enticing Oliver might be for his fortune alone. How difficult it could be to tell the truth of feelings when money was involved.

After all—she liked Earnest Allred. She could feel her attraction to him growing. But she wanted to make certain she liked him for genuine reasons, and not just what he could do for her. Or in exchange, she would come to no longer like herself.

Almost as though summoned by her thoughts, Frannie Allred appeared at the palace entrance dressed in a jewel-blue dress that set off her pale skin and auburn hair. Grace leaned forward and her heart rose, but the man on Frannie's arm wasn't Earnest. Instead he was a tall, handsome redhead that Frannie gazed at adoringly.

Grace felt the sharp prick of disappointment. *Careful*, she cautioned herself. *Don't get your hopes up.*

She'd been burned enough times to know that people in these circles worked with different sets of rules than she did. Perhaps, despite asking her to dance, Earnest wasn't coming tonight after all,

"Looking for someone?" Theodore asked wryly, appearing at Grace's elbow, sipping his yellow wine. She smelled a whiff of honey and smoke.

She didn't look at him. "For a man who hates parties you seem to attend a frightful lot of them," she said.

"With company this pleasant," he said smoothly, "who could blame me?"

She rolled her eyes. The air was pungent with floral scents of yellow wine and sprays of peach blossoms and chrysanthemums. Grace loved the smell of the intricately carved teakwood chairs, the rustle of the Chinese women's rich silks. The way she felt so far away from her real life. She plastered a smile on her face as Oliver and Lillie approached with a young Chinese man, trying to chase away the disappointment that Earnest was still not there.

"Grace. Theodore," Oliver said, "I'd like to introduce you to Mr. Wang. He was born and raised in Beijing and studies at Yale. This is my cousin, Miss Grace Covington."

"If this display is to be believed, your country is more beautiful than I can imagine," she said, curtsying.

He laughed a little, bowing in acknowledgment. "Even I still don't have a full grasp of my country's beauty. But we have done what we can to capture a faint breath of it."

"You would argue that these fair exhibits are hardly reality, then?" Oliver said. "We don't actually have temples of corn here in Missouri, after all."

"Perhaps they do not show the reality, but the ideal," Mr. Wang said. "And yet what we believe to be ideal shows the reality of who we are."

"I couldn't agree more!" Frannie's date said energetically, coming to join them. "That's what the fair is all about, isn't it? Picture this," he said, his blue eyes alight. "Tonight. A flying contest, pitting the newest machines and the best pilots. The winner has to get their machine around the course three times at twenty miles per hour. It can be a balloon, an aeroplane, a glider—the imagination, if you will allow the pun, soars."

"We'll allow it," Lillie said, smiling. "Won't we, Grace?"

"Ah, the infamous Grace," the man said, interest lighting his features. He turned to her with an appraising look. "Earnest has told me all about you."

Grace couldn't hide the flush she felt instantly sweep across her cheeks. Frannie's expression darkened like a storm.

"I'm Laurel," the man continued, "but everyone calls me Copper. Earnest and I row together. I'm his trainer."

"Don't say that," Frannie said haughtily. "It sounds so *common*. You're much more than his trainer."

"That's true, I'm also a runner," he said. "I'll be participating in the Olympic Games in a few months."

Frannie was incensed. "Earnest and Copper were school chums at University of Chicago, and he's the grandson of a *governor*," she said indignantly, sipping her rice wine.

"It's nice to meet you," Grace said.

She stole another look around the room. Theodore was speaking with Harriet and didn't seem to be looking in their direction at all. Something about that annoyed Grace more than she cared to acknowledge.

"Shall we head outdoors?" Copper asked, taking Frannie by the elbow. "The flight show is about to start."

They made their way outside. The night was mild, and lanterns hung from the eaves and lined the pathways to the rose gardens and the sloping roof of the teahouse. The cacophony from the heat of the day had quieted to a pleasant, dull chatter and the gentle tinkling of distant bells. The tea was warm and fragrant in Grace's hand—jasmine—and the air was pregnant with something. And that's why part of Grace still wanted to try to be in this world, even though it didn't want her back. There was always a feeling as though something magnificent could happen at any moment.

She looked over her shoulder again. Earnest was fascinated with aeronautics. He wouldn't miss this.

Was something wrong?

"Will Earnest be joining us tonight?" Grace asked Copper.

"Are you familiar with the Wright brothers, Miss Covington?" Copper asked, instead of answering.

She smiled. "Of course," she said. "Their aeroplane was all over the papers in December."

"I'm told that a new flying machine called the *Windshare* is going to attempt something similar tonight."

"Oh?"

Grace chanced one more look around the pavilion for Earnest's golden head, his bright blue eyes. Maybe he would show up at the last minute? Surely Frannie would have mentioned if he were ill?

"A dirigible called the *California Arrow* set the current record in the contest. It was airborne for thirty-seven minutes," Copper said.

The sun was setting in a striation of pinks to the west when a spotlight from the top of the Whitcomb Publishing building swung toward the sky.

The gathering crowd looked up, rapt, and applause rang out across the courtyard as something began a trajectory. It didn't look like a regular plane, but something made of silk and a bamboo-like scaffolding taking flight.

Prince Pu Lun stood next to fair President Francis on the pavilion, eyes trained on the sky.

"The future," Francis said, his eyes shining. "This is what it's all for."

Oliver slapped his knee, then put his arm around Harriet as if he'd forgotten he wasn't supposed to. "And hot damn! Here we are, right on its front porch, demanding to be let in."

Lillie did a slight double take when she saw him, taking in the intimate way he was holding Harriet. Her eyes widened.

"I can't believe it," Copper said, chuffing, shaking his head. "He did it. Earnest bloody well did it."

"What on earth do you mean?" Frannie asked, turning toward him. She choked out a laugh, as though the thought that occurred to her was absurd. "Surely you don't mean Earnest is *inside* that contraption?"

"I absolutely do." Copper raised his glass. "To the World's Fair!"

The crowd around them whooped and responded. "To the future!" they shouted.

And at that moment, the *Windshare* exploded.

CHAPTER FOUR

For a moment, Grace heard nothing but the tunneling of night, her heartbeat in her ears.

And then Frannie started screaming.

"You don't understand!" Frannie cried hysterically. "Earnest was in it. Earnest!"

The *Windshare* was falling from the sky in a golden blaze of sparks. It looked like a giant, burning coal.

"There's a parachute," Lillie breathed, her eyes trained toward a small, falling figure. She took off running.

Grace followed, panic spilling through her as they ran through the night in their gowns toward the place where the *Windshare* had fallen. A huge fireball went up when it made contact with the ground and forced them back. Frannie tripped and Grace stopped to help her to her feet. For the first time, she felt a stab of deep sympathy. This poor girl who had already lost her parents and maybe now her brother.

"Help!" someone screamed ahead of them. "He's alive! The pilot is alive!"

Oliver reached the scene first. There was a crowd gathering around a lump on the ground, the parachute spread out beside it like the tattered train of a gown. "The ropes!" Oliver yelled. "Cut him free! Get him away from the blaze."

Grace's lungs were heaving as Lillie pushed through the crowd and knelt beside Oliver. She had more medical training than most after shadowing the female doctors at the Evening Dispensary for two years.

"Earnest?" she asked, examining him. His face was dirt-streaked, sweating, and pale. "Earnest, it's Lillie."

"Lillie," he groaned. He met her eyes, and then he passed out.

Frannie ran toward Earnest, but Theodore grabbed her and held her tightly. She started to thrash against him. "It's going to be all right, Frances," he said as she broke down and sobbed. "Listen to me. He's alive."

Time was a kaleidoscope for Grace and came back into focus as the horse-drawn ambulance arrived and paramedics leapt out. Thirty yards away, firefighters fought to put out the blaze of the flying machine's wreckage. An enormous, frightened crowd had gathered along the periphery and police officers were attempting to cordon them away. Lillie talked the paramedics into letting her accompany them in the ambulance, displaying enough medical knowledge that they stopped arguing. She jumped inside.

"Frannie and I will follow in the carriage," Oliver said. He took off his coat and threw it around Harriet, who had tears in her eyes and was shivering.

"Theo, could you see them home?" he asked.

Theo nodded. He stripped off his own coat and wordlessly offered it to Grace.

The shock was translating into shivers that wracked her body. And yet still she hesitated.

"Don't be stubborn, Covington," he ordered.

She nodded, and he gently put it around her shoulders. She sunk into the warmth of the wool. The scent of him cut through the smell of acrid smoke. She tried to hide the way that she burrowed in deeper, breathing it in, so comforting. It almost felt as though he had taken her into his arms.

❧

The ambulance trundled away over the uneven dirt and the crowd began to disperse. Grace didn't much feel like returning to the party at the Chinese pavilion or like going home, especially to her aunt and uncle.

Harriet felt the same way.

"My nerves need a drink," Harriet said. "I know of a place. Are you game?"

For a moment Grace thought Theodore was going to decline. But the muscle in his jaw rippled with his curt nod.

Harriet brought them to Luchow-Faust's, the Tyrolean Alps restaurant on the Pike. They moved down the long stretch of Pike, more raucous in the night than it had been that morning. Theodore's hold on Grace's arm tightened near the dizzying entrance to the House of Mirth with its funhouse mirrors and the bars that spilled out with drunk patrons. Barkers were yelling into megaphones and from somewhere in the distance, Grace heard cannonfire. Eventually, upon entering the German portion of the fairgrounds, they passed through an alpine village complete with castles, a ridge of snow-capped, man-made mountains, and a group singing "Das Wandern."

By the time they arrived inside the restaurant, Grace's head was spinning.

"A table for three," Theo said to the host. "Somewhere private, please."

It was warm inside, and when Grace took off Theo's coat, she felt his gaze fall ever so briefly along her clavicle, the curve of her shoulder.

She relished a little of the power of it, that though he apparently thought her station in life far beneath him, he could still find her attractive.

"Did you follow me out here just to ruin my suit?"

The derision in his voice that night in Chicago flashed across her mind, razor-sharp and unbidden. It almost took her breath away. To be judged by someone and found wanting—it had made her feel so hollow, like a melon that had been scraped raw and clean.

She abruptly turned away.

The inside of the restaurant was an architectural marvel, with soaring ceilings and seating for 2,500 unobstructed by any posts. Grace's eyes scanned the room as they were led up to a large, more private room on the second floor. There was a gorgeous mahogany bar, and a Black man was playing the piano on an elevated stage.

"A Budweiser, please," Theo said after studying the extensive menu.

"I'll have a Roman punch and . . . a chocolate éclair," Harriet said. "My frazzled nerves want some chocolate. I'll share with you, Grace."

"Thank you. I'll have the Faust Blend coffee with cream."

"And some french fried potatoes for the table," Theo said. As the waiter left Theo excused himself to speak to someone he recognized at the bar.

Harriet leaned toward Grace as though she were sharing a secret. "That's Scott Joplin playing the piano over there," she said.

"He's good," Grace said.

"He better be. He's the King of Ragtime."

"I'd pay to hear him again. Is he playing at Festival Hall this week?"

Harriet shook her head. "Festival Hall is reserved for 'civilized' music. No ragtime allowed, except on the Pike."

"I thought the fair was supposed to be welcome to all," Grace said.

Harriet chuffed. "Tell that to the African American man I saw being denied a cup of water this morning. This is hardly the same experience for everyone."

"But—" Grace began. But wasn't the fair supposed to be about progress? Wasn't that the entire point of it?

Harriet took a strong sip of her drink. "You smell like Theodore, you know."

For some reason, Grace's face warmed.

"It's that distinct note of . . . something," Harriet said. "You know? Like cinnamon and smoke."

Grace did know. It was different than he had smelled in Chicago, and now, to her, he smelled like Christmas. Like when her father made spiced cider and they drank it in front of the fire. "It was kind of him to lend me his coat," she said, stirring cream into her coffee. She could feel Harriet's eyes on her.

"Ever think about taking my fake suitor as your real one?" Harriet teased, nudging Grace.

Grace almost choked. "Having oodles of money and smelling nice hardly make up for having the personality of a dishrag."

Harriet snorted, offering half of the éclair to Grace, who couldn't tell if she felt squeamish or starving. She hoped the sweet richness of the cream filling would fill the emptiness and calm her stomach.

It was as if Harriet could read Grace's mind. "What happened tonight was terrifying," she said quietly. "Wasn't it?" She hesitated, then put her hand gently over Grace's. Grace blinked up at the chandeliers.

"Do you think he'll be all right?" she asked.

She had worried that she might only like Earnest for what he could give her. A way to stay in her cousins' lives, to vindicate her mother, or the simple flattery of someone from his station paying attention to her. But the horror of that night had made her realize that she really did like him. She admired him. She liked his lack of pretense, his enthusiasm and joy, the way he threw himself headfirst into things. She liked—

"Harriet Forbes?" A man appeared at their table, making Grace startle. He was tall, with sharp cheekbones and wide-set eyes. There was a hungry look about him that immediately set Grace on edge.

"Sam Whitcomb." He stuck out his hand to shake, and it took Grace half a moment to place why his name sounded familiar. In her mind's eye she saw herself that morning, stooping to the ground. Smoothing out the crumpled paper.

The *Fair's Fare* by Sam Whitcomb.

"You publish the gossip rag!" Grace said in surprise.

Sam Whitcomb turned to her with a slow smile that built like a wave. Something about it attracted and repelled her at the same time.

Theodore was lighting a cigar at the bar. He sauntered toward them, taking his time, but he had a distinct mood about him. Like the dark cloud Grace had glimpsed at that party in Chicago the previous winter.

"Sam Whitcomb," the publisher greeted him, reaching out a hand.

"Theodore Parker," he replied coolly.

"Oh, I know who you are," Sam said, grinning.

Theo scowled, subtly touching the place on his chin where the port-wine stain stretched along his jawline. Almost as though he were self-conscious. The realization struck her with surprise.

"May I join you?" Sam asked, sitting down at their table without waiting for an answer. He signaled the waiter for a drink. "Everyone's talking about that explosion of the balloon tonight."

"It was a much more sophisticated piece of machinery than a mere balloon," Theo said witheringly. He might not have known Earnest for long, but it was apparent that Theodore Parker had a penchant for loyalty. He took a drag of his cigar, meeting Grace's eyes for a moment as if to say, *I wish this insufferable imbecile would leave.*

Surprised, Grace felt the ghost of a smile.

"It was your friend who was in it tonight, wasn't it?" Sam leaned forward, picking through their fried potatoes.

"Help yourself," Theo said with a perfected disdain.

"I'm hearing people surmise that it was sabotage," Sam said, chewing.

Grace's stomach turned. "People think the crash was intentional?"

A look of grotesque delight crossed Sam's face. "It wouldn't be the first mishap for that event. The only thing steeper than the ascent and the entrance fee is the size of the prize money at stake."

"How much is the prize money?" Harriet asked. She touched the heavy earrings that dripped from her lobes.

"One hundred fifty thousand dollars."

Harriet's jaw dropped. Theo's face remained unreadable.

"They have to complete a course that some pilots say simply can't be done," Sam continued. "Some dropped out, others are finding unfortunate mishaps are happening along the way."

"Mishaps?" Grace asked.

"Two of the other competing machines were balloons that were found slashed. Another caught on an errant nail and lost all its hydrogen. And tonight, Mr. Allred's machine falls from the sky in a blaze. Coincidence?"

The music was loud, the room growing warmer. Grace fought the feeling of dizziness again.

Harriet looked troubled. "What kind of a person would try to murder someone for money?"

"You must not read my paper much," Sam Whitcomb said with a dark laugh. A sick feeling settled into Grace's stomach, much like the time her grandfather had closed the door in her face when she was seven. Lillie had given her a hand-me-down doll that day with a delicate porcelain face and a satin dress. Grace had taken it back to Kansas City, where it made her own beloved muslin doll look so plain and pitiful.

In a rage, Grace had spat on her muslin doll and stomped on her face until she was ruined.

Then she had cradled her and promptly burst into tears.

The memory still filled Grace with shame, and she tried to shake it away. It helped that Mr. Joplin launched into a song that warmed the room like it had taken a sip of spirits. A woman sashayed past them toward the stage, radiating confidence. She had large brown eyes and olive skin and was wearing a lavender silk gown with a jeweled high collar that shimmered in the lights. When she opened her mouth, her voice had a tone one could drown in—deep, luscious, and rich. The lights went low, the conversations dimming.

"Miss Ethel Adams," Scott Joplin said. He raised a hand toward her and the crowd burst into applause.

"A rival of yours, isn't she?" Sam Whitcomb asked Harriet with a wolfish smile that made perfect sense on his face. He made his living looking for the weakest, most vulnerable parts of people to sink his teeth into and feed to the masses.

"How fortuitous for her that the foremost talent manager for the Chicago stage is sitting right over there," Sam continued, gesturing with his drink. "The one nursing a gin on the rocks. Word has it he's looking to make someone a star."

Harriet's face flushed.

Ethel caught Harriet's eye from the stage and winked. Her smile was dazzling, with a cut of edge beneath it.

Harriet gritted her teeth and gave her a delicate nod.

Grace tried to relax, to lose herself in the luxurious velvet of Ethel's voice the way others lost themselves in a drink. But all she could see was Earnest, falling from the sky. Lillie, rushing toward the burning embers of the flying machine, helpful in a way that Grace could only dream of being. And Theodore Parker lending her his coat, protecting her along the Pike and making sure to put himself between her and Sam Whitcomb.

She wished she could forget Frannie's heart-wrenching scream. The shiver of it curled through her insides. She could almost escape it in this room.

Almost.

When Ethel was finished, she bowed to thunderous applause. In response, Harriet threw back the rest of her drink and, almost shaking, sauntered toward the stage.

Sam laughed. "Careful, Mr. Parker. Might lose your lady to someone who can make all her dreams come true tonight." He rose, tipped his hat to them, and disappeared into the crowd, leaving Grace and Theodore alone at the table.

"What delightful American treasures we get to encounter at this fair," Grace said, turning to meet Theo's eyes. "I think that was the only man I've ever disliked as instantly as you."

"While your company, dear Grace, reminds me a little of these fried potatoes," Theodore replied.

Her thoughts caught on the words *dear Grace*. Something sparked within her. Why did it feel so good to challenge him?

"Golden and addictive?" she ventured. "The perfect companion for every meal?"

"Initially delightful," he said, "and stomach-turning when cold."

She snorted. "That's the first time a gentleman has ever likened me to soggy potatoes."

His handsome face broke into a half smile, and her chest warmed. She smiled back at him, and there was a moment of unsettling silence between them. The sharing of a secret—and now, a tragedy—was an intimate thing. She felt it melting away her rancor's sharpest edges. Theo cleared his throat. "I should pay the tab."

She tried to bring out her purse to cover her own portion, but he said, "Don't insult me, Miss Covington."

"More than being called a soggy potato, you mean?"

He left her with a low laugh, and she turned her attention back to Harriet. Where were Earnest and Lillie and Oliver right now, she wondered? In a hospital ward, while the three of them were lost in another world? That's what the World's Fair felt like. A dream. An immersive reality that wasn't, in fact, real. Harriet's voice filled her ears, her thoughts, magnifying her twisting emotions with a mournful, heartfelt ballad. It brimmed with such intimacy that an older woman near the stage raised a bejeweled finger to wipe tears from her crepey cheek.

When the song ended and the applause rose around them, Harriet turned toward the talent manager. Gone was the woman who had run through the fields an hour ago toward the horror of the burning crash with dirt on her face. She had shed that persona like a skin and became the actress she was known to be. Brimming with charisma. Shimmering like a diamond. Turning in the spotlight and the shadows to share endless facets of herself that she hadn't shown before.

It left Grace feeling uneasy. The same way she'd felt earlier, when the lies slipped off Oliver's tongue like smoothly polished stones.

It was clear that Harriet wanted that talent manager to see her, to pick her over Ethel. She wanted to *win*.

Grace's coffee had gone cold.

As for Ethel, she was glaring at Harriet with unvarnished displeasure that bordered on rage, clearly feeling as though she had been upstaged. She whispered something to a man sitting to her right.

"Are you all right?" Theodore asked Grace, appearing at the table. He was looking at her with a concern that she could not have imagined was possible after their exchange in Chicago.

"Fine," she said. "I'll just visit the ladies' room, and then we can go."

She brushed past him, feeling confused at the way everyone had shifted tonight, the very people around her warping like a funhouse mirror.

☙

Grace splashed cold water on her face. Her face was pale, and her eyes looked huge. She pinched her cheeks, unsure why she suddenly cared how she looked. When she stepped out, she glimpsed Harriet navigating to the back of the restaurant.

"Harri—" Grace started to say but stopped short. Someone was already speaking to Harriet ahead, half hidden in the shadows. He was too far away to make out, but Grace could tell by his build that it was a man.

She wasn't trying to eavesdrop, not really, but something stopped her from interrupting. Perhaps it was Harriet's look of surprise.

Grace listened to a sudden instinct and dropped back.

"I've seen you with him," the man said. "And I've got connections, too. If you want me to introduce you to that talent manager—"

The music began again, drowning out the rest.

The man, whoever he was, seemed to be growing more and more agitated. He was dressed in the fine clothing of a gentleman. He had a signet ring on his right hand, a crest impressed into onyx. But his face was flushed, and he was unsteady on his feet. Grace wished suddenly for Lillie and Oliver. None of this was her world. From ritzy parties to burning planes to expensive restaurants far beyond her father's, she felt so out of place.

And Harriet almost looked frightened.

Grace strode toward them, catching a glimpse of the man's profile as she neared. He didn't look familiar to her, and he was too intent on Harriet to notice Grace approaching.

"He owes me. You tell him," the man snarled. "Make sure he gets me that money."

He turned and staggered away in the opposite direction, and she could smell the alcohol in his wake. He was drunk.

"Who was that?" Grace asked.

"Just someone who thought he knew me," Harriet said. Her voice turned brittle. "He was mistaken."

"Are you all right?" Grace said.

Two splashes of pink had appeared on Harriet's face.

"I'm fine," she said. Grace examined her. Harriet was regaining control of herself, as any good actress could, but something had definitely spooked her.

"Are you certain, because—"

"It's nothing," Harriet said briskly.

"There you are," Theodore said, approaching behind them. "I thought you both had left me behind and Oliver was going to challenge me to a duel."

"Let's go home," Harriet said. She tugged on Oliver's borrowed coat, her face flushed. "This party has soured."

With a twinge in her gut, Grace followed Harriet and Theo to his waiting carriage. Someone Harriet knew owed this man money—enough to enrage him.

And for some reason, she was lying about it.

Grace leaned against the cushioned seat, deciding she needed to keep a much closer eye on Harriet Forbes.

Especially where her darling and very rich cousin Oliver was concerned.

CHAPTER FIVE

MAY 2, 1904

One Day Before the Murder

The next morning, Grace followed Lillie up the stairs of Earnest's house, letting her hands chase the gleam along the polished banister. The satin train of Lillie's dress trailed on the staircase just in front of her, lapping it like waves. In St. Louis circles, Grace often felt like a fraud. But—in her defense—at least she knew it. She dressed up in Lillie's clothes for weeks in St. Louis like she was putting on a costume. An actress, trying on a new life. But was Harriet, too?

Grace glanced at the imposing, aristocratic portraits of the Allreds on the walls.

She was aware of her own slightly mixed motives for wanting to marry someone of means. If someone close to Harriet owed a substantial amount of money, was Oliver merely a tool?

She'd thought that Harriet was her companion, a fellow outsider, but something about the previous night made her realize that she didn't know Harriet at all.

"Earnest," Lillie said, entering his room. "You gave us an incredible scare."

The morning light poured through the bedroom window. Earnest was starkly bruised, surrounded by white linens and pillows. A heavy wristwatch sat on the nightstand beside a vase of fresh lilies the shade of apricots. Frannie was wringing her hands, pacing. She looked as though she'd hardly slept.

"Did I fall from heaven?" Earnest said with a lazy smile. "Because you sure look like an angel."

"Not even remotely funny yet," Lillie said.

His smile cracked wider, his right eye a ghastly shade of purple. When he moved his hands, Grace noticed they were bandaged, as though they'd been burned.

"I missed that dance last night," Grace said lightly to him.

"Yes, well, things didn't go quite according to plan. I'd envisioned waltzing in triumphantly after a successful flight, but I ended up falling on my face. From quite a height."

He smiled at her, but his usual spark was dim.

"What happened?" Grace whispered, coming to stand near the bed.

"The machine seemed to be doing fine upon takeoff, and then something caught fire. I smelled the smoke and managed to bail with my parachute just before the damn thing exploded. Pardon my French."

"C'est bon," Lillie said. "Now, can we come to visit you again?"

"No need," Earnest said, sitting up with a slight grimace. "I'm not missing any more of the fair. I'll be back by tonight."

"Tomorrow, at least," Lillie insisted. "Surely you need to rest."

"Where's the fun in that?" He did look gray, though. As Lillie turned to leave, he caught her by the hand. "Thank you, Miss Carter," he said. "I believe I owe you my life."

She laughed. "Let's not be dramatic, I did very little," she said, but he held her tight.

"It meant a lot to me."

He gave them a hint of his old smile, then turned to look out the window.

Lillie was quiet in the carriage as they left Earnest's enormous house behind.

"Are you all right?" Grace asked her gently.

She had been planning to take this opportunity of a brief moment alone to tell Lillie about her to decision to leave. She felt a sudden sadness as the wheels passed the elegantly carved sculptures and blooming fruit trees of the Allred mannsion. Their time alone together was so little.

"You were amazing last night," she said instead, threading her fingers through Lillie's.

"I think there must be something wrong with me that I feel so alive when others are having their worst moments."

"Are you still planning to slip away tonight?" Grace asked. "When I distract Oliver with a game of croquet?"

Lillie threw a look over her shoulder as she always did when they discussed the Evening Dispensary, even though they were completely alone.

"I'm actually *helping*, Grace," she said, her face lighting up. "Dr. May has been training me. She helps prostitutes sick with venereal disease, girls and women who came to work at the fair. They're going to open a home for them so they have somewhere safe to go."

She laughed when she saw the look on Grace's countenance. "Don't look at me like that! I think what Dr. May does is so noble. And yet—can I be perfectly, dreadfully honest with you? Sometimes I don't know if I'm ready to give all of this up. Sometimes I think, perhaps I'll go into medicine myself. Nursing, if I don't have what it takes to be a physician. But Mother and Father would have a fit. They'd disinherit me, I'm certain of it. And so I pause. Isn't that selfish of me?

I like my pretty dresses and my clean food and a safe place to sleep at night. And it makes me ashamed."

"Those aren't bad things to want, Lillie."

"No, perhaps not. But then—it all starts to feel sort of dulled, doesn't it? When there are things to do out in the world that matter. That have to do with someone else and not just myself. People below my station."

Grace swallowed at that comment, but Lillie rushed on, not noticing. "Yes. Something beyond myself, and this circle that feels so suffocating sometimes, everyone curved in on themselves so that we've become something ghastly."

She finally caught the look on Grace's face. "Oh, darling. Grace. I know that expression. Of course I'm not speaking of you."

"You *have* always looked out for the charity cases," Grace said. She tried to laugh, but it came out brittle.

"I've never once thought of you that way," Lillie exclaimed, jumping to take Grace by the arm. "Don't be ridiculous."

"Lillie. It's all right. You aren't going to have to pull me along anymore, like a piece of dead weight," Grace looked out at the paved stone streets of the city, the trolleys and electric streetlights. "We're getting too old for it. It makes me feel ridiculous, and I think we have to face reality—"

"Don't say that," Lillie said, her alarm growing. "What are you saying?"

"I'm saying that this has to be the end," Grace said, tears springing to her eyes. "This week, this last, glorious week. I can't do this anymore, and it's not fair to do it to you either."

"I don't know what you're talking about," Lillie said, tears mirroring in her own eyes. "Please! What do you mean, this is the end?" She choked on a laugh. "We're going to be in one another's lives forever. I won't stand it any other way. You're more than my best friend—you—you know this—you're closer even than my cousin. You're my sister."

When Grace was younger, sleeping in the bed next to Lillie, she had often wished that they really were sisters.

"Besides, I like you better than Oliver anyway," she said, and Grace laughed.

"Your mother already thinks I've corrupted you. Your midnight medical adventures on Scab Row are not going to help things."

"She doesn't know a thing. She thinks I'm cross-stitching, but I don't even know how. I buy them from the women's league and pass them off as mine, and she's none the wiser." Lillie shook her head. "And I have *never once* thought of you as someone needing my charity. I've been grateful to you," she said, clasping Grace's hands, "for helping to keep my eyes open. You've made me simultaneously want more for my life regarding the things that matter and less for the things that don't. I will never forget the goodness you've brought me, all my life. Goodness—and grace," she said.

She reached out for Grace and embraced her, holding her tightly.

"I love you," she said.

"I love you, too," Grace said. "And I always will."

"Silly darling, imagining that you could get away from me that easily," Lillie said, squeezing her hands.

Grace smiled faintly, her throat going strangely dry. The thing was, Lillie had never once come to visit her in Kansas City. Grace knew it was because of Aunt Clove, and that now Lillie was finally old enough to start making her own choices. They both were. But this—whatever their life had looked like up to now—was ending. And as long as they were facing their ugliest secrets: if they couldn't without a doubt hang on to one another, Grace would rather be the one to cut the cord than the one who was left.

Lillie looked out at the city, seemingly convinced that all was intact and all would be well. Her face was clear and lovely, until her brow suddenly knotted.

"Also. While we're alone," she said, voice lowering, "I think Oliver has been acting quite strange lately. Have you noticed?"

Grace's heart fell. "Oh," she said, studying a fountain nestled between elegantly manicured parterres. Suddenly, she was eager to get back to the house. "What do you mean?"

"Just . . . odd. Sneaking off at strange times. His head in the clouds. Being a little, I don't know. Cagey."

"Maybe he, too, has secret forbidden medical aspirations," Grace said lightly.

Lillie laughed, pushing back strands of her hair. Grace's favorite sound.

She loved being with her cousins. Being between them had always been her favorite place in the world. Only recently, it had begun to feel like being pulled in two separate directions.

"So you haven't noticed anything?" Lillie prodded.

Grace glanced away, her throat uncomfortably dry as that pull threatened to break something that mattered dearly to her.

"No," she said. "I haven't."

❧

"You have to tell Lillie," Grace insisted to Oliver as soon as they were alone.

They stood together as the boats floated lazily below in the canals, the water reflecting the white columns of the Palaces.

"Tell Lillie what?" Oliver asked innocently.

"*Oliver*," Grace growled.

They moved through the exquisite gardens of the French pavilion, where Oliver had arranged for them to have a picnic lunch at a replica of the Grand Trianon at the Palace of Versailles. The scent of roses carried on the breeze, amid the pink marble fountains and espaliered trees. Harriet, Lillie, and Frannie were walking through the rows of fruit trees imported from Paris itself—apple, peach, pear, plum, and apricot. Frannie looked more recovered, as though being in the fresh air was reviving her.

"This way, sir," the guide greeted them. They were given a tour of the interior salon, with its damask-patterned walls and delicate murals painted across its high ceilings. There were circular sofas edged with blue fringe set beside a glass case displaying a single lock of Napoleon's hair. They were offered flutes of Veuve Clicquot as they headed out to the ornately manicured formal gardens. Grace politely declined hers, so Oliver took two.

Sometimes he reminded her too much of Walt.

"She is growing suspicious," Grace said to Oliver as the breeze ruffled her hair. "Why won't you just tell her about Harriet? This is miserable. And short-sighted. She's not stupid. She's going to find out."

Oliver chuffed. "Like she doesn't have secrets of her own."

"What do you mean?"

"I've seen her sneaking off. And you know of it already, don't you, you little minx?" He studied her over the rim of his glass. "She's meeting someone. Isn't she?"

Grace gave him a plaintive look and remained silent.

He took a sip of his champagne. "When did we start keeping all of these secrets from one another?" he asked.

"Are you saying there are more?"

He flashed her a wicked look. "Maybe."

She groaned and buried her face in her gloved hand. "Please don't tell me. I don't want to know."

"Too late," Oliver said, grinning. "It's a weight I've been carrying all myself and I simply can't bear it anymore."

He opened his suitcoat pocket and pulled out a small piece of gold.

She recognized it immediately. Their grandmother's ring. Grace remembered seeing it on her finger as a child, when her grandmother would sneak away and tut over her and wipe her mouth of chocolate. She got to see her grandmama only once or twice a year, when Grandfather Carter was away traveling and wouldn't know.

Grace couldn't help herself. She gasped loud enough that several people around them turned to look.

"Subtle," Oliver said, quickly tucking the ring back into his coat pocket. "You should really consider going undercover."

"Sorry! It's just . . . Does that mean . . . ?"

His eyes flashed with the mischief she'd known since he was a boy. "It's not for my mother, I'll tell you that much."

"Speaking of your mother, she's going to have a stroke."

"She'll get over it," he said, drawing deep on his cigar. "It's a new age."

"Not new enough," Grace said darkly, "I can assure you."

"I didn't take you for being a classist, cousin."

"Please. You know I wouldn't care if you married Harriet. She's lovely. I'm not a snob, I'm just a realist."

"And here I thought you'd be the happiest in the family for me," he said jauntily, nudging her.

"I'm overjoyed for you. It's just . . ." She trailed off.

What do you really know of her? she thought.

"When will you tell Lillie?" she asked instead. Stubbornly.

"Soon. I just wanted her to spend time with Harriet this week, get to know each other organically, have a friendship before they become sisters."

Sisters. That word touched something painfully tender in Grace, even while she was happy for Oliver. Harriet would step into the place that Grace was vacating.

"Besides, you know Lillie. She would give it all away too soon. She shows everything on her face, and then my mother would be even more suspicious."

One of the French pavilion guides was surreptitiously reading the *Fair's Fare*. He thought he was hidden behind the massive wrought iron gate that separated the French pavilion from the rest of the fairgrounds, but Grace could make out the bold type on the paper between his fingers.

BALLOON EXPLODES IN
FIREBALL AT THE FAIR;
PILOT INJURED BUT ALIVE

Grace shuddered, thinking again of Sam Whitcomb's theory that the episode hadn't been accidental.

Harriet looked over at them and waved.

❧

Grace grasped Lillie's hand, clutching onto her cousin for dear life as their roller-coaster cart crested the summit.

She squeezed her eyes shut just before the cart began hurtling down the track.

"I hate this!" Grace screamed with delight. She heard Oliver howling with laughter behind her, and next to him, Harriet scream-singing.

Afterward, they watched a naval battle reenactment with miniature ships in the Grand Basin, eating airy, spun fairy floss from a stick as shots rang out and smoke plumed into the sky.

"To the Observation Wheel!" Oliver cried.

"Nope," Frannie said flatly, looking up at the wooden monstrosity.

"I'll stay with you," Lillie offered.

"We'll go with Oliver, won't we, Grace?" Harriet asked, smiling sweetly at her.

The wheel was larger than Grace had anticipated, now that she was standing this close to it. She looked up at the compartments, which were roughly the size of a train car and could hold sixty passengers each. The wheel creaked as it spun and someone screamed. Her heart fluttered a little in her chest, and part of her wanted to stay on the ground. But it would give her a rare opportunity to observe Harriet and Oliver alone.

And now that she knew how serious Oliver was about a permanent future with her, the stakes had just gone way up.

"Sure," she said.

Oliver bought their fare. Fifty cents a ticket, the same as a whole day's admission to the fair, and they crowded on board.

"It's . . . festive, isn't it?" Oliver said. The car was filled with flowers and—

"Is that a piano in the corner?" Harriet asked.

"You could sing for us," Oliver said proudly. "I always love to hear you sing." And she beamed at him.

At the last minute, just as the doors were closing, Theodore ducked inside.

"What are you doing?" Grace asked.

He grimaced. "Something I'm surely about to regret."

He shifted, standing next to her longer than she expected him to, his hand splaying out on the banister.

The doors closed. The Ferris wheel box was enormous. The cars swung, some of the women letting out a screech somewhere between terror and delight. The lights were beginning to come on in the Palace of Electricity, reflecting in the Grand Basin like a hundred fallen stars.

Oliver turned around, surveying the car.

"Why are there so many flowers in here?" he mused.

"And is that a . . . reverend?" Harriet asked.

Somehow they had ended up in a special banquet car.

"Oh, good," Theo said. "We've managed to crash a wedding."

"That better be the only thing that crashes today," Harriet said.

Theodore gripped tightly to the handle above the window as the car swung. His face went white, the port-wine stain flushing even more crimson on his face.

"Not a fan of heights?" Grace asked, arching a brow with no small amount of pleasure.

"We had never been so well acquainted as we are right now." His jaw flexed, handsome as ever. "It's not giving the best first impression."

"You and heights have that in common, then," she said.

He swallowed, his Adam's apple bobbing. "There was a reason the inventor of this wheel died bankrupt and alone."

"You doing okay there, Theo?" Oliver asked above the din.

"Oh yes," Theodore said bitingly. "Having the time of my life, which I'm fairly certain is going to end at any moment."

Oliver threw back his head and laughed. Then he kissed Harriet.

In the corner, someone was playing the wedding march on the piano, and the reverend was addressing the bride and groom. Grace moved past Theo so she could see out the window. She never imagined she could view the fair from the air like this. The Ivory City, spread out beneath them in an endless maze of glowing palaces and canals, statuary and fountains, the people in their finest beginning to look like miniatures. Her stomach dipped a little, but she was determined not to show any nerves. She tried to memorize what it all looked like, as though she might paint it later. Maybe that's what she would do in Kansas City. Take up painting.

Meanwhile, Theodore was practically wheezing, bent over.

"Is he all right?" a woman next to him asked.

"Oh, he's always like this," Grace said cheerily.

But for an instant, she thought of Walt. He'd always been afraid of heights, too.

With a pulse of compassion, she sidled closer to Theodore. "You know, Mr. Parker, if you die today, at least it was doing something important. Riding a fair amusement while wearing expensive shoes."

"Ha." He laughed weakly, but opened his eyes. His white-knuckled grip on the side of the car tightened.

They were stuck on a moving car suspended hundreds of feet in the air together, amid the intense overtures of Harriet and Oliver, and an actual wedding ceremony.

Grace sighed.

"What helps me when I'm nervous," she said quietly, "is I sing a nursery rhyme for each letter of my name. So, yours would be 'Twinkle Twinkle Little Star,' and then, 'Here Comes an Old Soldier.'"

He squinted up at her. "Does that really work?"

She ignored him, prodding: "Here comes an old soldier from Botany Bay. Have you got anything to give him to-day?"

Theo sighed, gripping the edge. "I'll give him a hat."

"A hat. Right. Not terribly original, but I suppose given the circumstances, it'll do," Grace said. She turned to Oliver, who had just come up for air.

"What about you, Oliver?"

The woman beside them was now clutching her hat and giving him and Harriet a look of offended disgust.

Oliver grinned, his face blotchy. “I’ll give him a hat and this million-dollar view.” He winked at the woman, who huffed and moved toward another part of the car.

“Harriet?” Grace prodded.

She squinted, her eyes shining. She looked utterly, truly happy. “I’ll give him a hat, this million-dollar view”—she looked around the car and settled on the bride—“and that bouquet of baby’s breath.”

“And what will you give him, Miss Covington?” Theo said. A hint of color was beginning to return to his face.

“I’ll give him a hat, a million-dollar view, a wedding bouquet, and . . . a hearty dose of barbiturates to help for the ride back down.”

Theo snorted. “I never imagined the jealousy I suddenly feel for the soldier from Botany Bay,” he said.

Oliver took Harriet by the hand and pulled her closer to the window. He held her hand proudly as they gazed at the city below.

“Why on earth did you get on the wheel if you’re afraid of heights?” Grace hissed at Theo.

“First of all, it was only a suspicion unconfirmed until now,” he said crossly.

“Glad we’ve gotten to the bottom of that mystery.”

“And second of all, because I needed to talk to you.” He threw a look over his shoulder. “Alone.”

Grace’s stomach dipped. “Alone?” She got a whiff of that scent of him again, smoke and mystery.

Theo leaned close and whispered to her with a sudden, unexpected intimacy. “Do you recognize that woman over there?”

Grace subtly snuck a glance over her shoulder.

"Dark hair?" Theo asked. "Navy hat?"

A nondescript woman was standing on the fringe of the wedding party.

"No," Grace whispered. She couldn't help but notice that he was very close to her.

He whispered in her ear, his breath tickling her neck. "She's been watching us."

"I don't find that hard to believe, as you, Oliver, and Harriet have been taking turns making a scene."

He scowled at her. "But I noticed her earlier this afternoon, too, when we were at the Grand Basin, and she was watching us then. I actually think she's been following us since last night."

A warning prickled down Grace's spine. She didn't know if it was a lingering sense of unsettledness from the airshow explosion but she hadn't been able to shake her feeling of disquiet.

"Following who?" she asked. "You? *Me?*"

Harriet?

Was this somehow connected to the man who had approached Harriet last night?

Harriet seemed oblivious. Lost in love with Oliver.

But there was that strange interaction last night with the man she claimed not to know. Was she caught up in something else?

"I saw the woman board the car with the three of you and I just . . . bought a ticket and got on, too," Theo said. "Like a bloody *idiot.*"

Grace looked at his trembling hands clutching the side rail. So Theodore Parker was the sort of person who would face his worst fears to protect his friends.

To protect *Oliver.*

Her chest unexpectedly warmed again.

Grace stole another look at the woman, who did seem to be subtly watching Harriet and Oliver. But she just as easily could have been looking at the view of St. Louis out the window.

Perhaps they were all feeling paranoid, still unsettled by Earnest's crash, and that's all it was.

"Hurray!" The car erupted in cheers as the bride and groom kissed, and the guests threw rice into the air. The carriage creaked and came to a stop.

Theodore was the first to exit the car when the doors pulled open.

He was waiting for the rest of them at the ticket booth, clutching a brown paper bag when they disembarked.

"For you," he said to Grace. "A thank-you for helping me keep my wits about me up there."

She pulled out a small silver spoon with 1904 WORLD'S FAIR engraved in it.

"It's a souvenir," he said with a deathly straight face. "Given how you're so obsessed with cutlery."

"How thoughtful. I got you a souvenir, too," she said, thrusting the paper bag back into his hands.

"'World's Fair Gift Shop,'" he read the outside slowly. "You shouldn't have."

"It's a sick bag," she said, "to commemorate your Ferris wheel ride."

His jaw muscle flexed. "It's too bad such a devastating tongue hides behind such a lovely face."

She paused. For a moment, she was too surprised to say anything back.

He shot her a dry look, clutching his sick bag with as much dignity as he could muster, and strode away.

❧

"Try some Dubonnet," Oliver said that evening. Light from the setting sun poured into the sitting room, where they were lounging on the formal chairs.

Lillie let her overstuffed corgi Lulu climb into her lap on the settee, which she had been expressly forbidden to do. She had changed into a simpler day skirt and plain blouse because she was planning to help Dr. May later that night.

"What's Dubonnet?" Grace asked.

Oliver poured the drink into his glass. "It has herbs, spices, and a bit of . . . je ne sais quoi."

"Otherwise known as quinine," Lillie said.

"Quinine?" Grace asked. "You can't be serious."

"Mm. It's spicy. Almost bitter," Oliver said. "I like it."

Oliver poured the last of the bottle into Lillie's glass. "It's what gives it a bit of a bite."

Lillie dumped hers in the potted plant.

"I should go check on Frannie," she said meaningfully to Grace.

"That's a good idea," Oliver said, missing the glance that passed between them. "I'll come with you. I want to check in on Earnest. How about it, Grace?"

"Oh, let's don't. I'm sure he's sleeping, Oliver," Grace said quickly. "Besides, I was hoping you'd stay home with me. I want to play a game of chess."

"Well, if you're sure," Lillie said. *Thank you*, she mouthed to Grace.

And then she was gone.

"You wish a chance to win back your dignity?" Oliver asked, moving to set up the chess game.

"If it can possibly be reconstructed," Grace said. "Last time you left it in tatters."

Oliver was laughing into his Dubonnet when Aunt Clove suddenly appeared at the bottom of the stairs.

She moved into the sitting room, and it was as though a shadow passed. The laughter died on Grace's lips.

Aunt Clove stood and examined them. The silence was uncomfortable.

"I know," she said bitterly to them.

Grace's hand paused on a chess piece.

Oliver went a little pale, but he turned to face his mother with an attempt at his usual charismatic smile.

"You know what, Mother?" he asked.

"I know about your deceit. That you've been gallivanting around town like a *fool* with that harlot of an actress."

The color drained from Oliver's face. "M-Mother—"

"And you," Aunt Clove said, turning her wrath on Grace. "You knew. You ungrateful, scheming conspirator. This is your influence. Your bags are packed. You'll be leaving tonight."

"Mother, this is ridiculous. You're mistaken—"

"I saw you. You were hardly discrete."

Oliver laughed in shock. "You're not about to throw Grace out on the street," he said.

Aunt Clove's voice was like ice. "I am."

"Go ahead," Oliver said. "Then we can explain to Lillie exactly where Grace is and why she went."

He turned protectively to his cousin. "Don't worry, Grace. If she insists on carrying through with this nonsensical threat, I'll get you a hotel room in the nicest part of town."

"And whose money will be paying for it?" Aunt Clove asked. "You spend it like it's yours, Oliver. But it won't be, not until I'm dead." She took a threatening step toward him.

"And if you continue dallying with this girl, I'll make sure you won't see a dime of it."

"I'm going to marry her," Oliver declared.

"No," Aunt Clove said, her fury roiling like the hot breath of a bellows stoking a flame. "You are the future of this family, Oliver Henry Carter. And so no, you are not marrying that girl. So help me God, over my dead body, you are not."

CHAPTER SIX

MAY 3, 1904
The Day of the Murder

"I've paid for two nights at the hotel," Oliver said, handing Grace a key. "That's all the cash I had on me, but I'll get more."

"Oliver, you don't have to do this," Grace protested, grasping her carpetbag. She glanced at the potted palms set around the lobby of the Lamplighter Inn, the row of gleaming keys hanging in neat lines behind the front desk.

"Yes, I do. It's my fault you're in this mess," Oliver said. "I'm so sorry. We'll figure it out."

She kissed him goodbye and climbed the staircase to her room. The Lamplighter was a temporary, women's-only hotel that had been erected for the fair, and half of Grace couldn't believe that she was there—that her aunt had made good on her threat. Oliver had wanted to put her in the nicest hotel available, but they determined that one meant for women patrons only would be safest and most respectable.

Grace set down her carpetbag and locked the door behind her. It was just after midnight.

The room was a far cry from the lush trappings of her room at the Carter house. Gone were the heavy satin drapes, the four-poster oak bed, and the porcelain knickknacks above the carved fireplace. Grace stood in the middle of the room, suddenly feeling terribly alone. There was a single painting of irises hung on the wall.

The ones Walt used to paint were better.

Grace dressed for bed and brushed out her hair. She wondered, once again, where her older brother was. What he was doing. It used to break Grace's heart to hear her mother's keening cries in the night and even more when she showed up in the kitchen the next morning perfectly put together, the fake smile she used for everyone else on display there for Grace, too.

Don't push me away, Grace had wanted to scream at her. *Don't make me an outsider beyond your walls. I'm beyond everyone else's, everywhere. Don't keep me outside yours, too.*

Grace fell asleep clutching the brush to her chest, as though it could somehow ease the hollowness she could feel there.

She dreamed fitfully of herself as a young girl, with Oliver and Lillie, playing as children in a strange garden. Then the dream shifted to the night the police had come to her father's restaurant. Walt had broken into Moore's General Store down on Fifth and tried to steal a fancy clock to feed his morphine addiction, and the police were searching for him.

She remembered her mother's stricken face when they came to the door. The restaurant had gone silent and then its patrons had scattered, carrying with them a devastating stream of whispers about Walt.

In her dream, Grace let out a silent sob and twitched.

And then Walt reached out for her. His hand was ice-cold when it touched her face.

"Grace," he said.

She startled awake, soaked in sweat.

❧

In the morning, Grace melted into the thronging crowds outside the hotel as though she were walking with friends instead of alone.

She had no particular destination in mind, and no plans until she was to meet Oliver and Lillie for breakfast in an hour, so she followed the pathways down Skinker Road and passed the Ceylon tea pavilion, where waiters served visitors fragrant cups of tea while wearing snow-white jackets and sarongs. Beyond that was a Gothic-style, two-story Canadian pavilion with verandas and large wraparound porches. It would easily take a week to see all that the fair had to offer. She'd heard that some families planned to come for six.

Grace couldn't remember the last time she had done something as a family.

A familiar squeeze returned to her chest, as though she couldn't get enough air. She crossed the bridge over Arrowhead Lake to the Parian gate and a replica of the walled city of Old Manila. The Philippine exhibit was one of the largest parts of the fair, meant to be a testament to America's recent victory in the Spanish-American war. Inside the tribal villages there were Negrito people building thatched huts and demonstrating archery. Suyoc women, from one of the Igorot tribes, braced their feet against stones and wove cloth from vibrant yarn with their handlooms. There were lively dances and demonstrations of spear throwing. The Visayans had an adobe Catholic chapel. Young boys were whispering to one another and smiling and pointing, and once again, it struck Grace how many ways there were to live a life.

And yet it felt a little strange, that they were behind a fence. That she was observing their exhibit in much the same way she had the Persian rugs and new John Deere tractors.

She paused, considering this. One of the young boys waved at her, and she brightened. She waved back. But the sadness that she had hidden away so well, even from herself, suddenly welled up inside of her again.

She kept walking. The day after the police had come to the restaurant looking for Walt, her friend Ada had appeared at her front door. At first Grace assumed she had come to offer comfort, but then Ada had begun kneading her gloves in her hands. Her pretty ring had shone as she explained that her fiancé didn't want the focus to be on Grace with the scandal, and this was terribly awkward, but would Grace mind stepping down from the wedding party?

Grace had climbed the stairs, past Walt's abandoned bedroom, and cried while she wrote out all the words that raged inside her. She had to purge the anger so it didn't destroy her—anger at Ada and her fiancé, at Walt; but most of all at the world and its silly games of looking well for other people. Of ranking and devouring them, putting people in boxes and behind fences. The same world that had hurt her precious brother so much that he had to escape it somehow and, in the process, scattered buckshot and shrapnel in his wake.

She circled back through the fairgrounds and scanned the crowd for Oliver, raising her hand in a wave when she saw a different familiar face instead.

Harriet Forbes. Her head was down, and her face drawn, and Grace wondered if Oliver had told her about the previous evening's calamity. How had Aunt Clove found out the truth? Grace hadn't even had time to consider the answer to that.

But Harriet hadn't spotted her. Instead, she glanced over her shoulder nervously, as if she were anxious not to be seen.

Grace paused, letting her arm drop back to her side.

And then she watched Harriet approach a dark opening between buildings that Grace hadn't even noticed before.

With another quick look over her shoulder, she disappeared inside.

Grace picked up her pace, darting through the crowds of the Pike to follow.

She paused outside of the dark entrance. Water was draining down the slope inside, disappearing into a darkness that looked like a portal to the night.

"You don't want to go in there, dearie," a passing worker said. He had an Irish brogue and was carrying a piece of lumber on his shoulder. "It's where the unsavory things go on. Stay away. That's not a place for nice girls like you."

She knew instantly what it was, and where Harriet had gone. The Tunnels.

Grace's heart beat fast. Oliver was getting ready to throw his entire life and inheritance away for this woman. Grace had to make sure he knew what he was getting into.

She waited until the well-meaning worker had gone on. Then, she fought all the demons she felt rising inside of her and followed Harriet into the Tunnels.

❧

It was dark and damp in the Tunnels. A thin light made it through from above. The people there looked as though they'd been up all night and hadn't seen the sun in too many days. Though the fair had just opened and everything aboveground was sparkling and new, the Tunnels had already been there for awhile. Grace knew that St. Louis had networks of underground caves that formed due to the acidic water that cut through the limestone. They burrowed below the main thoroughfare of the Pike, spidering out into endless tight passages.

Grace's collar suddenly felt itchy. She hid her purse in the folds of her dress and kept her wits about her. Wearing one of Lillie's dresses, she looked especially out of place.

"You lost, missy?" someone asked to her right, leering at her with sallow skin and missing teeth. She couldn't tell if it was a man or a woman, but she didn't like the hollow note in the laugh that followed. It was disorienting here, as though time had been snagged somewhere between an endless dusk. How was the bright, gleaming Ivory City just above this place that felt like a tomb?

Her heart gave a pulsing throb as she passed by people who were lying in the alley's crevices as though they'd slept there that night. She could see Walt in all of them.

What happened to you? she wanted to ask. *What paths brought you here?*

But she pressed on, intent on following Harriet. She could just make out the top of Harriet's hat a hundred feet ahead, where she had stopped to speak with someone.

Was it the man from the restaurant the other night? The one she had claimed not to know, who wanted money?

Grace crept forward. She ignored the people who offered to show her a special deal, standing in front of makeshift stalls selling candles and barely concealed opium pipes.

Grace couldn't make out the person Harriet was speaking with. They were hidden behind some sort of column. But Harriet was gesturing, and after they exchanged words, she turned and came toward Grace.

Grace hid in the shadows and watched her go by.

Perhaps she should have confronted her. Perhaps, if she had, everything that happened after would have turned out so much differently.

Instead, she waited until Harriet had passed and then went deeper into the Tunnels, searching for a glimpse of the man from the other night.

But the person Harriet had met was gone.

❧

Grace worried the skin at her fingernails and thought over what she would say when Oliver arrived to meet her for breakfast. She sat beneath a lantern-strung garden until noon and finally gave up when it was clear that he wasn't coming. Annoyed and more than a little worried, she returned to her hotel, where she found a note waiting.

Mother's still having a fit and is holding us hostage.
Come with us to the Glass Ball tonight. I'll get you in.
—Oliver

P.S. And Earnest will be there.

She looked at the hurriedly crossed *t*'s, the way even Oliver's penmanship seemed to be rushing off the page toward the future. Though she was not anxious to cross paths with her aunt again, she had to tell Oliver what she had seen with Harriet.

Grace crumpled the note in her hand. She opened her carpetbag and decided that tomorrow, she would go home. She wouldn't take any more money from Oliver to keep staying at the hotel, wouldn't drag on this disastrous week just to keep putting off her goodbyes. Her eyes fell on the ridiculous souvenir spoon from Theodore Parker. It made her smile a little. Because tonight, she thought, pulling out her gown—her aunt didn't own her.

And nothing would stop her from spending one final, glorious night at the fair.

CHAPTER SEVEN

MAY 3, 1904
The Night of the Murder

That evening, Grace dressed in the gown, one of airy, rose-colored mousseline with a hem covered in spangles made from mirrors and mother-of-pearl. The sleeves cascaded from her bare shoulders like the fountains that drained into the Grand Basin.

She did her level best to create a formal pompadour without the help of Lillie or a maid, sweeping her hair into place with as many pins as she had, and draped a strand of pearls around her neck. They were paste, but no one need know that. It was no different than any of the ornate buildings of the fair, made of staff pretending to be Italian marble.

She twirled so that the delicate skirt flamed and fell around her figure. She was pleased. It was perfect for the Glass Ball, to be held in the columned halls of the Palace of Varied Industries.

Oliver had said he would pick her up at seven o'clock.

But when she came down the front stairs into the hotel lobby, she saw the dark outline of a familiar silhouette.

"Mr. Parker!" she said, moving toward him.

He turned and looked at her, his face unchanged save for the slightest twitch of his mouth.

"Miss Covington," he said, bowing.

"What are you doing here?" she asked. He looked sharply handsome, the way a well-crafted weapon could be, in his tailored frock coat and high white collar.

"Oliver was detained and asked me to ensure you arrived safely from . . . this place." He glanced around the hotel lobby with a distinct air of condescension.

"How generous of you," she said bitingly. "Can you manage to breathe in here without such rarified air?"

"Don't worry, I brought some along in that paper bag you gave me," he said.

She took the perfunctory arm he offered, hoping that Oliver had in fact secured her entrance to the party or this was about to be quite embarrassing.

Theodore hired a rickshaw to take them across the fairgrounds to the brightly lit Palace of Varied Industries. They crossed beneath the massive gate and made their way toward the Louisiana Monument and the Grand Basin, surrounded by fountains and the illuminated Cascades. She leaned forward, feeling the night breeze on her face, and he watched her with a bemusement that felt patronizing.

"Stop looking at me like that," she ordered.

"Like what?" he asked.

"Like I'm some sort of puppy," she said.

He snorted. "Then stop acting like one."

But the side of his mouth quirked in half a smile, and that place in her chest warmed. She didn't hate him anymore, she realized. She had almost come to like his aloof company, in those rare moments when he shed the storm clouds he wore like a cloak.

The air smelled like sugar and roses, and the Palace of Varied Industries felt even more massive in the night. It was lined with impressive columns, and intricately carved statues of men and women crowned the rooftop, perched above cornices and dentil molding. As the rickshaw drew closer, Grace caught sight of the vast arched windows above the carved double doors. A hundred evenly fitted glass panes glowed warm with golden light, beckoning them inside.

Theodore offered Grace his hand to disembark from the rickshaw.

"Mr. Gatewood!" she said with delight, stepping down. He was an old friend of her grandfather's, and she remembered a party she had once been to at his house where fir trees were lit with live candles. She and Lillie had found a fairy nutcracker and taken turns closing its mouth by pressing its wings. He had always been kind to her, asking about her mother when no one else would.

But this time, when she approached him, Mr. Gatewood looked at her like she was something on the bottom of his shoe. She had reached out her hand to greet him, but he regarded it with scorn.

"You have a lot of nerve," he said.

He took his wife's arm and they hurried into the Palace. His wife, Roberta, looked back with a troubled glance.

Grace was confused.

Had he not recognized her? Mistaken her for someone else?

A group of people around her were staring and beginning to whisper.

"I don't understand," she said faintly as Theodore appeared at her side. There were many people she expected unkindness from, but not Mr. Gatewood.

Theodore hesitated, then bent so that his voice grazed her ear. "He and your uncle had recent business interests that ended badly," he whispered. He caught her eye and added roughly: "It wasn't you."

There was a compassion in his voice that made her skin flush as they approached the entrance.

"Name?" the doorman asked.

“Theodore Parker,” Theo said.

“Grace Covington,” she said, hoping that Oliver had, in fact, secured her entrance. She was unsure she could handle any more humiliation at this point as she glimpsed the elegant array of guests inside, drinking flutes of champagne and dressed in the finest clothes Grace had ever seen.

She spotted Oliver with relief, who came to greet her.

“Cousin,” he said. “You look magnificent.” He ushered her past the doorman, nodding with the air of someone accustomed to being accommodated by people eager to do his bidding. It was endearing and infuriating at the same time, even when done on her own behalf.

“Thank you for helping me to be in two places at once,” he said to Theo. “Can you believe my mother cast her out?”

“Martyrdom looks good on her,” Theo said.

“I just had an unfortunate encounter with the Gatewoods,” Grace said, irritated that Theo had been dispatched to fetch her like an errand.

“Ah, such a shame,” Oliver said, instantly sobering. “I always really liked them—admired them, even. Alistair took me under his wing for an apprenticeship one summer when I was nothing but a knobby-kneed kid.”

“What on earth happened?” Grace asked.

Oliver’s brow knitted as they passed through a bazaar draped with billowing, jewel-toned silks, then climbed a wide, grand staircase to the second floor. “They think Father screwed them earlier this year with a large business deal—to the point they’ve made threats against our family.”

“Threats?” Grace asked, shocked. She could still see the anger that lit in a flame behind Mr. Gatewood’s eyes at her presence.

“I’m surprised they’re here, to be honest,” Oliver said. “They haven’t been as welcome in high society since that deal blew up and they defaulted some of their debts.”

Earnest came to greet them as they arrived at the top of the stairs. Dressed in tails, with a high white collar and bow tie, and carrying a dapper cane, he looked so much better than he had yesterday morning. His bruises had been covered over with a bit of powder so that they had almost vanished.

"Good evening, friends," he said, smiling. He opened his hands wide, the right one still heavily bandaged. "Grace, I've never seen anyone lovelier."

Grace curtsied. Her hearted lifted, and her eyes lit up to see him.

Theodore cleared his throat. "Mr. Allred," he said, bowing stiffly. He stepped away from Grace and excused himself to greet someone else.

"It's good to see you," Grace said to Earnest warmly. It *was* relieving to see him looking so much better, as though despite his dramatic fall from the sky and her being thrown out of her aunt's house, they were survivors, and everything was still going to turn out all right. She felt a kinship with him as she scanned the room for Lillie. Immense chandeliers dripped from painted ceilings with crystals and lush white flowers. The lighting was turned dramatically low, save for the displays of cut glass set as centerpieces on tables. These were illuminated so that they almost appeared to be floating.

And in the center of the room was the Libbey Glass Company's prized cut-glass punch bowl. It was 134 pounds of intricately decorated glass, shimmering with patterns of fleurs-de-lis that refracted the light. It was the largest single-cut glass object in history, and was accompanied by a sterling silver ladle with a matching cut-glass handle.

The Palace of Electricity shimmered beyond floor-to-ceiling windows, illuminating the fountains and boats studding the Grand Basin below. The floor beneath Grace's feet had been covered in a thick sheet of black glass that reflected the candlelight, as though they were walking across dark ice. It smelled like melting wax and unfurling flowers and smoke.

For a moment, Grace was overwhelmed. Most moments she lived melted away like snow on a fingertip. But a few seminal ones stayed. Captured in a globe, to be turned and examined from every angle.

Something in her sensed this night could be one of those.

"Allow me to introduce you to my good friend Copper," Earnest said, bringing her toward where Frannie nursed a drink at a standing table.

"We've met," Grace said.

"It's good to see you again, this time in better circumstances," Copper said, offering her a bow. His red hair was brilliant against his black tails. His eyes were a dark, striking blue.

Frannie was staring up at Copper with unmasked adoration. Poor Frannie. She always seemed to be hoping someone worthy of her fortune would notice her.

And this time, Copper turned and smiled at her. He bent his head to whisper something in her ear and she brightened. It was rare and then gone, like one of the flickering bulbs on the Palace of Electricity.

"Would you like to dance?" Earnest asked. A string quartet was situated in a dim corner, playing quietly as couples took to the dance floor.

Grace grasped his wrist, to avoid his bandages. His other hand slid around her waist.

"Where's Lillie?" he asked, looking around the crowd.

"I'm not sure," Grace said. "I expect she'll be here soon." There was a wistful look on his face that made Grace's heart fall with the weight of a feather.

He must have noticed. "She helped me so much that night, you see," he added gently.

“Of course. Do they know what happened yet?” she asked, studying his face.

“Surely you’ve seen the papers?” he said ruefully. “Bloody gossip Sam Whitcomb pretending to be a journalist.”

“We don’t have to speak of it, if it’s upsetting,” she said.

“I think it was a mechanical malfunction. Maybe a cracked cylinder in the engine caused oil to leak and ignite. Maybe the engine was overheated. But it’s possible it was sabotage. The police and my mechanic are looking into it. But with what’s left of the machine, I’m not sure we’ll ever know.”

At that moment, they both spotted Lillie.

She looked angelic, a vision in a silk and chiffon dress that glittered from shoulder to hem with iridescent beads. It was a shade between golden pink and peach, with a hint of shoulder peeking through the sleeve and gathers of delicate silk flowers stitched into the bodice. Grace felt the moment that Earnest noticed her cousin, and she should have known it was coming. As Grace stepped forward, she smelled something dark, pungent, and earthy. Something beautiful with a dangerous undertone. Something almost suffocating.

Aunt Clove stepped into her path, blocking her way. She wore a ball gown the color of green bottle glass with an elegant train and a furious look on her face.

“What on earth are you doing here?” Aunt Clove hissed.

“That’s no longer any of your concern,” Grace said. “As you made so *very* clear last night.”

Grace pushed past her.

“Would you be so good as to fetch me a drink, Mr. Allred?” she said to Earnest.

“What will it be?” Earnest said, though he seemed almost distracted. “The Dubonnet your cousin likes so well these days? A champagne?”

"A Dr Pepper, please," she said.

She crooked her head at Oliver. Without a word, he led her out onto the dance floor, looking jovial. They fell into their old steps, just as they had done when she was ten years old.

"I'm glad you're here, cousin," he said.

"Me too," she said. She glanced away. This was her moment alone with Oliver, apart from Harriet, and yet she was not at all looking forward to what she needed to say.

There was something off-kilter about tonight. The flickering of lights casting shadows, the fragrant white flowers floating in bowls. The dark glass floor was disorienting, a pit of darkness that could swallow them.

"You look like you ate something sour," he said.

"That's because I'm gathering my courage to say something unpleasant," she said.

"Surely it can wait, then," Oliver said, glancing over his shoulder. "It seems untoward to bring anything like that into such a beautiful evening."

"I'm afraid not," she said. She remembered the first time he dipped her, pretending to drop her, and how sorry he'd been when she'd grown teary. He had hugged her tight to his young, bony body. Reassured her that of course, he would never let her fall.

Now they waltzed around the black floor, the lights reflecting in it like stars floating atop a sea of ink.

"I saw Harriet this morning, when I was waiting for you," she said. "She went into the Tunnels and met with someone."

Oliver's steps faltered just slightly. Anyone watching wouldn't have even noticed before he slipped right back into the rhythm.

"You're sure it was her?" he asked. His jaw tightened. "You might have been mistaken."

"I'm certain. I followed her to be sure. I wouldn't mention it otherwise."

Oliver sighed heavily, his eyes looking heavenward. Then he scanned the ballroom, thinking.

"Did she . . . purchase anything?" he asked.

Grace gave a helpless shrug. "I couldn't tell. All I saw was her speaking to someone."

"So you have no real proof of anything?" he asked. His voice had a sharp undercurrent of hope.

She shook her head. It was all circumstantial, and yet none of it looked good.

"There's something else—" she said, ignoring Aunt Clove's glare. She braced herself as Oliver spun her, determined to be out with all of it. "The night of Earnest's crash, when you went to the hospital with Lillie, I saw a man approach Harriet. He seemed . . . angry about someone who owed him money, and she needed to pass along a message."

"Did you ask her about it?" he asked.

"I did. She claimed not to know him."

Oliver dipped her. "Then perhaps we should take Harriet at her word," he whispered in her ear.

Grace sighed as he righted her. Her head was beginning to pound a little. "You know that I, out of anyone, wishes it weren't true," she said, feeling a little dizzy. "I just wanted you to know. Whatever you decide, whatever you do, I'll support you." She squeezed his hand. "You're my blood."

He sighed. "I appreciate that you always tell me the truth. Even when I don't want to hear it."

Grace nodded. "What will you do now?"

"First I'm going to order a stiff drink, and then I'll talk to Harriet tonight. Hopefully it's all just a misunderstanding."

"Yes," Grace said faintly. "If anyone can get to the bottom of it, it's you."

He gave her a half smile as he walked away, and she wondered why the unburdening of truth had left her feeling worse than ever. The room was filling with more guests and with it, the temperature was climbing. Someone in uniform opened the oversized windows out onto the balcony, so that a blessed breeze came through. And then a beautiful woman passed by Grace, dressed in a vibrant peacock blue. At the last moment, Grace recognized her.

"Miss Adams," she said, stopping her. "I saw you the other night at the Luchow-Faust. You charmed us with a beautiful performance."

"Yes, I recognize you," Ethel said, pausing. "You were sitting with Harriet Forbes, weren't you? I'm Ethel."

"I'm Grace."

"I apologize in advance, but I can never hold on to names."

"And I can't carry a tune, so we can make up for one another's faults."

Ethel's eyes moved toward someone in the corner, and Grace recognized the talent manager from the other night. The one Sam Whitcomb said had come to the World's Fair to make someone a star.

The man took a slow sip of his drink, his sharp gaze raking the room. Ethel looked enamored, but Grace couldn't help but feel there was something predatory about him.

"Will she be here tonight, then?" Ethel asked delicately. "Harriet?"

"I'm not sure," Grace said. It was a question she wondered herself.

She hated to take Aunt Clove's side in anything, and she hoped that Oliver was right—that there was a perfectly reasonable explanation for all of it. But part of her worried, as she saw Oliver fail to meet her eyes, that she would take the bullet for delivering the message and burn one of the last bridges she had with the Carter family.

The music died, and at that moment, Harriet appeared at the top of the stairs.

"There she is," Grace said quietly. Ethel turned to look.

Aunt Clove's eyes almost bugged out of her head as Harriet entered the ballroom. If Grace thought her Aunt Clove despised her, it was nothing compared to the way she looked at Harriet.

And she wasn't the only one. It seemed that Harriet had inspired a range of reactions with her entrance.

Ethel's smile tightened, like a piece of porcelain that was about to crack. "If you'll excuse me," she said to Grace, and made her way a little more urgently toward the talent manager.

Copper had been in a lively conversation, listening to Frannie talk, but he too was distracted by Harriet's entrance. Frannie saw the way his eyes took her in.

She flushed with a sudden anger. Then, with a flick of her fan, she abruptly stalked away.

Harriet looked radiant, Grace couldn't deny it. She was wearing a burgundy evening dress set off by white satin gloves. Her hair was pulled into an intricate updo, and her ears glittered with chandelier earrings. Theodore Parker went to greet her, and, whether it was for show or because he couldn't help it, he looked truly happy to see her. As repayment, Aunt Clove shot Grace a look as though she should not even think about approaching Lillie. She whispered something in her husband's ear, and he brought Lillie out on the dance floor, ensuring that Grace couldn't speak to her.

But this was a battle Aunt Clove would not win. Talking to Lillie was the most important thing to Grace that night, because tomorrow she was going home.

"A Dr Pepper," Earnest said, offering her the drink in an ornate crystal goblet.

As she took it from him, Grace spilled a few droplets on her glove and hurriedly blotted it with her handkerchief. She knew she'd think of this week whenever she saw the stain.

"Looks like you'll be needing this back," Earnest said. With a theatrical flourish he returned her handkerchief, freshly white, without a drop of blood on it.

"So clumsy," she said, shaking her head at herself.

"Nonsense."

Her heart fluttered a little as he took her by the waist and led her past towers of flickering candles and lush vines of white flowers draped over chairs. And yet she couldn't help but notice the way Earnest stole another look at Lillie. Grace swallowed.

"I have an idea," she said, trying to smile. "Why don't you ask Lillie to dance? And since my aunt won't let me get near her, could you possibly deliver a message for me?"

"It would be a pleasure," he said enthusiastically. He gestured for Copper to take his place at Grace's side, then made his way toward Lillie.

Grace could almost feel the heat of Frannie's fury when Copper took Grace's hand.

"Who's that bloke with the camera over there?" Copper asked as they began a waltz.

Sam Whitcomb was turning the crank of a wooden cinematograph, filming the ballroom, much to the chagrin of the upper class. Aunt Clove looked disgusted.

"Oh. He publishes that gossip rag," Grace said. "The *Fair's Fare*."

Copper's eyes widened. "How vulgar. I'm surprised they let him in here."

"You sound like my Aunt Clove."

"That's the first time anyone's said *that* to me," Copper said with a sly grin. He tightened his grip on her waist. "Yet I have to agree with her. I wish he would leave."

"So you saw the things he published about Earnest and the accident?" Grace ventured.

"Except he claimed it wasn't one, didn't he?" Copper rolled his eyes as they whirled around the room. There were glassmakers next to the bar, dipping crystal into ruby-red glass to form a thin layer on top, then scraping it off in delicate designs. Guests were lining up to request personalized images and initials. The enormous, brilliant cut-glass punch bowl at the room's center refracted light in endless crystal patterns.

"Do you think it was . . . sabotage?" Grace asked. "Did someone really want to hurt Earnest?"

Copper's expression darkened. "People are never more driven than when the future's at stake."

Grace eyed the crystal staining red, like blood. "The fair will bring out the best and the worst in people, then."

"Earnest will be all right," Copper said firmly. "His ego and dreams were bruised more than his body, and he won't stop. I know, because I've been in the trenches with him. At school. In the crew boat. On his flying machine." He shook his head. "No, Earnest will be just fine. This was just a setback."

"His tenacity is admirable," she said.

She turned and startled at the sight of the woman Theo had followed on to the Ferris wheel. She was very good at blending in. Her dress was plain, but she must have means if she was there that night. She was standing innocuously beside Frannie, who was sulking in the corner.

Heart pumping, Grace searched for Theo in the crowd. He was speaking to a man in tails, sipping his drink. When he looked up, she subtly nodded toward the mysterious woman.

His eyes widened.

"Thank you for the dance," Grace said to Copper abruptly.

Copper understood the dismissal. "It was my pleasure. Enjoy the night, Miss Covington."

She caught Theodore's eye again and gestured toward the bar. He extricated himself from his conversation and sauntered toward her.

"Trouble in paradise?" he drawled. They looked to the dance floor, where Oliver and Harriet were dancing, and Harriet's face was flushed, her striking eyebrows drawn together in a frown. They appeared to be arguing, and quite publicly, at that. "They seem to enjoy dancing as much as I do," he added, and she smelled the cinnamon and woodsmoke.

"He was planning to propose," Grace said. It felt like a relief, to share the burden of that secret. She fought a sudden desire to take his arm.

"Hopefully he didn't," Theo said. "Or else we're witnessing an unpleasant aftermath."

Grace didn't want to admit that she was the cause of their argument. Instead, she lowered her voice. "Why is that strange woman here? Is she following us? It can't be a coincidence."

Theo sipped his drink. "No," he agreed. "Certainly not."

"Perhaps you should ask her to dance?"

He shot her a dirty look.

"She won't be able to resist your legendary charm."

"I think you're more like your cousin Oliver than you realize," Theodore retorted. "Somehow I've been relegated to do both of your bidding."

"Don't be silly. I'm much handsomer than my cousin Oliver," she said.

"At last, we've found something to agree on," he said in a low voice. He took a slow sip of his drink, his eyes glittering.

Her blood heated.

"Now, if you'll excuse me," she said quickly, "I have an appointment," and disappeared into the ladies' room.

She entered the sitting area, which had been decorated with sprays of white orchids and wallpaper patterned with birds.

"Lillie!" Grace exclaimed. Earnest had done his part to pass on the message.

Lillie stood to embrace her. "My mother told me you'd gone home early! I was devastated when I thought you'd left. And now part of me wants to throttle you and Oliver," she said, her cheeks flushing. "You *knew about Harriet*. How could you have kept it a secret from me?"

"I'm sorry, Lillie," Grace said, her frustration surging. "But you aren't telling Oliver important things either. You've both put me in the middle. And frankly, I've grown tired of it."

Lillie looked exasperated. "But I thought you'd choose me. Even over him. I thought we told each other *everything*." She gritted her teeth, her earrings dangling. "At least I did."

"I do tell you everything," Grace said. "This wasn't my secret to tell."

"Still. I'd do anything for either one of you. It hurts that you both kept it from me."

"I begged him to tell you."

Lillie opened the door and Grace followed her back out to the party.

Oliver was standing at the bar, holding one of the glasses that had been flashed ruby red. He gave it to Harriet.

Her face was still drawn, but she offered him a pinched smile, and they toasted.

Then Harriet knocked back the entire drink in one go. She grimaced.

"Is this your Dubonnet?" she asked. "It tastes more awful than usual."

"She's going to have to work on that if she wants to be a Carter," Lillie said darkly.

"Oliver looks miserable," Grace said. "This whole thing could be over just as quickly as it began."

"Well, good! You and I have looked forward to this week for so long and Oliver's made a right mess of everything. I came home last night and you were gone. It felt so awful, to see your room empty. And Mother is watching me like a hawk now. I think she's catching on about the Dispensary, and I'm going to have to be doubly careful—"

There was a loud noise behind them, an unnatural sound. Grace jumped. It had been glass, shattering. The orchestra stopped playing.

And then someone screamed.

They turned and saw Harriet fall to the floor.

She was frothing at the mouth.

"Help!" Oliver yelled. He bent over, and when he looked up again, his face was gray. "Help!"

Lillie gathered her dress in her hand and sprinted toward them.

Harriet was seizing on the floor, and Grace's head started to cloud with panic. The red glass was in shrapnel across the dance floor, glittering like rubies.

"What's happening?" Earnest asked, appearing at Grace's side. He looked horrified.

"Someone do something!" Frannie cried.

"Is there a doctor here?" Copper asked.

"I can help," a gentleman said. He swiftly parted the crowd and knelt beside Lillie. Lillie checked for a pulse in Harriet's wrist and neck, and the gentleman began to move Harriet from lying face up to her side, then back again, putting pressure on her thorax to resuscitate her.

A circle was forming around Harriet and a woman in a ball gown collapsed onto her knees, crying. Grace watched in terror. She'd never been any good in an emergency. She could feel the panic clouding her thoughts, darkening the corners of her vision.

"What's happened?" Ethel asked, coming to stand beside Grace. "Who is that?"

Grace couldn't speak. She could only see the hem of Harriet's gown from this angle, through the legs of the crowd.

"Someone fetch an ambulance!"

There was an eerie silence, save for the sound of the woman softly sobbing.

"Harriet," Oliver said. He stroked the end of her hair. "Harriet, it's all right. I'm right here."

Lillie stood up. She turned to Oliver, swaying.

"I'm so sorry," she said, her voice catching. "She's dead."

CHAPTER EIGHT

HORROR SPILLED ACROSS the crowd like a stain. The panic was thick enough to choke on.

The guests in their finery were being ushered downstairs by the St. Louis police to be questioned about what they had seen. There were sparkling pieces of glass scattered like rubies. The decorative punch bowl glinted eerily. The floor was littered with crushed flower petals.

Harriet's body was splayed on the dark glass floor.

"But I don't understand. How could this happen?" the woman in front of them asked.

Oliver pulled Grace aside. His eyes were wide with shock, his breathing shallow. His face was white. She felt frightened looking at him.

"Don't tell them about what you saw in the Tunnels," he said urgently. He held her arm a little too tightly. Like she was the last life raft, threatening to float away.

"Oliver, I—"

"Please."

"You aren't thinking clearly," she protested. She looked over and saw a policeman watching them. "This . . . don't you think this likely could have been an overdose?"

"It will make her look bad. I don't want her to be remembered that way." His voice caught. "Please, Grace."

Grace's head spun. She felt like she was caught in the middle of a turning kaleidoscope. She couldn't promise him this time.

"What happens now?" he asked wildly. "She was going to be my whole life."

He choked on a sob.

The police came to talk to him next.

"I can't believe she died," Frannie said. She was smoking a cigarette, her hand shaking. Copper was next to her, looking shell-shocked.

"What did the police ask you?" Copper asked Frannie.

"They asked me about Harriet's relationships."

Theodore was standing in the doorframe, a haunted look in his eye.

"I told them the truth," Frannie continued. She took a drag of her cigarette. "That Harriet was seeing Theodore Parker, but that Oliver seemed jealous of that."

"Watch your tongue, Frannie," Grace said sharply. "You do more damage with it than a bayonet."

She stalked away to find Lillie. Grace was done holding secrets on Oliver's behalf. Especially ones that only threatened to hurt him.

So when it was time to talk to the police, she told them everything.

Two uniformed policemen brought her into the ladies' sitting room, where she had just been not an hour before. Her heart raced. It was the same wallpaper patterning the walls. The same light scent of soap and lavender. She sat on the edge of the armchair, leaning forward, eager to tell them what she knew.

As she was giving them her name and temporary St. Louis address, another man entered the room. He was disheveled, as though he had been pulled out of bed. But she recognized his face. It was one of the main fair organizers who had been in the papers.

The man exchanged a nod with the head policeman, then leaned against the wall. Listening.

"I saw Harriet Forbes this morning, you see. In the Tunnels," Grace said. "And there was someone who threatened her about money the other night, at the restaurant."

"Who was it?"

"I'm not sure. A man. Tall."

"But you could recognize them?"

"Yes. I mean, I think so. It was dark."

"Was there anyone else with you who saw that interaction take place?"

"No," she said, faltering. "I was alone."

"Were there any other secrets Miss Forbes might have been hiding? Any reason for someone to kill her?"

"But surely you don't think she was *killed*? You think this was murder?"

She felt a chill go down to the deepest parts of her.

The policeman ignored her. "What was the nature of her relationship with your cousin, Oliver Carter?"

Grace felt the blood drain from her face. "Why do you ask?"

"There are witnesses that said they appeared to be arguing shortly before her death."

Grace's breath caught in her lungs.

"We've also been told that he was jealous of her relationship with Mr. Parker."

"No, but you see, it's all a misunderstanding. That wasn't a real relationship. They were hiding it on behalf of Oliver. He was the very one who asked them to do it, so you see, he wasn't jealous, he—"

"He asked them to *lie* while he saw Miss Forbes in secret?"

"Yes, but—"

"And who was the person who served her the glass tonight? Did you see, Miss Covington?"

Her heart fell, tumbling like it had tripped over a stone in the road she hadn't seen. "Yes. It was Oliver. But you must understand, he would never do anything to—"

"Thank you," the policeman said. He smiled tightly. "That will be all."

❧

By the time Grace returned to her hotel room, it was two o'clock in the morning.

She could vaguely make out the fair lights still glowing in the distance.

She took off her necklace made of paste and stared at her reflection in the watery mirror as though it should have changed. Splashed cold water on her cheeks until the horror broke through the dam she had carefully erected. When the sobs came, she held herself until she was spent.

Every time she closed her eyes, she saw Harriet falling. The ruby-red glass shattering beside her, scattering and crunching underfoot like pieces of a heart.

What if she had confronted Harriet yesterday?

What if she had told Lillie the truth earlier?

What if she and Theodore Parker hadn't agreed to keep Oliver's secret?

She felt a strange new terror, now that she knew life could change so drastically from one hour to the next. Harriet was alive, and then she wasn't. Could the decisions Grace made, no matter how seemingly small, have changed something?

For the second night in a row, she hardly slept.

The next morning Grace hurriedly packed and checked out of her room. People were gathered in the lobby, crowding together and reading the newspaper. She glimpsed the enormous font on the front page of the *Fair's Fare*:

DEATH AT THE FAIR

Actress Dies Under Suspicious Circumstances, Police Investigating

Grace turned in her key and half ran out of the hotel. On the corner, boys were holding fresh copies of the *St. Louis Post-Dispatch.*

"Death at the fairgrounds!" they called. "Was it murder?"

An anxious crowd was starting to form.

Grace reached into her purse. The coins there were thin. She needed to save enough for her train trip home. But she used some of the last of the money she had to hail a horse-drawn cab to the Carter house on Westmoreland Place.

She stood on the sidewalk beneath the dappled leaves of two wide oak trees. Though it was almost eleven o'clock in the morning, the windows were darkened with drapes.

"Miss Covington," the butler said solemnly, opening the door to greet her.

"Hello, Waters. I'm here to see Oliver," she said.

Waters bowed to her. "I hope you realize that I cannot directly disobey Mrs. Carter's orders," he said. "But I shall let Oliver know that he might do well with some fresh air outside."

"Thank you, Waters," she said.

Her heart twisted within her when Oliver slipped out the back door to join her a few moments later. He looked like he hadn't slept all night.

As soon as they were out of eyesight of the house, tears began falling down his cheeks.

"Do you want to talk, Ollie?" she asked.

She loved her cousin, and that love melted and found all sorts of new cracks within her to see him hurting.

"How can she be gone?" he asked. "I don't understand. I keep waiting to turn and see her face."

He let out heaving sobs, like the time as a boy he had fallen and impaled his leg with a stick and was trying to pull it out and also trying to be brave.

"Tell me what you loved about her," Grace said.

"The way she laughed." His voice sounded wooden, even while snot began to run down his face. "I loved her voice. It could touch something deep inside of me. She made me feel like a different version of myself. One who wanted to be settled down, one who cared about people more than how much money they had. I didn't want my parents' life, their marriage. I wanted her voice to be what I heard when I came home each night."

Grace's chest ached. The what-ifs of what she had done and not done over the past few days haunted her. "Do her parents know?" she asked.

"The police are contacting them. They live in Illinois."

"They think she was killed, Oliver."

His hand tightened into a fist. "I saw the papers. Those vultures, circling around like they were looking for meat."

"Do you think someone killed her?"

"She didn't overdose, if that's what you mean. I never saw her take anything, not once, the entire time we were together."

"But who would want her dead?" Grace asked.

"I don't have any idea."

They circled the block.

"Oliver, I want to stay to help you, but—" Her throat closed with the embarrassment of it all. She gestured to the carpetbag in her hands. "I've imposed on your generosity long enough."

"Don't go," he said. "Not now. I need you here. Your presence is worth more than a hundred days of hotels. I'll pay for the rest of your stay tonight. Don't worry, I'll build you a whole new one if it comes to that."

They looked up at the sound of a door slamming.

A group of black carriages were parked around the Carters' front stoop.

"Reporters," Oliver growled. "I'll give them a piece of my—"

He wiped his face and began to stride toward them, but stopped suddenly. As if realizing that they weren't reporters.

The man in front rang the bell.

He was wearing a police uniform.

Aunt Clove intercepted him before Oliver could.

"What is this?" she asked, frowning, standing in the frame of the front door. "Chief Harris? What are you doing here?"

The police chief sighed. He was a large man with pocked cheeks. "It's probably better if we do this inside, Clove."

Her voice rose in panic. "Reginald!" she yelled.

Grace could hear Lulu barking inside.

"Have you come for me?" Oliver asked.

The policemen turned around.

Oliver stood his ground bravely as they surrounded him on the sidewalk.

A neighbor opened their door, then abruptly shut it.

"Oliver Carter, you are under arrest for suspicion of murder in the death of Harriet Forbes."

Lillie dashed out of the house, wearing a hastily thrown on house jacket. She gasped as the handcuffs closed around Oliver's wrists, her hand covering her mouth.

The neighbors were starting to gather.

Lillie pleaded as they led Oliver toward the police carriages, trying to tell them, "He didn't do this. He would never do this."

"Well, right now it appears that he had some involvement," Chief Harris said. "And unless other evidence comes to light, the circumstances point to him."

Other evidence, Grace thought.

"Don't say anything at all," Uncle Reginald barked at Oliver, appearing on the sidewalk. "You'll be hearing from our lawyers."

"Surely that actress's death was an accident, she must have taken something herself," Aunt Clove was begging. "Chief Harris! You and your wife have dined in our home. How could you humiliate us like this?"

The chief sighed. He gestured the other officers to put Oliver in the carriage.

"I'm afraid not, Mrs. Carter," he said quietly. "Your son lied about having a secret romantic relationship with Miss Forbes that was going south. They had an argument, witnessed by many people, just before she died. The preliminary medical examination indicates that Harriet Forbes was poisoned."

He paused, as if pained.

"And by every account, Oliver was the one who gave her the drink."

❧

Grace could hear Aunt Clove screaming through the walls. Lillie had snuck Grace up to her bedroom. They lay on Lillie's bed together. Lillie's back was to Grace, but Grace could see the tears streaking down her cheeks like rain on glass.

"Your father is getting Oliver the best possible lawyer," Grace said, stroking her cousin's hair.

"But—Oliver. They think he *did* this," Lillie said.

"We will find out who really did," Grace said fiercely.

"Our family is ruined," Lillie said.

Grace didn't answer that. She knew it was likely true, and she knew intimately what that felt like. She could not bear to see it happen to Lillie, too.

Grace plaited Lillie's hair the way she used to when they were children. She didn't want to bother Lillie with the additional news that she had no place to stay. Aunt Clove would never allow her to remain in the Carter house, especially not now.

Should she call home and ask for more money?

Not that her parents had much to go around.

But—her mother. Her mother needed to know what was happening.

"Can I use your telephone?" she asked Lillie. "Somewhere private?"

"Father's office," she said.

Grace slipped down to Uncle Reginald's mahogany-paneled office. The lights were dim, and an unnatural sadness hung like a hush throughout the house. As if it, too, knew someone had died.

She saw the wooden secretary desk that Oliver had once carved his initials in as a boy and then tried to blame on Lillie. Grace ran her fingers over the old etching his small fingers had once made, then dialed her father's restaurant.

"Grace?" her mother said. "Are you all right?"

She'd seen the papers, but it wasn't until Grace told her that the police had come for Oliver that her mother gasped.

"Come home," Nell said immediately.

"I can't just . . . leave now, Mama. Surely you know that I could never leave Lillie and Oliver, no matter what."

"Put Clove on the phone."

"I don't think that would be a good idea," Grace said.

"Then you get on that train and come back here immediately," her mother demanded.

Grace heard the crackle of rage in her mother's voice, and it soothed her a little. It was that fire of her mother's that she loved and feared in equal measure, one that had dimmed to barely glowing embers after Walt's troubles. Hearing it again made Grace come alive.

But she was no longer a girl.

"I can't," she said. "Not yet, Mama."

"Grace—"

She hung up the telephone.

Grace sat down at her uncle's desk and contemplated her options. She knew staying at the Carter house was not one of them. What other females did she know? Frannie certainly wouldn't entertain the thought of having her—the idea almost made Grace laugh. Before, she might have asked to stay with Harriet.

But what was she to do?

She heard Waters answer the door, followed by the sound of voices in the foyer. When Grace slipped from Uncle Reginald's office, she was surprised to see Earnest, Theodore, and Frannie standing awkwardly in the sitting room. Frannie clutched her handbag in her gloved hands, glancing out the window, as though she already couldn't wait to leave.

"Miss Covington," Earnest said, greeting her solemnly. He and Theo removed their hats, holding them to their chests. "We heard that Oliver was taken into the police station and we came to offer our assistance."

"That's very kind of you," Grace said. "The Carters will be so grateful."

But what she thought was: *Word travels fast.*

"I apologize, but Miss Carter wishes me to convey that she needs to rest and is not feeling up to receiving visitors," Waters said. He sent an apologetic look to Grace, as if she were to be included in that category.

Of course, Lillie didn't know that Grace had nowhere else to go.

"Please let her know that we asked for her and we send our condolences," Earnest said.

"Good heavens, we did what we came for. Now let's go before we're seen by anyone," Frannie said curtly.

Earnest stepped toward Grace. He whispered gently in her ear: "We will find out who did this."

She nodded, eyelashes fluttering, and smelled a whiff of his cologne. She wanted to close her eyes and fall into his arms and have him assure her that everything would be all right. That this week wouldn't irrevocably ruin their lives forever. That someone who had more power than her would step in to fix it all and make it right.

"Please let us know if we can be of assistance to you, Miss Covington," Theo said formally. He gave her a small bow and exited the house, with Frannie hurrying on his heels.

Earnest glanced up the stairs. "Are you doing all right yourself, Miss Covington?" he asked.

She nodded, her throat narrowing at his concern. She didn't trust herself to speak.

He nodded. "I'll call again tomorrow," he said as she walked him to the door.

She fetched her carpetbag from where she had stashed it behind a plant and glanced up the stairs at Lillie's closed door. Did Lillie partly blame her for what had happened?

Grace chewed on her nail, flooded with guilt.

As Earnest's carriage drove away, she let herself out onto the Carters' front stoop.

She barely had the money for one more night at a cheap hotel, and then she wouldn't have enough for the train fare home.

She clutched her carpetbag, debating.

"Looking for a cab?" Theodore Parker called.

She whirled around, flushing.

She hadn't realized that he was still there, waiting in his own carriage.

"I can give you a ride," he offered.

"No, that's all right," she said hurriedly.

"I insist," he said. "No need to pay for a cab when you can suffer through my company for free."

He climbed out of the carriage and took her bag. "Where to?" he asked with unusual gentleness. "The hotel?"

She hesitated. Her face burned with embarrassment. And then he seemed to put it together, realizing what it meant that she had her bag with her and no clear direction.

He was delicate. And that made her want to die.

"My aunt has an artist's studio . . ." he began. "It's vacant. She didn't want to rent it out during the fair, but she hates crowds and didn't want to be here."

"Mr. Parker, I couldn't possibly—"

"It's nothing special. Small and rather quaint. She could use a house sitter. You would be doing her a favor."

Her pride flared up, threatening to consume her.

"Oliver didn't do this," she insisted. Tears pricked at her eyes.

"I agree with you," he said with conviction.

And so she accepted his hand and climbed into the carriage.

❧

The painter's studio was a short walking distance from the fairgrounds, barely two blocks from the entrance to Forest Park. She could see the Ferris wheel looming in the distance.

Theo unlocked the door and then waited outside of it. She set down her carpetbag amid the palettes and canvases. The studio smelled of varnish, and it had a bed, small bathroom, and a fireplace. She couldn't imagine what kind of wealth could afford an unused space like this. It was a bit chilly, but the blankets looked warm and cozy.

She smiled with secret pleasure.

She hadn't eaten all day and her stomach betrayed her with a loud grumble.

"Time for a meal, perhaps?" Theo asked wryly.

She dug through her bag for a notebook. "Only so we can talk about what to do next," she said.

They ended up at a restaurant down the street. Grace purposefully picked something outside the fairgrounds so she wouldn't have to pay the fifty-cent entrance fee or depend on him to buy dinner. Even so, her money was growing alarmingly low. The tomato soup and ham and cheese sandwich that was placed in front of her was warm and she was suddenly ravenous. She ate it without delicacy or care for what Theo thought. He watched her with that look of detached bemusement.

"Puppy no more," he said. "More like a mastiff."

"Your condescension is always so attractive," she said with her mouth full. "And may I suggest you refrain from comparing a lady—even one so below you in status—to any form of dog."

He flushed beet red. "I'm sorry, you're right. That hadn't occurred to me. I will refrain from such thoughtless comparisons in the future."

She arched an eyebrow.

"It's fine," she said, wiping mustard from her mouth. "I'm generally more bark than bite."

She winked and took another large mouthful, and he snorted.

She opened her small notebook, careful not to spill soup on it as she turned to a fresh page. She wrote LIST OF SUSPECTS across the top and underlined it twice.

"Am I dining with a detective?" Theo said.

"You're dining with someone who loves her cousins," Grace said. "And would do anything for them."

"Anything?" he asked.

"I didn't kill Harriet, if that's what you're asking," she said.

"Neither did I, for what it's worth."

"Then who did?" she asked, pen poised above the paper.

"Isn't this a job for the police?" he asked.

"Yes, they're doing such a fabulous job," she retorted. "Did you forget that they recently arrested *Oliver*?"

"To be fair, his actions leading up to last night do make him look like a prime suspect."

"I know." She sighed. "That's why we have to find the police a better one."

She tapped her pen on the page and examined Theodore's striking face as he stirred his coffee.

"We were the only two Oliver trusted with his secret," she said. "Did we do the wrong thing?"

"We couldn't possibly have known—" Theo said, frowning.

"I know," she said.

Theo looked away, his jaw tightening. "Before my mother died, she was sick for a week. My father wanted to call the doctor, but she insisted she was fine. I've always wondered, should I have called sooner?" He flexed his hand on the table and let out a humorless laugh. "I was old enough to know better, but young enough to simply obey. My father says I spend too much time living in the past."

The past. The clouds that surrounded him. Perhaps they were less the disdain she had marked them for and something more complicated than that.

She knew well what it was like to wish you could go back in time and change things. To save someone you loved.

"I know we can't change what happened before. But I don't want to spend the rest of my life second-guessing what I did now," she said.

He nodded. The dark clouds around him seemed to part, and for a moment, Grace felt an enormous sense of relief. He was going to help her. She wasn't alone. Her nose burned with the threat of tears.

She hurriedly cleared her throat.

"Right. Well. Let's compare notes, then. Harriet had two strange interactions in the days leading up to her death," Grace said.

She wrote:

1. *The man at the Luchow-Faust restaurant who demanded money*
2. *The unknown person(s) she met with at the Tunnels the morning she died*

"She went to the Tunnels?" Theo said.

"And I told Oliver. That's the reason why they were publicly fighting in front of everyone," she said miserably.

"Could numbers one and two have been the same person?"

Grace nodded. "It's very possible."

"And then there was that woman following us," Theo said. "She was there last night."

Grace's eyes widened. She wrote down:

3. *Unknown woman who was tailing us/Harriet? Who? Why?*

She finished her sandwich and began on her soup. "Was there anything else unusual that happened last night? Anything you saw?"

"I'm not sure." Theodore lowered his voice. "I just keep thinking—what are you supposed to ask when someone is murdered? Who benefited from it? Who would benefit from Harriet being dead?"

Grace wiped her mouth as a new thought came to her. "Ethel Adams, that singer. She was there last night. She had a motive. Beating out Harriet to become a star."

"But would she really kill Harriet over it?" Theodore sounded skeptical.

Grace shrugged and wrote down Ethel's name. "It could change the course of her entire life. I'd say that was big enough motive. Especially if she thought she'd lose out to Harriet. What did Copper say to me last night? 'People are never more driven than when the future's at stake.'"

She hesitated. "And speaking of Copper . . ." she trailed off.

"What?"

"No, it's too silly. You'll think it's ridiculous."

"That's very likely, but don't let that stop you."

"Well . . . Frannie wasn't happy with the attention Copper gave Harriet last night."

"Frannie?" Theo asked. He barked out a laugh. "Frannie Allred?"

Grace scowled at him. "I told you you'd say it was silly."

"Well, to be fair, you've never much liked her."

"With good reason!"

"That doesn't make her a killer."

"Envy is a powerful drug," Grace said. She ignored Theo and wrote down:

4. *Frannie Allred*

"Anyone else?" Theo asked, finishing his drink.

"I suppose we should clear ourselves," she said. She cocked an eyebrow. "Where were you?"

He looked vaguely amused, wiping his mouth, and cocked one back. "I was speaking with my godfather. My father wanted to make sure I was integrating well into St. Louis society, since I insisted upon coming here against his wishes."

"Your father wanted you to stay in Chicago?" Grace asked.

"He wishes I were more interested in carrying on the family name there, yes. But my mother was from St. Louis, and I'd rather do something more useful with my time than be a gentleman."

"Window washer?" she asked. "High-rise construction worker?"

"Your mockery is so charming. If you must know, I'd rather be a lawyer."

"And who is your godfather?" Grace asked.

"Thomas Squire."

"The robber baron?" Grace asked.

"I don't think he prefers that term," Theodore said, delicately folding his napkin and placing it on the table. "He is known for banking and steel, yes. And you?"

"I was with Lillie," Grace said. "We can vouch for each other."

Grace racked her brain, visualizing the other guests at the party. She saw Lillie stiffen at the sound of the scream. Harriet's body, seizing, the froth at her mouth. Earnest, rushing to her side.

"What happened?" he had asked.

Aunt Clove, looking stricken.

Grace froze. What had Aunt Clove told Oliver bitterly only a few nights ago? *You'll marry Harriet Forbes over my dead body.*

Grace hid a shudder.

Aunt Clove was driven and could be heartless. But surely she would never resort to murder. Would she?

Grace set her pen down.

"I think that's good enough for now," she said.

"So where does this leave us?" Theo asked. "Do we bring this list to the police?"

Grace eyed the uneaten pickle on Theo's plate. He placed it on her plate without comment. "I already tried to tell them some of this, but it seems they need something more substantial to take me seriously," she said. "Do you have any connections in the police department?"

"No. But perhaps my father or godfather does."

She finished the pickle, and the ache of hunger in her stomach finally eased. "Let's see if we can get in to visit Oliver—I'd like to talk to him," she said.

"And then what?"

She tapped her finger down the names on the list. "Let's start with Ethel Adams. I've met her, and hopefully she'll be willing to speak with me—especially if she's innocent."

Grace insisted on paying her own part of the tab, and Theo walked her back to the studio, unlocking the door for her. The fair was lit up in the distance, its palaces awash in a hazy, beckoning glow.

"Make sure to dead bolt the door tonight," he said, handing her the key.

"I think I saw a paint scraper inside that could function as a weapon," she said. "An intruder should be more afraid of me."

"I don't doubt it," he said.

She hesitated. "Thank you for helping me," she said.

The hint of his rare, true smile emboldened her.

"Would you like to pay a visit to Miss Adams together?" she asked before she could stop herself. "Tomorrow?"

His eyebrow quirked. "What are you going to do? Ask her if she poisoned Harriet and gauge her reaction?"

"No. But I'm hoping she might have seen something from the other night that will prove helpful. Even if she didn't realize it."

"I'll come by at nine," he said. He tipped his hat to her. "Good night, Miss Covington."

She nodded, and as he walked out into the night, she dead bolted the door.

While she washed up for bed, she thought of Oliver, alone, in prison. Grieving. Probably frightened out of his mind.

She thought of Lillie, a prisoner in her own house. Worried sick about her only brother.

Grace changed into her nightgown and sank into bed, hoping that Ethel Adams might have seen something that night.

Grace loved her cousins desperately. But she sensed that this went even deeper than that. It went down to the cracked depths of her, the parts that still grieved how she hadn't been able to save her brother. So she would fight even harder to save Oliver.

She turned off the lamp, pulled the covers around herself, and tried to get her racing mind to rest.

CHAPTER NINE

MAY 5, 1904

Two Days After the Murder

ETHEL ADAMS WAS set to perform at Festival Hall that evening, which meant, if they had any luck at all, she would be practicing there sometime in the morning.

Grace dressed in one of Lillie's most expensive high-necked lace blouses and a veiled skirt, examining her reflection in the hazy, full-length mirror in the corner of the studio. She picked a hat with delicate purple flowers and plumes. Because she knew that money talked.

And even more importantly, money got *other* people to talk.

Theodore looked sharp as well, in his black satin hat and tailored suit. He had the high cheekbones of an aristocrat. He was so handsome, especially when he shed his perpetual look of scorn.

"Sleep well?" he asked as they passed through the fragrant sunken garden on the way to Festival Hall. He walked by her side but did not offer her his arm.

"As well as can be expected," Grace said, breathing in the cloves mixed with the flowering fringe trees. In truth, she'd had awful dreams. Of Oliver in jail and Harriet in the morgue. Of Walt, reaching out for her with skeletal fingers.

The Cascades misted her skin as they climbed the palatial, curving steps toward the golden and teal dome of Festival Hall. She could hear a few distant chords of music from deep within the hall, but when she pulled on the doors, they held fast.

Locked.

"May I help you?" a smartly dressed attendant asked, striding toward them. He had on a dark uniform, a crisp white shirt and gloves, and a bow tie.

"We're unable to attend the concert tonight," Theo said briskly. "And were hoping to hear Miss Adams sing during her practice instead."

The attendant chuffed at the brazenness of the request, about to turn them away. Until Theo brought out a wad of bills.

The attendant's sneer turned into an obliging smile. "Right this way, sir," he said.

"That's right, I forgot," Grace said under her breath. "Only the rich get to be impertinent."

"Come now, Grace," Theo said breezily. "You seem to do a pretty good job of it yourself."

He held the door for her and she wrinkled her nose.

The sound of the door closing behind them ricocheted across the vaulted ceiling. Grace tried not to gasp at the gleaming white walls of the grand, circular dome, empty of people but with seating for thousands. She glimpsed the largest pipe organ she had ever seen. Its ten thousand gleaming, golden pipes made her wish she had Walt at her side. Walt loved music. He had loved the organ at their small church, and they had laughed at the petite, passionate woman who every Sunday had played it for all she was worth. One time, they had snuck in when no one was there and played the organ as loud as they could, pretending to be Mrs. Penelope T. Gottfried until their mother caught them. Grace wondered if, with the acoustics of this place, playing an instrument like this at the height of its volume could blow out her eardrums.

Theo's hand barely grazed her lower back as he ushered her toward the balcony, and an unexpected zing went up Grace's spine.

They sank into the plush box seats above the stage, fading into the shadows.

"All of this is to be temporary?" she whispered, gaping in awe at the splendor of the hall.

"*Life* is temporary," Theo said. "Might as well make it as beautiful as you can."

Ethel Adams appeared on the stage dressed in a white gown and sat down at a grand piano. Three women joined her onstage, and a single man sat in the audience.

"Can you hear me?" she asked, directing the question to the man.

He gave her a thumbs-up.

"There's someone I want to impress tonight. Let's make sure he gets the best seat in the house."

Grace exchanged a look with Theodore.

Then Ethel drew a breath and transformed it into a song that filled the room with something soft and velvet, something Grace could almost reach out and touch. Ethel was surrounded by pots of flowering trees and the train of her dress spilled around her ankles in an iridescent oyster silk, like molten mother-of-pearl. Draped banners swayed as the lights were adjusted behind her. For the first time, Grace felt as though a song could melt in the air, wrap itself around her, and then gently tuck her in.

Theo leaned toward her. "I forgot to mention that my father made a call," he whispered. "I can get us in to see Oliver."

"When?" Grace asked.

"Tomorrow."

She felt that pleasurable little zing again.

"Why are you doing all of this for Oliver?" she whispered. The fear of those zings made her voice come out sharper than she intended. "Playing along in his game with Harriet could have easily gotten the murder pinned on you."

His jaw twitched. "Don't think that thought hasn't crossed my mind."

"Then why?" she demanded. "Why are you being so good to him? Did he lend you money? Do you owe Oliver some sort of debt?"

"Your low opinion of me never ceases to amaze."

She turned toward the stage, not looking at him. "It just seems an awful amount of effort for someone you haven't even known a year."

Out of the corner of her eye, she saw him flush a little. "I'm not in the habit of making friends easily or quickly," he said. "I know well what it's like to be used for my name and fortune or mocked behind my back for the way I look." He flushed deeper, turning so that the birthmark was fully visible. "But Oliver was immediately my friend. He made other friends for me. He made my entering society in St. Louis so effortless. I may not have the gift of easily making friends, but I do have the gift of loyalty." He clenched his jaw, his profile limned in the light. And she thought of how alike they were, in some ways. Oliver had done the same for her. Instead of shunning her as an outsider, he had always brought her into the fold. Made her feel like she was wanted.

"So perhaps you're right," Theodore said. "Perhaps I am repaying a debt. But I like to think of it as more that I care. And when I care"—his eyes met hers, and something twinged inside of her—"I care to the depths of myself."

Her gloved hand grazed his and she immediately pulled it back. Hints of attraction were out of the question. This was all just a marriage of convenience. No, not that word. A *business arrangement* of convenience.

She turned over the thoughts in her head, playing with her pocketbook in her lap. Dear Oliver was always generous. Always willing to bring in people to the inner circle. But perhaps he had gone too far with Harriet.

Perhaps bringing her into the elite inner circle had gotten her killed.

When the next song ended, they made their way down the stairs to intercept Ethel as she took a break.

Ethel startled a little to see them approach, but quickly recovered.

"Ah. We meet again, Gretchen," Ethel said, eyeing them with suspicion.

"Grace," Grace corrected. "And this is my friend, Mr. Theodore Parker. You might remember him from the Luchow-Faust the other night, as well."

"Not to be rude, but I didn't realize we were opening rehearsals up to the public," Ethel said. She arched an eyebrow.

"We had to pull a few strings," Grace said.

"That desperate to hear me sing?" Ethel asked.

"And we were hoping to speak to you about something. Privately."

Ethel held their gaze. Then inhaled.

"Is it about Harriet Forbes?" she asked quietly.

Grace took that as an invitation to plunge ahead. "You might have seen that Oliver Carter was arrested on suspicion of Harriet's murder." She swallowed. "I'm Oliver's cousin. He didn't do this."

"I don't see what any of this has to do with me." Ethel's eyes darted toward the man doing the sound check, and he began striding toward them.

"You were there that night Harriet died."

"And I've already told the police everything I know."

"But there was another night I'd like to ask you about. Please."

It wasn't merely Grace's imagination that Ethel's eyes looked bruised and hollow. The makeup couldn't quite hide it, now that they were this close. She hadn't been sleeping. If Grace were a betting woman, she would say that Harriet's death had impacted her. But the question remained—was it out of grief or guilt?

Theodore shot Grace a wordless look that she was learning to interpret. He was offering to pull out his wallet again. But she didn't want to have to rely on his cash and connections at every turn. And Grace could tell that this was a woman who could not be bought. This time, it would be up to her.

"Listen. I don't have anything to offer you, I know that," Grace said quickly as the man approached them. "I have no money. No connections to help your career. All I can do is appeal to your better nature. An innocent man is being held. A man I love as dearly as a brother. If you had information that could set him free, would you give it?"

Ethel sighed. She held up a hand to keep the approaching man at bay. "Fine. My backup singers are practicing this song. You have three minutes until they're done."

One of them hit a wrong note and Ethel turned to glare at her.

"Or perhaps four," she said sardonically.

Grace pulled out her notebook. "That night we first met at the Luchow-Faust," she said quickly. "You and Harriet both performed, and Sam Whitcomb mentioned that someone important was there. A talent manager, looking for someone's career to invest in." She spoke quickly, but she was watching Ethel's reaction the whole time. Ethel remained impassive, her face not betraying a single twitch. But she was an actress, after all, Grace reminded herself.

Grace continued: "When Harriet exited the stage, she was approached by a man who wished to speak to her."

"Yes," Ethel said slowly. "I saw that."

Grace's pulse sped up. "Did you recognize the man?"

Ethel shook her head. "I did not."

Grace was undeterred. "But did you get a good look at him? Could you describe him? Or recognize him again if you saw him?"

"I didn't get a good look at him. And I don't know his name." Ethel hesitated. "But I can tell you who he was with."

Grace held her breath. Ethel reached for Grace's notebook and wrote down a name.

"Glen Perkins? Parkins? He works with the De Forest Wireless Telegraph Company. He wanted me to come and sing at one of their events next week. I spoke to him earlier that night, and I believe he left with the man who approached Harriet."

She turned the notebook around. "Find Glen Perkins, and he can tell you the identity of that man."

Grace felt a match spark of hope.

"Thank you, Miss Adams."

"Call me Ethel, Gretchen."

Grace smiled at Theo and gave Ethel a bow of gratitude.

"You better nail that note tonight, Bonita, or I'll have your hide," Ethel hollered toward the stage. "Let's take it from the top. And then I need a hot tea and a nap."

"Well, Miss Covington," Theo said, leaning to whisper in her ear. "I think you just got our first lead."

❧

Grace and Theodore were making their way through the verdant pathways of the sunken gardens when they ran into Earnest and Frannie. They were sitting on one of the many benches, chatting with Copper beneath the shade of Frannie's parasol.

"Fancy meeting you here," Copper said, noticing them. "Care to join us?"

"We're off on an errand, I'm afraid," Grace said. She met Earnest's eyes. "How are you feeling?"

"Like life has walloped me this week," he said. "Figured some fresh air at the fair would do us all some good."

Although perhaps by this point, we should all stay away, Grace thought.

"Where are you going?" Frannie asked. She directed her attention solely at Theodore.

"We have someone to speak with at the telegraph office," he said. He squinted, shading his eyes from the sun. "Someone who might know something about Harriet's death."

Earnest stood. "You're investigating?" he asked. "I'd love to join you. I have some thoughts of my own."

Frannie harrumphed, crossing her legs. "I couldn't be less interested in this and think it's all a terrible show of judgment," she said.

"Go ride some rides and have some fairy floss," Earnest said, waving his hand.

"What the lady wants, the lady gets," Copper said, offering Frannie his arm. She simpered, turning her back on them. "It's not that we don't care," Copper said, throwing an apologetic look over his shoulder. "We just have different ways of showing it."

Grace found herself between Theodore and Earnest as they turned toward the De Forest telegraph tower, which rose like a beacon in the distance, capped by a waving American flag.

News sellers everywhere were hawking special edition copies of the *Fair's Fare*. A few policemen were approaching the newsstands and appeared to be trying to shut down their operations. Grace caught the headline as they passed.

AUTOPSY RESULTS PENDING
OVERDOSE OR . . . POISON?

There was an image of Harriet's lovely face on the front.

Then beneath it read:

PROMINENT MEMBER OF ST. LOUIS ELITE
ARRESTED ON SUSPICION OF MURDER

Tears pricked Grace's eyes as she hurried past. People were lining up to buy the papers like they did to try ice-cream cones and iced teas. Her stomach soured at the gleeful way they consumed the gossip, made even more delicious by the featuring of someone rich. She felt an admonishment to herself, because of course she had participated before, too. But now it was Oliver, and Lillie, and yes—even Aunt Clove. Why were people so awful to one another—particularly among the classes? Why did they root for each other's downfall? Why must it—

"Why must it be so *tall*?" Theo groaned and pinched the bridge of his nose, looking up at the telegraph tower. Its wood structure was a lattice that stretched three hundred feet in the air. A box of glass windows glittered at the observation point.

Earnest laughed, but it was without cruelty.

"You stay, Parker," Earnest said, gently touching his arm. "Grace and I can handle this."

They left him behind and entered the line, then rode the elevators up to the 110-foot platform of the wireless telegraph observation office. The elevator opened into a room made of glass walls surrounding wooden desks, switches, and boxes of cylinders. It smelled like crisp paper and a hint of copper. There was a clicking sound as the dispatchers sent wireless messages to the *St. Louis Post-Dispatch* and the *St. Louis Star.* "Step right up and try it!" one of the uniformed workers encouraged the crowd. "Send messages across the fairgrounds and then go retrieve them yourself!"

Grace stepped closer to the windows overlooking the emerald, manicured strips that spilled over the grounds below, the streetlamps set like neat pins amid the lagoons and canals, the sculpted cupolas perched atop the ivory buildings. The Ivory City stretched on and on. The people below looked so small, walking the strip of the Pike. She could glimpse a bird's-eye view of Jerusalem, a massive holy city surrounded by walls that contained replicas of the Western Wall and the Church of the Holy Sepulchre's jewel-blue rotunda. Grace walked the periphery of the telegraph room, and in the distance, she glimpsed the Philippine Village, with young boys diving for coins in the lakes.

It was impossible to believe that soon, all of this would be gone. A brilliant matchstick whose flame drew the world close, and then snuffed out.

Through a partitioned window she saw another room, where a great spark appeared to accompany each signal sent through the air.

She cocked her head at Earnest, then raised a gloved hand to knock.

The man who answered looked annoyed. "Yes," he said through a bushy mustache.

"I'm sorry to disturb you," she said. "But it's urgent. We are looking for someone named Glen Parkins. We need to speak to him."

He scowled. "There's no one here by that name."

Earnest appeared at her side and Grace stopped the door from closing with her foot. "Perhaps it's Perkins?" she asked.

The man shook his head and shut the door roughly in her face.

Grace's cheeks burned. She took a step back, and Earnest gently touched her elbow.

Had Ethel invented someone? Made up a story and sent them on a wild goose chase?

Just then a young man in a cap tapped her on the shoulder. He was Latino and had a baby face, with the barest beginning of a mustache. "Ma'am. I couldn't help but overhear," he said. "Do you mean George Parsons?"

"Yes!" Grace said, turning on her heel. "Yes, that must be who I mean."

"There's a George Parsons who works here. But he left town. Had a family emergency."

"Thank you. Did he say when he would return?"

"I think the boss expects him back on Friday."

That was three days away.

"Could I leave my name and a way to get in contact as soon as he returns? It's really urgent we speak with him," Grace said.

"That's a good idea," Earnest said. "Let's leave him my address. It's a little more permanent."

"What's your name?" Grace asked the young man as she pulled out her notebook for a piece of paper.

"Santiago."

"Thank you so much for your help," Grace said.

Earnest wrote out his address and handed it to Santiago. "As soon as you can."

She kept waiting for Earnest to offer to pay him, but he didn't. He smiled at Grace and took her by the arm.

She stole a look over her shoulder as they made their way to the elevator. Santiago was slipping Earnest's address in his pocket.

A sixth sense was making her feel as though something weren't quite right.

Grace followed Earnest into the elevator, but at the last minute she stepped out.

"You go on," she said, as the doors were closing. "I forgot one thing."

She opened her purse. She had only a few dollars left. She hesitated.

Then she made her way back to Santiago. "For your trouble," she said, handing him a dollar. "And . . . could you send the message here, too? Just in case."

She wrote down the address to the artist's studio.

"Thank you," she said, and hurried back down to the ground to join her party.

❧

Lillie was dressed in a silk day dress when Grace stepped into the Carters' foyer later that afternoon. There was barely any color in her face. Her dress spilled around her in panels of embroidered flowers, while real ones were placed elegantly in her hair.

Lillie never cared what she looked like, unless she was really sad. And then she did it to cheer herself.

The sight of her in her fancy dress, sitting alone in the dim parlor, made Grace's heart fissure, a thousand delicate cracks.

"It's good of you to come," Lillie said bravely. She rose to greet them.

"Where's Frannie?"

"She couldn't make it," Theo lied. "Though she wanted to."

In truth, when they had met up with Frannie and Copper again outside of the Pike's "Creation" ride, she had forbidden Earnest to go to the Carter house.

"It isn't good for you to be seen with them," she said, pulling him aside. "Why do you do this? Put our family name at risk?"

He had jerked his arm away. "People remember who was there in their time of need. She was there for me. I'd like to be there for her."

But Frannie looked nervous. "Society will turn on them," she said. "You'll see."

Copper steered Frannie away from Earnest. "I'll see her home," Copper whispered.

"Better you than me," Earnest said angrily.

When he turned back to the group, he had muttered, "Is it possible to love someone and dislike them all at once?"

"It's more common than you'd think," Theodore said, catching Grace's eye with a dark smirk in a way that she was horrified to discover made lightning strike through her body.

She did not look at him again until they were standing together in the Carters' parlor.

"You were at the fair?" Lillie asked, looking at them in confusion. Unable to imagine that they could go and have fun, when her world had abruptly stopped turning.

Grace stepped forward and took her hand.

"We're looking into Harriet's death," she said quietly. She met her cousin's red-rimmed eyes. "Anything that might exonerate Oliver. We have a few leads. And we'll go visit Oliver tomorrow. Would you like to come?"

Lillie's gaze rose to meet Grace's. "My parents can't know," she whispered.

"Has that ever stopped us before?" Grace asked.

Flushing, Lillie reached out for Theodore's hand, too. Looking surprised, if not a little confused, he stepped forward and took it, so that they formed a broken chain of sorts. They just needed Oliver there to complete it.

And for the first time, standing in the fading light, Grace felt a fierce swell of belief that this small, unlikely group might actually do it.

CHAPTER TEN

MAY 6, 1904

Three Days After the Murder

Theodore's carriage stopped outside of the artist's studio at ten past ten the next morning. It was gray and drizzly, and Grace pulled down her hat. She had dressed conservatively for the visit: a crisp white blouse, unadorned with lace or embroidery. A wool skirt to keep out the chill, a gray hat with a spray of white flowers. If Lillie had been in a better mood, she might have called them drab. But Grace knew that the last thing she needed to do that day was draw attention to herself.

The door to the carriage opened and Theodore helped her inside to join Lillie and Earnest.

Lillie's face was shadowed, but she brightened perceptibly as she moved to make room. Earnest handed Grace a small bouquet of flowers that matched the one that Lillie was clutching in her hands. "A little something from our garden, in the hopes it might cheer you." He lowered his voice. "I hope it does, as I faced the wrath of our formidable gardener for picking them."

"How delightful. I am effectively cheered." Grace smelled the fresh tulips and Virginia bluebells. She squeezed Lillie's arm and asked, "How did you escape this morning?"

"I told my parents I was going to the fair with Mr. Parker and the Allreds," Lillie said. "I thought Frannie might come today, but she's been so scarce. She must be taking Harriet's death hard."

Grace wanted to tell Lillie that Frannie was no friend at all. But she couldn't very well say that in front of Earnest, no matter how much he might agree with her. She took one look at Lillie's anxious face and decided that she wouldn't add that burden to her now.

"Perhaps we'll see her today," Grace said. "I think we should go to the fair after our visit with Oliver."

"The fewer lies we tell the better?" Lillie ventured ruefully.

"And because of the people there we need to talk to."

Earnest helped them out of the carriage.

The Four Courts jail was an imposing building three stories tall and the length of a city block. It was made of buff limestone and its mansard roofs were topped with a decorative cupola. It would have been lovely save for the large, foreboding morgue on the northeast corner, and the gallows in the courtyard where the public executions took place.

When they stepped inside the first floor of the jail building, the doors slammed behind them and the air was laced with chill. Theo spoke to the head jailer and his clerk, exchanging words in low voices. The clerk glanced over at Lillie and Grace and Earnest.

Then the head jailer gave a dismissive nod, and the clerk walked them through the long corridor, their steps echoing. Earnest took Lillie and Grace on each arm, and Grace was grateful for his solid presence. Lillie seemed grateful for it, too, especially as the clerk unlocked a door and brought them into a private room.

Oliver was sitting at a wooden table. He was handcuffed and had an armed guard with him.

"Oliver," Lillie said. She ran forward to hug him, and the guard stared straight ahead.

Oliver wiped the tears falling from Lillie's face. "I'm sorry I have caused you all this pain," he said.

"We're going to get you out of here, Ollie," Lillie said. "Grace and me. Even if everyone else fails." Her voice became steel. "I swear to you."

"They won't let you post bail?" Earnest asked, joining him at the table. "Surely your parents would post it for you."

"They won't," he said.

"But why not?" Lillie asked.

"I'm up against bigger forces than even the Carter name can handle."

"What do you mean?" Grace asked.

"They need this to be a lovers' quarrel. Nothing more. Which means no one is eager to find another culprit."

"So they aren't even looking?" Lillie's face went white.

There was a beat of silence.

"It will be much better for you if it's an overdose," Earnest said quietly.

Oliver shook his head vehemently. "She wasn't on anything that night. Or any other. That just . . . wasn't who she was."

But how well had any of them known her? Grace wondered. Harriet had been hiding something, and it had gotten her killed.

"What were you arguing about just before she died?" Grace asked.

"I was inquiring about why on earth she went to the Tunnels. She told me she was meeting someone, but she couldn't talk about it there. I asked if it was romantic in nature."

"Did she deny it?" Grace asked.

"She was indignant. She said of course not. She insisted that it was something professional. But the argument began because she was insulted, and she also asked if I was spying on her."

Something professional, Grace noted. But why couldn't she discuss it that night? Because it was dangerous? Because the person she had met in the Tunnels was also there at the party? Could it have been the singer Ethel Adams? The talent manager? That man who had approached her at the restaurant?

Surely *someone* in the Tunnels must have seen who Harriet was meeting that day.

"Perhaps this was nothing but a tragic accident," Grace said to Oliver. "Perhaps the autopsy results will clear you."

He nodded, as though trying to appear hopeful for her sake. But the cousin she knew had faded into a wisp of shadow.

When their visit ended, the clerk escorted them out. Earnest tried to cheer Lillie, but it grated on Grace's nerves. For once she was grateful for Theo's dark, silent stoicism. As they waited for the carriage, a boy began to set up his newspaper wagon on the opposite corner.

"Papers!" he yelled. He waved a copy in the air. "Special edition!"

Lillie paled. She clutched Grace's hand, trying to read the screaming headline at the corner newsstand. "Look at the size of the font. There must be news."

She started to run forward, but Theo stopped her.

"Let someone else," he said gently.

"I'll go," Grace said. Earnest came with her and they strode over the gravel streets, kicking up dust in their haste.

Grace's hands trembled as she paid for the paper, taking the thin newsprint between her fingers. Letting the news sink through her.

"Oh, Oliver," she breathed.

"What does it say?" Earnest asked, his voice soft behind her.

She handed him the paper.

STRYCHNINE POISONING!
ACTRESS'S AUTOPSY CONFIRMS MURDER

"So Harriet was, in fact, poisoned," Earnest said.

Grace took in a deep breath. "And now they are really going to go after Oliver for her murder."

Earnest looked at Grace with a growing unease.

"But we both know he didn't do it," he said slowly.

"Yes," Grace said, swallowing. "Which means the real murderer is still out there."

❧

Grace believed, deep down, that Oliver couldn't have done this.

But she remembered, clear as day, him handing Harriet the glass just before she died. And she knew that meant that dozens of others did, too.

"We have to go to the Tunnels," she said. "Maybe someone saw who Harriet was speaking to that morning."

"Absolutely not," Earnest said. "I know I sound like Frannie, but no self-respecting lady can go into the Tunnels."

"Well, I've already been once before. I followed Harriet. It's my fault they were fighting before she died. I told him she had gone to the Tunnels and he confronted her. I have to do this for Oliver. And, with all due respect, no one here is going to stop me."

Earnest shook his head. "But think of Lillie. I'd argue that she can't be seen there. There are too many people who might recognize her. They'll jump to conclusions. Think she's . . . self-medicating after what's happened."

Lillie stuck out her chin. "I don't care about any of that. Not if it helps Oliver."

"Listen. I'm meant to meet Copper and Frannie at the Olympic track today so Copper can train. We could go talk to them. Ask them what they saw," Earnest said.

"I'll go with Grace," Theo offered quietly.

A look of anger and sadness flashed in Lillie's eyes. She pulled Grace to the side. "No more secrets between us," she said. "Us and everyone else—yes. But none between you and me."

"I promise," Grace said. And she meant it.

She felt the faintest twinge within her as Earnest put his arm around Lillie and led her away. She told herself she was being silly.

She turned around and was faced with Theodore Parker. Again.

"I don't have to tell you that this could be quite dangerous," he said.

"I know," she said.

"It's dangerous in the Tunnels. But it's also risky to be poking around this. If someone murdered Harriet, they probably wouldn't hesitate to kill anyone else who got too close to the truth." His eyes darkened.

"Does this mean you're concerned about me, Theodore Parker?" she asked.

"I'd hate for you to get murdered just when you're starting to grow on me."

"I have that effect on people," she said. "I'm irresistible."

"Hmm," he said. "Some would say tolerable."

"These are for purchasing and *then* reading," the newsstand man said curtly, stepping forward to block Grace's view of the newspapers. He crossed his arms.

"Leave her alone," Theodore barked, turning on him. "I'm buying whichever one she wants."

A ray of warmth winked through Grace and she selected one of the papers. "This is going to help us."

She showed him a printed image of Harriet's face.

Theo cocked an eyebrow. "Good thinking," he said.

He paid for multiple copies, and they began walking down the Pike, toward the Tunnels.

"Aren't you worried about your reputation?" Grace asked. "What will people say about you going into the Tunnels with a girl so below your station?" She kept her voice light, but they both knew the dark streak of truth that lurked beneath it.

He said with disdain, "I've better things to worry about than big mouths paired with small minds."

She snorted. "Those things do end up together quite frequently, don't they?"

"Here we are," he said. "Stay close to me." He took her by the arm, a little more forcefully than she was expecting. "I'm serious, Covington."

A cracking spark of electricity shot through her skin, her spine, the tips of her fingers. She stole a look at him and wondered again, *Why are you so different now than you were that night?*

"I won't leave your side," she promised."

Then she followed him into the deep shadows of the Tunnels.

❧

There were flickering lanterns and small alcoves tucked beneath the Tunnels' eaves. Most people eyed Grace and Theodore warily as they passed, slipping their drugs and paraphernalia away, but a few made to approach them with a hungry gleam in their eyes. Both the smoke and the laughter in the air held a sour undercurrent. The chambers were too crowded to walk shoulder to shoulder, so Theodore glanced behind him every few steps to make sure Grace was still with him—until finally he tired of it and took her hand in his. His palm was dry and warm, mostly soft but a little calloused. It felt like the embers of a fire in a grate on a cold morning, burning just bright enough to make her want to draw nearer to them.

Once they had made it deeper into the bowels of the Tunnels, the crowd began to thin a little. The air was dank and decaying and Grace attempted to breathe through her mouth. The smoke left a bitter, filmy taste in her throat.

"Where did you see Harriet?" Theo asked in a low voice.

"There," Grace said. With her free hand, she gestured to an alcove a few yards beyond them. She remembered the patterned silk banner that was draped above the makeshift doorway.

Theo led the way, navigating around people smoking in the alleyways.

"Excuse me," Theo said, ducking his head into the small shop. There were beads and small coin purses out for display, as well as a cluttered mass of pipes and ashtrays. The woman behind the display came forward. Her white skin was tinged gray, and her mouth was lined with wrinkles that looked like exaggerated parentheses. She narrowed her blue eyes as she inhaled a long cigarette.

"Yes?" she asked cagily.

"We're here to inquire about this woman. Have you seen her in the last few days?"

Theo held out the newspaper for her to consider. A man stepped from behind a draped area in the back, eyeing Theo's fine clothes. The woman gave a cursory glance at the image of Harriet and shook her head. "Never seen her," she said carelessly.

"What about you, sir?" Theo turned to the man.

"Nope." He shuffled a deck of cards between his hands. His nails were stained yellow. The walls around them were damp stone. Grace tried to breathe as her thoughts ricocheted. These were the kind of people who had given Walt the drugs that ensnared him.

She swallowed hard against the nausea, willing her compassion to rise.

These were people who had been ensnared, just like Walt.

Bloody hell, she absolutely hated drugs.

"Can I help you?" Someone sidled up behind them and Grace felt Theo stiffen. He moved imperceptibly closer to her. "I can't believe you came down here alone," Theodore said bitingly under his breath. "If I were your brother, I would have punched through a wall."

She opened her hand within his, just barely enough for him to feel it. She quietly said, "Good thing you're not."

"Are you and the lady looking for a score?" the man asked. He had beady eyes and a smile that reminded Grace of a shark.

"No," Theo said carefully, "but I'd pay handsomely for information."

He dropped Grace's hand and subtly brought out his wallet.

The man laughed with derision. "'Fraid you're in the wrong place, then."

He sauntered away.

Another man came close to them. His eyes were glassy, and his breath smelled like booze, but he said with concern, "You better get out of here. And for hell's sake, put your cash away." He staggered, steadying himself against a wall. "You're practically begging to get mugged."

"We just need someone to help us," Theo said. "We're looking for information about our friend." Though the man could hardly see straight, Theo thrust the paper toward him.

"Who is she?" the man asked, squinting.

"Something's happened to her. She met with someone here shortly beforehand. Please. If you know anything."

"Sorry. I've never seen her."

"I might have seen something," a woman said, coming toward them. She was wearing a ragged satin dress that spilled across her curves. Her eyes were bright and lined with kohl, and she looked at Theo hungrily. "Let's go this way and talk."

Grace suddenly felt like they were in too deep of the bowels of the fair. She couldn't see any daylight, and the smoke was making her eyes burn.

"This wasn't a good idea," Theo whispered into Grace's hair. He glanced over his shoulder, then shepherded her toward the exit. Grace could feel the prickling presence on the back of her neck of someone following them. Theodore must have sensed it, too, because he subtly took her hand again and they quickened their steps.

This stretch of the tunnels had thinned, making Grace feel exposed. They turned, expecting to see the exit out into the fairgrounds.

Instead, it was an empty alcove.

The footsteps were approaching, and slowing. About to catch up to them.

Theo dropped her hand and brought out a switchblade from his pocket. He flipped it open, stepping in front of her just as their tail turned the corner.

Grace let out a gasp that ended in a sob.

She fell forward, not believing her eyes.

"Walt?"

CHAPTER ELEVEN

"GRACIE?"

Everything about Grace's brother was too thin. His body, so that she could trace the bones of his clavicle. His hair, which had once been thick and wavy. The spark in his eyes, once vibrant, now flickering in and out like there was a draft within him. His clothes were slightly dirty and hung off his shoulders.

Tears sprang to Grace's eyes. She threw her arms around him.

He grasped her close, like she was the first day of spring after a long winter.

Then he pulled back from her.

"What are you doing here?" he asked angrily. He took in Theodore Parker, the sheen of his clothes, his finely tailored suit and hat. He knew this class well, and he charged toward Theo, regardless of the switchblade in his hand.

"What are you doing down here with her? That's my sister. Are you *mad*?"

"Walt, wait," Grace said, stopping him. "He's helping me. He's helping our family."

"Why? What's happened?" Walt asked. His brow knit together and he tensed, like he was expecting to receive yet another blow. That move cleaved Grace's heart clean in two.

"It's Oliver," Grace whispered.

Theo made a show of raising his hands in surrender, then putting away the switchblade.

"Dressed like that you should probably keep it handy," Walt said curtly. He turned back to Grace, examining her face. "It's so good to see you," he said, taking her in with brotherly affection. "You've never known how lovely you are, Gracie. You grow lovelier every year."

She flushed. Especially with Theo standing there, witnessing all the dimensions of this—these parts of herself she would have never allowed him to see.

"What's Ollie done?" Walt asked roughly.

"Can you come to lunch with us?" she asked. She glanced at Theo, expecting him to look repulsed, but his face was neutral. Even the usual look of disdain was under control. "We can get something to eat. Talk about what's happened."

Walt didn't spare a glance at Theo.

"Is *he* coming?" he asked.

"Yes. He's . . . my friend," she said. And as the words passed her lips, she realized it was true.

As Walt led them to the exit of the Tunnels, Theo whispered into Grace's ear, his breath a caress, "Do you want me to come? I'll leave you if you prefer—and if you'll be safe."

"Walt would never hurt me," she whispered. "But . . . I'd still like you to come."

Theo nodded, the flickering light catching the angles of his face, illuminating the way the birthmark spread across his handsome jaw like a map.

"Then I will."

❧

They ate lunch at a restaurant near the Cascades, where they could feel the sunlight and fountain mist on their faces. It washed away the dimness of the Tunnels like a clean cloth. Grace pretended to use the ladies' room, but instead she sought out the waiter and implored him not to bring their table any alcohol. When she returned to her seat, she snuck looks at Walt whenever she could.

She had been fed and clothed and raised in a house that had problems and love in equal measure. She had been loved and cared for. She cherished her childhood memories. They hadn't been perfect. There was a particular year her father's restaurant had almost gone under, and there were nights she'd pretended to be full when she went to bed hungry. Even as a girl, she could sense the tension that seeped through the house like moisture, molding the places where the love also grew.

But Walt. Walt had borne the weight of their family's failed expectations. He had felt them too keenly. He had been a thousand things. Drawn to melancholy, a nurser of wounds. Fiercely loyal and protective of her. Unsure of who he was. Her mother had tried to send him to their grandfather to learn business. Walt had come back worn down. He was an overthinker. His thoughts swirled around him, and he couldn't figure out how to fight them back. What was left behind were a thousand little cuts. She observed him now, while she pretended to study her menu. He was an artist who drew pictures for her on the glass in the mist left from the rain and built things with his hands. He had a temper. It had been a unique kind of agony to watch the brilliant colors in him twist and warp. He became volatile, a glass mosaic turning from its lighter sides to dark without warning.

He had done that to their home, too.

And yet she loved him. She had never stopped. His unresolved pain had cost her, too. These were the kaleidoscope parts of him, and almost none of them were things that Theo could see—nor could any of the other people sitting nearby, who were barely masking their distaste that someone like Walt was dining among them. She felt thrilled to see her older brother alive and fiercely protective of him, as well as embarrassed by him. She was embarrassed at *herself* that she felt embarrassed by him.

And yet always, always hopeful that he would return to her.

"What do you want, Walt?" she asked, pushing the menu toward him. "Don't worry about the money. It's my treat."

She'd have to borrow the money from Theodore, but she would give Walt a good meal. She could stomach facing the dank Tunnels for Oliver, and the depths of her own humiliation for Walt—hoping that this could be the first of many good meals for him. If only he could taste and remember what life could be like.

He ordered soup and a sandwich and bread and then, hesitantly, a Dr Pepper.

"Now," he said, massaging his fingers together and fixing a critical eye on Grace, "do you want to tell me what you were doing down in the Tunnels?"

She stole a look at Theodore, who shrugged.

"Like I said, Ollie's in trouble," she said, explaining what had happened. How Grace had tracked Harriet into the Tunnels the morning of her murder, and that they were hoping to find information that might somehow help to exonerate Oliver. But no one there would talk to them.

"Some friends of mine were mentioning that actress's death. I heard of this. I had no idea it was Ollie." Walt ate ravenously, still fixing a suspicious eye on Theodore.

"You don't really seem like her type," he said.

Theo chuffed, arching an eyebrow. "And what's that?"

"Pompous," Walt said. "Rich-blooded."

"Walt," Grace warned.

"Nothing she hasn't already called me, and worse," Theo said casually, leaning back in his chair.

Walt's mouth twitched. He gave Grace an approving look.

"Your sister is quite adept at handling herself, I can assure you," Theo said.

"And yet I swear, if you ever take her down to the Tunnels again, I'll use that switchblade on you," Walt said.

"Fair enough," Theo said. He narrowed his eyes. "Although you might consider what your own trips to the Tunnels are doing to her."

"Enough," Grace said curtly. She turned to Walt and abruptly changed the subject. "What do you know about strychnine?"

He shrugged. "Not much. It's not exactly my poison of choice."

"What is, these days?" she asked.

He shot her a look. "I thought we were having a nice lunch."

She paused, trying to decide how much she wanted to push him. It was a delicate balance. She decided to bide her time a little longer.

"Do they sell strychnine in the Tunnels?" she asked instead.

"I can look into it."

Walt took a sip of Dr Pepper, fixing his eyes on Theo across the table. Theo returned the stare.

"What exactly are your intentions with my sister?" Walt asked.

Grace choked on her drink. "He doesn't have any *intentions*, Walt. Trust me. He's helping me out of a bind like a gentleman and we both want to help Oliver. That's all."

Theo continued to stare back at Walt. He remained silent.

"Listen," Grace said, changing tactics. Gathering her courage, she turned to Walt. She said quietly, and urgently: "Lillie has some friends—doctor friends. I know she would love to see you, and she could bring you to some people who could help."

She felt like she was stepping out onto a paper-thin piece of glass. This was what had sent him running the first time—she and her parents had tried to get him help, but he had balked, and it was the last time they'd seen him. That had been almost a year ago.

She had to tread carefully.

"Still think I'm worth saving, do you, little sister?" Walt asked, shaking his head. His hands had a tremor to them. She clasped them in her own as her heart crumpled within her.

"Always," she said.

He squeezed her hand.

"So you're looking for whoever was meeting with that actress the morning she was murdered?" he asked, pointedly dropping her hand, and the subject.

Grace's hopes fell another notch. "We have this image of her, in the newspaper," she said, trying to mask her disappointment. She pulled out the picture. "If that helps jog a memory."

"I'll ask around," Walt said. "They're more likely to talk to me."

She swallowed, and reluctantly handed over the newspaper. She didn't want him descending into the Tunnels again, not for any reason. But she knew that he had to make his own choices. Even the ones that broke her heart without her permission.

"Bye, Gracie," he said. He kissed her cheek with his dry lips, and she could see the part of his eyes that were still him, his gaze lingering on her like she was Christmas morning. Her chest ached.

"Can we meet again to hear your updates?" she asked, grabbing out for him in a desperate attempt to keep him there, safe, with her. "Back here for lunch? Tomorrow?"

"I'll need a bit longer than that," he said.

"Two days' time?"

He nodded. And then he slipped into the bustling crowd and disappeared, just one more face among thousands, in a body that held part of her heart.

She bit her lip, staring down at the table, mortified that Theo had seen this part of her when he already had so much more power, commanded so much more respect from everyone in their world than she did. She looked for the waiter.

"Let's get the bill," she said briskly. "I'll pay for me and Walt."

He waved her off. "I already took care of it," he said. She began to protest, but he cut her off by saying, "What's the plan now?"

They stood, and she was secretly grateful she didn't have to ask him for a loan. "I'd like to talk to Lillie's doctor friend this evening," Grace said. "About strychnine, and where it might have come from." She thought of Walt, rejecting her offer of help. Tonight could have turned out so differently. It made her eyes prick and sting. As if he had rejected her, too.

"How long had it been?" Theo asked quietly. "Since you'd seen your brother?"

She shrugged. "About a year. He wasn't always like this," she said defensively, her voice betraying her with the slightest shake. She heard the drone of bees around them in the sunken gardens, could smell the hyacinths as they made their way toward the fairgrounds exit. It made her head pound to think about all the people whose depths were shallowed out to only be what others saw. The sheen of Wealth. The cracks of Pain. A shadow of people, not ever their true essence.

Theo paused. "What was he like before?" he asked. His voice was interested but rough, uncertain, as though he were making his way down a path he'd never been before.

"When we were younger," she said, "my parents were working late at the restaurant. Walt couldn't have been more than ten, and we were home alone. We heard some drunk, jangling the doorknob, trying to get in the house. And Walt hid me, sheltering me with his own body." Her voice dropped into a whisper. "I'll never forget the way his little-boy heart was beating, so fast." It had been a light and frantic thing. Like hummingbird wings. "He was so little himself, but he was determined to protect me." She scrunched up her nose, determined not to cry in front of Theodore Parker. When that failed, she tried turning the prick of tears to anger. "There is nothing more painful than watching someone you love drown in front of you," she said fiercely, "in an invisible water that you can't stop."

And yet the tears were rising, threatening to spill out. There were three safe places for Grace to cry—with her mother, with Lillie, and with her pillow—and she feared she wasn't going to make it to any of them. Theodore Parker was the very last person she wanted to cry in front of.

Thankfully, they passed beneath the fairgrounds gate and she quickened her pace.

"Please go," she said. "I'll meet you tomorrow."

He hesitated, seeing her blotchy face. Then he tipped his hat with a stiff bow and obeyed, striding away from her.

She crossed the street and ducked into an alley, feeling the sobs rise. She wasn't going to make it to her safe place.

She cried, covering her face with her hands. And then she felt someone's strong arms wrap around her.

She knew it was him by the scent. Cinnamon and smoke. He didn't say a word, because she would die of embarrassment, and he knew it.

But in that moment the last thing she wanted was for him to leave. This realization was made infinitely easier because she couldn't see his jaunty, arrogant face. Instead she melted into him, and he instinctively tightened his arms around her. She nestled in closer. She had no pride left. She just wanted someone to hold her.

"You're going to be okay, Covington," he whispered roughly against her temple. She felt his voice on her skin, sending a spray of sparks down her spine.

She took a deep breath.

By the time she opened her eyes, he was gone.

❧

That night she was dressed in her nightgown, wrapped in a blanket, when there was a knock on the artist's studio door.

She froze.

"Who's there?" she asked. She grabbed the painter's tool and threw on a robe, relaxing when she heard a familiar voice.

She opened the door to find Lillie standing outside in the rain.

"I got your message," Lillie said.

Grace ushered her inside.

Grace lit a fire in the hearth, and they sat cross-legged on the bed.

"Now what's this about?" Lillie asked as Grace set out small, chipped teacups from the cupboard and heated a teapot over the fire.

"I promised you no more secrets," Grace said.

Lillie arched an eyebrow. "Yes," she said.

"I went to the Tunnels today in search of answers about Harriet," Grace said. "And instead . . . I found Walt."

"Walt?" Lillie cried with a start. "Oh, Grace. In the Tunnels?" Her eyes widened. "How is he?"

"He looks terrible," Grace said, this time letting her tears spill freely. Lillie slipped her hand in Grace's.

"Poor Walt," Lillie said. "Poor you, Grace."

"Our brothers," Grace said.

"What's going to happen to them?" Lillie asked.

"Do you blame me for what happened, Lil?" Grace asked quietly. "Even a little?"

Lillie sighed and hesitated. "No. That would be ridiculous. You were loyal to Oliver then, just as you're being now. That's all I see."

The weight in Grace's lungs lifted. It felt so good to have Lillie there. Her presence filled the room like light filled a lamp.

Grace wiped her cheeks with the base of her palms and rose to pour them tea. "Walt's agreed to look into some things I hope might help Oliver."

"How good of him," Lillie said.

"In the meantime, I was thinking you and I could pay a visit to your doctor friend." She offered Lillie a steaming teacup. "Would she answer questions for us?"

"I'm certain she would," Lillie said, accepting the hot tea.

"Should we go tomorrow evening?" Grace asked. "Could you slip away again?"

"Not tomorrow," Lillie said. She sighed, taking a sip of tea. "There's a ball I'm expected to be at. Mother thinks it's important we still go to functions, to show that we believe the charges against Oliver to be meritless. But she won't admit how drastically our social status has fallen since his arrest." Lillie wrapped her elegant fingers around the teacup. "So far that I'm not sure I can get you in this time."

"That's all right," Grace said, heart sinking. She had been hoping they might be able to interview some of the people who had been there the night of Harriet's murder. "Let's speak with Dr. May the night after, then."

"Yes. I'll send her a note arranging it."

"How was your day?" Grace asked. "Did Copper, Earnest, or Frannie see anything of note?"

Lillie took a short sip. "Frannie didn't seem much interested in my company," she said delicately. She gave a little laugh, the way she did when she was hurt but trying not to show it. "I suppose she was just tired today."

Grace's eyes narrowed, her anger rising like a roused animal. She'd had more than enough of Frannie Allred.

"Please allow me to inform you that Frannie Allred is a notoriously heinous stuck-up *shrew*, Lillie."

"Grace!" Lillie said, shocked into laughter. She covered her mouth. "What do you mean?"

"She just is," Grace continued. "I'm sorry you finally witnessed her true colors, but I'm afraid this is how she's always been."

"To you?" Lillie's face fell. "Has she treated you badly, Grace, and I didn't even notice?"

"You don't notice anything but the good in people, Lillie, and I can hardly fault you for that." Grace squeezed her cousin's hand.

Lillie frowned. "I can forgive a slight to myself but not to you," she said. "I hope you know I would heartily run someone through with a sword for you."

"Oh, I count on it. And in Frannie's case, I'd happily supply one for the job."

Lillie laughed. "It's her loss," she said, shrugging, with a jutting chin. "You're my favorite person in the world. Anyone who doesn't see that is beyond my help or good graces."

"Something you might find from this unfortunate incident with Oliver is that misfortunes come with one benefit. They're like a lens, showing who the people in your life truly are."

Lillie drained her tea to the dregs, and Grace paused, clearing her throat.

"But Earnest still treated you well today?" she asked carefully. She stole a glance at Lillie's face.

Lillie flushed, and Grace's stomach turned a little. With what? she asked herself. Jealousy?

"He was kind," Lillie admitted.

Grace looked at Lillie's face in the firelight. She was so lovely. Grace had always adored her, thought she was the most enchanting person she'd ever known. She could hardly blame Earnest for feeling the same way.

"It's all right, Lillie," she said gently. "I've seen the way he looks at you."

Lillie's mouth twisted. "Grace, I don't know what's wrong with me." She buried her face in her hands. "I truly want him for *you*. It would solve everything."

Grace slowly set down her teacup. It was true. Earnest had been a dream she had hoped would resolve all her problems, and part of Grace wasn't eager to let that go. After all, she liked Earnest. He was funny and clever and attractive. He had demonstrated good character. Her mother would be overjoyed. She could stay in Lillie and Oliver's lives. And the petty part of her loved the way his attention toward her drove Frannie Allred mad.

It all worked so well on paper.

But perhaps, even given all of that, she liked the idea of him more than him.

"I would never stand between him and you," Grace said. "Especially if you have feelings for each other."

"But I don't *want* to have feelings for him," Lillie said, her voice muffled from where her face still lay in her hands. "So how can I?"

She lay her head down on Grace's shoulder. "Perhaps it's just because it's all been so confusing this week."

Yes, Grace thought. Perhaps that's all it is, for both of them.

Her mind turned toward what Theodore Parker felt like, his heart beating strong and steady through his coat, his comforting arms wrapped around her—first that horrible night months ago at the winter ball, and then on the street corner only a few hours ago. The memory of it set off a thousand glittering stars, erupting like fireworks in her night sky.

She rested her own head on top of Lillie's. Why couldn't she have fallen for Earnest?

And he for her?

It would all be so much easier.

She stifled a groan at the utter inconvenience of it.

That she might be developing feelings for the last person in the world she wanted to. That arrogant, irritating, and utterly bewildering Theodore Parker.

CHAPTER TWELVE

MAY 7, 1904

Four Days After the Murder

The next morning, Lillie, Earnest, and Grace hired a boat and rowed along the canals. Steepled buildings rose around them in a dreamlike, temporary city. Their gondola rocked as Grace unwrapped a croissant and spread it with fresh strawberry preserves. She drank a thermos of hot coffee and Earnest held an umbrella over their heads to shade the morning sun. The crowds streamed by on flower-lined paths beneath the Palaces.

Lillie was wearing an intricately embroidered pink dress that cinched at the waist and a matching hat with crisp white gloves. Grace had washed her blouse in the sink, hoping that no one would notice that it was still slightly damp.

"My parents are visiting Oliver with his lawyer this morning," Lillie said.

"I heard they hired Clive Marpels," Earnest said. "He's supposedly the best money can buy."

"And yet I think we can help," Lillie said, wiping her mouth with a handkerchief. "I'm planning to talk to people tonight at the ball. Inquire if they saw anything useful."

"That sounds like an excellent plan," Earnest said. "The three of us can cover a lot of ground if we divide and conquer."

"Oh, I'm afraid I won't be there," Grace said. She smiled ruefully. "Even the Carter name won't be enough to get me in this time."

"Then I'll take you," Earnest said. "I'll bring you both. I can get Grace into the ball."

"Thank you," Lillie said with genuine surprise.

Earnest smiled at Grace, but his eyes drifted to Lillie. And Grace understood that it was a kindness to her, but it was perhaps more a kindness for Lillie.

She looked away. She was happy for Lillie. And yet she tried not to wonder what it might feel like, just once, to be the one chosen.

Her eye caught on a familiar silhouette walking along the canal banks, almost shrouded beneath the flowering trees. It was Mr. and Mrs. Gatewood.

Grace stiffened a little, remembering the way they had been toward her that night at the Glass Ball.

The night that Harriet had died.

She blocked the sun with her hand.

"Lillie," she said slowly. "What if we've been thinking about this wrong?"

"What do you mean?"

Grace swallowed. "I just had a thought. What if the murderer wasn't someone who actually wanted to hurt Harriet, but wanted to hurt *Oliver*?"

"But who would hurt Oliver?" Lillie asked, her brow creasing.

"Someone who was angry at your family," Grace said. "And wanted to see them suffer."

Earnest followed Grace's gaze to the banks.

"The Gatewoods," he said, grimacing. "They were there that night."

Lillie shook her head. "No. Absolutely impossible."

"Well. Perhaps not *impossible*," Earnest said.

"No. They were our *friends*. No one could be that cruel," Lillie insisted.

But Grace took note of it, believing the thought warranted at least consideration. Perhaps she would pay another visit to Oliver and ask him what he thought.

The gondolier rowed them to the shore, bumping into the banks. She almost fell over, but a hand caught her just in time.

She looked up into the face of Theodore Parker.

"You seem to have a recurring issue with boats," he said dryly. "Namely, balancing on them."

He pulled her back onto solid ground, so that their bodies almost collided. Her gaze drifted along the birthmark on his jaw. He was beginning to grow a beard over the mark, which looked like a bear's claw, swiping across his cheek and down his jaw. She wasn't sure what she was expecting from him this morning. She felt that something must have changed between them after what happened in the alley.

But he kept her at a careful distance. He was back to being his formal self, despite the way he had held her so intimately yesterday. And so she followed his lead.

"Perhaps you should stick to dry land," he said, eyeing her.

She stuck her chin in the air. "Spoken by someone who can't stomach being more than a foot above it."

"Yes, I believe my limits have been well-established," he said. "Now we need to locate yours."

"What brings you here today, Parker?" Earnest asked. "Care to join us for a trip on the Creation ride?"

"Actually, I need to borrow Grace for an errand." He looked at her. "Do you mind?"

"Of course not," Earnest said, believing the question to be directed at him. "Lillie, we can discuss how to plan our approach tonight, if you'd like."

Lillie leaned in and whispered to Grace, "I'll have Earnest pick me up at the house on the early side so we can bring you a dress. Look for us by six."

Grace kissed Lillie's cheek. "I've never deserved you," she whispered.

"You deserve *everything*," she said. "I wish someday you'd realize that."

She felt Lillie's observant eyes on her as she took Theodore's outstretched arm.

"Did you actually fall out of the boat?" Theo asked, frowning at her sleeve. "Your blouse feels damp."

"Never mind that," Grace said quickly. "Am I to believe you need a favor?"

"I had an idea," he said. They strolled down the Colonnade of States through gently falling blossoms. The air smelled like sugared almonds as they came to a stop in front of a caricature artist.

"Here," he said.

"You'd like to remember me forever?" she asked dryly. "But with horrifically exaggerated features?"

"I can assure you, Miss Covington, that you need no exaggeration," he said. "You are more than enough to handle as it is."

"You have such an elegant way with compliments," she said. "You might want to reconsider the way you ask for a favor."

"I don't need a favor, exactly," he said, frowning. "What I need is your memory."

The woman sketching the pictures turned to them. The tips of her agile fingers were stained with charcoal.

"Could you do something a little unorthodox for us, perhaps?" Theodore asked her.

"Unorthodox," the artist said. She smiled, showing ragged teeth. "Another word for 'it'll cost you.'"

"That won't be a problem," Grace said sweetly, jabbing Theodore with her elbow. "He just *loves* to spoil me."

He rolled his eyes.

"If we described someone to you, could you draw a sketch of her?"

Grace's understanding dawned.

"That woman," she said, turning toward Theodore. "The one who was following us just before Harriet died."

He nodded. "Do you remember her well enough to describe her?"

"I think so," Grace said, furrowing her brow. She closed her eyes, mining her memory. She remembered the woman's navy hat and suit, her profile as she turned to look at them on the Ferris wheel, with her sloping nose and ruddy cheeks. She did her best to paint a picture of the woman with words.

Theodore added in his own details, and between the two of them, the woman that appeared on the page in front of them was vaguely recognizable.

"Thank you," Theo said, nodding at the sketch. "You've captured what we need."

"This was a good idea," Grace admitted as Theodore paid the sketch artist handsomely.

"I want to talk to Oliver again," Theodore said, tucking the sketch into his pocket. "See if he might recognize the person who was following us."

"Let's go together, then," she said. "I have some questions to ask him myself."

❧

They passed Oliver's lawyer, Clive Marpels, on their way into the jail. Theodore spoke to the front guard in lowered tones, and then they were led once again into the interrogation room.

Oliver looked pale, but he instantly perked up when he saw them. He rose, his wrists handcuffed.

"Theodore," he said. "Grace. You're a sight for sore eyes."

"We've come bearing questions that might help your case. Do you recognize this person?" Theodore asked, laying out the picture in front of him.

Oliver looked at it carefully. After a long moment, he shook his head. "Should I?"

"She was following us in the days before Harriet died," Grace said. She watched him closely as he took in the sketch. He was quiet for a long time.

But then he shook his head. "I was so caught up in the fair, in being with Harriet. I wasn't paying attention to anything else. It all feels like it was a haze."

When he looked up at them, as forlorn as a child who thinks he failed an exam, Grace tried to hide her disappointment. She said, "It's all right. We're just exploring every possibility. And I had another thought. Why would the murderer kill Harriet in such a public place? Why do it when it would draw so much attention?"

"I've been wondering that myself," Oliver admitted.

"The only thing I can think of is that someone clearly set you up to take the fall for it. They put something in Harriet's drink, then had you hand it to her. Could it have been the bartender? Are the police looking into that at all?"

"There were two bartenders working that night and they were right next to each other. They both vouched for the other that neither put anything in the drink," Theodore said.

"That doesn't mean that they didn't," Grace said.

"Except that neither has any connection to Harriet. There's little to no motive, so the police dropped it," Theo said.

Grace sighed. "So the real question is, who benefits if you are accused of murder?"

Oliver blanched, leaning forward.

"You think someone was coming for me? And Harriet just got in the way?" He looked like he was about to be sick.

"It's worth considering," Theodore said.

"The only people I can think of are the Gatewoods. Father screwed them with a business investment. They might have seen an opportunity to make us pay."

"I know about that," Grace said. She quickly scrawled it in her notebook. "I'll see if I can talk to them tonight."

"If I'm the reason Harriet was killed . . ." Oliver said. His face had taken on a gray tinge, his unwashed hair falling into his eyes.

"You didn't do this," Grace said. With a look to the guard for permission, she knelt beside him. "Whoever did this bears responsibility for their actions. They and they alone."

Theodore carefully tucked the image of the mysterious woman into his own coat pocket for safekeeping. He stood and conversed with the guard in the corner, giving Grace and Oliver a moment alone.

"Grace," Oliver said, turning to her urgently. "I remembered something that I need to tell you. I've been going over and over it in my memory."

Her stomach sank as he bent forward to whisper into her ear.

"The night Harriet died," he whispered, "it was Earnest who handed me the glass."

CHAPTER THIRTEEN

Dressed in one of Lillie's lush lavender satin gowns, and elbow-length white gloves, Grace jumped as the carriage wheels jolted over a pothole that night. Her chandelier earrings jangled against her throat.

"Are you all right?" Lillie asked.

"Just a little on edge tonight," Grace said. She stole a look at Earnest, who was seated across from her. He gave her an unassuming smile that she tried to return.

But her mind was flush with questions.

She tried not to flinch when he offered his hand to help her down from the carriage, his palm brushing the small of her back. She had promised Lillie no more secrets.

But she needed Earnest to get her inside the Ball, first.

And she couldn't very well say anything to Lillie about Oliver's claims right in front of him, now could she?

Earnest flashed an invitation and ushered them inside before the guard could question them. Grace's breath caught in her chest like a trapped bird as they stepped into the magnificent Sculpture Hall in the Palace of Fine Arts. It was the only structure built to last beyond the fair. Everything else would be turned to dust, but the marble floors and the dramatic, soaring ceilings, modeled after the grand public baths in Rome, would remain. To house the world's most precious treasures, it had to be fireproof.

Grace paused in front of the museum's facade, reading the words etched into it: ART STILL HAS TRUTH. TAKE REFUGE THERE.

She followed the sound of rushing water and the train of Lillie's emerald dress as it swept across the gleaming floors. Inside the museum, Roman arches and white walls were framed with blood-red roses and burgundy leaves. One of the walls was covered with plush moss, and in the center of the hall was a stone fountain filled entirely with floating peonies and lilies. There were sculptures by Rodin and works of art hung in gilded frames by artists like Winslow Homer, Hokusai, and Juan Luna de San Pedro y Novicio Ancheta—not to mention a seventeen-foot portrait of the Empress Dowager of China.

It felt as though gold dust glittered through the air.

The crowd parted to let them through. Earnest led the way, but once he had passed, the glances became decidedly sour. Women in satin and tulle turned their backs to snub Lillie, whispering as she walked by. Grace was used to it, but she felt proud to see the way that Lillie's head remained high.

Lillie's parents stood at the far end of the room, apart from the crowd. Aunt Clove was sipping a drink as though she didn't have a care in the world, but her mouth was tight.

As Lillie went to greet her parents, Grace dropped away.

And to Grace's surprise, Earnest came with her.

She stiffened, instinctively searching the room for Theodore. But all she saw were unfamiliar faces, many of them frowning back at her. Her heart sank a little.

"I know we all spoke to the police that night, but it wouldn't hurt to hear what happened from other people's perspectives," Earnest said, surveying the room.

Grace eyed him. "It's a good idea."

Her pulse skipped a beat, and she pondered asking him about Oliver's revelation, but at the last minute she said, "I'll start with the Gatewoods."

"Their daughter had quite an advantageous proposal," Earnest whispered covertly in her ear. "From someone close to the fair's head, David R. Francis. That's why they are back on the map, like chess pieces."

Grace ordered herself a flute of sparkling lemonade from the bar and made her way through the labyrinthine galleries, trailing Mr. Gatewood at a distance.

She watched him, sipping her drink, until he stopped in front of a Caravaggio painting.

She bit the inside of her cheek.

She would do this for Oliver.

Gathering her courage like it was the dress in her hand, she approached, joining him to admire the artwork side by side.

For a moment she stayed quiet. She thought he hadn't noticed her. A small bead of sweat began to slide down the curve of her back. Until, without deigning to look at her, he drawled in the direction of the painting, "Did you have something you wished to say to me, Miss Covington?"

"Perhaps," she said. "I've heard my family may have something to apologize for."

He seemed surprised.

"You'd be the first of them to admit it," he said.

"It probably doesn't mean much coming from me," she conceded. "I'm hardly the family figurehead." She cleared her throat.

He turned and finally looked at her. "No," he seemed to agree. "You hardly speak for them. And yet, it does mean something."

Grace's lips were dry. She drank in the rich colors of the painting in front of them. It was the opposite of comforting. In fact, it was quite gruesome—a depiction of Salome with the head of John the Baptist. She forced herself not to look away from the severed head resting on the platter.

"Are you still angry with them?" she asked steadily.

Mr. Gatewood sighed. "After what happened to that poor girl, I can't find it within myself to be angry anymore," he said, swirling the gin in his glass. "I will admit that in my darker moments, I might have wished tragedy upon your family. Betrayals, particularly around money, can short sight you. But now I think that they are going to suffer more than even I wanted them to."

Grace held her tongue as he shook his head.

"People tend to get hurt around that family. Particularly the ones closest to them." He drained his drink and looked at Grace sadly. "Be careful."

Grace stood alone in front of the painting long after he walked away.

She could hardly cross Mr. Gatewood off her list of subjects based on his own word, and yet she felt herself mentally doing it anyway. Perhaps she was naive. But she believed him. His last words to her hadn't been a threat. They had been a warning.

"It's an interesting painting to be examining this closely," a voice murmured near her ear.

A thread of icicles formed along her spine. She turned slowly.

"A little bloody. People might start to get ideas," Earnest said. He flashed her a charming smile, but this time she realized that she'd never noticed how smooth it was, almost like a Cheshire cat. "Would you like to dance, Miss Covington?"

He held out his hand.

The bandages had been removed, and he wore formal gloves now, hiding the skin beneath that was pink and new.

"Yes," she said, ignoring the fear that rose in her throat.

She was conscious of his every move. The way his hand slid around her back. The way he breathed, his breath tinged with something sweet. Out of the corner of her eyes she could see Lillie standing on the sidelines of the ballroom, sipping her drink. Alone. For the first time in her life, no one in this fickle crowd had asked her to dance.

Grace felt a red rage creeping along the back of her eyes.

"Were you at the police station today?" Earnest asked. Just beneath his cologne, she could smell the hint of alcohol on his breath.

She tried to keep her own breathing steady.

"I went to visit Oliver," she said carefully. "How did you know?"

He tightened his grip on her. Subtle, but noticeable. "I thought I saw you there," he said.

"And yet I didn't see you," she said. For a fleeting moment of fear, she wondered if he somehow knew what Oliver had whispered in her ear.

But that was ridiculous.

She and Oliver had been alone.

"What were you doing there?" she forced herself to ask. She faltered a little, her mind tripping on the dance steps.

"The police called me in with their findings about my flying machine," he said. "They didn't think the crash was malicious. Just a good old-fashioned engineering failure that almost killed me."

She paused, her mouth going dry.

"And what do you think?" she asked.

"To be honest, I think they're wrong," he said. He said it with a smile that felt bright yet was tinged with bitters. The bruises on his handsome face were fading, almost imperceptible now beneath the powder. "I think someone was trying to make sure I didn't win that prize money, or maybe even make it out of the sky alive. But—" He twirled her, and for a moment Grace felt like she might fall, but at the last moment he caught her. "What can you do?" he said low in her ear. "There are bigger problems we're dealing with here. As we are both well-aware."

Aunt Clove was watching Grace from the dance floor, over Uncle Reginald's shoulder. While dancing, it was harder to tell that no one was eager to speak with them. Grace could feel Aunt Clove's glare cut through her, silently blaming her for the way Lillie was standing alone.

How does it feel, Grace wanted to ask her, *when people treat you badly for something you had nothing to do with?*

"I saw you speaking to Mr. Gatewood," Earnest said. "Do you think it could have been him?"

Grace's eyes slid back to Earnest.

"I'm not sure," she said faintly.

She caught a glimpse of Frannie over Earnest's shoulder. Frannie Allred wasn't traditionally handsome but there was something about her that night that was glowing, as she smiled without a care in the world, twining her fingers through Copper's red hair. He said something that set Frannie to laughing, and they walked past Lillie with no acknowledgment. Doing nothing to save her from the ridicule and loneliness she must be feeling.

Grace gritted her teeth. Frannie Allred was selfish, utterly lacking in compassion, believing others to be beneath herself. She had wanted Copper or Theodore or even Oliver for herself. What if she simply couldn't stand for Harriet to be in her way? To get something Frannie didn't believe she deserved to have? Could it have pushed her to murder?

With a deep pang Grace imagined Harriet and Oliver together on the dance floor, where they should have been. Twirling. Laughing. Young, and in love.

"You seem like there's something on your mind," Earnest said.

Grace chewed her lip. "It's just . . ." she said. "I've been racking my brain to remember that night. And I came up with something I just can't understand."

Earnest nodded his encouragement. "What's that?"

"I remember the bartender pouring a drink. But the thing I've just remembered is . . . well, that it was in *your* glass, Earnest. You're the one who handed it to Oliver."

Earnest's face looked surprised.

He stopped short, chortling in incredulity. The rest of the dance floor continued moving around them.

"Wait. Are you saying—you think *I'm* the one who poisoned Harriet?" he asked. He looked at her in disbelief, a confused smile dawning on his face as if he hoped she was kidding.

"I'm not saying that, exactly," she said, trying not to lose her nerve. "I'm just trying to follow the truth. Weren't you the one who handed Oliver the glass? And do the police know that?"

As people continued to swirl around them, the look in his eyes darkened to anger.

"Is—I'm sorry, but—is this because of Lillie?" he sputtered.

"What?" Grace asked, taken aback. "What do you mean?"

"Are you making this ridiculous accusation because—" His gaze darted over to where Lillie stood. "Are you jealous?"

Now it was her turn to be offended.

She took a step back, her face flushing. "I can assure you that all I want is my cousins' happiness. *Both* of them. I don't generally go around accusing people of murder just because I want to keep them for myself," she said.

He snapped, "Well, I certainly didn't do it. What reason would I have for wanting Harriet dead?" He gestured toward his fingers. "Besides, I could barely do anything that night, I had clumsy bandages on my hands. You think I'd be able to subtly add poison to a drink when I could barely tie my own shoes?"

He chuffed, as though she were small and ridiculous, and perhaps she was. She had found his confident assurance charming before but now it grated on her.

"Well. This was certainly an illuminating turn on the dance floor. Enjoy the rest of the party, Miss Covington," he said curtly, letting the unsaid between them—*the ball you wouldn't even be at without me.* He bowed to her and walked away.

She took a deep inhale, her face flushing hot.

Just then Theodore Parker appeared, parting his way through the crowd like a shark fin cutting through water. He had a distinct aura of power and wealth that surrounded him, turning the heads of the men and women he passed. Even despite his resting face of disdain, Grace's heart rose unbidden in her chest.

She pretended not to watch as Theodore came to a stop in front of Lillie. He bowed slightly, then offered her his arm. Lillie smiled genuinely, a look of relief crossing her face. In response, Grace felt something blooming within her that she'd barely thought possible.

Intense gratitude for Theodore Parker, as he led Lillie to the dance floor.

Only—she realized—it *wasn't* the first time she'd felt that. She'd felt it many times over the last few days, which was incredibly inconvenient, given that he'd accused her of being a shallow gold digger a mere few minutes after they'd met.

Grace stood alone, miserably sipping her drink. Looking around at the couples twirling on the dance floor. Mentally tallying who else was there the night of Harriet's murder. If only she could go back in time and see it play out again. But it was hazy, her memories flickering like a light.

Oliver thought that Earnest had handed him the glass.

She tried to remember, but she couldn't.

Earnest, with his bandaged hands.

Who else had been there?

Frannie and Copper.

Mr. Gatewood and his wife.

Ethel.

The talent manager.

Lillie.

Theodore Parker.

And then, suddenly, there he was, standing in front of her.

"You look . . ." he said, a slight frown crossing his brow.

"Beautiful?" she supplied wryly.

"Like you're plotting something."

She huffed. "Can't I be both?"

"Indeed." He offered her his gloved hand, and, with a spark of surprise, she took it.

"May I offer you my condolences, Mr. Parker," she told him as he led her to the dance floor. "You're dancing with the pariah of the Ball. I'm afraid your social standing is dropping by the moment."

"You seem to mistake that I care."

She flushed, her eyes catching on the way Earnest was taking Lillie by the hand and leading her to the dance floor.

He seemed to be purposefully ignoring Grace.

"Did you find anything out?" Theo asked, following her gaze.

"I'm not sure," she said. "I might have mended one bridge, but I burned another."

Her mind was reaching for something.

But she could feel the whispers, the murmurs of the crowd, closing in like shadows in her periphery. He read it on her face and dipped her.

"Are you trying to make me ill?" she asked.

"Don't go soft on me now, Covington," he whispered roughly. His mouth was at her throat.

"I wouldn't even know how," she breathed.

When he brought her upright again, his lips barely grazed her neck. She was trembling, her breath hitching. His hand tightened across her bodice.

No one had ever done this to her mind, her body before.

She was turning to melted gold. There were explosions of fireworks in her head as though she had stared too long at the sun. Champagne bubbles tingled just beneath her ribs, and the glow of euphoria was an undertow, pulling her in the longer she looked into his eyes and felt the grip of his hand on her waist.

He would never believe you wanted him for anything other than his money, she told herself. *Even if it wasn't true.* And that, her pride could not bear.

That was the dash of ice water that cut through the haze.

She returned to herself.

Theodore Parker was not why she was there.

She forced her breathing to slow. Coaxed her mind back to the task at hand.

"I just keep going over who was there that night," she said.

"That woman who followed us isn't here," Theodore said, glancing over his shoulder. "I've been keeping my eye out for her all night."

Grace's disappointment deepened. She was hoping the mysterious woman would appear and they could question her together—at the very least to determine her identity, if not uncover what she wanted.

Why had she followed them when Harriet was with them, and then stopped as soon as she was murdered? That woman was rising to the top of Grace's suspect list.

Situating her right next to Earnest.

But suddenly, the thought she had been searching for earlier dropped like a lazy feather, just within her reach.

"There is someone else who is conspicuously absent tonight," Grace murmured. "Someone who was there for the night of the murder but isn't here now."

"Someone other than Oliver, you mean?" Theodore asked.

She smiled. "Someone who had a camera."

Theodore arched an eyebrow at her in understanding. "That gossip columnist for the *Fair's Fare*."

She nodded. "Sam Whitcomb."

She felt a warmth rise within her as another lead unfurled itself, beckoning her to follow it like a road paved with gold.

CHAPTER FOURTEEN

MAY 8, 1904

Five Days After the Murder

GRACE WANTED TO alight to Sam Whitcomb's offices first thing the next morning, but Lillie had arranged for them to meet with Dr. May instead.

Grace tightened her hat as she stepped out into the cool morning breeze. She locked the studio door behind her, her eyes narrowing. She would have just enough time to speak with Dr. May that morning, meet with Walt for lunch on the fairgrounds, and then pay a visit to Sam Whitcomb's offices. But she startled a little when a carriage came around the corner.

Because it wasn't the Carters' carriage that she had been expecting.

It was Earnest Allred's.

Her face promptly flushed, embarrassed about how badly things had gone last night. She braced herself as the carriage door opened.

"Grace!" Lillie exclaimed. "Earnest agreed to give us a ride to Dr. May's on his way to a business meeting this morning. Wasn't that kind of him?"

"Miss Covington," Earnest said in greeting. His smile was brittle.

"Mr. Allred," she said. She fiddled absently with the large flowers pinned at the throat of her blouse, hoping Lillie didn't pick up on how noticeably strained things were between them.

"I wasn't sure if I was even going to convince Mother to let me leave this morning," Lillie said as the carriage trundled over the paved stone roads. "Her nerves are fraying. But with Earnest's help, she finally relented."

"Then we thank you for your service, Mr. Allred," Grace said stiffly.

He tipped his hat sarcastically at her.

"Was Aunt Clove upset about the party last night?" Grace asked, turning to Lillie.

"Livid," Lillie said.

They left the bustling streets surrounding the fairgrounds and drove to a place called Scab Row. The sunlight was weaker here, the smells stronger. The streets seemed glazed with something sticky and wet. It was not a part of St. Louis Grace had ever been to before.

There was a small, almost-hidden sign outside the building. THE EVENING DISPENSARY FOR WOMEN.

Earnest eyed the street. "Are you certain you'll be safe here?" he asked, frowning as he helped Lillie from the carriage.

"We'll be fine," Lillie assured him. "We'll hail a cab for the way back."

Earnest turned to help Grace from the carriage. He gripped her arm perhaps a little tighter than necessary, fixing his blue eyes on her.

When she stepped to the ground, he drew her in close.

"It's true. I remember now. I did order a drink for Harriet that night," he said roughly, his voice low. "But I was having a conversation with someone before I could give the glass to Oliver. If someone put something in it, it was probably then."

He dropped Grace's arm and climbed back into the carriage. He shut the door, giving two smart raps on the carriage's ceiling, without looking at her again. Grace fought an unsettled feeling as the driver pulled away.

She followed Lillie, climbing the brick stairs lined with rusting wrought iron, and Lillie knocked on the door. Grace covered the rumble of hunger pains in her stomach by feigning a cough.

"Dr. May and Dr. Baker opened this. They were two of the first female physicians in the state of Missouri," Lillie said as they waited on the stoop. "Remind me to tell you later how Dr. May tricked the all-male St. Louis Medical Society into letting her in by submitting her name with only a first initial."

"Lillie," a woman said warmly, opening the door to them. Her hair was pulled up into a chestnut bun streaked with the beginnings of silver. Her eyes were overlarge and soulful, and though her face was lined with wrinkles, something about her appeared strangely youthful.

"Dr. May! This is my cousin, Grace Covington," Lillie said. "Thank you for agreeing to meet with us. I know how busy you are."

"Of course, my dear," Dr. May said. "Come in."

Dr. May ushered them inside the clinic. It was dim, with the drapes pulled closed, but sparkling clean. They sat on worn chairs, surrounded by bookcases and glass cases of medicines and plants. There was a faint smell of woody tea and iodine.

"Dr. May opened the Emmaus House for young women who come to the fairgrounds and work long days with little or no family," Lillie said as the doctor disappeared into the small kitchen. "She's made her career seeing mostly working women and"—she dropped her voice—"prostitutes."

Grace looked around the room and took out her small notebook.

"Does she treat addicts?" Grace asked.

At least the murder had something Grace could grasp and get her hands around. It was information and clues and motives, and she would get down in the dirt of it all, feeling the grime of it beneath her fingernails. It felt good, to chase down an enemy she could take on for Oliver. Because it was something outside of him.

Not inside. Not something that became intertwined with himself that she couldn't kill the monster of it without hurting him too.

"What would you like to discuss?" Dr. May said, appearing with a tray of tea.

Lillie accepted a steaming cup. "Thank you for your concern about my brother Oliver. We're not convinced we have the full story, and we're looking into it a little ourselves. We'd like to hear more about the kind of poison that was revealed in Harriet Forbes's autopsy."

Dr. May's face was serious. "Go on."

Lillie nodded at Grace, who took out an ink pen and cleared her throat.

"Strychnine," she began. "We're wondering, what does it look like, and how would it be administered?"

"Yes. Let's see. Well, strychnine is sourced from the seeds of the *Strychnos nux-vomica* tree," Dr. May explained. She stood and pulled a book from the shelf, flipping through its pages. "It's a neurotoxin, a white powder that is odorless, and quite bitter." She paused on a page. "In fact, I'm surprised that Miss Forbes would have consumed it without noticing it, unless it was administered in a very strong drink."

Grace and Lillie immediately looked at each other. "Dubonnet," Lillie said, her eyes wide with horror. "Oliver had recently begun drinking Dubonnet."

The intensely bitter drink was another detail not in Oliver's favor.

"And how would strychnine be sourced?" Lillie asked. "Would it have been difficult for the murderer to acquire?"

"Unfortunately, no," Dr. May said. "It can be used as a rodent poison, which means it's likely being used in abundance during the Exposition. It's also used as a stimulant for the heart and bowels, and it rapidly metabolizes in the human body. Fatal doses cause severe muscular convulsions that eventually paralyze the respiratory muscles, causing asphyxiation. The autopsy would have shown concentrations in the blood, liver, kidneys, and stomach wall."

Grace shuddered.

She remembered Harriet, so alive on the roller coaster as she laughed and screamed, clutching Oliver's hand with delight. Singing at the restaurant with that fire in her eyes; thanking Grace that first night in the boat. Dreaming of her future.

Who did this to you, Harriet? Grace wondered.

"So there is no way to track the particular kind of strychnine?" Lillie asked. "No variants to help determine where it came from?"

"I'm afraid not," Dr. May said.

"What about drug addicts?" Grace asked quietly. "Do they use it?"

"Not usually," Dr. May said. "No. I've heard of some cases where strychnine can be used to adulterate drugs like heroin and cocaine, but then ingestion is accidental." She paused thoughtfully. "Well. But then there's the Keeley Cure."

"The Keeley Cure?"

"It's a treatment for addicts. Concoctions that contain gold, strychnine, and alcohol that are injected into those battling addictions. To be honest, I have my suspicions about it. I wonder if it does more harm than good."

Lillie stole a glance at Grace, and the questions Grace had been prepared to ask suddenly died.

Other questions, the ones she most desperately wanted to know, rose up within her, coating her mouth like bubbles. Could this woman tell her—were the truest, loveliest parts of Walt still safe and hidden away somewhere? Able to be unfurled and reached again? To be coaxed back out and into the sunshine?

"My brother—" Grace paused. "He . . ."

"What can be done to help an addict?" Lillie asked, jumping in for her. "What resources are there?"

"Unfortunately, there are too little right now," Dr. May said. "I know of some doctors exploring treatment options in New York City. There are a few private options available for those with a substantial amount of money here in this city. But I'm seeing a need for a clinic or something to help those without as many resources. It's something I'd like to look into after the fair."

Dr. May's eyes blinked at them behind her large glasses like a small, inquisitive bird. "I'll need to get back to the hospital soon. What else?"

Grace watched the sunshine and shadows dance over her fingers. "Do you ever feel overwhelmed by all of the hurting people?" she asked.

Dr. May touched her hand gently. "Life often feels like one long, dissonant chord, waiting for release, doesn't it?" she said. "Well, I look for those places I can create a little relief for people. Brief moments of harmony." Her face melted into a glorious smile. "And what's been most unexpected is that the notes end up playing a melody in my life as well."

Grace held on to that, as though Dr. May had given her a life raft, a rope made of light to cling to.

"Thank you for seeing us, Dr. May," Lillie said, standing. They helped bring the teacups to the sink.

As Dr. May walked them to the door, Lillie asked, "One more question. Is it possible that the strychnine was administered earlier in the day? How long until the onset of symptoms?"

Dr. May shook her head. "The onset is quick. It would have had to be administered in that room. And it would have had to be put into the victim's drink specifically, because no one else at the party was affected."

"Interesting," Grace said.

"If I were you, I'd get a list of who was in that room that night. And then find out if any of them knew Harriet Forbes before."

"Thank you, Dr. May," Lillie said.

"You're good sisters," Dr. May said. She smiled at them with a tender understanding that touched something buried deep in Grace's heart.

"It's clear that you would do anything for your brothers," she said, meeting Lillie's eyes. "Both of you."

❧

Grace and Lillie hitched a trolley ride back to the fairgrounds.

"I'm meant to meet Walt for lunch," Grace said with a glance at the beating sun as they walked through the turnstiles into the Exposition. They made their way toward the restaurant where she had seen Walt two days ago.

"A table for three, please," Grace said. This time, they were seated beneath an umbrella and Grace skimmed the menu—but really, she was glancing over her shoulder every few minutes, searching the throng of humanity beyond the fence of the restaurant's outdoor seating. There were women in long skirts and fancy hats, children in sharply tailored sailor suits; members of the Philippine Constabulary band and Indian women in gold-threaded saris. Accents and languages wove through the air, intertwining like strands in a tapestry.

There were clusters of pigeons and bits of trash and scattered petals on the walkway.

But there was no Walt.

"Well, perhaps we should go ahead and order," Lillie said with a forced brightness when they'd turned the waiter away for the third time. "We can pick something out for Walt."

Grace nodded but worry gnawed at her stomach. Did Walt forget how to find the meeting place? Had something happened to him? Was he blacked out somewhere? Overdosed? Hurt? Too drunk or high to remember the plan?

Her brow knit. Grace's mind had traveled down these paths so many times. She tried to stop her anxious thoughts from slipping like oil over the well-worn grooves.

"I can see why you love Dr. May," Grace said instead, sipping her glass of iced tea. The wind blew the branches of a nearby tree and sent shadows spattering across her face.

"I just want to be around her," Lillie said. "It's like she has her own gravity."

Grace agreed. When their food came, she half-heartedly ate her club sandwich and drank her sweating glass of iced tea, and Lillie paid for all of it, and Grace was grateful. She no longer knew when her next meal would be. She would need to find some sort of paying job at the fair if she was going to continue on like this.

She knew she could tell Lillie she was falling dangerously short and that her cousin would happily lend her the money. She knew she had promised Lillie no more secrets. But she'd rather feel the pinch of hunger and keep hold of her pride.

She eyed a bird pecking at a crust of bread, wanting to stall. Just in case Walt came.

"Where would one get rat poison, do you think?" Lillie asked.

"Vermin powders are sold at any drugstore," Grace said. She knew her father kept them in stock for his restaurant.

She looked one more time over her shoulder for Walt.

"We can meet here again tomorrow," Lillie said, quietly noticing Grace was upset. "Maybe he'll come then." She checked her timepiece. "I have to get back home. We're going to visit Oliver this afternoon."

They walked arm in arm to Grace's studio, the hems of their skirts brushing together, and Lillie hailed a carriage to take her home. Grace kissed Lillie's cheek and brought out her key to unlock the door.

When she pushed it open, she almost didn't notice the folded piece of paper at her feet. As though someone had slipped it beneath the door.

She bent to retrieve it.

The message was from Santiago, the young man who worked at the wireless telegraph tower.

She read:

> *Mr. Parsons has returned to St. Louis and is expected back at work tomorrow.*

She crumpled the note in her hand.

She was itching to find out what Mr. Parsons knew, to fill in the gaps between the man desperate for money and what that had to do with Harriet.

❧

Sam Whitcomb's press office was north of Delmar and overlooked the fairgrounds.

It was impressive, she would give him that: five stories and shaped like an octagon, with American flags gracefully draped from its windows. The building was built on a hill, and before it he had erected a massive, temporary tent city. "Camp Whitcomb," it was called, with lodging for three thousand people. It had been a brilliant strategy move: subscribers to Whitcomb's publications could stay there for much cheaper than any of the surrounding hotels.

Grace felt the folded creases of Santiago's note in her pocket as she briskly walked through the tent city. The tents were almost like cabins, with wooden floorboards and potted plants and electric lights strung along their ceilings. She could hear the distant roar of the crowds at the fair, the brassy sounds of marching bands. There was a hiss of grease as she passed one of the many kitchen tents, and near the showering tent, she smelled the lather of soap.

For a moment, she paused with the prickling sense that someone was following her.

She slowed, then snuck a glance over her shoulder.

There was no one there.

Stop being silly, she told herself.

She clutched her hat to her head and quickened her pace. She spotted Theodore just where they had planned yesterday—leaning beneath the flags of the Whitcomb building.

Her heart started beating traitorously at the sight of him.

He arched an eyebrow when he saw her, and for a moment she thought of what it would feel like for him to slide his arms around her waist again, the weight of his hands grazing the curve of her rib cage, making her breath hitch—

She stopped, flushing. What was wrong with her?

"Covington," he said shortly.

"Parker," she said.

"Did you meet with Walt?" he asked. "What did he say?"

"He didn't show," she said. She pulled open the door to the publishing office before Theodore could frown or, worse, show her any pity. "Shall we?" she asked briskly.

They entered the foyer together, then rode the elevator to the fifth floor and announced themselves to Sam Whitcomb's secretary.

"We're here to see Mr. Whitcomb," Theodore said.

"Do you have an appointment?" she asked.

"No," Grace said. "But we have information about Harriet Forbes's murder."

The secretary ducked into Mr. Whitcomb's office, then reappeared with a smile.

"You may proceed," she said.

They stepped inside the large room, which was covered in mahogany wood and flanked with file cabinets. A wastebasket was overflowing with crumpled sheets of paper. The room smelled like stale coffee, and there was a typewriter and a dim, bronze harp table lamp on the desk.

"You have intel for me?" Sam Whitcomb said, rising to greet them. The windows of his office showed an expansive, bird's-eye view of the fairgrounds and the stretch of his tent city below. "On the murder of the actress?"

"The police have made an arrest in the poisoning death of Harriet Forbes," Grace said. "But we don't believe they have the right man."

With ink-stained fingers, Sam Whitcomb gestured them toward the chairs set before his desk.

He sank into his own chair, purposefully set above their eye level, and smiled at them with teeth that were big and overly white. He made Grace's skin crawl a bit. Grace glanced at Theodore out of the corner of her eye.

For once, she was glad to see his unvarnished look of disdain.

Whitcomb raised an eyebrow.

"You're friends with the accused," he said. "Is that right?"

"Yes," Grace said firmly. "And we'd like to talk to you. Off the record."

Whitcomb set down his pen and gestured at her. There was a glint in his eye. "By all means. Proceed."

Grace shared a look with Theodore, and he rolled out the caricature of the woman the fair artist had drawn.

"Do you know who this woman is?" Theodore asked.

Whitcomb gave him a skeptical look, then examined the sketch for a long moment.

"No," he said. "Should I?"

"This woman was following Harriet relentlessly in the days prior to her murder."

Whitcomb scoffed. "A caricature? You can't be serious," he said.

Grace scowled, rolling up the paper. "So that's a no, then?"

Sam Whitcomb sneered. "This is what you've brought me? A woman who may or may not have been following Harriet, whose name you don't know, and a sketch that could be of any number of the tens of thousands of women at these fairgrounds?"

He stood, as though dismissing them.

But Theodore remained sitting, his fist flexed on the table.

He spoke slowly, his derision matching Sam Whitcomb's own.

"We have a mysterious woman who tailed Harriet Forbes multiple times in the days just prior to her death," he said, his handsome jaw twitching as he counted on his fingers. "A verbal threat was made to her about money, with some sort of message she was expected to deliver to someone else. Then, Harriet Forbes secretly met with someone in the Tunnels, all in the days leading up to her death—which I think we can all agree is unusual for a woman of her stature. There's a bigger story here than a mere romantic tiff gone wrong."

Whitcomb leaned back in his seat, his eyes narrowing thoughtfully. "I'm listening."

"Anyone could have put something in her drink besides Oliver Carter," Grace said. "All we know for certain is that it was someone at that party."

"And *you* were the only one filming that night," Theodore said.

Mr. Whitcomb templed his fingers. "The trouble is, I've already watched the film from that night and shared it with the police. It doesn't show much of Miss Forbes's death, or anything that could exonerate Oliver Carter. It cuts to Miss Forbes right when she's dying and then ends."

Grace hesitated. "Could we see it anyway?"

Mr. Whitcomb's lips parted in an amused smile. "I don't think so."

"What if we could give you something in return?" Grace asked.

"Such as?"

Theodore began shifting in his seat, but Grace shot him a look.

"What if I wrote an article about this for you?"

Whitcomb's smirk deepened. "You're hardly unbiased."

"That's the point. It will be an inside scoop detailing all the things we think the police missed. What we are doing to prove Oliver's innocence, because we believe that the police got it wrong. Which means the *real* murderer is still out there."

She watched as a calculating gleam entered Whitcomb's eye. It was the sort of thing that would stoke public fear and sell out his newspapers, and they both knew it.

He stroked his chin and studied her. "Your ilk doesn't usually want to be associated with my newspaper."

That was true. If she thought Aunt Clove was angry with her before, this might be enough to turn her murderous.

But everything Grace would write was the truth. And it might help Oliver.

"I don't live my life by what other people think of it," she said.

It was a half-truth that she hoped might become whole someday, and she saw the quirk in Theodore's eyebrow that, in some lights, might almost be mistaken for admiration.

He gave her an encouraging nod.

"So you agree to write up a piece for exclusive publication in the *Fair's Fare*?" Sam Whitcomb asked. "You will raise enough questions in the minds of the public to sell papers and possibly force the police to take another look."

Grace answered without a second thought. "I'll do it."

Whitcomb smiled and rose. "Let's take a look at that film, then."

CHAPTER FIFTEEN

Grace had seen only one moving picture in her life before, and it was hard not to gasp when the scenes from the Libbey Glass Ball reappeared on the projection screen like a living memory.

The images were grainy and silent, but they showed the doors opening to the Palace, the guests climbing the staircase. The glassy floor, the gleaming contrasts of the crystal, and the ruby flash glass being made. The film panned over the dancing, and Grace hurriedly took out her notebook and wrote down every person she could recognize.

She saw Theodore in the corner, talking with his godfather. Thomas Squire was respected for his endeavors in philanthropy, feared for his ruthlessness in all manners of business.

The kind of person who might vouch for his godson if it pleased him, and whose word would not be questioned.

She didn't know where the thought had come from.

After all, why would Theodore Parker want Harriet dead?

"That's Donald Ogle and Doris Pote," Theodore said as Grace scribbled furiously. "They are from Chicago. There's Prince Pu Lun. Adolphus Busch. William H. Danforth. And—there—look. That's her, isn't it?"

The woman who had been following Harriet managed to skirt just around the camera. She always had her face turned the other way.

"Darn," Grace said.

The camera panned past the musicians and the bar, and in the background, Grace could just make out Earnest accepting the glass. To the left, Ethel was dancing. Earnest appeared to set the glass down and then speak with someone just off-camera. The quality of the film wasn't clear, and Earnest himself was quite blurry in the background.

"Look!" Theodore said.

Someone was approaching. A shadow, too difficult to make out in the grainy footage. A shadow that passed by Earnest, when his back was turned, and paused ever so briefly over the drink.

Just long enough to possibly put something inside of it.

Exactly like Earnest had guessed.

"Damn. That's not enough to prove the poisoner isn't Oliver," Theodore said.

"That's what the police said, too," Sam Whitcomb said.

"But who is it?" Grace whispered. She drew closer to the screen.

It couldn't have been Oliver, could it? she wondered. She hated that the thought could even occur to her. And yet, she had seen people she loved become someone else entirely in the right circumstances. Oliver had loved Harriet to the point of infatuation, and he wasn't used to being told no. What if he had found out that she was using him for some reason or another? That his love for her was real but hers was merely expedient, a stepping stone to something else?

One thing was clear. The murderer was definitely not Earnest.

She could cross Ethel off the list, too. The singer was plainly visible in the foreground.

Grace's face flushed.

"The police have seen the footage. It wasn't enough to exonerate Oliver. As far as they were concerned, it very well could have been him," Sam Whitcomb said. "Trying to put the blame on Earnest."

"Thank you," Grace said, stepping back.

"You won't forget our little agreement?" Sam asked.

"I'm good for my word," Grace said. Theodore's hand brushed the small of her back as he escorted her to the door. "I'll have the article to you soon."

❧

They walked briskly in the direction of the fairgrounds Grace's thoughts were racing. If it wasn't Earnest, then who had poisoned Harriet?

"Are you sure you want to do this?" Theodore asked. "If the murderer is still out there, he won't be pleased by that article. And it could lead him straight to you."

"This again," she said airily.

His face darkened. "I understand you are quite capable of defending yourself to the death with wits," he said. "But even the sharpest words are no match for an actual sword."

"Don't worry," she said. "Thanks to a certain gentleman, I am also in possession of a very dangerous spoon."

He rolled his eyes, then followed her into the shaded ivory columns of the Manufacturing Palace. They walked through the bustling corridors, past exhibits of hats and typewriters, crystals and window dressings, until they reached the massive display of textiles. There was a small shop decorated with felt and paper flowers. She looked through its beautifully bound journals and ink pens, fingering the coins in her hand. The small notebook she owned was really only appropriate for scrawling lists and snippets of thoughts.

She didn't even have enough money to buy paper and ink to write the article.

She tried to keep her voice nonchalant. "Is there any paper to be found in your aunt's studio?"

"Probably. Check the corner desk," Theo said distractedly, examining a leatherbound notebook. He paid for it and tucked it into his waistcoat. "Now, may I see you back?"

"My company has proved too stimulating already?" she asked.

"My brother has forced me into a dinner this evening with a family acquaintance who has the personality of wet paper," Theo said. He shot her a look as she opened her mouth. "Don't say it," he added.

"What?"

"Something devastating about how I'll fit right in."

"As though I could ever say something to devastate *you*."

He snorted and turned away, flushing.

Had she said something in the past that had truly hurt him? The thought confused her. She thought she was the only one with scars borne from his words.

"Besides—wet paper hardly suits," she said, almost before she could stop herself. "As you're neither mushy nor do you fall apart easily."

He turned back to her. "What, then?" he asked, studying her. His eyes were dark and glittering.

"Sandpaper, perhaps." She reached up, dangerously close to his cheekbone.

"A little rough around the edges, but . . ."

She trailed off, her hand faltering as she glimpsed Frannie in the distance.

Regret flooded through her every time she thought of what she had said to Earnest. She had all but accused him of being Harriet's murderer, with no actual proof. And now that evidence on tape had refuted it. She needed to gather up every scrap of pride she had and apologize. To try to mend the damage she'd caused with her meddlesome tongue.

"You don't need to worry about seeing me home," Grace said hurriedly. "There's Frannie Allred coming this way. I need to speak with her."

Theodore took a step back.

"You make interesting friends," he said lightly.

"Frannie and I have never been friends," she retorted. "And we're going to be even less so after what I have to say to her."

Theodore tipped his hat toward Grace in goodbye and bent, slowly, to kiss her hand. He held her eyes, as though challenging her to avert her glance.

But this time, she didn't.

It felt more vulnerable than the time he'd seen her cry over Walt, more intimate than a caress.

A feeling of pleasure flushed through her like a fever.

She could feel the brush of his mouth. Burning.

Her face.

Burning.

He wasn't wet paper, or sandpaper. He was kindling, and her body was set alight.

"Take it easy on Frannie," he whispered, his voice catching.

"Enjoy your dinner," she said hoarsely.

She turned away and hurried toward Frannie before he could witness the effect he had on her. It was too mortifying to bear.

Her breathing was heavy and fast, and she had the most delicious lift in her stomach—the way she felt just before the roller coaster plunged over the edge of its track.

This was the last thing she wanted. And yet she was tempted to draw even closer to it, feeling the warmth she knew could leave only burns.

"Frannie," she called out across the crowded chamber. She emerged from behind the column, waving to draw Frannie's attention.

Frannie turned and when she registered who the voice belonged to, her face soured.

She attempted to keep walking, but Grace took her skirts in her hand and wove quickly through the thick crowds of the Palace, keeping Frannie's ridiculous bird-topped hat in her view.

"Excuse me," Grace said, making her way past a group of people who had gathered to look at an exhibit displaying thousands of handmade shoes from Mexico.

"Frannie, this is ridiculous," Grace called ahead. "Are you actually trying to run away from me?"

"It doesn't benefit me in the least to be seen talking to you," Frannie said over her shoulder, not slowing.

"Fine." Grace quickened her pace even more. "We can have this conversation loudly or quietly, it's up to you, but it *will* be said."

People were starting to turn as Grace parted through the corridors, following Frannie out of the Palace and into the fresh air.

"You're making a scene," Frannie hissed.

"Some things are worth making a scene over."

Frannie finally stopped walking. When she turned to Grace, her green eyes blazed, but they were no match for the fire that was heating within Grace, licking up her spine.

Frannie opened her parasol and brought it up to block them from view.

"What do you want, *Miss Covington*?" she asked Grace through gritted teeth.

"I have something to say to you. About your treatment of Lillie."

Frannie pursed her lips, as though she were bored.

"You were shockingly rude to her at the party last night. Lillie—who has always, against everyone's better judgment, been your friend. And you publicly shunned her in her moment of need," Grace said.

"There are *rules*," Frannie hissed. "Social rules you've never abided by. You *or* your mother. Rules are what keep society running. Your impertinence to believe you are above them is unsurprising but no less disappointing."

"There are rules of decency, too," Grace said, sharpening her words like claws. "They matter most of all. And those are the rules you apparently never bothered to learn."

Frannie snapped her parasol closed and Grace walked away, chest heaving.

❧

That evening, Grace found paper in the drawer of the desk, just like Theodore had said. She thought of the way he had held her gloved hand earlier that day. The way a thrill had shot up her spine when he had brought his mouth to it. She settled in with her small notebook, going over her notes. There was nothing to eat for dinner, but she made herself tea and lit a fire in the hearth. She had gotten a small loaf of bread they were giving out for free from the Pillsbury counter that would carry her through. The spring rain outside was coming down in sheets, and though she was hungry, the studio felt cozy and warm.

She changed into a nightgown and took down her hair so that it fell in honeyed swells around her shoulders.

Just then, there was a bold knock on the door.

She jumped. Heart racing.

She wrapped a blanket around her nightgown and suddenly wished she really did have a weapon. What a stupid quip she'd made about that spoon.

She grasped the pen to use as a last resort—it could probably take out someone's eyeball with a well-aimed thrust, at least—and strode toward the door.

"Who is it?" she asked through the wood.

"Miss Covington?" a voice shouted from the other side. "Are you there?"

She let out a breath. She recognized that voice.

She opened the door slowly.

"Mr. Parker," she said in surprise. "What are you doing here?"

The rain was streaming down his face, running off his coat. His shirt was plastered against his chest. He held a large object beneath his right arm, shielded by some sort of tarp.

He handed it to her, using both hands, and it was surprisingly heavy.

"Careful," he said. Her hand brushed his as she took the bundle from him. The cold, wet touch of him sent a shiver down her, in the best possible way. "I bought a little something for my aunt," he said. "Maybe you could use it too. While you're here."

She looked at him from the doorway, where she was wrapped in a warm blanket, her hair tousled and her face flushed.

He seemed to be trying to keep his eyes fixed on her face, or the space next to her head by the door. His wet clothes moved against him with every breath.

There are rules, Frannie's voice said in her ear. Social rules. Rules of decency.

And she had already broken so many of them.

"You're going to catch your death," she said, looking at the sheets of rain behind him. She hesitated. "Do you wish to come in? You could get warm for just a minute."

"What I wish is irrelevant. Warmth hardly seems like a fair exchange for destroying your reputation," he said.

"We both know there's not much left of it to save," she said.

"I beg to differ," he countered, with an unexpected ferocity. He bowed to her, the rain streaming from his hat down his strong nose, his sculpted cheekbones. "Good night, Miss Covington."

She swallowed, nodding, and he raised his hand to keep his hat on and began striding through the dark streets.

She closed the door behind him and locked it.

Then she padded to the middle of the floor and gently set the package down.

She pulled the cover off, the raindrops dripping in rivulets onto her bare feet.

She gasped, grinning in shock.

It was a typewriter.

She slid down and ran her fingers along the keys, excitement stirring within her. Her very own typewriter to use.

Because she was alone, Grace let out a delighted squeal.

She moved the typewriter to the desk and found fresh sheets of paper, feeding one into the roller. Then, drawing the blanket around her amid the low-burning candles, she began to type the words she hoped might save her cousins.

CHAPTER SIXTEEN

MAY 9, 1904

Six Days After the Murder

GRACE STAYED UP late into the night writing the draft of her article, falling asleep just as the morning began trickling through the gaps of the curtains.

When she woke, there was ink on her cheek.

She scrubbed it in the sink until her skin was rosy but clean, and got dressed. She tucked her small notebook into her waistband along with the draft of her article, ignored the gnawing hunger in her stomach, and tied on her hat.

Then she strode down the street toward the fairgrounds to meet Lillie.

A lingering hope pricked the back of her mind. That maybe Walt would come today.

Lillie greeted her and after showing their ticket booklet for entrance, they crossed through the Exposition turnstiles. Lillie looked tired and a little gaunt. Her hair was pulled up beneath her hat, her embroidered gown and gathered skirts draped to accentuate her figure.

Grace's stomach chose that moment to growl noisily.

Lillie laughed. "That was rather monstrous," she teased.

Grace smiled, laughing it off. But Lillie caught something in her face. "Wait. When was the last time you ate something?"

Grace swallowed, her mouth dry. She had promised she wasn't going to lie to Lillie, not anymore.

"Our lunch yesterday. I may have . . . recently run out of money," she admitted. Her pride made the words feel like nettles on her tongue.

"Grace Covington!" Lillie said, looking horrified. "Are you saying that you would rather go hungry than ask your own flesh and blood for help? I've never been more offended in my life."

"Be gentle," Grace said. "My pride already feels quite wounded, and you know how beastly I get when I'm hungry."

Lillie marched them through the fairgrounds to one of the two restaurants flanking the Cascades and ordered Grace a feast. They had steaming coffee and popovers with sweet raspberry jelly. Thick slices of maple bacon, cinnamon buns, salty smoked salmon, and plates of fresh fruits arranged like flowers. Grace ate until she was stuffed.

When Lillie paid the check, she also slipped a coin purse across the table.

It was flush with cash.

"You're looking into things for Oliver," Lillie said. "Let me at least pay you for that service."

Grace was drowsily full. "Lillie—"

"Please let me do this. Money is a small thing for me, but it's a big thing to be able to help you."

Grace sighed and tucked the purse into her bag.

"Thank you," she said. "This will quite literally buy me several more days."

"Good." It was the first time Lillie looked truly happy in the last week.

They stood, and Grace took Lillie's arm. With her hunger quenched and her cousin at her side, Grace could almost forget all the rest of their troubles. As they walked, her eye caught on the front page of the new *Fair's Fare.*

The seller seemed prepared to repeat his threat from the other day, but she didn't give him a chance.

She had already seen that Harriet Forbes would be buried tomorrow.

"The funeral is at First Lutheran," Lillie said, noticing her interest.

"Will you go?" Grace asked.

"Mother, of all people, insists we should," Lillie said, holding her parasol so that Grace could join her beneath it.

"She's found her compassion at last?"

"I'm not sure that's a bone she was born with. No, she thinks it will look worse if we don't go."

"Ah," Grace said. Children were laughing and flying kites in the breeze. As she passed the lagoons and the gondolas that were floating beneath the Cascades and Festival Hall, Grace made plans to be at Harriet's funeral herself. She wanted to say goodbye, to pay her respects to a girl who had been like a brief, bright flare in her life.

And because Grace had a sneaking feeling the murderer would be there, too.

"It does grow tiresome, living life not by doing what is right, but by the filter of how it appears to other people," Lillie sighed. "Ah, Earnest!"

Grace's face promptly heated when she saw Earnest. He was leaning against a lamppost, and he appeared to be waiting for them.

"Lillie," he said, smiling. He gave a curt nod to Grace, his affect flattening. "Miss Covington."

"I didn't realize you were meeting," Grace said, taking a step back. "Please go ahead, I don't want to intrude."

"Nonsense!" Lillie said. "We're going to discuss the lawyer Daddy hired for Oliver. Earnest is talking with the aeronautics engineers at lunch, and Mother insists we're seen out enjoying our lives, rather than holing up as though we have something to hide."

"Please join us," Earnest said, but it was without conviction.

Grace hesitated. Lillie took her by the arm and Grace followed Earnest, shame-faced, to a concert on the pavilion, shrouded beneath trees on a hill. They sat on blankets and listened to the Mexican artillery band with Ricardo Pacheco. The men were dressed in formal military regalia but bore instruments in place of weapons. There were clarinets and trumpets and cornets that played lively polkas.

The breeze ruffled Earnest's hair beneath the brim of his hat. He didn't look at her.

Grace sat in awkward silence until she couldn't stand it anymore.

"I'm so sorry, Earnest," she said, lightly touching his sleeve to draw his attention. "I should never have accused you of something so heinous. I was deeply wrong, and I hope you will forgive me."

He shrugged. "Thank you for the apology," he said. Which she understood was not quite the same thing as forgiveness. Especially when he glanced away, so as not to have to look at her. Whatever fledgling magic had once been between them was now entirely gone.

She sighed. She was sad that her tongue had ruined their friendship. Especially when he was one of the first of the group who had been kind to her.

But at least it made it a little easier to bear the way he looked at Lillie. He had engaged Grace before with interest. With flirtation. But the way he was looking at her cousin was something different.

It made Grace's heart fall like a whisper, even though she couldn't blame anyone for adoring Lillie. After all, *she* did.

Earnest leaned to whisper in the curve of Lillie's ear. A pleased flush spread across Lillie's cheeks and lit her eyes. She edged her hand slightly closer to his, where it was splayed in the grass.

The truth was, Earnest had proven himself to be worthy of her beloved cousin. Sticking close to Lillie when everyone else turned away.

Although, Grace thought pettily, she wasn't sure any man would be worth a lifetime tied to that shrew Frannie Allred as a sister-in-law.

She closed her eyes and felt the sunlight spackle her face. She listened to the music, wondering what Walt was doing right then, and why he had failed to show up this time. Why Harriet had followed a path into the Tunnels that led to her death.

Grace opened her eyes with a thought. She extended it to Earnest, as an olive branch.

"I was thinking I'd head over to the wireless telegram tower today, if you wanted to come," she said. "Follow up on that lead we were chasing before."

"Oh," he said. "Glad I could spare you the wasted trip, then. I received a note from the message boy just yesterday. He said that George Parsons decided he wasn't coming back."

Grace paused, confused.

"He's not?" she said slowly. Her thoughts shuddered together.

"Sorry," he said. "I guess that lead turned into a dead end."

Mind whirring, she felt the corners of her own note from the messenger in her pocket. The one that said the exact opposite information.

Why was Earnest lying to her?

She watched him carefully. "So I guess there's no way to find out what he would have said, then . . ."

He shrugged. "I'm just passing along the message. I wasn't there when it came," he said, turning his face back to the music. "Frannie was."

❧

Grace was troubled as she parted ways with Lillie and Earnest.

She strongly disliked Frannie and knew her own biases. Grace thought Frannie was a terrible snob with no character and even less integrity. But that didn't mean that Frannie was a murderer.

Right?

The spring breeze was heavy and hot as she felt the corners of her article in her pocket. What would murdering Harriet do for Frannie, anyway? What would she possibly gain from Harriet's death?

Grace strode toward the wireless telegraph tower on the edge of the fairgrounds, but when she saw the line snaking and looping back on itself, she decided to head straight to Sam Whitcomb's office first. She wanted to make sure she could hand in her article to run before the next paper was printed.

She exited the fairgrounds and made her way toward Delmar, where she wove through the neat rows of the tent city. There was an area for babies to be left and attended to while their parents were visiting the fair; a barbershop where men could get a haircut and fresh shave. She smelled bacon wafting from one of the kitchen tents.

And this time, when she rode the elevator to the top floor of the octagonal Whitcomb press building, the secretary waved her in.

Grace found Sam Whitcomb at his desk, sorting through stacks of paper. There was smoke curling from the cigar on the ashtray, and mottled light from the harp lamp on the desk.

"My article," she said, retrieving it from her bag. "As promised."

He took the article and read it in front of her, which made her feel surprisingly vulnerable. She shifted her weight, and he made a few sounds accompanied by strikes of words with his red pen. That slow, unnerving smile spread across his face.

"Good," he said. "Very good. It will run tomorrow."

She nodded. "You showed me the tape, I wrote you the article. We're even now. If you want more, you'll have to pay me for it next time."

“Such a shrewd little reporter, aren’t we?” Sam Whitcomb said. His condescension was irritating. He picked up the cigar and ashed it in the crystal tray. “I think you’re getting more than enough benefit from my newspaper telling your side of the story.”

“I think you’re going to sell more papers than ever with this angle.” Grace set her shoulders. After all, she couldn’t live off of Theodore and Lillie’s charity forever. “And a girl’s gotta eat. Your choice.”

He narrowed his eyes.

“Keep bringing me the juice and we’ll talk.”

She pursed her lips and nodded. “I’m just about to follow another lead now.”

He smirked at her. “You’re a sharp one, aren’t you? Wouldn’t want to get on your bad side.”

“So don’t,” she said.

She picked up a copy of the day’s *Fare* for herself on the way out.

“Good day, Mr. Whitcomb,” she said.

❧

Grace read the paper from cover to cover while she waited in the snaking line for the De Forest wireless telegraph tower. There was Harriet’s smiling face. It hit Grace anew like a punch to the gut. This bright, alive woman was gone. How could a life be snuffed out like a candle?

She jumped a little at the boom of cannons shooting from a distant battle reenactment, the screams of people riding the roller coaster on the Pike, and felt a fresh determination buzzing in her veins to find the person who had killed Harriet. What were they doing now, while Oliver sat in prison and Harriet was going to be placed in the ground?

Grace rode the elevator up to the observation deck, tucking the folded newspaper beneath her arm as she asked one of the workers for Mr. George Parsons. The man pointed her toward the separated room at the back of the observation deck, where there were warning signs displayed amid coils, levers, and sparks.

She knocked on the door and tried to appear confident.

This moment was going to prove key to the next part of the investigation, she could just tell.

A man she'd never seen before came to the door. He appeared to be in his mid-thirties, with dark eyes and blond hair. He looked harried and irritable.

"Mr. Parsons?" she asked.

"Yes?" he said, his brow knitting suspiciously.

"Hello," she said. "My name is Grace Covington, and I'm looking into some background details about Harriet Forbes's life in the days before she was murdered."

Was it just her imagination, or did Mr. Parson's face turn a grim shade of white?

"You were with a man last week at the Tyrolean Alps restaurant, the Luchow-Faust, on the second floor," she continued. "He spoke to the actress Harriet Forbes. We're trying to get in touch with him."

The man shook his head, backing away.

She made to follow him.

"Please," she said, pulling out her notebook. "It's very important. A man has been wrongfully accused. He's—"

"You need to stop looking into this," Mr. Parsons said, his voice deathly quiet. "Or someone else is going to get killed."

She stopped short. "What?" she breathed.

"Don't come here again," he said. "Or it is probably going to be you."

He slammed the door in her face.

CHAPTER SEVENTEEN

THOUGH SHE WASN'T remotely hungry, Grace made her way toward the Cascades restaurant and asked for a table. She ordered an iced tea and waited for Walt, just like she had for the last two days.

She wasn't sure what to do now. She brought out her notebook and scribbled, looking over her shoulder, scanning the crowds milling around the Grand Basin, the gondolas cutting through the canals.

She was admittedly spooked by the man's warning. But this was proof, wasn't it? Real proof that Oliver was being framed. That she was on the right track. After all, if they already had the right person, then why would anyone threaten her for looking into it?

She felt a tingle of dread as she returned to her list of suspects. She crossed off Earnest's name and that of the singer Ethel Adams—they both had alibis, clearly visible in the camera footage when the shadowy figure put something into the drinking glass.

The rest of her list remained frustratingly the same and had even grown. Half of St. Louis's high society had been there that night.

Then there was the someone who met with Harriet that night at the restaurant and wanted money.

There was still the mysterious woman following Harriet and Oliver.

Who did Harriet meet with in the Tunnels?

And why had Frannie lied about the message?

Grace pressed her pen against the page, watching it bleed ink like a clot. She was coming up with more spidering directions to pursue, not less.

And then, when she turned her head, she saw Walt.

"Walt!" she cried, bursting to her feet.

He was walking with Lillie, who had him clasped by the arm, guiding him toward the restaurant.

Lillie's tired, lovely face lit up when she saw Grace. *I have him*, it said. *He's alive, and he's with me, and he is all right.*

Grace rushed to greet them and threw her arms around her brother. He smelled a little sour and she felt that familiar rush of conflicting emotions. Joy and sadness and a slight revulsion that made her disappointed in him and in herself. Anger at him for disappearing again and making her worry. And then back to joy again, that he was all right.

"I'm so glad to see you," she said. "I was worried about you." Both were equally true.

He smiled at her, somewhere between charm and shame. "I lost track of time," he said.

"Come sit," she said, leading him to the table.

They ordered roast beef sandwiches, potato salad, and iced teas in jewel-tone glasses to cool off from the midday sun. Grace waited until the food had been served and the edge of hunger had waned to broach any real attempts at conversation.

"How are you, Walt?" she said.

"I did what you asked," Walt said, chewing. "I found a guy who saw Harriet meet with someone that day in the Tunnels."

"Who was it?" Grace asked, her dashed hopes instantly rising. "A woman or a man?"

"He said it was a man. Listen. I have the source. But he says he won't talk without . . ." He trailed off. Shrugged, and took another bite.

Grace's heart sank. Of course. She glanced at Lillie.

Could she trust that Walt was telling her the truth? Was this merely an addict's way of twisting the circumstances to manipulate her and get money for a score?

How horrible, the way thoughts themselves turned to snakes when you could no longer fully trust a person.

"How much would he need to talk?" Grace asked. Her voice sounded brittle.

"Five dollars."

She inhaled sharply. That was a lot.

Was she really about to hand over money to her brother to potentially give to a drug dealer in exchange for information? Or money that could be wasted on something that would only hurt Walt more?

"Will you come and stay with me?" she asked. "I've got a clean room and a safe place for you to sleep for the night."

"I'm good, Gracie," he said. His voice was gentle, but firm.

She remembered him as a little boy, his heart hammering over hers the night that man had tried to break into their house.

"*It's going to be okay, Gracie,*" Walt had whispered fiercely in her ear. "*I've got you.*"

She felt rage and disappointment that he never let her help him, even now, when he needed it so much. Should she yell, cry, scream? She could hardly force her brother to do anything. And yet part of her knew she shouldn't offer the studio without talking to Theodore first. Theodore had given *her* permission to stay there, not her and Walt.

She thought of the new typewriter Theodore had gifted to her, and how much Walt could sell it for to use for drugs.

She shook her head, trying to clear her thoughts.

"I'll give you the money," she said slowly. "Try and get a detailed description of the person. A name would be even better." When she placed the money in his hand, she met his eyes. "This is for Oliver," she said. "This is about Oliver's *life*."

Walt nodded solemnly, his face a shade of gray. He slipped the money in his pocket.

Grace felt uneasy. She didn't know if she had done the right thing.

"Walt," Lillie said, folding her napkin. "Where have you been staying as of late? Are you enjoying the fair?" She asked Walt kind, gentle questions. He gave straight answers to a few of them. He was staying with some friends in the Tunnels. He hadn't left the fairgrounds for weeks, so that he wouldn't have to pay the fare to get back in. He enjoyed the John Philip Sousa band and the artists' booths, and he was getting enough to eat. Not the finest food, but it kept him alive, and he didn't have much of an appetite these days anyway. In talking to Lillie, there was a flash of his old wit.

Grace had barely touched her lunch, but Lillie ordered them all chocolate ice creams anyway. The dish sat in front of Grace, melting in the sun, and she poked at it with her spoon, pretending not to be listening too closely. Lillie talked to Walt about Dr. May, and what she was learning by apprenticing with her. "You could come in with me sometime," she said. "I'd love for you to meet her."

He nodded noncommittally, but he finished the ice cream and then sketched a little drawing on the paper napkin. It was of Lillie, lounging like she was the woman on the fairgrounds poster, and it had the silhouette of the Ferris wheel behind her. It had taken him five minutes, and it was extraordinary.

"Thank you for lunch," he said. He handed the napkin sketch to Lillie, as though it were payment, and Grace wanted to snatch it and keep it for herself. He had so much promise and it brought up so many feelings.

She knew that Walt went through the world constantly feeling too much, that living often felt like a knifepoint pressed against the pad of his thumb. Bringing the blood to the surface, all the time, without relief.

But hadn't part of him chosen this path he was on, too? And kept choosing it?

"There's one more thing," Grace said.

The drawing had reminded her of something.

She pulled out the caricature that she and Theodore had commissioned. Slowly, she unfolded it and showed it to Walt.

"Do you recognize this person? Perhaps while you're asking around, could you see if anyone knows who this is?"

Lillie caught sight of it as she put a bite of ice cream in her mouth. She said, "That looks like Ms. Lackey! How do you know her?"

Grace's heart stilled. "You recognize this woman?"

Lillie studied the drawing. "Well, the nose is a little wrong, but otherwise, it looks just like her."

"Who is this?" Grace asked.

"Our former butler's daughter. She used to come to the house sometimes when I was growing up and her mother was ill. Mother paid for her schooling. Her name is Vera Lackey."

Grace turned to her cousin with a mix of dread and excitement. "Lillie, this woman was following Harriet and Oliver. She was spying on Harriet in the days right before her death."

Lillie went a little pale. She set the spoon down as gently as a whisper.

"Do you know where we could find her?" Grace asked. "I'd like to talk to her."

"Oh, we're going to talk to her," Lillie said, trembling a little. She summoned the waiter for the check. "But we're going to confront my scheming, meddling mother about it first."

❧

Grace made plans to meet with Walt again tomorrow, which she knew all too well may or may not actually happen. She had hugged him for a second longer than was natural, feeling his ribs too keenly beneath his worn suit, the sour smell of sweat, and held on to the scrap of hope that he would come through with the information she had asked for. She slipped him the address of the studio where she was staying, so at least he would have a way of contacting her.

"Tomorrow," she said meaningfully, looking into his eyes.

He wiped a bit of ice cream from her cheek.

She still felt the touch of his fingers when Lillie's carriage moved through the shadow-spackled streets around Forest Park.

The Carters' brick house loomed as the carriage approached, and along with it rose up Grace's complicated memories of being there. She had played hoop and stick with Oliver and Lillie, just there, and eaten creamed lemonade with honey. Oliver had fallen from the front railing after trying to balance on it like an acrobat and, instead of being comforted, had been scolded for tracking blood in the house.

Now Grace followed Lillie up the front steps, Lillie striding with purpose. Lillie was usually the calmest, gentlest person Grace knew. Which made her the most frightening person imaginable when she was angry.

But they weren't alone. There was a woman standing at the door, waiting. Her back was to them, as though she had just finished ringing the doorbell.

Grace had a sinking feeling in her stomach as she faintly realized the worn spots on the woman's coat. The pattern of the bag that was clutched in the woman's hand. She was out of place on the Carters' front porch, and yet Grace would recognize her anywhere.

Grace stopped short, and the woman spun around.

Eyes just like her own, echoed in another face.

Nell Carter Covington.

Her mother.

❧

"Thank God! Grace Carter Covington. Where have you been?" Grace's mother asked angrily.

Her eyes filled with tears, caught between relief and fury, the same way that Walt had just made Grace feel. Grace was pierced with guilt as her mother grabbed her, hugging her hard enough to make it hurt.

"Aunt Nell," Lillie said warmly. "It's so good to see you. Let us go in."

Lillie led them inside, deftly removing her hat, and instructed Waters to inform her mother to come down.

He gave an uneasy look in Grace's direction, but Lillie's voice turned to steel. "Now, please, Waters."

He hurried away.

Lillie brought them into the sitting room, fussing over Nell and calling for tea. There were flowers starting to droop in their crystal vases—the only sign that things were not truly right in the Carter home.

"Mother, what are you doing here?" Grace said.

"Looking for you," Nell said sharply. "Clove refused to take my calls. I had no idea where you were. At this fair, with hundreds of thousands of strangers. You have no idea the agony you have put your father and me through these last few days."

"I'm fine, Mother. I'm sorry. I should have let you know that I was all right." It was strange to see her mother in this house. She looked like her older brother Reginald, but she had their mother's high cheekbones and deeper lines etched around her mouth. Grace could see the resemblance all the more clearly in the large portrait of her grandmother that hung in the hallway.

"I couldn't reach you," Nell said. "And with this terrible mess Oliver is caught up in . . ."

"He didn't do it," Grace said, reaching to squeeze Lillie's hand.

"Of course he didn't," Nell snapped. "But reason stands that if it wasn't Oliver, that means someone else is still out there . . ."

She trailed off as Aunt Clove appeared at the landing above them. She had dark circles under her eyes, and she looked irritated as she came down the stairs in her dressing robe.

"Nell," she said curtly. "I wasn't expecting you."

"You wouldn't take my calls. I understand you're up against it with everything that's happened, Clove, but for goodness' sake. When you refused to communicate with me and no one would let me speak with Grace, I had to come out here myself to make sure my daughter was all right."

"Your daughter is no longer welcome in this house thanks to the part she has played in all of this. Or did she not tell you?"

There was a beat of silence. "Excuse me?" Nell's voice dropped.

"Ask her yourself about the role she played in deliberately concealing the nature of Oliver's relationship with that actress—"

"*Harriet*, Mother," Lillie said loyally.

"Which has now destroyed my son, his future, our family name. I never should have let her step foot in this house."

"You think that Oliver's choice to hide a relationship from you is somehow Grace's responsibility and not his own?" Grace's mother was incredulous. "That's fine. Grace, go fetch your bags. We're going now."

"My bags aren't here, Mother," Grace said calmly. "Didn't you hear what Aunt Clove said? I'm no longer welcome in this house."

Nell's voice dropped to an octave Grace had never heard before. Her crisp, upper-class enunciation drew out each word. "What do you *mean*, your bags aren't here?"

Grace didn't answer.

Nell turned to Clove, biting out each word. "Where has my daughter been, if not under your roof?"

Aunt Clove stared coolly back at Grace's mother without answering.

The tension stretched between them, building until Grace could bear it no more.

"I've been staying in a friend's vacant apartment," she said. "It belongs to his aunt."

"Oh, good heavens," Aunt Clove said, turning away, as if this were the most shameful thing she'd ever heard. As if she had nothing to do with the necessity of it.

Nell was shaking with rage.

"You turned out my daughter, your husband's own flesh and blood, to fend for herself in a city flooded with hundreds of thousands of people. You refused to take my calls to admit this. My daughter, who I entrusted to your custody?" Nell's voice was rising to hysterics. "Money cannot buy decency. Or integrity. Or even the barest scrap of sense. You should be ashamed of yourself."

Grace barely had time to relish in her mother's takedown of Aunt Clove before she turned on Grace next, her face pale with rage but pricked with red.

"And you. You are coming home with me."

Grace planted her feet in the plush carpet, feeling it sink beneath her.

Her grandfather's imposing gaze settled on her from the oil portrait.

"I'm not leaving until Lillie and Oliver are all right," she said softly. "Both of them."

Nell laughed, as if she could not believe what she was hearing. "What did you have in mind, Grace? Being some sort of detective?"

She said it like it was the most ridiculous thing she'd ever heard. Grace's face stung like she'd been slapped, but she wouldn't let it show.

Especially in front of Aunt Clove.

With as much dignity as she could muster, she picked up her mother's bag.

"Let's talk over dinner," she said, as though Aunt Clove were not there. "I have some information that might be of interest about Oliver's case."

"If you have something that could help Oliver, you should be sharing that with his *lawyer*," Aunt Clove said.

"I'm sorry. This information is for family only," Grace said, turning her back on her aunt. She called over her shoulder as she sailed out the door, "And you've made it very clear that we are not that."

❧

Nell's ire had cooled a little by the time they'd walked several blocks and the revolving silhouette of the Ferris wheel came into view.

"You have to at least see it," Grace said, wheedling. "Since you're here."

"Fine," Nell said, fixing Grace with a steely gaze. "But you're telling me everything while we do."

They entered the fair's turnstiles and, seeing it through Nell's eyes, Grace was hit anew by the wonder of it all. It washed over her in a wave of elation, flooding her with the feeling of possibility. The energy was electric. It felt like watching thousands of flowers suddenly erupting into bloom at once.

"How many buildings?" Nell asked faintly, glancing up at the towering Tyrolean Alps.

"More than a thousand."

"And how many countries are here?"

"Sixty-two."

"It would take weeks to see it all."

"A month, at least," Grace countered. She breathed in the sugar-scented air and thrust the program into her mother's hand. It was astonishing what human beings could collectively do when they put their minds to it. Fossils of dinosaurs! A blue whale's skeleton! Live reenactments of military battles and firefighters putting out blazes! Premature infants in incubators! Elephants that went down slides! Morocco's twenty-five rare Arab stallions!

It hit Grace's veins like a drug. She wanted to see it all. Take it inside of herself to carry around like a cupboard of secret, hidden treasures that she could take out and look at until the day she died.

She felt something that was almost like pride as Nell admired the fair's architecture, the pottery and looms, the women they passed in traditional Irish and Japanese dress. They found a restaurant modeled after a coal mine and examined the menu, commenting on the way Grace's father would have liked the ham and fried egg sandwiches. As the heaping plates appeared in front of them and grease dripped from her fingers, Grace told her mother everything that had happened.

For the first time, it tumbled out of her. The way Oliver had gotten her into the party. How it had felt to watch Harriet die in front of her. Being thrown out of the Carter home, and all the reasons she believed Oliver was innocent. How Theodore had provided the use of his apartment.

"Time to come home," Nell insisted. "I'm grateful that this gentleman helped you, but the arrangement is unseemly. You're a smart girl, you must know what this looks like."

"He's Oliver's friend. And since when have you cared what others think?" Grace asked.

"I always care more for my children than I ever have for myself," Nell said crisply. "Now, there's a train home tonight and I expect you to be on it with me."

Grace was quiet. She suddenly felt guilty that she'd forced her mother to come looking for her. It had been irresponsible and unkind, and the train ticket, the restaurant meals, were all things her parents couldn't really afford.

And yet something hidden deep within her healed at the knowledge that her mother had dropped everything to come for her. Nell had been a shadow of herself ever since Walt left. But this had brought her flickering back to life, into something solid Grace could hold again.

She stole glances at her mother as they paid the bill and walked out to the Music Pavilion. For a moment, she looked a little more like the woman in Grace's memory.

"Your father would love this," Nell said wistfully, taking in the thousands of incandescent bulbs that lit up the Palaces. They dimmed and changed in colors of red, white, and green, electrifying the sky. Grace fixed her gaze on them, knowing better than to tell her mother about the *Fare* article she had written; that she was perhaps going to provoke a murderer. And that at that very moment, Walt was likely wandering in the Tunnels nearby.

Grace felt the guilt of that settle in deep and squeeze her chest, making it hard to breathe. But she suddenly couldn't bear to bring him up, to reveal that nothing had changed, and see the way her mother's heart would crack just a little more all the while pretending it wasn't. Perhaps it was selfish, but she had relished the way her mother had listened with full attention, reaching out to stroke Grace's hair when she told her how it had felt to see Harriet die. She hadn't known how much she needed it until she felt herself soaking up her mother's attention like a sponge.

And she wanted to hold on to that for just a little longer.

"We should go," Nell said, checking the time. "Let's get your things. The last train is leaving soon."

They walked beneath the city's leafy trees and misty streetlamps, Grace leading the way through the streets until the train station appeared, glowing in the night. A light rain had begun to fall.

"But this is the station," Nell said, frowning as the realization dawned. "I thought we were going to the apartment to collect your bags."

"I know. I'm sorry."

"Grace—"

"I can't go with you tonight," Grace said. "They're burying Harriet tomorrow. And as much as I want to make you happy, there are things I need to do here first." Grace wrapped her arm around her mother's waist, smelling the rosewater of her hair. "I'm an adult now, may I remind you," she said, already feeling Nell beginning to argue. "But I'll be better about being in touch, so that you won't worry."

"Of course I'll worry," Nell snapped.

"I promise I'll be careful," Grace said.

Grace handed her a piece of paper with the studio address on it.

Nell clutched it in her hand.

"I can't lose both my children," she said. Her eyes welled with tears.

At the sight of them, Grace's suddenly filled, too.

"I am the person you taught me to be," Grace said. "You do what your heart says is right, no matter how it looks to other people. And I am your daughter."

"And look at you go," her mother said. She smiled, watery and brave. "Go, and go, and go. And then come back to me," she said.

She cupped Grace's cheek.

"In the meantime, I'll be having a word with my brother Reginald," she said. She gathered her dress resolutely in her hand. "If you prefer not to witness the aftermath, I'd stay clear for a few days."

Grace snorted. "I love you."

Her mother embraced her, then whispered fiercely into her hair. "No one tells of the freedom you have when you're no longer bound by society's opinion."

"I'm afraid that some days I'm not there yet," Grace said.

"Nor am I. But I'm on my way."

Grace watched her mother buy the train ticket, feeling something within her fissure.

She'd been the reliable one, the responsible one, for years now. That had been a gift she could give her parents, becoming one less weight for them, in case they collapsed under what they already carried.

And yet this had been a gift her parents had given back to her, too. That she was worth fighting for as well. Worth worrying over.

Grace waved fiercely, stepping on her tiptoes and watching the train pull away, as though it could go back to the place where her father still sifted flour like snow in the kitchen, where Walt papered the walls with his drawings and she hid in the knotted boughs of the juniper tree. Back to childhood and all the versions of herself that didn't exist anymore.

She waved at the train until it disappeared.

And then she went home to try to catch a murderer.

CHAPTER EIGHTEEN

MAY 10, 1904

Seven Days After the Murder

In the morning, Grace dressed in formal black for Harriet's funeral and stepped out to hail a carriage. But as the carriage drew near, her eye caught on something.

"Explosive new claims!" a news seller shouted from the corner. He held a paper in his hand, showing its bold headline: IS A MURDERER STILL ON THE LOOSE AT THE FAIRGROUNDS?

It was her article.

A crowd was already beginning to gather like finches to birdseed. Newspapers were flying off the stands. She felt a special jolt of pleasure, standing anonymously amid dozens of people devouring her words.

It was power. She was entering their minds, beckoning their thoughts where she wanted them to go. They didn't have to follow, but for a moment she was a prosecutor, presenting her case, and they were the raptly listening jury.

"Is it true? There might still be a murderer on the loose?"

"A *poisoner*."

"That's it. We're only eating sandwiches we brought from home."

She walked through the invisible perfume of their words, folding her article beneath her arm, and climbed onto the trolley, exiting at the stop nearest the Four Courts jail building.

Her ears turned pink when she entered the prison and saw that even the guard manning the front desk was reading her article, though he was trying to pretend that he wasn't.

Grace found herself in the same windowless room she had been in before, waiting for Oliver. Her shoes clicked against the tile. The room smelled like loneliness, sterile and gray. She drew a breath when the guard brought Oliver in handcuffed.

His eyes looked hollow, like endless mirrors. His skin was drab, as though he'd not seen the sun in months, though it had really been only a matter of days—and she knew the prisoners were taken outside to exercise in the courtyard, even though it was in full view of the gallows. She longed to take his face in her hands. To tease each other and hear him laugh again.

He eyed her dark funereal clothing and the corner of his mouth twitched downward.

"They're burying the woman I love today," he said softly, "and I cannot be there."

"I will go in your stead," she said.

"I dream about her," he said. "I dreamed of her last night. She was dancing and laughing."

Grace had known he would be in agony today, sitting helplessly in his cell while they buried the person he had wanted to spend his life growing old with.

She unfolded her article and pushed it across the table. His face flickered with surprise.

For a moment, there was almost the hint of a smile on his lips.

He picked up the article and read it hungrily.

His face had changed by the time he looked up again. He'd shed years like layers.

"You're fearless, Grace Covington," he said. "I always knew you were formidable."

She flushed, embarrassed. "Come, now, Oliver. You'll give me a big head."

"It's true. I've seen you face things that would make others cower, including two major cities' high societies and my own mother. But this—you're a lionheart."

Instead of brushing him off, she let his words go down deep into the soil of her heart, where they might take root. She brought out her notebook. "I'm still just getting started. Can you help me? I have a few more questions."

"Anything," he said.

"Where was Harriet living until recently? What was her last known address?"

The color came back into his face as he gave her Harriet's address, the name of her roommate and a description of the girl. "Her roommate is Caroline," he said. "Caroline Locke."

"I'll plan to speak with her today at the funeral," Grace said. "See if I can find out anything the police might have missed."

"Good." Oliver rubbed the bridge of his nose, a strange look crossing his face.

"What is it?" Grace asked.

Oliver hesitated. "Just . . . watch carefully today at the funeral. I've read that guilty people tend to insert themselves into the investigation. They want to appear helpful, but really, they're just waiting to strike next."

Grace felt the slightest chill curl around her heart at his warning.

Who had been helping her the most in this investigation?

"I'll be looking," she promised.

Then she kissed his cheek and made her way to the church.

❧

The First Lutheran church was a towering brick Gothic building flush with sprays of fresh lilies and tolling bells. Black-clad mourners spilled down the front steps as the sun limned the stained-glass panels above two large, iron-strapped doors. Grace slipped into the line filled with Harriet's family, friends, and fans. There were voyeurs, people who had come for the spectacle. Reporters. Other actresses and people from Harriet's theater company. Grace spotted Ethel, draped in a black veil.

Inside the church, Grace took a seat in the pew beside Lillie, who had purposefully sat apart from her parents. The church smelled like a mix of must and heady roses, and Harriet's casket was draped with a white pall. Lillie was rigid, staring straight ahead as the pastor performed the service. Late-morning sunshine shone through the stained glass, its colors melting in jewel tones along the walls and floor. It was jarringly cheerful amid the congregation's stark black.

"Everyone is looking at us," Lillie whispered.

Grace clasped her cousin's arm. She was painfully aware of the people whispering behind cupped hands, their eyes wandering toward Lillie, or toward Aunt Clove and Uncle Reginald. As the mourners sang the hymn "Abide with Me," Grace saw Earnest and Theodore sitting together. Theodore gave her a short nod when their eyes met, and warmth instantly pooled through her.

She realized in that moment that she had never formally thanked him for the typewriter.

She continued to scan the crowd, her eyes falling on a woman in the second pew who matched the description of Harriet's roommate. Caroline Locke was scant and pale and had white-blonde hair that looked like fairy floss. She kept a pinched look on her face throughout the service, her eyes fixed on the hymnal in her lap, while Harriet's father and her older sister Penelope wiped tears from their faces with handkerchiefs.

At the service's conclusion, Grace followed the procession of the closed casket to the graveyard. She gave her condolences to Harriet's family.

"I'm Grace," she said. "I was a friend of Harriet's."

Penelope, Harriet's sister, looked strikingly like Harriet. Her hair was darker, her eyes slightly closer to the bridge of her nose, but the physical similarities were enough to make Grace dizzy.

"Thank you for coming," Penelope said. Her brown eyes were swollen and rimmed with red. She looked past Grace, as though she were not fully there.

Grace didn't want to imagine what it would feel like to bury a sibling.

She moved from the line and again spied the roommate Oliver had described. Grace parted through the solemn crowd, wanting to ask permission to possibly examine some of Harriet's mementos before they were all collected or given away.

But the grounds were thick with people milling around the old trees, sharing condolences and smoking cigarettes, and she didn't reach Caroline in time.

She watched the girl climb into a carriage and drive away.

Grace made her way toward where Theodore Parker was leaning against a tree, looking dapper in his black suit. The scruff was starting to fill in over his birthmark, and part of her was sad that it was disappearing.

She hesitated. "Would you like to go somewhere with me?" she asked.

He said yes before she even told him where.

❧

The carriage wove through the narrow streets as Theodore and Grace navigated to Harriet's former address. The route ended in front of a small, brick apartment building beside a general store. There were pots of cheerful flowers peeking out beside the cracked steps, but the building looked like it had seen better days.

Grace climbed the stairs resolutely and knocked on the door.

There was a long beat before Caroline Locke answered. She slid open the door slowly, still in her mourning clothes.

"Caroline?" Grace asked.

Caroline's eyes narrowed as she looked between Grace and Theo. "Yes?" she asked warily.

"I'm Grace Covington, and this is Theodore Parker. We were friends of Harriet's. We saw you at the funeral earlier today."

"Grace Covington." Her eyes narrowed further as she thought. "The Grace Covington who wrote that article in the paper this morning?"

Grace nodded. "Yes."

"What do you want?" Caroline's affect grew noticeably flatter.

"I was hoping we might be able to take a look at Harriet's things," Grace said quickly. "Before they are all boxed and taken away."

"I don't think so," Caroline said.

She began to shut the door in Grace's face, but Grace stopped it.

"Please," she said. "It might help my cousin. Don't you want the person who killed Harriet to face justice? The *true* murderer—not the person who loved her?"

"Listen," Caroline said. "All you're doing is stirring things up. I don't want to end up in the paper, or have any attention drawn to me at all. Especially if the murderer is still out there. Harriet and I weren't that close. I definitely don't feel like putting myself in any danger for her. Just let this be buried with Harriet."

This time, Caroline shut the door resolutely before Grace could stop her.

Grace sighed heavily.

"Now what?" Theodore asked. He leaned against the door and looked at her with something that bordered on amusement.

"Now it's your turn. You didn't think I brought you along merely to look at, did you?"

"I'm beginning to think you had something more calculating in mind."

"In fact, I do," she said. "I need you to distract Miss Caroline Locke for me."

"And how, pray tell, are you expecting me to do that?"

"By using your considerable charm."

He frowned. "Have you forgotten who you're talking to? Perhaps sustained a recent head injury?"

She glanced toward the fire escape.

Oliver had told her he once used it to get into Harriet's room: the first window on the second floor.

"Would you like to climb this ladder instead?" she asked sweetly. "I know how much you enjoy heights."

He scowled at her.

"Thank you for the typewriter, by the way," she said. "Now go make Caroline Locke fall in love with you."

She didn't miss the flush that rose to his cheekbones as she hitched up her skirt, showing a bare sliver of ankle, and began to climb.

❧

Grace jangled the window open and climbed inside. Closing it behind her, she heard Theo's knock, and then the distant timber of his voice as Caroline answered the door again. Grace stood in the middle of the room, turning in a circle to look around it.

Harriet's room had already been thoroughly searched. It was clear by the way things had been pulled out, rummaged through.

There was a twin bed with a faded quilt in the corner. A clock on the nightstand, and a small lamp. A bureau, with clothes sorted through and hastily put back, and a rose that was starting to wilt in a vase. Tucked beneath it was the talent manager's card. Grace's eyes fell on a magazine with starlets on the cover. A perfume bottle, and a tube of lipstick.

She felt a wave of grief. She was doing this for Oliver, but she was doing it for Harriet, too. She had been a girl with a full life, overflowing with dreams.

Grace looked through Harriet's wardrobe, at the dresses she had just seen Harriet wear not a week before. She forced herself to focus and quickly scoured beneath the bed, running her hand between the mattress, opening the drawers of the nightstand and bureau. Harriet's nightstand held a small book with her handwriting in it.

Grace fished it out and sank down on the bed.

Tucked inside were old performance programs, notes from Harriet's grandparents. A write-up in the newspaper about her performance in *A Doll's House.*

Love notes from Oliver.

Grace felt conflicted about reading the woman's private diary, but at the same time—she was dead. She wasn't coming back. And even from the grave, Grace believed Harriet would want to help Oliver.

Grace flipped through the pages to the back, finding the most recent entries. The last ones Harriet would ever write.

I never want Oliver to think I want him for his money, she had scrawled. *I don't even want him to know I need money—makes things too complicated. No, I need to get it from someone else.*

Money—for what?

Grace skimmed through earlier pages, looking for any mentions that might shed light on what Harriet needed money for.

Oliver wants to keep our relationship a secret for a little bit longer, she had written. *I'm dying to marry him, but if that's what he wants, I'll play along.*

Sometimes I think I'll retire from the stage and start a family. But the way it feels to perform, to feel the crowd's applause—it feels like falling in love. It feels like the way I feel when I'm with Oliver. I hope I don't ever have to choose between them. Although I know his family will never accept me unless I do.

Finally, Grace found an entry dated five weeks back.

Her heart sank.

My theater is in desperate trouble, Harriet had written. *If it doesn't find an investor soon, it will likely go under. I've given them everything I could manage to part with myself, because our fates are tied together*, Harriet surmised. *Should I ask Oliver for help with it? Any of our friends?*

With a pang, Grace recognized herself in this, even though it seemed so silly now. Oliver would have loved to help Harriet. Just like Lillie loved to help her. Just like she loved to help Oliver when he needed it. Pride was such a silly thing.

A pebble hit the window.

She looked up sharply.

That was Theodore's cue. Someone must be coming. Perhaps it was Harriet's family, there to finish gathering her things now that the funeral was over. Grace hurried to put the diary back. But her gaze caught on something else hidden in the drawer.

It appeared to be a small datebook.

There was another ding of a pebble against the window.

Grace drew out the datebook. It was barely bigger than her palm.

She hesitated, and slipped it into her pocket.

Then she opened the window sash and began to climb onto the fire escape.

"Hurry," Theo hissed from below. She quickened her pace down the ladder.

She neared the end of the fire escape just as Caroline came around the corner.

Without hesitation, Theodore wrapped his arms around Grace's waist, pulling her from the escape, as though they were lovers, merely out for a walk.

"I'm afraid I failed your task," Theodore whispered roughly.

"Nonsense," she said.

"That was too close, Covington," he breathed into the curve of her ear as Caroline passed.

"I found something," she whispered, hiding her face in the hollow just beneath his jawline. She inhaled his heady scent, and the feel of his hands instinctively tightening around her waist sent a shimmer of sparks down her neck. She fought against the almost incontrollable urge to kiss along the roughness of his throat, trailing up to the cut of his mouth. He scowled and swallowed hard, holding her tightly, and the look on his face said he was annoyed at having to be this close to her. But she could feel his heart beating hard and fast, betraying him through the fabric of his shirt.

She waited until Caroline's footsteps had faded and Theodore's grip began to loosen. When he pulled away from her, she felt flushed and bothered. She tried to hide it by fussing with her dress and bringing his attention to the book in her pocket.

"Look what I found," she said. "It's Harriet's datebook."

They moved to the shade of the elm trees and she riffled through the pages, tracing the days before Harriet's murder.

"There—" he said, pointing. "The day she met someone in the Tunnels, right?"

"Yes," Grace said. Harriet had scrawled something down as if she were in a hurry. It said:

Fairgrounds ↓ 9 a.m. —Jenny

"Jenny?" Theo asked.

"No," Grace said, squinting, bringing her face closer to the page. "I think that's a *P*."

So Harriet had needed money for the theater, and she had gone to the Tunnels that morning to meet a woman named Penny.

A woman.

Not a man.

So either Walt had lied to her, or his source had made up the information to get money.

She fought against the crashing wave of disappointment that threatened to overtake her.

"Do we know someone named Penny?" Grace whispered. Theo met her eyes and want surged through her.

"Harriet's sister at the funeral," Theodore said. Without the telltale hammering of his heart, he seemed largely unaffected, and she almost wondered if she had imagined it. "Wasn't her name Penelope?"

Grace nodded. "But why would she need to meet her own sister in the Tunnels?" she asked.

"I think that's something only Penelope could answer," Theo said. His pinkie grazed hers with a touch as gentle as a whisper, raising every nerve ending she had.

"Well," she said hoarsely, "then let's find out what Penelope knows."

CHAPTER NINETEEN

"Why would you need to meet your own sister in secret?" Grace mused aloud. It seemed an odd place to meet, unless one really didn't want to be spotted. Could she really have been talking to her about money?

"It's strange," Theo agreed, directing his carriage driver toward Lillie's house.

"Harriet's theater needed money or it was going to close," Grace said. Was it possible that the man who had threatened Harriet at the restaurant was part of her theater somehow?

People did unimaginable things when their dreams, livelihoods, or families were at stake. Perhaps, if it involved all three, it could even drive someone to murder.

But why would you kill your own star?

Lillie had changed out of her funeral clothes and seemed in good spirits when she accepted Theodore's hand and climbed into the carriage.

"Earnest got us tickets to the orchestra at Festival Hall tonight," she said to Grace. "He thought we could use some cheering."

"That was kind of him," Grace said. She turned to Theodore. "Are you going?"

"I hadn't planned on it," he said.

"Unfortunately, I think they're sold out," Lillie said apologetically.

"I could use a quiet night at home anyway," Theo said. "Between the fair and a murder investigation, I've been rather inattentive to Sesame."

"Sesame?" Grace asked.

"A small black puppy I recently acquired. Destroyer of slippers and Persian rugs."

"Perhaps while you and Sesame are having a raucous night at home together, you could look into contacting Penelope Forbes," Grace said.

She filled Lillie in on what they had found in Harriet's apartment, and Lillie reciprocated by showing Grace a small, handwritten piece of paper tucked into her handbag.

"I decided not to confront my mother about the woman she hired to follow Harriet until I did a little snooping of my own," she said. "The woman's name is Vera Lackey and this is her address. I'd rather catch her off-guard and get the truth from her lips before she can be tipped off by my mother."

Grace touched the page with a slight thrill. "Can we call on her now?" she said.

Theo rapped twice on the carriage ceiling, directing the driver to the new address.

"Shall I come in with you?" Theo asked as the carriage pulled to a stop.

Grace examined the small, tidy home. It was a gray, timber-framed hall-and-parlor house in a slightly better neighborhood than Harriet's had been and was situated next to a church.

"No need," Grace said. "And if we don't come back out, you'll know we found the murderer."

"Your humor is disturbing," he said. "But, Grace," he said, reaching out for her. "You're taking a lot of risks right now."

She quieted. "I'll be careful," she promised.

And yet, she felt a fresh hunger surge within her. She was going to do this.

Lillie waited to ring Vera Lackey's front bell until Grace was out of sight. From this angle, it was apparent that the house was in worse shape than Grace had first thought. The roof, at the very least, needed replacing. She could smell a lilac bush blooming just beneath the rotting window.

The white curtains flicked, and then the door hesitantly opened.

"Miss Carter?" Vera asked with surprise. "What are you doing here?"

When Grace appeared next to Lillie, she paled.

"I'm Grace," Grace said. She smiled thinly. "But I think you know that already."

"Come in," Vera said, looking furtively over their shoulders at Theodore's waiting carriage. Its presence provided Grace with a comforting sense of protection. "We can have tea."

The shifty look she gave them was less than assuring, but Grace followed her into the dim hallway anyway. There were knickknacks on every surface, cluttered but immaculate, and Grace examined them on the way into Vera's small parlor. Wallpaper was peeling around framed baby silhouettes and through the window, Grace glimpsed a small vegetable garden.

Vera sat. "What is this about?" she asked.

"We need to speak to you about Harriet Forbes," Lillie said.

Thankfully, the woman didn't try to play dumb.

"What do you want to know?" she asked. Her eyes shifted from Lillie to Grace and back again.

Grace's neck prickled as she felt something watching her. She turned her head to see a cat, staring at her from the basement stairs.

"You were following Harriet Forbes," Lillie said. "Spying on her."

"Oh, come," the woman said with a nervous titter. "'*Spying*' is a little sensational."

"I disagree. Not when that same woman was murdered not long after," Grace said.

When Vera remained silent, Lillie prodded, "Did my mother hire you?"

Vera cleared her throat. She seemed young for the gray beginning to streak through her mousey brown hair. "Yes. I was hired by your mother to watch Harriet and Oliver."

"Why?" Lillie asked.

Vera clasped her hands. "She suspected there was something going on between them, despite their claims to the contrary. I was merely to follow them and report what I saw."

"And then she wound up dead. On a night you were there," Grace said.

Lillie shot her a look from the corner of her eye, and Grace backed off.

"Mrs. Carter didn't hire me to *kill* her, if that's what you're inferring," Vera said coldly.

"I just think the timing is interesting," Grace said. "Do the police know about this arrangement?"

"You think turning suspicions from one family member to another is going to help your case?"

Vera laughed and stood, picking up the cat. It slunk beneath her, rubbing its face along her neck and purring. There was a doll in the corner, looking at them with dead glass eyes.

Lillie touched Grace lightly on the hand, and Grace knew she had to tread carefully. Her cousins wouldn't want to see their mother wind up in jail, either.

"When you were following Harriet, did you see her go into the Tunnels at all?" Grace asked.

Vera shook her head.

"Did you see her meet with her sister, Penelope Forbes?"

Vera shrugged.

"I don't have anything to hide," Vera said, but the way she said it sounded almost like a threat. "I told Mrs. Carter that Oliver and Harriet were in a relationship, and that you knew about it, Grace. And she paid me handsomely for it. But I didn't have anything to do with killing Harriet Forbes."

She showed them to the door. "Go ahead, tell the police. But you'll only be creating more problems and more suspicion for your family."

Grace knew that was true.

She believed Oliver would never have killed Harriet.

But as she climbed into Theodore's carriage, she realized she wasn't so sure about Aunt Clove.

❧

Grace's mind sorted theories that night at the orchestra concert in Festival Hall. She tested them, rolling them around like marbles, as she slid back into the half-waking dream world of the fairgrounds. Being there felt like putting on a coat of mist and champagne bubbles.

Lillie sat beside her, wearing a midnight satin dress and a glittering neck of jewels. Grace was re-wearing the rose-colored mousseline dress, but she didn't care because it made her feel so effortlessly lovely.

She was irritated to realize how much she wished Theo could see her in it.

Frannie was there too, swathed in sea-foam tulle, her hair glittering with pins. She was on Copper's arm, his red hair slicked back and his suit looking sharp and expensive. They ignored Grace entirely and gave Lillie an only slightly warmer reception. Earnest seemed annoyed by this and made up for it by showering Lillie with attention. He reached for her hand as the violins swelled.

Grace clasped her own palms in her lap.

She watched the orchestra responding to the conductor's effervescent direction, the musicians moving in choreographed tandem like wind over grasslands, or what Grace imagined the waves of a sea might look like.

As the evening went on, she felt like her heart might explode in her chest. The musicians played as though their instruments had souls that could be brought to life beneath their touch. She felt that quickening again of being near to the pulsing heart of being alive, and rose to her feet, applauding. Perhaps she felt it even more keenly because she had witnessed death, and this felt like the opposite of decay: explosions of color and sound ripping through cobwebs of sadness.

"Shall we walk?" Earnest asked after the final encore. The evening outside was a perfect spring temperature, a cool breeze rustling the tree branches and the light fabric draped along Grace's arm.

Festival Hall and the four major Palaces around it were illuminated with incandescent bulbs, so that each became slashes of ivory marble against the velvet sky. The fountains erupted from the Grand Basin in sprays of mist and light. Above it, the moon was a crisp slice.

They walked past Jerusalem's walled gates and eventually turned off into the cool quiet of the Japanese Pavilion, with Earnest leading the way. They passed a bazaar with hand fans and silks for sale and a teahouse offering green tea and tea cakes, instead choosing to wander dreamily across a bridge set near a waterfall. There was a replica of a temple from Kyoto alongside two-hundred-year-old imported bonsai trees, their twisted limbs set among cool stone lanterns. Grace relished the quiet stillness that stood in such contrast to the rest of the fairgrounds. She caught the look on Lillie's face that meant she was pondering, and she pulled her back from the group.

"What are you thinking? About Oliver?"

"I think we find Penelope Forbes next. Ask her about the meeting with Harriet," Lillie said.

"Maybe she knows something about the man who threatened Harriet at the restaurant, too," Grace said.

And Grace still planned to have a talk with her dear aunt Clove.

"You're writing about all of this for that gossip rag, are you?" Earnest asked Grace, looping back toward them. He lit a cigarette, shielding it from the breeze as it sparked.

"A little ironic, that," Copper said through the side of his mouth, stopping to light his own cigarette with a sardonic grin.

"Ironic? How do you mean?" Grace asked.

"Well, the autopsy showed it was strychnine that killed Harriet, wasn't it?" Earnest said.

"Yes," Lillie said.

"And strychnine is often used as a rat poison, right?"

"Right . . ." Grace said.

"And do you know who just happens to be a former insect extermination salesman? A firsthand seller of rat poison?"

Grace stilled. "Who?" she asked.

Copper grinned, taking a deep drag of his cigarette. "The publisher of the *Fair's Fare*. Your very own Sam Whitcomb."

A deep chill raised the flesh on Grace's arm. She felt Oliver's voice come to whisper in her ear: *Keep an eye out for someone close to the investigation*, she thought.

Sam Whitcomb had been there that night. Supposedly he had been filming. But what if he hadn't? What if he'd handed the camera off for a brief moment?

She was beginning to hate being suspicious of everyone—of "seeing a devil behind every bush," as her mother used to say. People were mostly good, weren't they? Wasn't that what this fair showed?

They wandered deeper into the gardens. The paper lanterns were dim, and the evening was beautiful. The air seemed fresher here, somehow, and in the distance, someone let out a scream as the roller coaster rumbled down its tracks.

A koi fish flipped in the pond, sending out expanding ripples.

Grace jumped a little, then chastised herself for being so jittery. These thoughts weren't helpful. She told herself to ignore them when she saw something move in the shadows just ahead.

That was, until Frannie let out a sharp yelp. Her instinctive sound of fear instantly turned Grace's blood to ice.

"Don't move," a voice threatened.

The first thing Grace saw was the knife, gleaming in the moonlight.

And then a man emerged from the shadows.

He wore a mask, but it didn't hide the fact that his eyes were a piercing green. He was tall and well-built, and dressed completely in black.

Frannie covered her mouth to muffle a scream.

Earnest was quick as lightning. He stepped in front of Lillie and Grace. Copper made a protective move toward Frannie, to shield her, but the masked man held out his knife in a warning to stop him.

Copper put his hands up in a show of surrender.

"Your jewels," the man ordered. He pointed to Frannie. "Take them off and hand them to me. Now."

Trembling, Frannie tried to comply, but her hands were shaking too much to unclasp the jewels from around her neck. Grace looked wildly to the teahouse, illuminated and quiet in the distance. There was faint music playing in the air, but the fairgrounds suddenly seemed all too far away. She felt in the dark for Lillie's hand and Lillie squeezed back frantically.

Frannie finally managed to untangle the jewels from her neck and tossed them to the burglar.

"Now yours," he said, swiveling to point the knife toward Lillie.

Lillie's face was white as bone.

"Listen—" Earnest said, stepping forward.

"Shut up," the thief snapped. Grace tried not to make eye contact with him, but when he turned, she stole a brazen look to profile him.

She waited for him to approach her next, to demand that she give him any jewels she was wearing. Of course, she didn't have anything valuable on, but he couldn't know that.

When he whirled around toward Grace, she was ready. But Copper got in the way. He attempted to take the man's knife, but the man was too quick. "What are you doing?" the thief barked. Copper winced and drew back his slashed hand. It was bleeding.

The thief turned and approached Grace, holding out his knife with Copper's blood still on it.

He was close enough that she could smell his sweat and her own.

She kept her eyes on the knife, swallowing a sound of fright when he brought it near her face.

But instead of cutting her, he lowered his mouth to her ear.

"*Stop looking*," he hissed.

The air around her stilled, so that she almost imagined she could see the dust swirling in the night air, the spring petals falling slowly around her like confetti. And that was the moment when she realized that this was not just a random robbery.

The masked man stuffed the jewels into his bag and as he drew his hand away from her face, she noticed that he had a ring on his finger.

She recognized it.

It was a signet ring, set with onyx.

This was the same man who had threatened Harriet about money at the restaurant.

He disappeared into the night just as a fresh group of revelers turned the corner.

There was a beat of stunned silence.

Then Frannie collapsed on the ground in sobs, her gown spilling around her as she clasped where the jewels used to be around her neck.

"Give me your tie," Lillie ordered Earnest.

He ripped it off without hesitation and she wrapped it around Copper's hand to staunch the flowing blood.

Earnest tried to chase after the thief, but by the time he reached the gardens' exit, the man was gone.

❧

Later that night, Grace pulled the heaviest furniture she could drag in front of the studio's door. She lit candles and kept the lights blazing and stayed up all night writing.

She composed a draft by hand first, then typed up a second, cleaner draft on the typewriter. Even though they had spoken to the police about the robbery and the officers had promised to look into it, she couldn't stop shaking.

She finally fell asleep at dawn and woke several hours later to sunlight streaming in through the slats of the windows.

She washed, dressed, and resolutely marched to Sam Whitcomb's office with the freshly typed pages in her hands.

The clock on the wall said it was eleven o'clock in the morning.

"I was threatened as a result of looking into this. Twice," she said, thrusting the new article toward him.

Sam Whitcomb looked surprised. He took the article from her and moved his glasses from his forehead to his nose.

"Why threaten me if the right person is in jail?" she asked.

"That's a very good question," he said slowly, sitting down to read the article at his desk.

"There is more to this story," Grace insisted. He nodded, making fewer marks with his red pen this time.

Then he stood and paid her in cash for the article.

"It will run tomorrow," he said.

"Not to be rude," she said, counting the money, "but is this it? I'm risking my life for this."

"You can take your article elsewhere, if you like," he said, arching an eyebrow. But they both knew he was calling her bluff. The *Fair's Fare* was her best chance to get this information out and start to change public opinion.

She glared at him, undeterred.

"Fine," he said, sighing. "I can't offer you more money. I have to turn a profit, you know. But as a favor, I'll show you something else that just came in."

He hesitated, and her hackles instantly rose when his smarmy nature turned to something almost apologetic. What did he know that she didn't? Something that made him feel sorry for her?

"There's a lot of attention on this case," he said. "It's sensational. A beautiful young actress murdered at the beginning of the World's Fair. The powers that be need to show they're in control. That this was some domestic issue gone wrong, not a serial killer stalking the fair. For once, this goes much higher even than a wealthy family can pay off. You can't imagine the amount of money invested in this exposition.

If it flops, if people are scared of a murderer on the loose and public opinion turns against the fair, the entire city could collapse."

She suddenly felt ill.

He flipped over the typecast for tomorrow's news.

TRIAL DATE FOR ACCUSED
MURDERER SET

Oliver. It was Oliver whose trial date had been scheduled roughly a month from now.

Her eyes fell to the line beneath it, and she felt the bile rise in her throat.

PROSECUTION TO SEEK
EXECUTION BY HANGING

CHAPTER TWENTY

MAY 11, 1904
Eight Days After the Murder

Grace was so tired.

She trudged out of Sam Whitcomb's office, away from the fairgrounds and through the quiet, tree-lined streets to the Carter mansion.

She felt the breeze on her face.

How could she go up against an entire society that had already determined Oliver would take the blame? A society that had never given her a second look in the first place?

Had she done the wrong thing by writing the articles?

No. The only way Oliver had a shot was to place a seed of doubt into the minds of the public, rather than let him hang before there was even a fair trial.

She turned her head toward the fairgrounds, its silhouette of palaces, Tyrolean Alps, and roller coasters stark outlines against the sky. It was a slice to the gut to remember the way that she and Lillie had watched the grounds steadily rise, their hopes and dreams and fantasies building along with it. They had never been able to even imagine that the fair would bring such horror within its gates.

She turned down Westmoreland Place and knocked on the Carters' massive front door.

"I need to speak with my aunt," she told Waters when he answered. "It's urgent."

He brought her into the sitting room. She looked at the heavy green curtains, the imperial urns, the ticking brass clock on the mantel. Remembering the way she and Oliver had played in the massive fireplace when it was swept clean each spring.

She was startled when Aunt Clove appeared in the room behind her.

"For someone who was explicitly uninvited to this house, you certainly make frequent appearances," Aunt Clove said.

She was wearing a tea gown trimmed in ribbons and black satin. There was a slight scent of laudanum. Her face looked haggard.

"They're seeking the *death penalty* for Oliver," Grace said. She choked on the words.

Aunt Clove didn't flinch. She was a mask.

She played with the heavy rings on her fingers, leveling Grace with an even stare.

Grace stared back.

"You may not believe me, but I'm doing whatever I can to help him," Grace said. "Do *you* want to help him?"

The look Aunt Clove gave her in return could wither fruit on the vine. "Don't act simple," she said. "It doesn't suit you."

Grace took a step toward her.

"You hired someone to follow him."

"I hired someone to follow that *actress*."

"And you must understand how that looks now, given everything that's happened. Perhaps you had more motive than anyone to make sure Harriet was gone."

Aunt Clove gestured toward the fringed sofa.

"Sit," she said curtly.

There was no offer for tea to be called. They both knew what this was. Not a social call, but hostilities edging closer to a declaration of war.

"I would do anything for my children," Aunt Clove said with precise enunciation. "Anything at all. Except for that."

Grace sat down on the sofa. "Then why were you having Harriet followed, if not to kill her?"

"I wanted to observe them," Clove said. She slid into the fringed armchair like it was a throne. "I wanted to know the truth, when everyone around me was intent on deceiving me. What a way to repay me after everything I've done. Just look where all that deception has led us now."

"And what was your plan once you discovered the truth about Harriet and Oliver? He wanted to marry her."

Clove sniffed bitterly. "I would have done the sensible thing and paid her off to leave him. Not *killed* her. There's a difference between being cunning and being a monster, though I know you love to paint me as such in the stories you tell yourself."

Grace braced herself against the condescension. She took a deep breath. They had danced around this confrontation for as long as she could remember, and it felt good to finally be having it. She leaned forward.

"Why have you always hated us so?" she asked. "My mother? Me and Walt? Harriet? What threat have we ever posed to you?"

"You pose a threat because you are ideas. Allowing *you* in our lives was a doorway, opening paths I never wanted my children to walk down. My children decided that they loved you, and that was the first seed. Oliver should have felt more misgivings in that initial tug of misplaced interest in Harriet. He should have known that she was not his future and turned away. But you, Grace, had already opened the door to loving someone beneath their station. Walt had already begun walking that path, and it was much harder to turn back.

"So yes. I regret not fighting my husband harder when you were children. That was an enormous mistake. I had to correct it."

"And now we're adults," Grace said coldly. "These are no longer your choices to make."

Aunt Clove waved off the sentiment. "Spoken like such a child."

"Have you ever paused to consider why your own children hide things from you, Aunt Clove?" Grace asked sharply. "Do you hope to have any relationship with them at all?"

"Love would not hesitate to take down any obstacle that stands in her children's way. Especially when they don't see the harm it will cause them. *Your* mother, on the other hand, was selfish and shortsighted. She thought only of her own happiness. I make my choices by thinking generations ahead." Her voice dropped to a lower register. "Even if they cost me."

"You forfeit your own choices to take someone else's," Grace said, trembling with fury that this insufferable woman dared to call her mother selfish. She stood to go. "I don't think that's as honorable as you think it is."

Aunt Clove rose to match her. "Is it not love to set someone up for their best possible chance at life?" she challenged, seething. "Even at great cost to yourself? When you have children one day, you'll remember me. You'll remember this conversation. And then try to tell me differently."

She exited the room with great, self-righteous dignity, and glided up the stairs.

There would be no convincing Aunt Clove that she was wrong. And yet, Grace knew at that moment that Harriet's death was not ordained by Aunt Clove. Aunt Clove gained nothing from this. She would never have had a murder orchestrated so publicly, especially when it could so easily point to Oliver, dig up sordid information, and embarrass the family name. The stakes were entirely too high for Oliver and for the Carter family. They got caught in the crosshairs of whatever else had happened here.

As Aunt Clove climbed the stairs, wrapping her arms around her rib cage like she was protecting a gaping wound, Grace quietly brought out her notebook and crossed her aunt's name off the list.

❧

Grace felt the way the time was slipping away, the shadows of an impending night lengthening for them all, even though the floral clock showed that it was barely after noon. She sat with Lillie, Earnest, and Theo for lunch in the Flight Cage restaurant across from the caged aviary in Forest Park. It was a huge structure built by the Smithsonian Institute with a dome fifty feet high. Inside, swans and herons swam in ponds, and they glimpsed peacocks between ferns as they sipped iced tea and ate Waldorf salad.

"Have we all mostly recovered from the terrible shock of last night?" Lillie asked them.

"Hardly," Earnest said.

"What happened last night?" Theo asked quizzically.

"We were jumped," Earnest said. "Mugged."

Theodore grew quite still.

"Are you joking?" he asked, turning abruptly toward Grace. As if expecting to see a mocking smile on her face.

She shook her head.

"Frannie and Lillie had their necklaces stolen. Copper was slashed with a knife. And I was threatened to stop looking into Harriet's murder."

Theo was silent, his eyes darkening. His fist curled on the table.

"Someone threatened you?" he asked Grace.

She shook her head irritably. "He should know it had the opposite intended effect. Fear only fuels my stubbornness."

"Did you go to the police?"

"Of course," Lillie said. "They took down a report, but they don't expect to recover the jewels."

"They also seemed eager to keep the incident quiet," Earnest said. "It can't look good for the fair."

That's exactly what Sam Whitcomb said, Grace thought.

"This is crazy. Perhaps it's time to stop investigating this," Theodore said.

Grace frowned at him. "Why would you say that?" she asked.

"Grace—" Theodore said, exchanging a look with Lillie.

"No," she said stubbornly. "I'm going to push even harder now. What happened with Penelope?"

Theo sighed. He had hardly touched his salad. He pushed his hair back from his forehead and said, "I tried to find her all morning, but she's gone."

"Gone?" Lillie asked.

"She left after the funeral. She lives in Chicago."

"Can we find a telephone number for her?" Grace asked. "An address?"

She sensed a strange feeling from Theo. The shadows swept across his face, caressing them. He seemed distracted.

"Yes," he said. "I'll keep looking into it."

"They probably aren't very happy that you're stirring things up right before the big dinner with the president," Earnest said. "You told your father you'd go, didn't you, Theo?"

Grace tilted her head. She'd read about it as she'd scoured the papers—one of the biggest events of the fair, happening the day after tomorrow—but she hadn't realized they were all going. Once again, she felt the pinch of time.

She was running out of threads to chase. And when that happened—what would she do?

Oliver would be lost. Thrown in jail to rot, or worse. And there would no longer be any good reason for her to stay.

"I haven't felt much in the mood for fancy dinners as of late," Lillie said grimly.

"That's exactly why you must go," Earnest insisted.

Theo glanced over his shoulder more than once.

"I have to go," he said.

"Where are you off to this afternoon?" Lillie asked.

"Meeting a friend of the family," he said.

But he didn't meet her eyes.

He wiped his mouth with his napkin and stood. Grace watched as he subtly paid for their lunch on the way out.

"Lillie," Grace said. "Is there any way Oliver's lawyer can get us a complete list of the guests who were present at the Glass Ball on the night of Harriet's death?"

Lillie nodded. "I'm sure he must have one. I'll see if he would be willing to make a copy for us. But—" She hesitated. Grace knew what she was going to say before she even opened her mouth.

"I'm not stopping. We have to keep trying," Grace said. "For Oliver."

"We will. You've been stubborn and strong-willed for as long as I've known you, and I love you for it. But, Grace—I can't lose you in the process."

"Let's go to the baby incubators on the Pike," Earnest gently interrupted. "Figured Lillie might like to see something medical."

"Yes," Lillie said, standing. "I would."

They made their way toward the Pike, where they found the baby incubator exhibit in a large, flag-topped building with two U-shaped columned floors. It was situated next to Cairo and cost twenty-five cents to enter. They stepped inside a crowded, narrow room with white-capped nurses tending to premature babies in twenty-four metal boxes with glass windows.

Grace peered inside the first incubator, at the baby's small, rosebud mouth. It was twisting, writhing its little legs. Flies were buzzing around the incubators, some even caught inside of them.

"Step right up and see how this little mite, Jack, weighs less than three pounds!" a male announcer exclaimed. "The baby incubator is truly the highest attainment of human achievement. These weaklings hardly stood a chance without this intervention."

Some of the babies were listless, their cheeks flushed. They stared out at Grace with glassy eyes.

Lillie began fanning herself.

"It's too hot in here," Lillie said, her voice rising in panic. She waved down one of the nurses. "Excuse me, but this child looks like it needs help."

"I can assure you that Mr. Bayliss has taken care of everything," the nurse said curtly.

"Is he even a doctor?" Lillie shot back.

Grace felt that familiar panicked feeling of not being good in a medical situation, and she began to walk backward, tripping on someone as she made her way out of the exhibit.

She passed the shop where she could buy a soap baby souvenir, and then through the exhibit's themed café. She didn't start breathing normally again until she was out in the sunshine. She found a bench beneath an awning toward the end of the Pike, where they held reenactments of the Great Galveston Flood of 1900. She pulled out her small notebook and revisited her original suspect list.

This—this she could do.

Her breathing steadily slowed. She stared at the names on the page.

There was the robber who had first discussed money with Harriet and then threatened Grace to stop looking into the case. He was the prime suspect in her mind. Had Harriet borrowed money from him to help save her theater? Had he been there at the Ball that night? Grace didn't remember seeing him, but that didn't mean he wasn't there.

And what about Harriet's sister Penelope? Why had Harriet met with her in the Tunnels?

There were the Gatewoods, the betrayed family with a possible revenge motive against Oliver himself, but Grace no longer thought of them as prime suspects.

She could almost definitively say it wasn't Aunt Clove, or Vera Lackey, the woman who had been following them.

The publisher Sam Whitcomb had been there at the party that night, but he had supposedly been filming, hadn't he?

Earnest Allred was definitively on camera, holding the drink with his bandaged hands, not putting poison in it.

Who else had been there that night?

Lillie had been at Grace's side, arguing with her in the ladies' room.

And then there were Frannie and Copper. What about Frannie? Why had she lied about the message that had been left for Earnest and Grace? Was she merely being a thorn in Grace's side or was it something more sinister than that?

There was something Grace was missing.

Then there were any of the other guests—fifty, a hundred more—who had been present that night, who would show up on the list Lillie would get from the lawyer. And of course . . . Theodore.

She instantly began to banish the thought as ridiculous, but a small piece of it caught like a tangled ribbon in a branch. She let her mind wander toward it. Theodore Parker. Present at all these events that were burned in her mind. The Winter Ball, where he disparaged her so cruelly, only to turn up later and begin to change his tune just as everything began to disintegrate around them.

She paused, feeling a growing numbness. He was the only person who was there all three times. The only other person who knew the truth about Harriet and Earnest. He had been present for Earnest's explosion, when he fell out of the sky. Then Theodore had led them to the restaurant, when the thief had found and threatened Harriet. He had been there at the Ball on the night when she was killed.

But he was conveniently away when the thief found them in the Japanese gardens to rob and pressure them.

Grace shook her head. This was silly. She had forgiven Theodore for that horrible night back in Chicago—she hadn't realized it until that moment, but she had. At least almost all of her had.

He seemed so different now from the dreadful person she had first met. Still prickly, yes, but also strangely thoughtful, to the point of deeply caring. Had he changed in such a short time? Which Theodore Parker was the real one?

This was ridiculous. He had tried to help her every step of the way, hadn't he?

Look out for someone who is involved in the investigation, Oliver had warned.

She couldn't believe she was actually suspecting that Theodore had played a hand in Harriet's murder.

She brushed the thought away. She would not think about it any longer.

She was about to walk on when Earnest suddenly came out of the baby incubator exhibit. But this time, he was without Lillie.

He looked furtively over his shoulder.

"Grace," he said in a low voice. "Can we talk?"

❧

Grace cringed a little. She quickly shut her notebook, where his name had recently been crossed off the pages. Things were still slightly awkward between them, and it reminded her again how stupid she was to be suspicious of Theodore. After all, look where that had gotten her with Earnest. But he seemed to have softened toward her, as if he had forgiven her accusations. Perhaps after the scare they had experienced last night, all could be put behind them.

She nodded and smiled.

"Of course," she said.

He gestured toward the notebook that she had set on the bench beside her.

"I saw the article you wrote. And it got me thinking."

She moved so that he could take the seat next to her. "All of these things that have been happening. First, the plane I'm in explodes. The police say they think it was just an engineering failure, sure. But then Harriet dies. And then we get mugged and threatened. And the thing is, Grace, I just keep thinking about how I'm the one who handed Oliver the glass. But someone put the poison in the drink when it was with me.

"What if they thought *I* was the one who was going to drink it?"

Grace turned toward him in surprise.

"You think that poison was meant for you?" she asked, aghast.

"Perhaps someone was trying to kill me when the plane exploded. And then"—his eyes grew wide—"after the balloon sabotage didn't work, maybe they tried a second time. Maybe *I* was the real target all along."

It was an angle she hadn't thought of before. And yet she should have. It made so many of the pieces fit together. What if she had been looking at it the wrong way round this entire time? What if Harriet was never supposed to be the one dead?

What if the real target had been Earnest?

"But who would want to kill *you*?" she asked.

She stood as Lillie came out of the exhibit, and Earnest shot Grace a look that he wanted to stop talking.

"That was atrocious," Lillie said furiously, marching toward them. "They clearly have no business taking care of those babies. It's inhumane."

"I'm sorry, but I need to go meet Walt," Grace said, standing. "I told him I'd be at the restaurant to see if he had any updates."

"All right," Lillie said hesitantly. She turned to Earnest.

"Shall we go to the Philippine Village?" he said. "It's supposed to be huge. It would take us all day to see, at least. You should come meet us afterward, Grace."

"Sure," Grace said, nodding. "Hopefully with good news."

She turned the corner, still dazed by what Earnest had said, and almost ran into a small electric autobus, packed with riders.

"Watch it!" the driver barked.

"Sorry," she said. She hurried on into the Pike, chastising herself for letting her imagination get away from her.

That was when she saw a familiar silhouette.

She stopped short.

It was Theodore Parker.

Theodore Parker, who had told her less than an hour ago that he had to leave to meet with a family friend.

But instead, he was at that very moment emerging from the dark shadows of the Tunnels.

❧

Grace hid behind a column, her heart hammering.

What was happening?

Why would Theodore lie to her?

She turned slowly.

Should she confront him?

By the time she peered out from the column, he was gone.

She adjusted her hat, taking a few deep breaths, and went to wait for Walt.

Surely there was some way to explain all of this, she thought.

But the truth was sinking through her as she waited and he didn't come. She was too hot. The crowd around her was pushing, the music from the marching bands too loud.

Theodore Parker had gone into the Tunnels.

Was it possible that *he* was the person Harriet had been meeting that morning?

She sat on a bench just outside the restaurant, feeling vaguely nauseous. She left briefly to get some water, then came back and resumed watching. But it was soon apparent that Walt wasn't coming.

After forty minutes, she gave up and began walking toward the Philippine Village.

She had just crossed over Arrowhead Lake into the village's walled city when she heard a familiar voice. It was beastly hot and thick with humidity, and the water shimmered. Divers were plunging into the lake looking for pearls. Junks dotted the water, and the grounds were thick with banana trees.

"Grace!"

She turned.

"Grace," Lillie said, hurrying toward her. Her face looked pained. "It's Walt."

She grabbed Grace's hand and together they pushed through the masses heading to see the village's Model School, the sea-shelled windows of the Women's Building, the Agriculture Building made from bamboo and nipa.

Walt was sitting amid the crowds on the street in front of the Samal Moros's stilt houses. He was like a stone set in a river, making the people part around him. Earnest was beside him, looking distinctly uncomfortable.

Earnest leapt to his feet as soon as he saw them.

Grace could tell before she knelt beside him that Walt was drugged out of his mind, drunk, and incomprehensible.

A policeman was eyeing them on his patrol of the grounds. He slowed his walk, keeping them in his sights.

"It's a zoo," Walt said, gesturing toward the Philippine Village exhibit. "Can't you see? They put them out here for display just like the animals. They've *ranked* them, for God's sake. It's wrong."

Grace said, "Please come with me."

He pulled his arm away.

"Dammit, Grace. Stop trying to save me," he slurred. "This is my choice."

We're adults now, she had told Aunt Clove that morning. *These are no longer your choices to make.*

She heard Aunt Clove's voice echoing in her head. *Love would not hesitate to take down any obstacle that stands in her children's way. Especially when they don't see the harm it will cause them.*

"You're destroying yourself," she said, a heavy lump rising in her throat. "And you're destroying me, too. I want a choice in that."

She knew she wasn't physically strong enough to force him to do anything. She felt so helpless. She wanted to scream.

Lillie and Earnest stepped away to give her some semblance of privacy, even though this meltdown was happening amid the most crowded fair in the history of the country.

Is this rock bottom? she wondered desperately. *Will he even remember we had this conversation?*

She changed tack and turned her voice to soothing. She gently touched his arm. "Walt," she said. "Did you find anything for Oliver?"

"I was supposed to find something for Oliver?" he asked. His eyes were dull.

Her heart sank. She felt something crumble within her.

"I can help you," she said fiercely. "*Please.* Let me help you."

She cried then, the tears bursting forth from somewhere long-buried. They were streaming down her face, mixing with snot. People were staring. St. Louisans in long skirts and oversized hats. Bagobos wearing beads and knee pants and carrying bolos. Visayans in puffed white blouses with sleeves. Bontocs in cloth sashes and bead necklaces. She was making a scene in front of them all. She didn't care.

Walt looked at her with a cruel disdain brought out by the drugs, the brother she once knew now so far away she couldn't reach him anymore. He shoved her aside, staggering to his feet, and bent to snarl in her ear, "No."

CHAPTER TWENTY-ONE

THAT NIGHT, Grace dreamed she was going to die.

She was next to Harriet in the fair's roller coaster, but their harness was broken. It crumpled away like tinfoil and as the coaster fell, there was nothing to hold her in. She felt her stomach drop as her body jolted up into the air like a limp rag doll. She tried to reach out for Harriet, but she couldn't.

Harriet was screaming, then laughing.

And then Harriet turned into her sister Penelope.

"I met with her in the Tunnels," Penelope said.

"Why?" Grace asked. Penelope was opening her mouth to answer, but it was too late.

Grace braced herself to hit the ground.

Instead she gasped and sat up in the small bed, sweating.

She reached out to the nightstand for her glass of water. Gulped it down to the dregs.

Her eyes focused and she forced herself to reorient to the small room. The desk and typewriter in the corner. Her clothes, where she had left them on the chair last night. The fireplace, and the smell of paints that always greeted her when she first opened the door.

She could feel how swollen her eyes were from crying herself to sleep.

She swallowed, listening to the sound of her heartbeat as it steadily began to slow.

Harriet was dead.

Oliver was imprisoned.

The Walt she knew was gone.

But she was alive, here. In this room.

And that's when she heard it.

There was movement just on the other side of the door. A slight scratching sound.

Or was it?

She listened intently.

It sounded as though someone were trying to pick the lock.

She hurriedly pulled on a dressing robe. Then she crept to the door, her heart rocketing.

She heard muttering just beyond it.

Something told her not to cry out. She grabbed a heavy candlestick from the fireplace mantel and held it aloft, ready to strike.

The doorknob slowly turned.

She covered her hand with her mouth in fear.

But as the door tried to push open, the dead-bolt lock held fast. It caught the door with a catch.

The knob stopped turning.

Grace adjusted her grip on the candlestick, her hands sweating.

She stayed there like that, breathing heavily, straining her ears above the sound of her own heartbeat, until the footsteps finally turned and walk away.

She leaned her back against the door. Then she slid down it, dropping the candlestick with a thud, and cried muffled sobs into her hands.

❧

In the morning Grace cleared off the desk and sat down to write her mother a postcard. *Doing well!* she wrote. It wasn't entirely the truth, but it sounded a bit more optimistic than *Still alive!* So she scribbled,

"Keeping busy with visits to the Colonnade of States and trying hundreds of different types of food. You'd be impressed by the pyrheliophor covered in thousands of mirrors—and perhaps even more so by Missouri's elaborate temple display made entirely from corn. Give Papa my love. Be home soon."

She slipped it in the postbox and returned just as Theodore came to her door.

"Brought you something you were looking for," he said. He held out an envelope. "The complete guest list from the night of Harriet's death."

"Thank you," she said, taking it from him cautiously. "Did you . . . come here last night?"

"What?" he said. "No." She watched the realization as his face darkened. "Why? Did someone visit you?" he asked.

"Never mind," she said.

"All right . . ." he said, studying her. "That's the guest list from the night of the party. Lillie got it from Oliver's lawyer, but she was busy with something this morning."

"Thanks for bringing it by," she said. "Have you seen it yet?"

"No."

They walked a little and took a seat on a bench beneath a tree that was dropping pink petals like fat, lush tears. She opened the envelope and unfolded the list so they could look at it together.

There were a hundred names on it. Her suspect list just kept growing.

She snuck a glance at Theo, who was examining the list beside her. She could smell the mint of his breath. The cinnamon spice of his skin.

"You know, it's interesting," she said. "But Earnest is wondering whether he might have been the real target."

She shifted to put a little more space between them. Could Theodore be the murderer? Surely not. Surely there was some good explanation for what he had been doing yesterday. Sneaking away to a nefarious place and lying about it.

"You're kidding." He seemed genuinely surprised. "Does someone have it out for him?"

"I'm not sure. We'll have to ask if anyone comes to mind." She paused. "How was meeting with a friend of the family yesterday?" she asked carefully.

"Tedious," he said. His face remained blank.

She continued to scan the list and decided to push her luck. "Where did you go?" she asked.

But he merely smiled at her. "I got an address for Penelope up in Chicago," he said. "A friend of a friend tracked it down."

"That's good," she said. She smiled weakly back. "A telephone number would be even better. I'd love to talk with her in real time."

"I'll see what I can do. In the meantime, did you know that President Roosevelt is coming to town? It's my last contractual event that my father expects me to attend at the fair. It's supposed to be at least two hours of a banquet followed by dancing."

"Sounds like your own personal hell," Grace said. He had changed the subject first about his outing yesterday and then about Penelope, and she hadn't neglected to notice.

"And no one appreciates my suffering more than you," Theo said. He swallowed, his throat bobbing. "Would you care to go with me?"

"You do make a convincing argument," she said.

"So is that a yes?" he asked.

But she merely smiled, arched her eyebrow, and stood.

Lord knows he was making her wonder about all kinds of things. At least he could wonder a bit now, too.

She walked back to the studio and locked the door behind her, sneaking one last look over her shoulder at him.

Because all his arguments were so smooth and convincing, and that meant she was starting to suspect him all the more.

❧

Grace pored over the list in the studio, making notes until hunger began to gnaw at her.

They still didn't know who Harriet had met with at the restaurant that night. That, along with the multiple threats for her to stop looking into that part of the case, still made her think that it was Harriet who was being targeted, not Earnest.

But none of the names from the list jumped out at her. Lillie and Oliver would know more about them than she would.

She could ignore her hunger no longer. She locked the door behind her and walked to the diner she had eaten at with Theo a few blocks away from the studio. She ordered the same thing, and then her gaze fell on an abandoned newspaper someone had left on the diner's counter.

She stood and took it for herself, opening it across the table to read as she ate.

When she turned the fold, she gasped.

MAN FOUND DEAD IN THE MISSISSIPPI, the paper said.

Sylvestor Watson, age 30 years, was found floating in the Mississippi River early this morning. The victim was found with blunt force trauma to the head. The cause of death was drowning.

It is unclear whether he sustained the injury from a fall or if it was the result of foul play.

Beneath the article there was an image of his face. She recognized him immediately.

Her stomach turned. She delicately sat her spoon down on the table.

It was the man who had robbed them.

She looked for a waiter so she could ask for the bill. There were two people she wanted to talk to about this development, as soon as possible.

The first was her cousin Oliver, and the second was the newspaper man Sam Whitcomb.

She folded her napkin.

But the waiter had disappeared.

As well as almost every other customer in the place.

She glanced around. There had been several people in the diner when she arrived, but they were all gone now. It was eerily quiet.

And then the bell rang as the front door opened.

She looked inside her purse for cash to leave on the table.

A man slowly began to approach her.

She wasn't paying much attention until he stopped at her table.

"Miss Covington?" the man asked.

She looked at him, suddenly wary. Her senses were on alert.

He was charismatic in a way that intimated great power. He seemed out of place in the diner.

"Yes?" she asked.

He gestured to the diner table.

"May I have a word?" he asked.

But his tone of voice, and the way he was physically blocking her from leaving, meant it wasn't really a question.

She glanced around her.

The diner was empty.

There had been a cook behind the counter. He disappeared into the kitchen. The host had stepped outside for a cigarette.

"How do you know my name?" she asked.

"Word gets around when you're a famous columnist," he said. But his face was flat as he slid into the seat opposite her.

"And you are?" she asked.

"Someone who would prefer to stay off the record."

She nodded. Her mouth had become bone dry.

"Do you have information for me, then?" she asked. She gripped her napkin under the table.

"Not information, not exactly. But I do have an offer for you."

"An offer?" she asked.

"A deal to propose. To put an end to you publishing these salacious rumors."

"They're not rumors," she said, frowning. "Everything I've written is the truth."

"You're stoking fear, and therefore tainting the experience of thousands of people. Maybe even millions. And that has its consequences."

"Financial consequences, you mean," she said. "For the fair."

"And financial incentives to cooperate," he said. "For you."

He pushed an envelope across the table at her.

A thick-looking envelope.

She eyed it.

"Do you know who killed Harriet Forbes?" she asked in a low voice.

"No, and I don't really care. What I care about is making sure this goes away. That's what I do. I make the bad publicity go away."

She saw the money, stuffed into the envelope. Just within reach.

It appeared to be enough that she could afford to live in St. Louis for years. Maybe even at the level that Lillie did.

It was enough that she could get Walt into the best possible treatment center.

She could pay off her father's restaurant.

But she would have to turn her back on Oliver and therefore Lillie. And if she did that, she would never forgive herself.

"I'm afraid I can't accept that," she said.

The man seemed surprised. His face of pleasantries disappeared.

"It's a highly generous offer already. This isn't a negotiation."

"No, it isn't," she agreed.

"I see you're determined to be unreasonable."

"I'm quite reasonable," she said calmly. "My integrity just isn't for sale."

The man glowered. "Then I regret to inform you that you're hereby barred from entering the fairgrounds. If you're seen there, you will be promptly removed."

"For what?"

"For public disruption."

She reached out and delicately touched the envelope. Like a caress. As though she were reconsidering.

He paused for a moment. His eyes watching her very carefully.

She picked up the envelope and handed it to him.

"You wouldn't want to forget this," she said.

He snatched it from her hand, his mouth tightening into a slim line, and stalked with as much dignity as he could muster out of the diner.

She gathered herself. Then she knocked angrily on the window to draw the attention of the host.

"Check, please," she yelled.

❧

Oliver's head was bowed over the wooden table when she came into the small jail room.

The guard sat in the corner.

She took the seat across from her cousin.

"Oliver," she said.

He was staring at a knot in the wood.

He looked five years older than the last time she'd seen him.

"Grace," he said, but he didn't look up to meet her eyes.

"You look defeated," she said. "Don't you dare give up on me now."

"Give up on *you*?" he said, with the faintest hint of spark. "Never."

She slapped the newspaper down on the table and sent it across to him.

"Have you seen this?"

"I haven't received my daily newspaper delivery, no. Nor my room service tray this morning, either. I'll have to speak to the manager."

"But your daily attitude quotient has been quite filled, I see," she said, turning the newspaper to the second page. It revived her a little, to see that the ember of him hadn't completely gone out.

She pointed to the headline:

BODY DISCOVERED IN THE MISSISSIPPI

"Great. Another death. Are they going to try to pin this one on me, too?"

"Considering that it happened just last night, I doubt it."

"What does this have to do with me?" he asked.

"The deceased is the man who threatened Harriet at the restaurant the night you went to the hospital with Earnest." She tapped the accompanying image. "Do you recognize him?"

"No," Oliver said. His brow crumpled. "I've never seen him before. I have no idea what he wanted with Harriet."

She snuck a look at the guard, who was watching them closely.

"Not that I want to rejoice in the death of a human being, but"—she lowered her voice—"this could be good news for you. It could be over now, right?" she said hopefully. "Maybe they'll find some evidence that connects him to Harriet's murder."

Oliver shook his head. He suddenly seemed far away again. "Sometimes my mind gets to me in here. I find myself wondering, did she ever even love me? Was I nothing but a mark to her?"

"She loved you," Grace said. "I saw her diary. And there is not a doubt in my mind, she really did love you."

She reached out for his hand, ignoring the guard, and squeezed it fiercely. And at her touch, Oliver—her carefree, charismatic cousin—broke down and cried.

She sat with him, holding his hand, until his sobs were spent. Neither of them put on a falsely brave face or offered platitudes. They sat with the heaviness together, and that seemed to lessen its power.

She wasn't certain how much time had passed when the air shifted, and she knew it was safe to speak again.

"I have to go. But there's another question for you to consider," Grace said. "I need you to be very honest with me. What do you think of Theodore Parker?"

Oliver opened his palms in surrender. "I admittedly haven't known him for that long, but I've always liked him. Since that first night when he stepped in to help you with that aggressor. He's guarded and a bit standoffish, but he has a lot of integrity."

But you didn't see the other sides of him, Grace thought. *The sides that disparaged me so harshly. That lied and went into the Tunnels.*

The coin that kept turning to show different faces.

How many sides did Theodore Parker have?

She was still pondering that when she said goodbye to Oliver and stepped out into the evening air.

She wanted to talk to Sam Whitcomb at the publishing office, but it was now too late in the day. She was curious what he thought. If he had heard any outside gossip about the dead man. If his own sources thought it was an accident or murder.

Night was falling quickly, and she increased her pace as she walked the streets. The streetlamps were turning on and she was careful to stay away from the dark maws of the alleys.

Someone catcalled her and she bristled. Perhaps she should have taken a cab.

She glanced over her shoulder.

She really shouldn't be alone. She had felt momentary relief when the man who had robbed them and intimidated Harriet was found dead. But that wasn't her only threat. What if that man from the diner was still watching her?

And if the thief himself had been murdered, then . . . who had done that?

She approached the studio and as she brought out the key, she saw that something about the door was wrong.

A piece of the mat was caught at the bottom. She had not left it that way. She would have seen it when she locked the door from the outside.

Someone had opened this door since she had last been there.

Her heart thudded.

She kept her key in her fingers to use as a weapon and pounded with her fist.

"Who's there?" she called.

She heard movement. There was someone inside.

The door opened, and the light shining from the studio was so bright it took Grace's eyes a second to focus.

A woman stepped forward.

"Grace?" she asked.

It was Lillie.

*

Grace let out a huge sigh of relief and fell forward into her cousin's arms.

"What are you doing here?" Grace cried.

They stepped inside and Grace quickly dead bolted the door behind her.

"I had it out with my mother," Lillie said. "I couldn't stay there any longer. I thought I could be with you for a few nights."

"Of course," Grace said, taking off her hat. "But how did you get in?"

"Theo let me in."

"He isn't here, is he?" Grace asked, her pulse skipping a beat as she scanned the room.

"No," Lillie said. "Come in. Get cozy. I have some really good news."

"About Oliver?"

Lillie shook her head. But her eyes danced.

Grace washed up and changed into her nightgown as Lillie put on a teapot over the fire.

Grace climbed into bed next to her, just like they used to do when they were little.

"Your feet are hideously cold," Lillie said.

"That's because my shoes are atrocious. Did you bring your hot water bottle?"

"Please. It was the first thing I packed."

As Lillie got up and poured hot water into a ceramic water bottle for their feet, Grace told her about seeing Oliver and the interaction with the strange man at the diner.

"Grace, this is frightening. You've rattled them," Lillie said.

"I just want to shake things up so that the truth comes out." She stretched her feet, pressing against the water bottle and letting its warmth spill onto her.

"Is it wrong that I feel relieved that man is dead?" she whispered into the dark.

Lillie hesitated. "I feel it, too," she said. "Is it wrong that I want him to have been the one to kill Harriet? That would mean this nightmare could finally be over."

"Will the police search his home?"

"Oliver's lawyer says they already have."

"Wait—" Grace said, turning over to clasp Lillie's hands. "I know! They found your necklaces at the thief's place, didn't they? Is that the good news you were going to tell me?"

"No," Lillie said. "They didn't say anything about the necklaces being there."

"Oh," Grace echoed. She frowned. "What's the good news, then?"

"Well, it's a little bit of bad news followed by good news."

And suddenly, by a twitch across Lillie's lovely face, Grace knew.

"Walt," she whispered. Her heart faltered.

"First, you need to know that he was in really bad shape, Grace. Got into a fight sometime after we saw him. He's really banged up. But . . . he's agreed to try getting some help."

Grace shot up. "Where is he?"

"At a beautiful facility. The top hospital in St. Louis. There's a trial program just beginning. Dr. May knows someone who works there and was able to pull some strings."

"But . . . how did this happen? He just . . . decided?" Grace asked. She still remembered the way he had turned on her with such fury, the spittle on his lips when he had snarled at her. It had left wounds deeper than claws.

"Well. Sometimes you can run and run away from something until you run right into reality. And often reality can really hurt. Besides, there was a bit more of an incentive this time."

"What happened?" Grace asked.

"The police were going to take him and book him for disturbing the peace, but after a bit of skillful negotiation"—Lillie cleared her throat—"Walt agreed to seek treatment if the police would drop the charges."

"Skillful negotiation?" Grace knew how that worked. "So you helped strike a deal for Walt? A monetary deal?" Grace bit her lip. "That must have been considerable."

Lillie looked flummoxed and waved it off.

Grace shook her head. "But, Lillie. My family can't afford any of this."

Lillie swallowed. "It's taken care of," she said softly.

Grace felt a sob rise in her throat. She choked it down. "Is this what you and your mother fought about?" she asked.

"That and other things," Lillie said. "There were many to choose from."

Grace let out a small laugh. "Thank you, thank you, my darling." Grace hugged Lillie, the soft weight of her like a solid anchor, and Lillie hugged her back.

"I really can't take much credit, Grace."

"Can I see him?" Grace asked, wiping her eyes with the heels of her palms.

"I'm not sure. You can try. I think he's sorry for the way he treated you yesterday. He can't remember much of what happened, but he knows he hurt you. He gave me something in an envelope to give to you—I think it's an apology."

Lillie climbed from the bed and rummaged through her bag. "Oh, blast. In my rush to pack, I must have left it at home."

"Will we have to climb into your bedroom window from the tree like we used to in order to retrieve it?"

"I'd like to see you try. But I already need to return home tomorrow as it is. I didn't bring my gown for the president's dinner, so when I go home to dress, I'll find it."

"The president's dinner . . ." Grace said, trailing off. She bit her lip. Her heart lifted like sprays of dark butterflies when she thought of arriving there on Theodore's arm. And yet, she still hadn't decided whether she was going to go.

Lillie wrote down the name of the hospital where Walt was staying. "Here," she said. "You're helping my brother. And I got a small chance to help yours in return."

Grace took the slip of paper from Lillie, feeling awash with gratitude. She fell asleep holding her cousin's hand, wondering if perhaps something good might finally come out of the World's Fair, after all.

CHAPTER TWENTY-TWO

MAY 13, 1904

Ten Days After the Murder

In the morning, Grace stared up at the face of the St. Louis Sisters Hospital. It was an impressive building with white columns that stretched three stories tall and was flanked by mature oak trees.

"I don't know if they'll let you see him," Lillie had warned that morning as they parted for the day. "I wouldn't get your hopes up." But Grace had come anyway. She strode through the doors and approached the front desk, explaining that her brother had been brought in for treatment and she needed to see him.

The nurse looked him up in the files.

"He's in detoxification," she said curtly. "Visitors are not typically permitted at this time."

"Could you please ask?" Grace said.

The nurse didn't glance up. "It might be a while," she said.

"That's fine," Grace said, staring at the top of the woman's small white hat. "I'll wait."

She took a seat in the waiting room. She would wait as long as it took. And once she had seen Walt, she would find a way to call her mother and tell her what happened.

She played nervously with her handbag and glanced around the waiting room, taking in the wallpapered walls and tile floor. There were newspapers on the coffee table. A man was smoking a cigarette.

Eventually he extinguished it in a crystal ashtray and was called back to visit someone. For awhile, Grace was alone, and she sat for roughly half an hour before someone else joined her.

It was two visitors, actually. Two women who appeared to be around thirty years old and looked suspiciously like they could be twins.

They spoke to the nurse and then took a seat near Grace. One of them had a hole in her stocking that she kept touching subconsciously. Grace stole glances at them and then went to check in with the nurse again.

"The doctor is very busy today," the nurse said. "Perhaps you should come back tomorrow."

"No," Grace said firmly. "I'll wait."

When she returned to her seat, the two women were twittering on about something to do with the upholstery and then mushroom stew and she was ignoring them quite successfully until she heard the word strychnine.

Her ears pricked. She instantly looked up.

They were talking between themselves, though not particularly quietly. "Strychnine is for rat poison," one of them was saying. "Not people. And he took it *voluntarily.*"

Grace's interest piqued. "I'm sorry," she said. "I don't mean to pry. It's just—did you say something about strychnine?"

"Our idiot brother."

"Victoria!"

The one named Victoria continued. "He's a runner. Training for the Olympic marathon. They give them strychnine to run faster. I'm glad he's alive. Idiot."

"They give the athletes strychnine?" Grace asked. "Why on earth?"

"It's a cocktail of raw eggs and brandy. And strychnine."

"Don't they know that could kill them?" Grace asked.

The one not named Victoria shrugged. "The price of glory."

"Paid for by idiots," Victoria added.

Interesting. That was yet another use for strychnine that she hadn't heard of before.

So presumably, someone could get strychnine in the athletic department.

She was about to write it down in the list in her notebook when she glanced up and saw a familiar face.

"Dr. May!" she called.

She hurriedly put away her notebook and caught up with the doctor.

"I remember you," Dr. May said. "Lillie's friend."

"Her cousin. I'm Grace. I wanted to thank you so much for helping my brother Walt. It means a great deal to me."

"It was clear from our first meeting how much he means to you," Dr. May said. "How is he doing?"

Grace swallowed. "They haven't let me see him yet."

Dr. May glanced toward the front desk and sighed.

"Bertha. She's a real piece of work."

"Is there anything you could do? I just . . . need to see him."

Dr. May narrowed her eyes.

"Follow me," she said.

She led Grace through the winding, white corridors and up two flights of stairs, where she spoke with another doctor. They conversed quietly and then the other doctor walked away.

Dr. May gave Grace a brief nod.

"You can have five minutes," she said.

"Thank you," Grace breathed. "For your great kindness."

She braced herself and stepped through the door.

Walt was lying in a bed, his eyes closed.

Lillie had warned her, but Grace was still taken aback by the state of his face. Mottled and purpled, with a few stitches around his mouth.

"Do you see?" he had once said, holding her up when she was about six. "The birds made a nest in the house I built. I wanted their babies to be safe."

She stood watching him for a moment. And she could have cried.

Why did Grace carry wounds around like bruises and Walt like gashes, gashes that grew untended and infected, spreading throughout him like poison?

She had known her parents loved her and each other. And she had known that Walt loved her. Had Walt's love as her older brother been the extra cover of protection for her? Had it acted as just enough of an added buffer for her to make up the difference between them?

Or maybe they were just different people who made different choices. Either way, she wanted to help him.

He opened his eyes and saw her there.

"Grace," he said. He sat up a little straighter in the bed and a smile came to his face, slowed by the pain in his stitches. "You came."

She took a step toward him. "I wanted to see you."

"Did you get my letter?" he asked.

"I haven't read it yet."

"I'm sorry. I don't remember a lot. I think I hurt you."

She hesitated. There was no point in shielding him from his actions. Not if she wanted him to change. "You did," she said. "But I'm glad you're here. I'm glad Lillie found you and brought you in."

He shook, his thin hands tremoring, and sweat was pouring down his face. He grimaced.

“Does it hurt terribly?’ she asked.

“The withdrawal is agony,” he said. “I apologize if I throw up on you.”

“It’s worth it if it makes you better,” she said.

He was quiet. He looked out the window, his mouth twitching. “For the first time in a long time, I actually want to.”

“What happened?” she asked. “Why were you fighting?”

“I got into it with someone,” Walt said. “About money. About the drugs. It’s all blurry. I don’t remember much after I started throwing punches. Until I saw your friend Theodore.”

Grace’s heart flipped. “Theodore?” she asked.

“Oh.” Walt grimaced and let out a low curse. “You weren’t supposed to know. My memory is trashed right now. You can’t let on that I told you.”

“Wait. Theodore was the one who brought you here?” Grace asked.

“Yes. He talked to the police. Made a deal to bring me here. He said he’d take care of everything.”

“Theodore Parker? Are you sure?”

“Isn’t he the one with the birthmark on his face?”

She nodded slowly, dazed. It was Theo.

She sat down abruptly on the chair. Her face flushed. Her heart flooded with something that felt like light and song were sweeping through her.

Theodore Parker must have paid a huge sum to help her brother.

“I’m going to make this right, Grace,” Walt said. He held out his hand to her. “You don’t have to believe me until I show you,” he said. His lips were pale, his teeth almost chattering.

She laced his fingers through his as he whispered, “I don’t want to make you promises I can’t keep. But I can tell you, from the depths of me, I don’t want to be that person anymore.”

❧

Grace’s heart couldn’t stop beating furiously. She picked up her skirts, walking briskly through the streets.

Where did Theodore live?

She had to find him.

She burst into the artist’s studio.

The studio where Theodore had found her somewhere to live.

Paid for many of her meals.

Held her while she cried about Walt.

Bought her a typewriter.

Saved her brother.

Lillie might know where Theodore Parker lived, but she wasn’t there. So Grace began to tear through the studio, looking for any scrap that might tell her his address.

There were letters in the desk, and she riffled through them with great haste.

Finally, she found a return address from Theodore’s father scrawled at the top of one of the envelopes.

7120 Meadow Place.

She dressed in her favorite gown—the one she had worn the first night of the fair. She pulled it tight around her waist, admiring the way the skirt fell.

Then she hailed a cab.

“7120 Meadow Place,” she said.

The carriage wound through the cobblestone streets as the lots grew larger and the houses grander.

This was a neighborhood even Aunt Clove would aspire to.

The cabbie let out a low whistle as they pulled to a stop.

“That’s a pretty pile of bricks right there,” the cabbie said. “Is it yours?”

“No,” Grace said, faintly touching her collarbone. “I’ve never seen it before in my life.”

The house was made of a stunning pink-hued granite and fronted by carved arches. Chimneys rose from the slate roof and sprays of alyssum spilled over from the balcony’s banisters. The grounds were lush with grass, manicured tulip beds, and towering elm trees lined in columns. Grace composed herself and took a breath before she walked up the front stairs.

“Good afternoon,” the butler said when she rang the bell.

“Hello. Is Mr. Parker home?” she asked.

The butler let her inside, where a chandelier glittered from the vaulted marble foyer. There was a massive fireplace in the entryway set below intricate plaster rosettes that looked like they had been sculpted from cream.

Theodore came down the staircase.

“Grace?” he asked, astonished. “What are you doing here?”

“I came to talk,” she said. “There’s something I must know.”

His jaw twitched.

“Tea, please, Doyle,” he said to the butler. “We’ll have it on the veranda.”

He led her through the brightly lit hallways to the back gardens. There were shocks of pink tulips and irises hedged by dwarf boxwoods and an elegant fountain. He gestured to a wrought iron table, where they sat.

“Meet Sesame,” he said as an energetic black pup bounded toward them to lick Grace’s wrist. She pulled him into her lap, despite her gown.

He licked her face.

"May I take it that you've decided to join me for dinner, then?" Theo asked, eyeing her dress.

"That will depend entirely on how you answer my questions," she said.

"I'll take care to only tell you what you want to hear then," he said.

"No," she countered. "I just want the truth."

She set Sesame on the ground.

"I saw you yesterday, after you left our lunch," she said. "You said you were going to see a family friend."

He remained expressionless. "In a way, I was."

"And yet you went to the Tunnels."

He was so handsome in the golden light of the afternoon, surrounded by the scent of roses and the drone of bees—his dark lashes lining his eyes, the shadows cutting like a delicate knife along his cheekbones.

"I was trying to help someone who was in trouble," he said.

"An honorable thing, to be sure," Grace said. "Then why lie about it?"

The familiar storm cloud passed over him, and she saw the look of arrogant disdain in his features. But it was something else this time. Something warring within him.

"When I heard that you had been robbed and threatened—that someone could have hurt you—I . . . snapped," he said, his jaw twitching. It was a confession, unhidden by banter, a lifting of his armor to the softness underneath. "I wanted to undo it in some way. I wanted to help. And I knew the best way to do that was . . ."

"To help my brother."

Their fingers were a whisper's breath from touching. She felt pulled to him, as powerfully as a magnet.

"Theodore," she said faintly. His hand reached for hers.

And then the butler emerged with a tea tray, and Theo abruptly stood.

"Thank you, Doyle," Theo said, turning to him stiffly.

Doyle took the hint and left the tea, but Grace joined Theo in standing.

He had helped to get Walt off the street and keep him out of prison. It was a risk to his reputation and assuredly an enormous sum to get him the best care.

Something was smoldering inside of her. It must have come out like shadows in her gaze. She drew toward him but kept a tantalizing distance.

"You're a difficult man to really know," she said.

He stiffened at her words, as though they were raised weapons.

She tilted her face up. Her lips were just close enough to his, without touching. "Like a storm that tries to warn people away," she said in a husky voice. "But what you really are . . ."

He traced his thumb down the curve of her jaw. ". . . Is the shelter from it," she finished.

He kissed her. Softly, more softly than she ever would have expected. He had formerly been all angles and sharpness and shadows but not here. He was delicate and gentle, and she was heat and sparkles, a firecracker that blazed right after it had been lit. She kissed him back, melting at the pressure of his lips on hers. It lit a hunger in her she had never known before, a taste for something that was instantly her favorite. He slipped his hand around her back and everything in her came alive. She let out a small sigh and he abruptly pulled back.

"I'm sorry," he said breathlessly. "Forgive me."

Her heart beat so fast she felt like she could fly.

"Perhaps I should go," she said.

"That bad, huh?" he deadpanned.

She laughed, low and hoarse. "On the contrary. I think it's entirely too dangerous to be alone with you."

He cleared his throat with a look that sent a shimmering tingle of light through her entire body.

"Or perhaps you could stay, if I promise to behave," he said. "I could give you a tour?"

She jumped at the chance. "Yes," she said.

She smoothed out her dress and clasped her hands behind her back, following him around the grounds.

"My mother used to love this garden," he said, careful to keep an arm's distance between them. He showed her a lush boxwood knot garden with carved ivory statues studded throughout the greenery, their crisp white echoing the bursts of cream-colored hydrangea. Thorndale English ivy threaded amid fixtures of patinated bronze, all encircling a three-tier, Parisian fountain. It was the garden of her dreams. If she lived there, she would situate herself on the wrought iron bench with a book and never leave.

"My father is coming into town next week," Theo said. "He hopes that my time in St. Louis has changed my mind about wanting to find some sort of occupation rather than merely be a gentleman."

"You wish to work?" she asked. She couldn't believe how handsome he was. That she was in Theodore Parker's gardens. That he had just *kissed* her.

"I'd like to do something meaningful with my life, yes," he said.

He turned, suddenly close enough to graze her. "How admirable," she said, lightly teasing, but all she wanted was for him to kiss her again. He swallowed, searching her eyes. When she bit her lip, he guided her a step backward until Grace felt the brush of the stone fountain behind her.

"You were saying?" she asked faintly.

"My father thought I'd change my mind, living the life of a gentleman here these last few months. But if anything, it's made me want something real even more." His voice was dusky as he leaned toward her. "The fair has shown me glimpses of what is possible. And how short life can sometimes be."

"Working or not, you've shown you will always be a gentleman," she said, feeling lightheaded and dizzy, as though she were about to swoon. His hands tightened on her ribs.

"I'm trying very hard to behave, Miss Covington. You're making that difficult."

She lifted her lips to his ear. "You must know by now that I'm not much for following rules."

He made a sound somewhere between a low laugh and a growl.

"May I assume this means you've accepted my dinner invitation for tonight?" he said.

Her soaring heart promptly sank.

"I can't. My intrepid reporting has gotten me barred from the fairgrounds," she said. "I don't think they'll let me in."

"Well, who needs it? We'll go somewhere else, then," he said. "I'd rather dine with you than the president tonight."

"If I had a penny for every time I've heard *that* before," she said.

He laughed, low and curling, like smoke and touched the bow of her lips.

"I'll change and we can go," he said. With a bow, he left her sitting along the fountain, letting the faint mist wet her skin.

❧

They decided on the restaurant Piccadilly at Manhattan.

Theodore gave the directions and his carriage turned west.

He looked debonair. He wore a coat with tails, a white tie, white gloves, and a silk top hat, and was carrying a cane.

He kept stealing glances at her from across the carriage.

"You have always driven me a little crazy, Miss Covington," he said. "Since that very first night."

"At the Fair?" she asked. "In the ill-fated little canal boat with Oliver and Harriet?"

"No," he said softly. "Even before that. In Chicago."

She went a little cold and shifted in her seat. "Let's not speak of it," she said, suddenly unable to meet his eyes. "It has taken me a long time to get over that night."

She glanced out the window. But it hung in the air between them now.

"What changed between us, since then?" he asked.

"I could ask you the same question," she said.

"You decided you could look past my flaws?" he said. "You made it quite clear that there would be much to overcome."

"We have different recollections, then," she said, a flush starting in her chest. "I came out to the balcony and found that you were a different person."

He frowned. "Only because of what you had said to Frannie about me."

A creeping sensation made its way up Grace's neck.

The carriage jolted.

"What do you mean?" she asked.

His expression darkened. "I will admit, I acted so beastly that night. I apologize. I've never gotten over the shame of it. But your words had found their exact mark."

"What did Frannie say?"

He narrowed his eyes. "You're going to make me repeat it?"

"Tell me," she said urgently. The carriage lurched again, and she grabbed the seat.

"She had overheard you and Lillie. That I might want to watch myself around you because of your family station and your . . . desperation."

"That's exactly what I thought she said," Grace said. Her hand tightened on the cushion. The warmth of the coals within her at his presence had died.

"But that wasn't all. She said you laughed that it was a good thing I came from money, that otherwise no one would be interested." He gestured toward the port-wine stain on his cheek with his gloved hand. "Because marked men made for easy marks."

The blood drained from Grace's face.

"I lashed out because I was humiliated, but it was unacceptable. Your words felt like poison going down. I've always been rather . . . vulnerable there and you struck that soft place right between my armor. I reacted badly, and I've been ashamed ever since. I have regretted those words every day. That's partly why I wanted to help Oliver so much. To make it up to you."

Grace let go of the seat, her hands tremoring. "She lied to you. I never said that. I thought . . . I thought you were *handsome.* I thought you genuinely liked me, the way I genuinely liked you, until you found out I didn't have money."

He scowled at her furiously. "What?"

"I saw Frannie talking to you and I assumed she was telling you about my family, my station, my brother's scandals. And then the way you reacted confirmed my worst suspicions. You only were interested if I had money and status like yours. My places of weakness. My biggest fears."

He sat back roughly. "She exploited them against us both," Theo said.

He looked at her sheepishly and rubbed his hand over his handsome mouth. His mouth that had just been on hers.

"There's going to be another murder on the fairgrounds because I think I'm going to kill her for this," Grace said.

"Can you stop looking so attractive while you're plotting?" he said. "It's hardly fair."

The warmth kindled like fire through Grace again.

He slid across the carriage so that he could sit beside her.

She took his face in her hands. Gently stroked the birthmark on his jaw.

"I have never once thought of you as marked," she said. "Only extraordinarily handsome, snobbish, and maybe a tiny bit brooding."

"Brooding, afraid of heights, and angry with you for being poor. Got it."

"Frannie Allred lied to you about me. Poisoned you against me."

"She turned against Oliver and Lillie as soon as Oliver was a suspect."

"And she lied to Earnest about the note I'd had sent to her house."

"She tried to misdirect the investigation about Harriet."

It all came back to Frannie.

Grace looked at him with a growing sense of horror.

"What else has she lied about?" she whispered.

"There's only one way to find out," Theo said.

He rapped on the top of the carriage.

"Change of plans, Bert," he ordered.

The carriage turned back toward the fair.

CHAPTER TWENTY-THREE

"I have an idea," Grace said. "But we'll need to make a stop first."

She directed him to the location she had in mind and hopped out. Made a transaction. Safely hid it within her purse.

Then they were on their way again.

They disembarked at the Lindell turnstiles, and Theodore hired a gondola to take them the rest of the way through the fairgrounds. The teal and gold dome of Festival Hall loomed over them when they came to a stop in front of the Palace of Electricity.

There was a line forming in front of a security detail at a private entrance for the dinner.

"No safer place to confront a murderer," Theo murmured as he helped her out of the boat. "There will be so much security there tonight."

"That is, if I can get past it," Grace whispered.

"We'll invent an alias for you," he said, drawing out his invitation. He whispered into her ear, "Think of something outlandish."

She scoffed. "As if I would miss this opportunity."

"Theodore Parker," he said to the guard, flashing his invitation. "And this is my guest . . ." He turned to Grace.

"Mitzi Ramsbottom," she said primly.

Theodore's eyes widened. He choked on a cough, and she waltzed in front of him with a straight face.

They stepped inside and were thoroughly frisked for weapons. She held her breath, waiting for the guard to find the purchase she had just made, which would lead to some uncomfortable questions, but ultimately it remained hidden in her makeup compact and he let her through.

They were escorted through the palace to the second floor, which had been transformed. Grace had been to many fancy balls at the fair, but this one surpassed them all. There were fountains where the water had been almost entirely replaced with flowers. Sharply dressed waiters with trays of appetizers that looked like crystallized candy. Candelabras studded with orchids and draped with crystals. Fizzing drinks in elegant, impossibly long-stemmed glasses. Butter that had been pressed into delicate molds to resemble swans. There were ambassadors and diplomats mingling amid famous families swathed in jewels and silks from New York, Chicago, Philadelphia. She spotted the Chinese prince Pu Lun, Thomas Edison, the vaudeville performer Will Rogers, and the Chiricahua Apache Chief Geronimo, who was both a guest and a prisoner of war, and therefore accompanied by his own guards.

"Grace!" Lillie said, parting the crowd. "You're here!"

"I'm afraid you're mistaken," Grace said in a low voice, glancing over her shoulder. "It's Mitzi tonight."

"Well, Mitzi, it's a pleasure to meet you. I brought the letter from Walt. Maybe you can give it to Grace when you see her," Lillie said.

Lillie slipped the envelope out from her handbag. Grace recognized Walt's handwriting on the front.

"I'll get you a lemonade," Theo whispered into her hair. His hand grazed the curve of her back.

Lillie looked between them and gave Grace a single, subtle look. She accomplished it with the slightest lift of her eyebrow.

"There's a lot I need to tell you," Grace said, biting her lip.

She trailed off as Earnest came up behind them.

"Grace, I didn't realize you would be here tonight," he said, smiling.

"It's Mitzi," Grace and Lillie said at the same time.

He didn't miss a beat.

"Rumors are that President Roosevelt isn't here yet, but he will be arriving soon. In the meantime—care to dance?" he asked Lillie.

She took his hand. "I want to hear everything," she said to Grace over her shoulder as he led her away.

Grace wove through the crowd, past the formal musicians with their gleaming instruments. All the while, she was surreptitiously looking over her shoulder for Frannie.

Instead, she caught the profile of the man who had approached her at the diner. She froze. He was turning toward her.

She backtracked, whirling on her heel until she found the ladies' room. She slipped inside and locked herself into a stall so she could think.

How much trouble would she be in if they found her here? Could she be arrested?

As she waited, heart hammering, she reached into her bag and slit open the envelope Lillie had put into her bag.

Walt's handwriting was still the same, albeit a little shakier.

I'm sorry for everything, Gracie. I did get some information—writing it down before I forget. I found someone who saw Harriet Forbes that morning in the Tunnels. She met with a man and spoke to him for five or ten minutes. The man was tall and had no distinguishable features other than reddish hair. Not bright red but reddish gold.

Hope this helps.

Walt

She looked up.

Red hair.

So Harriet hadn't gone to meet her sister Penelope in the Tunnels. Grace thought back to what she had seen written in Harriet's planner. Harriet had secretly planned to meet someone named Penny in the Tunnels.

Grace stood.

Penny.

Red hair.

And suddenly, it clicked.

She emerged from the ladies' room, keeping her head down and skirting along the wall.

As the crowd parted, she saw him. A tall, handsome man with red hair.

Of course. Penny. A clever pseudonym for *Copper*, if you didn't want anyone to know.

Harriet had gone and secretly met Earnest's friend Copper.

Copper, who trained with the athletes. Who would therefore have had plenty of access to strychnine.

And the man had been by Frannie's side this whole time.

They must have been working together.

Grace moved toward the door.

But for what purpose? What was their motive?

There was still a piece of the puzzle she was missing.

She smiled demurely as she approached Theodore. He was talking to someone she didn't recognize, a drink in his hand. She pulled him aside and whispered into his ear.

"I'm even more certain now that it was Frannie," she said. "But she wasn't working alone. Can you get her upstairs?"

She'd seen a large balcony that wrapped around the circumference of the palace, overlooking the Grand Basin and Festival Hall. It would be a good place to have a private conversation—and stay hidden from the man who had tried to bribe her in the diner.

"Grace—" Theo said. "Be very—"

"I know," she said. "I will."

Her anger quietly simmered as she gathered her gown in her hand.

She found Lillie next. "Can you do something for me?"

Lillie smiled. "Anything for Mitzi."

"I need you to find Copper and send him upstairs. Tell him that Frannie wants to speak to him privately," Grace instructed. "And if we don't come down in twenty minutes . . . send a policeman up."

The smile faded on Lillie's face. She paled. "Grace . . ." she said.

Grace kissed her cheek.

"For Oliver," she whispered.

She climbed the stairs to the balcony, feeling the weighted tug of her gown trail behind her. The fair was lit up around her with the incandescent bulbs of the electric lights. They dimmed and glowed like lanterns and fireflies, glittering in the dark as night fell. The Cascades were illuminated as they rushed down their banks into the Grand Basin. It was dark and cool up there on the balcony, enclosed within a rim of carved ivory balustrades and unfurling flags. There were guards stationed below, but they looked small from this distance. No one could spot her standing in the shadows.

The president was arriving in a cavalcade, but on the other side of the palace.

All attention would be on him for at least a few moments.

When Grace turned the corner of the balcony she came upon Theodore. He was speaking quietly with Frannie, and the moment caught her breath. It was just like watching them through the hours and months that had transpired since December that fated Chicago evening. Frannie glanced up and, seeing Grace, scowled. She was wearing a teal oyster silk gown with pearls dangling in her dark red hair. She touched the place at her neck where her stolen necklace should be, as though surprised to find it still missing.

Frannie looked at Theodore.

"What's *she* doing here?" Frannie asked.

"We wanted to talk," Grace answered coolly. She was having an almost visceral reaction to the sight of this beautiful, venomous woman. She had hurt everyone Grace loved in different ways, like the shards of an elegant vase that shattered out and cut wherever they landed.

"Well, I can hardly stay," Frannie said, shifting. She glanced behind Grace, as though hoping someone else would come up behind to save her. "The president is almost here. We can't miss that."

"Actually, I think we can," Theodore said.

Her face whipped toward his, and for the first time, she saw his cool disdain directed toward her.

"What is this about?" she asked, face flushing.

"I know you lied to Theodore about me that night at the Winter Ball in Chicago," Grace said, taking a step toward her.

Frannie let out a mirthless laugh, but she almost seemed relieved. "Is that what this dramatic confrontation is about? A tiny white lie I told months ago?"

"And yet it was much more than that. You tried to poison Mr. Parker against me," Grace said, taking another step toward her. Frannie retreated with one of her own in response. "But that isn't the only person you poisoned. Is it?"

Frannie's eyes narrowed for a split second before Grace's meaning hit home.

"You think I killed Harriet?" This time when Frannie laughed it was laced with genuine surprise. Her eyes widened. "She was climbing well beyond her social bounds but that doesn't mean I wanted her *dead.*" She shook her head as if they were ridiculous. "Fine, I'll admit that I lied to Theodore about you that first night at the Chicago Ball. It was clear you had set your sights on him, and it bothers me when people don't abide by the social rules. They are there for a reason. But that doesn't make me a *murderess.*"

She laughed again, still shaking her head in reproach. She began to walk away, but Grace stopped her.

Grace thought quickly, reaching for another card to play.

"And yet, we don't think you were trying to poison Harriet. We think you were trying to poison Earnest. After all, it was his drink that was poisoned, not hers."

"Earnest?" For the first time, Frannie's composure faltered. She paused. "Someone was trying to poison my brother?"

"The murderer put strychnine in Earnest's drink, and then he gave it to Harriet by accident."

"But I would never . . . Earnest is my . . ." she trailed off. But her face paled. As though in that moment, she had realized something. There was a faint twitch by her eye. She reached up to touch it.

"What is it?" Theo asked sharply. "You've put something together just now, haven't you?"

Frannie swallowed. She looked dizzy.

"What does strychnine look like?" she asked, her voice faint.

Grace pulled out her makeup compact. Hidden inside was a small bag of crushed white powder.

"Like this," she said.

Frannie took it from her. Stroked the bag with a finger that betrayed the slightest tremble. She was silent for a tense moment.

"It wasn't me," she said fiercely. "I would never, ever hurt my brother. He's all I have left."

"But you know who did it," Theodore said. "Don't you?"

Frannie exhaled, looking at the bag. "I saw this once. They use it for running, did you know that? He was trying to get Earnest to use it for rowing. I saw it but I didn't realize until now that it's what strychnine looks like."

"Who, Frannie?" Grace asked.

Frannie closed her eyes. She whispered, "Copper."

Theodore frowned. "But why would Copper want to kill your brother?"

"Why does anyone kill?" Frannie asked bitterly. She tightened her grip on the bag of strychnine. "To get to our money somehow. Now that my parents are gone, we're all that's left." Her face looked pained. "Copper must have been courting me and planning to marry me for my inheritance, especially with my brother out of the way." Her mouth turned down into a sad, resigned grimace. "Well, I'll be *damned* if that happens."

Grace glanced over her shoulders at the sound of approaching footsteps.

"Here he comes," Grace said.

"Quick," Frannie said, scowling. "Hide. I'll get a confession out of him. Just you wait and see."

She pushed them into the shadows and smoothed her face into a mask. Then, when she had composed herself, she turned and welcomed Copper with a smile.

He strode toward her, leaning down to greet her with a kiss.

She managed to turn her face at the last moment.

And it was at precisely then that Grace realized that Frannie was still holding the little white bag.

"Were you talking to someone?" Copper asked, glancing over her shoulder.

Frannie shook her head and laughed. There was a coldness in it that he didn't seem to notice.

"No. It must be the echoes from the party." She glanced over the edge of the balcony toward the waterways and lagoons beneath them. "Has the president arrived yet?"

"He was just coming in," Copper said. "Lillie said you wanted to see me?"

"I just needed a moment alone," Frannie said, smiling sadly. "With you."

He took her hand, then seemed to realize what was in it.

He stilled.

For a long moment, he was quiet.

"Why do you have that bag, Frannie?" he asked slowly. Grace could just see his face, limned in the light. He almost looked frightened.

The organ pipes began to ring out in the distance from within Festival Hall.

"That night of Harriet's murder, you put this in my brother's drink," she said. "Why?"

A look of disbelief crossed Copper's face.

"Is it possible you were the one to kill Harriet?" she asked. "Even accidentally?"

The athlete stepped toward her menacingly. His face twisted into something cruel. "You're not going to try to pin this on me, are you, Frannie? I'd stop looking, if I were you. If you don't, you're not going to like what you find."

"What are you saying?" she asked.

"What do *I* gain out of Harriet's death?" Copper shook his head, his smile dark and glittering. "I thought you were ruthless," he said. "And then I met your brother."

He turned his head as Earnest stepped out from behind him.

Grace bit back a sound. Theodore grabbed Grace by the waist and held her to him. She could feel his heart beating hard beneath his shirt.

"Don't. Move," he whispered on the barest hint of breath into her ear.

She nodded, her hand pressed to her mouth.

Earnest walked toward where Frannie and Copper were standing.

"Frannie," Earnest said. "You look cold."

But it was his voice that sent a chill down Grace's spine. She shivered and Theo pulled her closer to him.

"What is this, Earnest?" Frannie asked. She stole a glance over her shoulder, where Grace and Theodore were hiding. Her voice was shaking. "Did you know Copper was going to kill Harriet?"

"Whose idea do you think it was in the first place?" Copper said roughly.

"I don't understand," she said.

"I never wanted you to know about this," Earnest said, sounding apologetic. He frowned. "Did you come up with these accusations all on your own?"

"Earnest, no," Frannie said desperately. "What are you saying? You couldn't possibly have done this. What reason would you have?"

"Why do you think, darling sister? It was the only way I could see to save our family from ruin."

"From ruin?" Frannie asked faintly. "Surely you don't mean that."

"I can assure you that I do. Our beloved late father squandered our entire fortune."

The breath that came from Frannie was like a candle being blown out. "What?"

Earnest sighed. "When Mother and Father died, there was almost no money left. I met with Father's attorney to discuss the state of our affairs only to discover they were in shambles. Our house has been mortgaged and mortgaged again. Unless I did something drastic, we were about to lose it and everything else we had."

Frannie blanched. "But . . . what does killing Harriet have to do with any of that?" she whispered.

Grace leaned forward. Theodore's fingers tensed on her waist.

"I invested everything we had left into the flying competition, and then borrowed more. The aeronautics prize would have been enough to get us back on our feet again. I tried to sabotage everyone else to make sure we would win, but then the bloody machine exploded on me. Perhaps it had been an engineering failure. Perhaps someone had sabotaged me back. I'll probably never know the truth."

Frannie was holding her head in her hands as though she were faint, and breathing quickly.

"You borrowed money?" Frannie asked. "From whom?"

"A schoolmate of ours whose family had also fallen on hard times. He understood what it was like, to have to keep up appearances when the family fortune was gone. I told him I could win. We pooled the last of our finances to enter the competition. Think, Frannie—it was more than the prize money. There would have been opportunities to take the plane on the road for paid exhibitions. We were dreaming big."

"Instead it blew up," Frannie said. "And now we truly have nothing?"

Earnest raked his hand through his hair. "The truth was going to come out. My co-investor sought out Harriet the night that I crashed. He'd been keeping tabs on me throughout the Fair and had seen us all out together. Sylvestor was desperate that night and he told Harriet that I owed him a lot of money. She was supposed to pass on the threat."

"Which she did, through me," Copper said. "She had wanted to talk about money and whether Earnest was in trouble. He'd promised her that he would invest in her failing theater."

"And she was worried that I was as broke as Sylvestor claimed. But she was too close to our circle—one word from her, and then the whole thing would come crashing down."

"So you killed her?" Frannie asked coldly.

"I didn't jump to that plan right away," Earnest said. "Killing Harriet Forbes wouldn't do anything to help restore our fortunes, after all. But there was another way. A narrow, delicate way. The only way out."

"And that way was the Carter family," Copper said.

Earnest scowled. "Cripes, don't look at me that way, Frannie. Killing Harriet accomplished the only things that would save us. Save *you*. It kept her mouth shut from spilling that we were frauds and utterly broke. And if Oliver Carter could take the fall for her murder—it was perfect. He would no longer be able to inherit the massive Carter fortune. And because of the scandal, no one would want to marry Lillie."

"Except for you," Frannie whispered.

"Except for me. Waiting in the wings to comfort her. To look past the scandal and marry her anyway, bringing together their good money and my good family name. It was the solution that solved everything."

Frannie was aghast. "But—this isn't what we do, Earnest," she said, frantic. "We follow the *rules*. Everyone else bends them but we don't. They're there to keep society functioning." She stumbled backward, landing on the balustrade.

Copper snorted. "That's sweet, Frances. But a little naive. Everyone twists the rules. Those who don't get run over and left behind."

"Do you think I wanted to be put in this situation?" Earnest said sharply. "I never wanted to become the man of the house in my twenties, or to shoulder the immense burden of our parents' mistakes and ruined fortunes. But this was the hand I was dealt. This was the only way I could see to save us."

Anger surged through Grace like molten gold. She could feel it burning in her veins. Earnest had played all of them for fools. He had come up with a malicious plan to save his family that in turn ruined hers. Her beloved cousins. Destroyed by this man's pride and greed.

"So Copper got you the strychnine and put it in the glass?" Frannie asked slowly. She turned to Copper. "You were willing to risk being caught for murder for us?"

He shrugged, but there was something in his eyes. He didn't quite meet her gaze.

Grace saw the moment that the realization hit Frannie. "No, wait . . . I see. You would never marry me if this didn't work out. The Carter money was for you, too." She stumbled a little, as though he had struck her.

"Frannie—" Copper said, but she turned away from him. Angry tears were glittering in her eyes.

"Like I said, Frannie. I never wanted you to know any of this." Earnest turned softer, pleading. "I wanted this for your happiness, and mine. And now it's done. As long as I can continue to successfully court Lillie, you can live the life you're accustomed to. So, on that front"—he laughed bitterly—"you might want to start being a little nicer to her."

Frannie swallowed hard.

She looked once more toward where Grace and Theodore were standing. Where they had heard everything.

"Earnest," she said. "I didn't know."

He froze. Seeing the guilt in her face.

"Is there someone there?" he asked.

He strode toward the place where Theo and Grace were hiding, pulling out a flask from his inside pocket as he walked. His nose was beginning to bleed, crimson trickling to his lip.

"Earnest!" Frannie screamed. "Don't!"

"Get her out of here," Earnest snarled to Copper.

Copper grabbed Frannie, pulling her arms behind her back.

"You don't want to see this," Copper said. "Go down to the party and make sure no one comes up here."

He pushed her toward the door. But first, he wrenched the baggie of strychnine from her hand.

Frannie turned and ran.

"Stay hidden," Theo whispered roughly at Grace as Earnest came closer. Then he stepped out of the shadows.

"Theodore?" Earnest asked in surprise.

Theo threw himself at Earnest, tackling him with his full weight. Grunting, they struggled against each other, rolling on the balcony floor.

"Theodore!" Grace cried.

Copper came up behind her, trapping her arms behind her back. He pulled them tight. She could barely breathe.

"You couldn't stay out of it, could you?" he hissed in her ear. "Even after all of those warnings."

Copper and Earnest had seemed so brave that night at the Japanese gardens, winning her trust and her esteem when the robber approached them. Now she knew why. They had arranged it all with him beforehand. She could see it now—Earnest inviting them to the concert, knowing they would be dressed in their finest jewels. Telling Sylvestor right where they would be, so he could rob them and take the jewels as repayment for the money Earnest had lost. And deliver a warning to her at the same time.

"Did you kill him, too?" Grace asked. "The thief who threatened me?"

"Grace," Theo gasped, struggling with Earnest. Her eyes fell on the flask, where Earnest pulled out a hidden knife.

Copper's arms tightened around her, wrenching her shoulders out of place.

"Copper will give her the strychnine unless you sign a confession that you killed Harriet," Earnest said.

"I'll do it," Theo wheezed. "Don't hurt her."

"Good," Earnest said.

Then he turned and stabbed Theo in the leg.

Theodore bit down on his fist and muffled his scream. Grace cried out, seeing the blood immediately begin to flow from his thigh. The sound of it was drowned in the crescendo of the organ from Festival Hall.

"That will keep you from getting any ideas," Earnest said, pulling the knife from Theo's leg.

He brought out a small notebook and pen and stood over Theo while he shakily wrote a confession. Grace's eyes filled with tears, spilling over and slipping down her cheeks.

"Good," Earnest said, tucking the note into his waistband. The stress seemed to be getting to him. He was sweating, and trembling, and all Grace could think about was Lillie, unwittingly marrying the murderer who had framed her brother. He had fooled them all, pretending to look at automobiles he could never afford; pretending to consider Harriet's plea to invest in her theater. Just like Sylvestor had conned poor Harriet into believing he was a connected, wealthy gentleman who could introduce her to the talent manager if she passed along his threat. "Now this whole mess can be put behind us," Earnest said. He stole a look at Copper. It seemed to be a signal of some sort.

Copper loosened his grip on Grace, and she took in a gasping breath.

But then he opened the bag of strychnine.

It was in her face before she could take another breath. Coating her nose. Being shoved down her throat. She was coughing, choking on it.

"Grace—" Theodore cried. He tried to stagger to his feet but couldn't.

"It was a sad end to the affair, with a murder-suicide. But at least now there will be no evidence." Earnest wiped the sweat from his face. He swayed a little.

Then he turned and stabbed Theo again. He was aiming for Theo's heart, but Theo rolled at the last moment, and the knife hit him instead in the side.

Grace collapsed to the ground.

Copper released his hold on her and stepped over her spasming body.

She folded, trying to clutch her arms to herself. Knowing what was coming next.

Instead, her hand grazed a door stopper.

It was made of iron and shaped like a ship.

Her fingers closed around it.

"How long does strychnine take to be fatal?" Copper asked.

She could see, hazily, through the balustrades. The lights in the Grand Basin shimmered like fireworks.

"She'll be dead within fifteen minutes," Earnest replied. He bent down as she was spasming. Tucked Theodore's written confession into where her handbag had fallen open next to her.

Grace's hands closed around the door stop.

She whirled around with all of her might and brought it against his head.

It made a sick cracking sound.

"What?" Copper cried in disbelief as Earnest crumpled next to her.

She picked up the doorstop and rose to her feet.

She had brought the strychnine herself, and it was fake. A mixture of flour and powdered sugar. It hadn't felt good to breathe it in to her nostrils and airways, but it certainly wasn't a neurotoxin paralyzing her spinal cord.

She heard the distant pounding of footsteps, but it might have been her imagination. She held up the doorstop, preparing. "You can try to fight me," she said. "But you have a better chance if you run."

Copper looked at Earnest's body, knowing that their tidy explanation was no longer an option.

He swallowed, then stepped forward and grabbed Earnest's knife where it had fallen.

Grace couldn't help Theo in time and fight off Copper simultaneously. She sank down beside Theodore and tore off pieces of her dress to bandage him. There was so much blood everywhere.

Copper began to approach them, his knife out.

"Don't you see?" he said, snarling. "I can't run if there's still someone left to talk."

"Please, someone, help us!" Grace screamed.

She bent down as Copper neared, raising the knife. She sobbed, trying to staunch the bleeding from Theo's leg, his side. It was impossible. She could feel Theo's pulse flagging, hear the organ notes and the distant cheers of the crowd below. The president must have arrived.

And then the door exploded on its hinges.

"Get down!" someone yelled. The police poured onto the balcony.

Grace held desperate pressure on Theodore's wounds as someone knelt beside her. "Please. He's been stabbed, he's hurt," she said.

Theodore's face was white. His blood was everywhere.

Theo reached for Grace's wrist with his hand. His grip was growing weaker. She had to lean down to hear him.

"I need you to know," he said, his voice faint and raspy, "that I've always wanted you. Since that very first night."

"Shh," she said. "Please."

She couldn't stand that the words he was saying to her might be draining what life he had left. They had used their words against each other so many times, to spar and to wound. But now he was speaking his life into her. Using his last bit of strength to tell her who she was and what she was worth.

"It's done," he said. "You did it."

He was slipping away. She leaned down, bringing her ear to his mouth. He closed his eyes and then his fingers around hers and used his last breath to say the words she had always most wanted to hear.

CHAPTER TWENTY-FOUR

MAY 20, 1904

Seventeen Days After the Murder

THEY FOUND THE stolen jewels in Copper's possession.

He had lured his old schoolmate Sylvestor to the river and killed him to keep the truth from coming out, then had taken Lillie's and Frannie's jewels back. He had planned to sell them to help Earnest keep up the appearances of having money until he could marry Lillie.

By then it would be too late. The Carters would be forced to help their new son-in-law financially to keep up appearances. Their name couldn't handle another scandal. Or, if that failed . . . Well, Earnest had killed before. He had come too far and done too much to be ruined now. If he had to, he would do it again.

The irony of it was not lost on Grace. That her aunt would banish her from the family but welcome a well-bred murderer right through the front door.

It had been a week since the president's dinner, and the first time Grace had returned to the fair since that dark night. It looked so promising and innocent in the daylight, with the boughs of its trees skimming along the paths like a lace hem. She shivered a little. She stood outside the fence and heard the distant screams of the roller coaster, saw the Ferris wheel and the telegraph tower, the Alps and the glinting Festival Dome in the distance. Beyond it would be the Chinese summer palace, the Japanese gardens, the sprawling Philippine Village with its various tribes. The palaces, the massive pipe organ, the X-ray machine, the newest inventions in automobiles, trains, flying machines, appliances, and city planning. The art and animals and transplanted trees, the beauty of dancing and culture. The wonder and the *joy*. The Pike, with its endless restaurants and performances and zoos and baby incubators.

Lillie said that some of the smallest babies in the incubators had died. Dr. May was outraged, claiming that the man running the exhibit was not a doctor but a charlatan moneymaker. The fair had passed over the doctor who had run previous exhibitions in favor of someone who was willing to give them a larger percentage of the profits. Grace could hardly think about it. The tiny babies with their rosebud mouths, dying alone in their cases while people paid money to look at them. She thought of the men who had fallen to their deaths attempting to build the Ferris wheel. The Philippine tribes, lined up to be ranked like animals.

Grace watched the people pour in through the front gates. The fair was so much like humanity itself, infinitely complex in its light and shadows. It drew the world, showing the heights and depths of what people were capable of in their ingenuity and cruelty. Was she allowed to love something that was so complicated? And even more importantly, was she allowed to love such complicated some*ones*?

Or were the faultless the only ones worthy of being loved?

She clutched her final article in her hand, moving through the gate. She'd written the full story and tried to do it justice. She wanted to vindicate Oliver, first and foremost, and restore the Carter name for his sake and for Lillie's. She'd wanted to capture how heroic Theodore had been that night.

And she'd done it to finally be the one holding the brush stroke in her hands. All her life, other people's words had defined her like a painter using negative space. Filling up the places around her with vague shadows that actually didn't capture her at all. She thought of Walt, smashing the window of the general store, and lifting her up to see the bird's nest. Oliver, who always raised Grace's social standings and also put her in the worst positions. Theo, saving and destroying her in the course of a single Chicago night.

And Frannie.

Grace could acknowledge their fault lines and their propensity for good, sometimes tangled frustratingly together. It was painstaking work, pulling weeds without uprooting the gentle flowers that grew beside them. It was always easier and lazier to simply raze a thing to the ground. But without nuance there would be nothing left to love—within herself, included.

Love, after all, required grace.

She spotted Frannie Allred, sitting alone at a table in the Beer Garden, beneath a parasol.

Frannie turned her face toward Grace as she approached.

"May I sit here?" Grace asked.

"I'm fairly certain you won't have to fight anyone for it," Frannie said dryly. Her lips were pursed. "My social card has been rather empty since my brother was arrested for murder."

Grace resisted the temptation to make any snide comments about how Frannie had treated Lillie exactly the same way when their situations were reversed

Instead she bit her tongue and pulled up a chair. "You know I've never cared about any of that."

Frannie chuffed a little. She examined the menu.

"Just a coffee," she said to the waitress. She closed her menu.

Grace ordered enough food for both of them. When it came, she artfully passed some of the plates over to Frannie's side of the table.

Frannie hesitated.

Other than the necklace Frannie was getting back, and the other jewelry she already had in her possession, Grace didn't think there was much for her to live on.

"Thank you for meeting me here," Grace said.

"Why are you doing this?" Frannie asked, frowning. She still looked displeased to be seen with someone like Grace. Grace tried not to bristle.

"I could ask you the same question," Grace said. "I know what you did that night. I thought Lillie was the one who sent the police up to the balcony to save us. But it wasn't her. It was you."

Frannie stared stonily at her coffee cup, stirring it.

"Why did you do it?" Grace asked her. "You knew what it would mean for you, for your brother. You could have turned on us. And then I would not even be here."

Frannie shook her head with an exaggerated sigh. "You've never understood. I tried to tell you before. You don't follow the rules. You don't see how necessary they are. But rules are what keep society functioning. No one gets to bend them just for their own sake. That's what your mother was always trying to do. And that's what Earnest so foolishly did . . ." Frannie looked off in the distance, her mouth twisting into a grimace. "Thinking the rules somehow didn't apply to him."

"But you follow them," Grace finished softly. "No matter what they cost."

"Yes. For me or anyone else. I don't know any other way to live with myself."

Grace paid the bill and requested bags for the leftover food. Frannie finished her coffee and stood.

"Thank you," she said, as though it pained her.

"I'll be seeing you, Frannie," Grace said. She pushed the bags of food in Frannie's direction.

Frannie shook her head with a wry smile on her face. "I very much doubt that."

Grace watched as Frannie straightened her shoulders and walked into the oncoming crowd. Alone, resolute, and with her head held high. She raised her parasol and disappeared into the wave of humanity, letting it swallow her.

She'd left the bags under the table.

EPILOGUE

DECEMBER 1, 1904

Seven Months Later

The wisteria was draped just the way Grace had instructed. Purple, and wisping, and light as lace, even though it was frigid outside.

She stood in front of the gilded mirror. It was wintertime, she was going to a floral ball, and she was dressed in many layers of luxurious clothing—but this time, every layer belonged to her.

She examined the rich silk gown that trailed in heavy pleats at her hips, and the embroidery that knit along the train.

It was astonishing what a difference a year could make.

"My darling," a man said from behind her.

He was sharply handsome. He still limped from the scars on his leg, the occasional pain in his side.

"I never knew how much you truly loved me," she said to him. "Until you voluntarily agreed to host this party."

"I'd almost rather be stabbed again," he said.

He kissed the skin on the back of her neck, and she smiled. She turned around and straightened his tie.

"I thought I hated parties. As it turns out, I just hadn't found the right person to endure them with," he murmured, admiring her dress.

"Though I hope you'll still glower at everyone from the staircase," she said. "Your black cloud is so . . . mysterious."

She kissed his jaw, tracing her fingers across his birthmark.

"Stop," he said in a low voice, gently turning his mouth toward hers, "or we won't make it to our own party."

When she pulled away, his hands reluctantly trailed after her. On her dressing table, he picked up a small, gilded spoon.

The gold caught the light. It was painted with the words 1904 WORLD'S FAIR.

"For better or for worse," he said, turning it in his fingers. "It brought us together."

And after tonight, for all its beauty and horror, the fair would close forever. The buildings of the Ivory City would soon be razed. The Ferris wheel would be disassembled, its parts sent elsewhere. The winding canals would be filled in, to be erased by the growth of new earth and flowers. It had been a temporary moment in time that forever impacted the people who had walked through its gates.

"After you," Theodore said, his gaze falling to the ring he had given her. It sparkled on her hand. "Mrs. Parker."

Grace made her way down the massive staircase. Her train spread out behind her, a ripple of echoes down the stairs. It never ceased to amaze her when she took the turn on the landing that this was all hers.

She surveyed the house, with its arches of blooming flowers, lanterns, and luminaries that lined the sweeping front hallway.

She took a moment to appreciate it, but also to remind herself that she didn't *need* it. She was determined never to be a slave to wealth, but to make it work for her. To use it to reshape the world more how she wanted to see it.

Which was why they were holding the ball that night in the first place.

She adjusted a hanging bough of dew drops along the edge of the banister.

"Lillie," she said, her stomach filling with warmth at the sight of her cousin.

Lillie turned. She was a vision in soft pink, her silk sleeves falling from her exposed shoulders in arcs of gold- and rose-colored beads like freshly dropping petals.

She greeted Grace with a kiss on the cheek. She smelled like narcissus.

"Thank you for the dress," Lillie said.

Grace squeezed her. "Only twenty more and I'll have repaid the favor," she said.

She was happy that her cousin looked lovely. Lillie was glowing. She held a fizzing drink in her hand that almost matched the color of her gown.

"Where's Oliver?" Grace asked.

"I believe he's showing the kitchen staff how to make a proper peanut butter and pickle sandwich," she said.

"Oliver!" Grace said, sighing. She shook her head as though warding off a headache.

"What?" he asked, sauntering up behind her. "I know how much you've always loved my PB-and-pick-which," he said. "Or are they not sophisticated enough for you now, my darling?"

It had taken months, but the color was finally returning to his face.

"You look dashing, and a little impish, and that always looks good on you," she said.

He kissed her cheek. "To be honest, I think I'll feel better tomorrow, when this fair is finally behind us."

She squeezed his hand. In the days to follow, workers would demolish the building where Harriet died, as though it had never been there. The city would move on, even if Oliver had not yet. But for the first time, his eyes lit up when Theodore offered him a box of cigars.

"He looks better tonight," Grace commented as the two men ambled away.

"He does," Lillie said. "His appetite has finally returned, and my mother is keeping him well-fed. Or so I hear."

Lillie's smile was bittersweet. Grace squeezed her hand. Lillie had chosen to officially study and work with Dr. May, despite her parents' threats to cut her off. She was no longer living at home or within her parents' means. Someday, when Oliver inherited it all, he would assuredly share their family fortune with her. But Theodore and Grace quietly supported Lillie now, by asking her to live with them and funding a new women's house she was working in with Dr. May.

It was strange, how their positions had shifted. And yet it was fitting. They both recognized the joy of giving generously to someone they loved and the humility it took to receive it.

"I think someone's looking for you," Grace said, glancing over her shoulder.

A strikingly handsome man was glancing their way. Thomas Kenton was someone Theodore had known since childhood and heartily approved of. Someone kind, with a proven character that was *almost* worthy of Lillie.

Lillie smiled and Grace said behind her gloved hand, "He's already requested strong interest in your dance card."

"And should I take him up on it?" Lillie asked with a faint touch of wariness.

She had become much more guarded in friendship and in love. Grace worried that Frannie and Earnest had forever ruined the delicate something in Lillie that made her so special, but somehow Lillie had come out the other side with a toughness that made her even lovelier.

"I think he's the exact opposite of Earnest," Grace said firmly. "And therefore, a good man in every way."

Lillie threw back her drink, shot Grace a mischievous glance, and accepted Thomas Kenton's hand onto the dance floor.

In the far corner, Harriet's sister Penelope was also present, swaying as she listened to the voice of Ethel Adams fill the ballroom. She had agreed to come when Grace explained that the Ball was given in honor of Harriet—a benefit in her name to save the theater she had so loved.

Grace came to stand beside Penelope.

"That's beautiful," Penelope said, glancing up at a framed painting.

It was new. It was a scene of the fairgrounds at daybreak, when the sun was just awakening, and the rest of the grounds were still hidden in shadows. It had captured the whole experience, with its light and darkness, so exquisitely.

Grace had climbed up the ladder herself and hung it, replacing a large portrait of one of the Parker ancestor's dogs. Theodore had slow clapped.

"Thank you," Grace said now to Penelope. She smiled and added proudly, "My brother did it."

Her eye caught on someone who had just arrived. "Excuse me," she said, and went to greet Frannie Allred with genuine warmth. "Welcome."

Frannie glanced stiffly around the party. "Thank you," she said.

She had been summarily turned out of all other social circles after what Earnest had done came to light. He and Copper were in jail, awaiting trial for the murders of Harriet Forbes and Sylvestor Watson, and the attempted murders of Theodore and Grace Parker. Frannie had no fortune and no family name or reputation left to speak of.

But what she had done that night at the fair had likely saved the Parkers' lives, and they would never forget that.

Grace took Frannie by the arm and introduced her to a few people who might be willing to look past the surface stories and actually see the faceted, frustrating, more complicated woman for who she was.

"Is that Frances Allred?" an older woman to Grace's right sniffed. She pulled Grace aside, a concerned look further creasing her lined face. "I know you're new to these circles. Would you accept a little friendly advice?" Giant diamonds sagged from the woman's ears. "I am not sure I can stay if this is the company you choose to keep."

Grace shrugged. "Our butler would be happy to call your carriage, if you prefer. I'd advise you take some of the pecan buns for the road. They're divine."

The woman looked stunned. "Well, I never." She grasped her husband's arm and backed away.

"Becoming better and better at gardening, aren't we?" Theodore came up behind her, wrapping his arms around her waist.

She turned toward him. "Gardening?"

"Helping people to weed themselves out," Theodore said.

Grace snorted. She loved Theodore Parker. She felt it in every part of her body. And she was willing to spend the rest of her life enduring society gossip about her motives for marrying him when the truth was, she had fallen in love with him despite herself. She felt a new kind of freedom now to let people believe what they wanted. They could run and run with false versions of the truth until mercifully, reality sometimes intervened—just like it had with Walt; just like it had with Earnest.

Fantastical worlds could be built temporarily, but at some point, they always had to come down.

As the night wore on, Ethel sang, they held a moment of silence in Harriet's memory, the head of Harriet's theater proposed a toast, and Oliver convinced enough people to pledge donations that Harriet's theater would be saved for the immediate future, if not many years to come. Grace leaned into her role as mistress of the house with the grace and poise of her mother, who looked utterly at ease back in high society. Nell Covington smiled as the exquisitely cultivated appetizers were served around her.

"These bacon-wrapped dates are divine," Lillie said.

"Your uncle made them," Nell said proudly.

"If anyone ever wondered why you married him, they won't now," Lillie said, nudging her.

"It's almost as delicious as watching them eat their words." Nell raised a glass of sparkling punch to Grace as she took to the dance floor with her husband. Grace's parents had traveled to St. Louis to attend the party and visit Walt, who had decided the fête would be too much of a temptation for his tenuous sobriety.

Grace had asked for their help in planning, and they had executed their roles with resounding success, given how many guests stayed well into the morning hours.

Finally the last song played, goodbyes were said, and the final carriage departed. Grace saw her parents to bed, then took off her shoes and traipsed up the flower-draped stairwell.

"Mrs. Parker," Theodore said, leading her outside, where the air was cold but his arms were warm. "As memory serves, momentous things seem to happen to us on balconies."

He kissed her.

"Was it so torturous tonight?" she asked, nestling in closer to him.

He wrinkled his nose. "I largely married you because you claimed you don't like parties."

"I solemnly promise to only use them for good causes."

"Your cousin is Lillie Carter," he said dryly. "I hardly think we'll want for good causes."

She gave him an impertinent smile. "You may want to rip out your hair, but at least you won't ever be bored."

"Never," he deadpanned. "My hair is my best feature."

"That's debatable." She touched his handsome face. Kissed his birthmark. The scar on his arm. The parts of him that were the most beautiful to her.

"And now it's all over," she murmured as he led her in a private slow dance. She turned toward the fireworks that were beginning to explode over Forest Park, lighting up the sky. "How unbelievable, that for a few months, the entire world was encompassed in the span of a few blocks."

"And yet I found my whole world there," he whispered roughly against her temple, "encompassed in a single person."

Grace was surprised by the sudden tears pricking her eyes. The fair had changed her life irrevocably, and she would never walk its paths again. There were things about its passing existence she would miss and return to often in her memory. Stories she would tell her future children, and some she would hold close to her own heart. Horrors she had witnessed and scars she would likely carry for the rest of her life. She would walk its paths in her dreams, and perhaps, a few nightmares.

She took Theodore to bed as the fireworks fell, the city darkened, and in the distance, the Ivory City shut its gates for the final time.

AUTHOR'S NOTE

I am incredibly grateful to all the people whose time and previous study made researching this novel such a joy, and at times, a heartbreak.

Some of the resources I have found helpful in researching this novel include *Inside the World's Fair of 1904, Volume One* by Elana F. Fox; *From the Palaces to the Pike: Visions of the 1904 World's Fair* by Timothy J. Fox and Duane R. Sneddeker; *Meet Me in St. Louis: A Trip to the 1904 World's Fair* by Robert Jackson; *Bradford's World's Fair Bulletin, Volume 4*; *The Textbook of Medical Jurisprudence and Toxicology* by John J. Reese; *The 1904 St. Louis World's Fair: 100 Years of Memories* by Mike Truax; and the documentaries *The World's Greatest Fair* and *That Fabulous Summer.*

A significant amount of information came from Missouri History Museum's 1904 World's Fair exhibit. I am forever indebted to the public historian Adam Kloppe for the generosity of his time with in-person meetings and email exchanges. This novel would not be nearly as rich or accurate without his invaluable help. An enormous thank-you to Janna Añonuevo Langholz from the Philippine Village Historical Site, who took me on a tour of the former Philippine Village and is doing tireless work to honor the memory and experience of the 1,204 Filipino people who were part of the fair.

Thank you to Bill Stanard from the Chatillon-DeMenil Mansion (and his dog Lulu) for the tour of the mansion's 1904 World's Fair souvenirs collection at the very beginning of my research. Thank you to bookseller and public historian Amanda Clark for the tour of the World's Fair grounds, and her generous early read of my manuscript. I have tried to do as much research as possible to accurately capture the fairgrounds and the cultures represented there responsibly. All errors are entirely mine.

A few notes on the historical framework behind the novel:

The fair drew nearly 20 million visitors from all over the world to St. Louis. The 1904 Olympic Games really were held in tandem with the St. Louis World's Fair and strychnine really was given to some of the Olympic athletes to help their performance.

The aeronautics competition that Earnest competed in is loosely based on a competition that actually happened, and although several flying machines were slashed or damaged before the competition, no machines are reported to have exploded like Earnest's did.

Prince Pu Lun and Thomas Edison really did visit the fair. Prince Pu Lun was there for several months and lived at the Chinese Pavilion, which was a smaller recreation of his summer palace, and he really was gifted a carriage from Adolphus Busch.

President Roosevelt did attend the fair in person, but not until after his re-election in November 1904, because he did not want to be seen as using the event for unfair political advantage. Other notable visitors to the fair were Helen Keller, Grover Cleveland, and T.S. Eliot. Almost all of the structures from the fairgrounds were destroyed, save for the St. Louis Art Museum in Forest Park and the Flight Cage that resides in the St. Louis Zoo, which you can still visit today.

I have loosely based several characters on real people. Dr. May is based on Dr. Mary Hancock McLean, a female physician and surgeon who opened an Evening Dispensary for Women to provide low-cost or free medical care for working women in St. Louis in 1893, as well as the Emmaus Home for Girls, which provided a place of residence for women working at the fair. Her character is further inspired by my great-great-aunt Katherine Bain, the sole woman in her 1925 medical school class at Washington University School of Medicine in St. Louis. She and my great-great-uncle, her brother-in-law, Park J. White, ran the first racially integrated medical facility in St. Louis.

The newspaperman Sam Whitcomb is loosely based on a man named E.G. Lewis who did exist. He sold questionable extermination products before publishing an array of newspapers and magazines and erecting a tent city known as "Camp Lewis" near the fairgrounds for his subscribers.

While there are underground limestone caves beneath the city of St. Louis, the tunnels themselves are completely fabricated. In addition, there was a ride on the Pike called Under and Over the Sea, but it looked more like a simulated trip to Paris than a ride through various countries with individual gondolas. I took some liberties with both these elements for the sake of the story. In addition, strychnine would usually take a slightly longer time to manifest fatal symptoms—from fifteen to sixty minutes. I thank Dr. Katherine D. Watson, FRHistS, for her paper "Poisoning Crimes and Forensic Toxicology Since the 18th Century," and for her kind email pointing me to several helpful articles and the book *Doctors and the Law: Medical Jurisprudence in Nineteenth-Century America* by James C. Mohr.

The ice-cream cone, iced tea, and Dr Pepper, while likely not invented at the World's Fair, were popularized there. The same is true for the X-ray machine, the electric typewriter, and the wireless telegraph. Ruby-red "flash" glass really was a big part of the World's Fair experience, and the souvenirs are still passed down by St. Louis families and World's Fair enthusiasts today—though they would not have been used as drinking glasses like they were at the Glass Ball. In addition, St. Louis's city water supply was significantly cleaned up prior to the fair, leading to improved health for both visitors and residents.

A better author than me could have incorporated even more of the fair's complexities into this story. As it is, I need to give ample space in this Author's Note in acknowledgment of the beauty and triumphs and horror and mistreatment we are capable of, which exist side by side in all of our history. In the case of the preemies on display or the zoological exhibitions of people groups that the fair organizers considered to be more barbaric and uncivilized—something that we now, ironically, consider to be barbaric and uncivilized itself.

For instance, Ota Benga was an Mbuti man with sharpened teeth who was advertised as a cannibal at the fair. Afterward, he was put in an ethnological exposition at the Bronx Zoo Monkey House in New York. He committed suicide in 1916.

Equality for entry to the fair was emphasized for African Americans, Native Americans, and other Indigenous people, but it was often not their experience within the fairgrounds. Scott Joplin, the "King of Ragtime," wrote a song inspired by the fair called "The Cascades." It is not confirmed that he was at the fair—but if he was, he would only have been permitted to play his music on the Pike. A planned Negro Day was canceled in response to the unequal treatment people experienced at the fair.

The Philippine Village was one of the largest exhibits at the fair, and it functioned as a way for the United States to show off the colonization of its recently acquired territory. Many different Filipino and Indigenous tribes were displayed and ranked in degrees from "most" to "least" civilized, with a model school that was meant to demonstrate the superior benefits of a Western education. Seventeen people died as part of the Philippine exhibit, either from pneumonia, malnutrition, or suicide. Some were trafficked to the fair under false pretenses. Some contracted pneumonia because they were forced to travel to the fair on cold train cars without adequate heat. During the fair, they also married, loved, worked, and had babies. Janna Añonuevo Langholz has done significant work researching this and you can find her work at philippinevillagehistoricalsite.com.

The Baby Incubators were another exhibit that was meant to showcase the progress of humanity and instead demonstrated facets of horror. Reportedly, thirty-nine out of forty-three premature infants displayed in the exhibit died because the contract was awarded to a man who was willing to split more of the profits with the fair organizers than the doctor who had traditionally overseen these exhibits. The premature infants were fed cow's milk, eggs, and cereal, and the incubators sometimes reached 105 degrees. Eventually, after public outcry, a separate doctor took over and the babies under his care fared much better.

In evidence of the myriad complexities of these stories, a St. Louis policeman brought an abandoned baby weighing less than three pounds to the incubator exhibit, where she was cared for and miraculously survived. The policeman and his wife visited her for several months, and eventually adopted her as their own daughter. They brought her home and named her Frances.

The fair is a microcosm of humanity itself—in every facet of our collective glory, our shame, the ways we displayed and denied dignity, the ways we made the world better and worse for each other. My hope is that even something as small as a murder mystery story can bless the people of St. Louis, especially those who may have historically been hurt by the more horrific parts of this fair. I include them because light comes through honesty, even in—and sometimes especially in—works of fiction.

Thank you for being my readers.

With much gratitude,
Emily

ACKNOWLEDGMENTS

Whenever it comes time to write my acknowledgments, I am always grateful for the chance to reflect on how many people have blessed my life.

Thank you to my children: James, Cecilia, and Liv. You bring so much joy into my days, and being your mom is my favorite.

To my parents, Kevin and Sarah Bain: Thank you for your lifelong encouragement and belief in me. Thank you, Mom, for always being one of my first readers and biggest cheerleaders. Thank you, Dad, for our meaningful conversations, which I treasure. To my parents-in-law, Mark and Barbara Murphy: My books could not be written without your love and support. I am blown away by your servant hearts. To Hannah, Andrew, Angie, Silas, Hazel Bain, and Janlyn Murphy—I love you. Thank you for loving me so well and for being such a precious part of my life.

To my cousins: It was a joy to grow up with you! Beth Nelson, thank you for having my back since you were three months old. To the Bain, Goldman, Murphy, Nelson, Shane, Spragins, and Westwater families: Thank you for your endless love and support.

To Pete Knapp—will there ever be enough words to say thank you? Ten years, seven books, so many conversations that have meant the world to me. I'm grateful for your guidance, wisdom, care, and the fingerprints you've left all over my life. To Stuti Telidevara, Danielle Barthel, Olivia Valcarce, and everyone at Park, Fine, and Brower: I pinch myself that I get to work with such kind, immensely talented people. Thank you for all of your work.

Mika Kasuga: I know I've said it before, but I hit the jackpot with you! Thank you for caring for this story and for me. Thank you to Mahalaleel M. Clinton—it's been an absolute joy to get to work together. Laura Schreiber: Thank you for seeing the potential in this one! Hugs! A huge thank you to the rest of the team: my publicists Alex Serrano and Nathan Siegel, my copy editor Diane João, cover designer Erik Jacobsen, interior designer Christine Heun, Margaret Moore, Alison Skrabek, and everyone else who poured into this book at Union Square & Co./Hachette Book Group.

An enormous thank-you to the time, patience, guidance, and expertise of Adam Kloppe, public historian at the Missouri History Museum; Amanda Clark, public historian and community tours manager at the Missouri History Museum and co-owner of Leviathan Books; and Janna Añonuevo Langholz, who runs the Philippine Village Historical Site.

To Kayla Olson: I'm so grateful for your friendship and encouragement. Thank you for always just getting it and always being there.

Catherine Bakewell: You have brought so much joy to my life. Thank you for our writing times, discussions, and a trip to Paris that I'll never forget. Thanks especially for loving my kids so well.

April Welch: Thank you for your friendship, which is truly one of the greatest gifts in my life.

Britteny Hess: Thank you for all of our hangouts, game nights, and child swaps, which helped me get this book over the finish line!

Thank you to Andrea, the Emilys, Heather, Karen, Kristine, Michele, Rinkal, Vickie, the Hess and Vaden families, my small group and church family, everyone at Renovaré and especially the Phoenix RI, Chrystal Schleyer, Autumn Krause, Katie Allen Nelson, Erin

Phillips, Ande Pliego, Jaime Gross, Michelle Collins Anderson, Emily Schroen, Cassandra Hamm, Michelle Mason, and our friends at the Carver Project and the Missouri House Rabbit Rescue Society (particularly Joanna Wurth). Thank you to Gabby Nickel, Sarah Dill, Alex Nesbeda, Caitlin Dalton, Wendy Huang, Anna Delia, Kristen Wade, Yomei Kajita, Dani Rose, Wendy Stanton, Nanette Pink, Susi Thannhuber, and all of my friends in Connecticut, Indiana, San Francisco, Tokyo, Hong Kong, Massachusetts, and Missouri. Thank you to Tom and Julia Bakewell for letting me use their house as a writing retreat!

A massive, heartfelt thank-you to the St. Louis community—especially all of the rich cultural places that have inspired me over the last eight years of calling St. Louis my home. I'm so grateful for the Missouri History Museum, the Missouri Botanical Garden, the St. Louis Art Museum, the St. Louis Zoo, Forest Park, the St. Louis symphony, the Muny, the Cathedral Basilica of St. Louis, the Mercy Conference and Retreat Center, and the Bach Society of St. Louis. Thank you to the Novel Neighbor, Main Street Books, Leviathan, Left Bank, Subterranean, and all of the other incredible independent bookstores in this community.

I am grateful to Dallas Willard for the concept I reference of reality being something we run into when we're wrong, from his book *The Allure of Gentleness*—"Truth reveals reality, and reality can be described as what we humans run into when we are wrong, a collision in which we always lose."

To Greg, my best friend and my greatest romance: Thank you for your support, for being my first reader, for all of the things you do behind the scenes to make my dreams come true. I love this beautiful adventure with you.

To Jesus: You are everything. Thank You for all of the butterflies.

And finally, to my readers both old and new: Thank you, thank you—you are who all this is for.